Sunday *Times* bestselling author Carmel Harrington is from Co. Wexford, where she lives with her husband Roger and two young children. Her books have been published worldwide and translated into eight languages. She is a regular on Irish television as a panellist on TV3's *Elaine Show*. In addition, she is Chair of Wexford Literary Festival, which she co-founded.

You can discover more about the author at www.carmelharrington.com

COLD FEET: THE LOST YEARS

Reeling from the sudden death of Rachel, his beloved wife, Adam has no time to grieve. He has to keep going, for the sake of their baby son . . . Jenny moves back in with her ex-husband Pete, eight and a half months pregnant with another man's child. Can their relationship overcome past jealousies? And Karen and David agree to an amicable divorce — but that's before he sleeps with the divorce lawyer . . . From Manchester to Belfast and back, these tales of the original characters from the hit TV show bridge the gap between the old series and the new — with plenty of tears, laughter and friendship in true *Cold Feet* style.

CARMEL HARRINGTON

◆

COLD FEET: THE LOST YEARS

Complete and Unabridged

CHARNWOOD
Leicester

First published in Great Britain in 2017 by
Hodder & Stoughton
London

First Charnwood Edition
published 2018
by arrangement with
Hodder & Stoughton
An Hachette UK company
London

A catalogue record for this book is available
from the British Library.

ISBN 978–1–4448–3834–3

Published by
F. A. Thorpe (Publishing)
Anstey, Leicestershire

Set by Words & Graphics Ltd.
Anstey, Leicestershire
Printed and bound in Great Britain by
T. J. International Ltd., Padstow, Cornwall

This book is printed on acid-free paper

For my daughter
Amelia Rose

PROLOGUE

The trip down memory lane and a black cab farewell to Didsbury

Adam and Rachel's house, Didsbury, Manchester
September 2003

Adam looked down to his right, to the spot on the floor where his wife and he had sat, side by side, planning their future. They'd just moved in together and surrounded by packaging boxes, she'd rested her head on his shoulder and said, 'You know what I'm looking forward to the most? Us not having to be apart again.'

Rachel.

Now, those once beautiful words seemed barbaric and cruel, taunting him.

He rocked his infant son Matthew in his arms and took a final look at the house they had once shared. It was time to go.

'All loaded up, ready when you are,' the taxi driver's voice shouted through his front door.

'On our way.'

It was the most difficult decision of his life, selling this house. But he knew that he couldn't stay here. Not without her.

This home had been a silent witness to all their moments, whether mundane or momentous, yet always unforgettable. Make ups and break ups, laughter and tears, infidelities and lies,

1

heartbreaking fertility issues, Adam's cancer, their marriage and finally the joyful arrival of Matthew. They finally had their happy ending.

Until a cruel twist of fate snatched Rachel away from them both.

The moment his wife died, their house ceased to be a home for him.

Yes. It was time to leave.

He hadn't told his friends he was going today. He couldn't handle the emotional goodbyes that would have ensued.

Rachel's death had cast ripples throughout each of their lives. It made them re-evaluate things and changes were already apparent. Jenny, recently returned from New York, with her little boy Adam, was pregnant. The baby's father was not on the scene. Adam's best friend and her ex-husband, Pete, had also just split up from his Australian wife Jo. Jenny once said that she thought it was possible to fall in love all over again with the same person. And it appeared she was right, because that's exactly what was happening over in the Gifford house. Jenny had moved back in with Pete.

To everyone's relief, Karen and David had called a cease fire on their acrimonious divorce. David was now dating his divorce lawyer Robyn. He liked to live dangerously that fella. Karen was in Spain with her children, visiting her mother, trying to make sense of the loss of her best friend Rachel and her newly single status.

'It's time.' A voice said.

He looked up and saw her leaning against the doorframe.

Rachel.

His wife might have died, but she never left him.

'You're coming too,' he said to the ghost of his wife. It wasn't a question. It was a statement.

'Of course.'

'So what happens now?' Adam asked.

'It's time for a new beginning,' Rachel replied.

'I'm not ready for that,' Adam said. He felt panic begin to bubble its way up inside him again.

'Well, for now, let's just go to your dad's in Belfast and see what happens next,' Rachel said.

Her voice calmed Adam, as it always did.

It was time to leave.

1

The quicksand and the wet facecloth

Bill's House, Malone Road, Stranmillis, Belfast, Northern Ireland October 2003

Adam ran down the long corridor, scanning the closed classroom doors as he went. All empty now, save for the echoes of its past. He knew he was getting close. His feet sank into something cold and mucid. It crept its way up his body.

Matthew!

He looked around, desperately searching for something to help haul himself out. He needed to reach his son. Matthew was in danger, the dark figure on its way to take him. His mind was now fully alert.

He turned to his left, slower than he wanted, because his body was now swathed in quicksand, up to his chin. The more he fought to free himself, the more he began to sink, lower and lower, until the muddy, unrelenting sand filled his mouth and nose. He felt hysteria threaten to overtake him. His heart rate doubled in speed, hammering inside his chest. Both ears thumped fiercely in protest at the assault.

Matthew!

'You're dreaming,' she whispered in his ear.

★   ★   ★

His eyes flew open. He was back in his room. He'd escaped the quicksand, but his body still felt heavy and uncooperative. With every ounce of his strength, he forced himself to twist towards his son. As his mind reeled through possible horrors he might find in his cot, terror overtook him. And then the figure emerged from the shadows, dark and menacing.

His face was nasty and mean.

'You're still dreaming, none of this is real. Wake up,' she said again.

Moments passed, intolerably slow. Adam fought to open his eyes, to escape from the darkness, to save his son from that ominous figure.

Matthew!

Finally his eyes opened wide and he gasped out loud.

Matthew was unharmed — of course — asleep on his back, arms above his head, starfish-like. He was oblivious to the hell his father had just been through. Satisfied that his son was safe, relief came crashing in and Adam broke out in a cold sweat, shaking from head to toe. He pulled his duvet up high, under his chin.

His eyes never left Matthew and, as the warmth of the duvet helped quell his shakes, he scanned the room once more, looking deep into the dark corners. Only then was he satisfied that danger had not crept into this room in the darkness of the night to steal his son.

He reached over to touch his face. For the millionth time since Matthew's birth, he felt bewildered awe and gratitude that this little thing, this perfectly wonderful little man, was theirs.

Only his now.

Fresh pain clipped his body.

'He's fine, love,' Rachel said, her voice steady and calm. Then she continued, her voice still gentle but now with a note of concern in it, 'You have to stop having these panic attacks. You'll not make it to forty if you continue the way you've been going these past few weeks.'

The last of his fear — irrational, maybe, but very real to him — disappeared at the sound of his wife's soft voice. He rolled on to his right side, towards her, leaning his head on his arm. Seeing her there, watching him with great tenderness, made everything all right again.

He was back on solid ground, the quicksand gone.

'Hello, you,' he said, grinning like a schoolboy. She was the only woman he'd ever met who made him feel young and old all at once.

'Seriously, Adam, you've got to stop getting into such a state. I'm worried about you,' Rachel said.

'I know,' Adam replied. 'Don't be. I'll relax. Honest.' It felt good having her worry about him all the same.

She was the keeper of all his secrets, she knew every single irrational fear he had.

'Was it that same dream again, or something new this time?' Rachel asked.

Adam nodded. 'Same one, Rach. Like clockwork, every night, since I arrived at Dad's house. I never had dreams like this before in my life. It must be something to do with the air here in Northern Ireland — the land of mythical stories and all that!'

'That's as maybe, but you do know that it's highly unlikely that you'll ever see your old high school again. They've torn it down. It doesn't even exist any more. So unless you go back in time, you're safe enough.' She smiled, reading his mind. 'And Marty McFly isn't going to rock up to your front door in his DeLorean to take you back to your old school.'

'Killjoy!' He stretched his arms above his head and grimaced at a new twinge in his back. His dad's spare bed had seen better days and his back was beginning to complain. 'Right now, my body is telling me it wouldn't mind being fifteen again! Mind you, I was a good-looking lad back then. I was well fit, as the young wans would say.'

'I don't doubt it,' Rachel replied, amusement dancing in her eyes. 'And if I may be so bold, you're still fit now.'

Adam smiled his thanks and his body flooded with love for this woman. How did she do that? Manage to make him feel loved and safe and secure in just a few moments?

'If I had a time machine, there's only one time I'd go back to,' Adam said.

He closed his eyes, but couldn't close his mind to the image of Rachel's car being smashed by a lorry, then battered by an oncoming car.

Yes. If he could go back in time, he'd make sure she was never behind a wheel that day, and he'd make it his life's work to keep her safe.

'Was he there again? Your old headmaster, Mr

8

Irwin?' Rachel asked interrupting his thoughts. A frown creased her forehead.

The shadowy figure in his dreams was that of his old schoolmaster. 'Yep. Auld bollicky Will himself. I'd never forget that face. Like it was yesterday I can see him standing at the top of the class, ruler in hand. Ready to beat ten shades of shite from me and Pete. The old bollox.' Adam shuddered at the memory.

Rachel's laugh filled the room. How Adam loved that sound. How he missed it.

'He was a tyrant and a monster, by all accounts. And there wouldn't be a bit of exaggeration on your behalf at all, Adam Williams, I'm sure.' Indulgence and amusement was written all over her face. She was half-teasing him, half-agreeing with him, in the way she'd done for years. And he loved it.

'Oh, trust me, I don't need to make up anything when it comes to that fella. He had a fair right arm on him. One belt of that ruler and you'd be scarred for life,' Adam said.

And then a memory that he'd long since buried surprised him.

He was nine or ten perhaps, dark unruly hair framed his young face. He was standing in front of his mother, sobbing. She gently patted his arm, with a damp facecloth in an effort to soothe the red welt that had been inflicted earlier by Mr Irwin. His mother was a great woman for the facecloth — a firm believer that it was the cure for all injuries. Headaches, falls, bugs, all made better with the gentle placement of that cloth on his forehead. Followed by a kiss.

He reached up and touched his face in the memory. He was thrown by the look he remembered on his mother's face. When he thought of her, her face was pinched in a sad frown, earned from the many disappointments of her life. It looked different in this memory. Her face was softened with concern for him, her only son.

Somehow or other over the years, he'd forgotten that there was a time that she'd loved him.

And he loved her.

'Go on then, show me your battle wounds,' Rachel said, peeking over his shoulder. Adam sent the thought of his mother back to whatever part of his mind it had been hiding in these past ten years. He didn't want to think about her. Not now.

He scoured his arms. He was sure he had a big scar there somewhere. He'd been belted enough times by Bollicky Will Irwin. 'Ha!' he said, triumphantly. He pointed towards a teeny pink line.

'I've got bigger stretch marks,' Rachel said dismissively. But before Adam could retort with something really witty, the door to his bedroom creaked open.

'Everything all right in here?' Bill asked.

Adam's father looked around the small room, wondering who on earth his son was chattering away to.

'All's good,' Adam said. He felt guilty. He shoved that emotion away, refusing to dwell on it any further. He was talking to his wife, and there was no law against that.

'Tea's made, porridge is cooling, it will be the

perfect temperature for his lordship in ten minutes or so,' Bill said, nodding towards his sleeping grandson. He turned to walk away, then thought better of it, moving closer to Adam in the bed. 'I thought I heard voices as I came up the hall. I was sure you were chatting to someone.' Confusion clouded his face.

He waited for Adam to answer, but his son remained silent.

Bill continued, 'Matthew's asleep though, so it's a bit of a puzzle as to who you were talking to, all the same.'

'The wee man is great for the sleep,' Adam said, deciding it best to just ignore the comment about the chat. 'I'll get him up now. We'll be down in a bit.'

Bill didn't move, his face twisted with worry. He looked like he was about to say something again, so Adam decided to cut him off before he had the chance to ask any more questions he could not answer. 'Thanks, Dad. See you in a bit.'

Bill walked out, with one last furtive glance behind him, before he closed the door.

Rachel started to laugh, clutching her chest in mock pain. 'My heart! Gosh, it's been a long time since I was nearly caught in a man's bedroom by his parents!'

They giggled at this for a moment. Then Matthew began to stir, kicking his little legs around the cot.

'All his granddad's talk of food has woken him up,' Adam said, feeling his heart leap in joy. It always felt like the first time all over again, when he held his son in his arms each morning.

'I'd give anything to hold him,' Rachel whispered, and the yearning in her voice cut holes in his already splintered heart.

He tried to respond, to say something that was understanding and supportive, but his words were strangled by a sob. Instead he picked up Matthew and held him close, closing his eyes as he breathed in his baby smell. His little head, soft and downy, nestled under Adam's chin and a pudgy hand reached up and honked his nose.

'Oi!' Adam said, pulling his hand away. Adam's nose was Matthew's new favourite toy.

The tug worked like a slap to the face. Adam was okay again.

The fear, the profound grief that felt like it could gobble him up whole, subsided once more.

He knew it hadn't disappeared, he knew that it was one thought away from jumping back up to attack him. But for now he was fine. He had to be. For Matthew's sake.

He turned to Rachel, determined to offer some form of comfort to her, but the room was empty again, bar him and Matthew.

'Let's get you washed and dressed,' he said to his son, who gurgled his appreciation.

When he made his way downstairs, Bill reached out and took Matthew from him. He started to sing the song that he'd made up, to the tune of the beautiful melody of 'Danny Boy'.

He remembered that morning, when Adam and Matthew had walked down the stairs for their breakfast. It was their first time in Belfast and they were all awkward with each other.

Neither Bill nor Adam knew what to say nor how to behave. This was new territory, son visiting father as an adult. In fact, he had never been in this house before. Adam was raw from all the changes in his life.

Added to that, the last time they had been together was at Rachel's funeral in Manchester. So on that first morning they both felt unsure of themselves. As they stood awkwardly in the kitchen, Bill said, 'I used to sing this silly ditty for you, when you were a baby, same age as him.' He nodded towards Matthew. He coughed, clearing his throat, then he started to sing. Bill's strong, beautifully timbred voice filled the kitchen, making both Matthew and Adam turn to stare at him.

'*Oh Matty boy, the porridge, the porridge is ready.*
The tea, is wet and waiting for your daddy and me.
And when we've eaten and stuffed all our faces,
we'll change your nappy and wipe your little bum till it's shite free!'

By the time he got to the final line, Adam yelped with laughter. He'd not expected that!

And so, a new tradition for the three generations of the Williams boys was created. Adam now sang harmonies and this week, to both their amusement, Matthew had started to sing along too. There was no doubt about it, he was definitely trying to join in, humming and making noises, in an attempt to form words and notes.

'That bloody tune. Can never get it out of my

13

head now,' Adam said, as the last note rang round the room. Adam watched Bill secure Matthew into his high chair in two quick precise moves.

'Look at granddad, a pro now,' Adam remarked, and Bill laughed, remembering his dire first few attempts.

'We never had anything so complicated when you were a baby,' Bill said. 'You sat on my lap most of the time. And you had the boniest of arses too, I might add!'

★ ★ ★

Adam always found it bittersweet when Bill mentioned his childhood. It was a subject that he found difficult to think about, even though he'd forgiven his father for walking out of his life when he was a teenager. '*Have you, though?*' a voice in his head asked.

At the very least Adam understood a little bit more why Bill had left. He had no choice. He now knew that Adam's mother had made it impossible for him to see his son, once news of his gay love affair became common knowledge. But despite Adam knowing this now, he still didn't quite understand it all. And the nagging feeling that Bill had given up on him too quickly heckled him. Now that he was a father himself, he knew that there wasn't a reason in this world that he'd be parted from him.

And the flashback to his mother earlier this morning had unnerved him. He'd trained himself to not think about either of his parents for years. Self-preservation, it hurt too much. Rachel had been estranged from her parents too, so they'd joke together that they were well met. They had each other. They were all the family that they needed. But Bill was back in Adam's life now and it appeared that his mother wasn't as banished from his head or heart as he'd liked to think.

They sat down and started to eat their breakfast in companionable silence. Adam spoon-fed Matthew, who greedily ate each mouthful like it was his last. Well, the bits that went into his mouth. He still managed to get a lot over his face and hands.

Adam felt his father's eyes resting on him and he snuck a glance from under his curly dark hair. Bill looked worried again. Damn it. Adam hated that his actions were resulting in his dad stressing himself out. He kept telling him that he was fine. And he thought he was doing a pretty good job of going through the motions, showing him that he was coping okay.

When he was in Didsbury, at their home, he used to talk to Rachel all the time. But nobody was there to question him. Here he had to remember he had an audience. He would have to make his conversations silent. They would become telepathic communicators. Ha! That could be a name for a great sci-fi movie. He must remember to tell Rachel that one, next time she came to visit.

'You were away with the fairies there,' Bill said.

'I was always a day-dreamer. That's what Mum always told me anyhow.'

'I've not heard you mention your mother in a long time,' Bill said. When Adam ignored him, Bill continued, 'Anything on your mind that you want to talk about?'

Adam wondered what his father would think, if he asked him what the correct etiquette was on having a relationship with a ghost. He figured some things were better left unsaid.

'More tea?' Bill held up the brown teapot.

Adam nodded, passing him his cup. Something told him that his father, in fact nobody, would understand about Rachel. They'd try to tell him it wasn't 'normal'. That he should 'let her go'. It was best to keep Rachel and their chats to himself.

Even so, he was grateful to Bill. He'd have been lost without him this past few weeks. Not just for his songs and tea-making, which in all fairness were excellent. It was more than that. He wouldn't have survived those days after Rachel died and then the funeral, without his daddy by his side.

And the more time he spent with him, in particular here in Belfast, just doing normal everyday things, the more he liked him. They were becoming more than father and son. They were becoming friends.

When he was feeling fanciful, usually after a second can of lager, he began to suspect that something else governed Bill's decision to come back into his life, exactly when he needed him most. Some might call it fate, others might just say it was dumb luck.

Whatever it was, Adam was thankful for it.

16

2

The ducks and the Dolly Parton fan

Botanic Gardens, Belfast

'It's a nice day out there,' Adam remarked when they'd finished breakfast. He looked out through the kitchen window into the long, narrow garden at the back of Bill's terraced house. He'd lived on this street, close to Queen's University where he lectured, for nearly ten years now. The garden didn't have much in it. As Bill himself said, he wasn't very green-fingered. Plus, they were only a short stroll away from the Botanic Gardens, which already had become a firm favourite of the trio.

Bill had plans to get more lawn laid out the back. He wanted Matthew to have a place to play football in as he got older. This made Adam nervous. He had no idea how long he was going to stay with Bill. Right now, it was as if he had no anchor and he was drifting along, at the mercy of the tides of his grief.

He wasn't sure he'd ever find a safe harbour again.

When Adam tried to say this to Bill, he just shrugged and said that they'd still want somewhere for a kick-about, even if Matthew only came once or twice a year to visit.

Adam liked that Bill wanted a future with

17

them both in it. That *he* saw beyond the next few weeks, which right now was all Adam could get as far as.

'Will we go to the Botanic Gardens for a walk?' Bill said. 'We should take advantage of the nice day that has presented itself to the world. I've no lectures until this afternoon.'

'Let me check my day planner,' Adam joked, pretending to open a fictional diary. 'Would you credit it, Matthew and I are wide open. Who'd have thought it. We're in!'

'Good man,' Bill smiled.

Matthew was now ten months old. He already had a strong personality and knew what he liked — or didn't like, as the case often was. And as far as the local park went, he was totally enamoured with it. They could navigate their way around the circular walk in under an hour. Bill always saluted the statue of Lord Kelvin when they passed it. He almost had Matthew trained to do the same. It was the Rose Garden that Adam loved though. Something about walking down the steps and then through the stone pergolas always reminded Adam of his favourite child-hood book, *The Lion, the Witch and the Wardrobe*. It was Narnia-like. It was as if he stepped into another world each time he walked down those steps.

Adam could see why Bill loved living here. His house was a few minutes' walk to the university where he lectured. And a brisk walk had him into the centre of Belfast.

It was very different from Coleraine, where Bill and Mary had grown up. As a boy, Adam had spent the greater part of his own summer holidays there, visiting his four grandparents. Most of those memories were filled with laughter and craic, courtesy of his many Irish cousins.

Now all of them were grown up with their own lives and families, scattered all over the world. He'd lost touch with that part of his life, his heritage.

He needed to talk to his dad about Coleraine at some point. He needed to understand why Bill never went there any more. But not today.

'Hey, you big slacker,' Bill's voice teased him. 'That child won't get ready himself.'

Adam mock-saluted him. 'Your granddad is a right auld bossy boots,' he whispered to Matthew as he picked him up. He changed his nappy, then once dressed, he put his jacket on. 'Hat or no hat, son?' He waved the woolly red Fireman Sam hat in front of Matthew, who snatched it and stuffed it in his mouth. 'Hat it is,' Adam said, laughing.

Adam grabbed some bread from the kitchen. While a park with a large playground was in the not-too-distant future, for now it was all about the ducks for Matthew. He particularly liked pegging bread in their general direction and the more they squabbled and squalled as they fought over a crust, the more Matthew enjoyed himself.

Adam added cooled-down water from the kettle into three bottles. He poured three measured scoops of formula into one and shook it vigorously over his head, while he made faces at his son.

Matthew appreciated a good show.

He remembered shaking a cocktail for Rachel and Jenny, years ago, at the Giffords' house, after they'd watched the Tom Cruise movie — *Cocktail*. Rachel and Jenny had howled with laughter. He smiled at Matthew, committing the memory to his mind. He'd tell him about his mother's laugh one day. Her wicked sense of humour.

Bill walked back into the kitchen and said, 'Nappy bag is now replenished and good to go.' He peered inside the contents, checking off each item as he did. 'Muslin cloths, baby wipes, Sudocrem, nappies, nappy bags, all present and accounted for, in their correct position.'

'He'll surely work up a thirst halfway around, so bottle made too. Have you a spare set of clothes in there?' Adam asked. They both shuddered as they remembered the previous week's poonami incident when they were out. They had no choice but to wrap Matthew in Adam's sweatshirt and hightail it home.

'Affirmative!' Bill replied, placing the folded vest and babygro into the bag. 'That bottle ready?'

'Check.' Adam squirted a drop on to the inside of his wrist, nodding in satisfaction. 'Will be a perfect temperature by the time we need it.'

As Adam picked up Matthew from the floor, Bill unfolded his stroller from under the stairs and they high-fived each other.

'All set to go for the royal walk, with his lordship,' Bill said, looking down at his pride and joy. Matthew rewarded him with a toothless smile and both men felt their hearts constrict in love.

All things considered, the three generations were doing very well. In many ways it was hard to fathom that it had only been two weeks since they arrived. At first, it was difficult, as they all adjusted to their new normal. Bill's house, with over a decade of life with only a bachelor to consider, wasn't child friendly. Certainly not for a curious ten-month-old who was on the move all the time. But Bill never once complained, he just got on with the business of child-proofing the house. In fact, he was never off the Internet, reading advice from mother and baby forums. He joked that he was going to set up a grandfathers' forum, because he'd noticed there was a gap in the market for that.

Adam and Matthew had slept in the same bed, that first night they arrived, for ten hours straight. Adam had given Bill no time to prepare the house for their arrival. But when they awoke, they found a note from Bill, who said he had gone shopping. A couple of hours later, a taxi pulled up outside the house, and Bill came in with half of Mothercare in its boot. He had bought a cot, high chair and enough nappies to last Matthew until he was in long pants.

So while they had a few false starts as they got used to living side by side with each other, the three generations quickly settled into their new normal. And somewhere along the way, they had become a perfectly coordinated tag team.

'We're doing all right, aren't we, son?' Bill asked, his voice trembling with emotion.

'I think we're doing just fine, Dad.' Adam nudged his father's shoulder with his own. Then, before things got too emotional, he said to Matthew, 'Right, let's go find those duckies.'

'He loves pegging bread at them, doesn't he?' Bill said.

'The bread!' they both shouted together.

Bill went back into the kitchen to get the bag of crusts Adam had left on the counter.

As they walked towards the Stranmillis entrance to the park, Adam realised he was smiling. Today was turning into a good day. The sun had a way of doing that, bringing light into a sometimes dark mind.

Within a few minutes, they arrived at the large wrought-iron gates of the park. The sounds of children playing together on the green drifted towards them. Students in between lectures sat cross-legged on the grass.

'Everyone's got the same idea as us,' Bill remarked. 'Suppose it would be a shame to let a good day like today go to waste.'

They started their walk around the circumference of the park.

'Won't be long before we'll have to find a park with a playground for his lordship,' Bill said.

'I used to love the swings,' Adam said.

'I remember,' Bill replied.

Adam looked at him in surprise. Adam had no recollection of ever being in the park with his dad. There were a lot of blanks in his head from his childhood. It was as if, when Bill walked out of his life, he took a lot of Adam's memories with him too.

As if reading his mind, Bill continued, 'We used to go to Fletcher Moss Park in Didsbury.

Do you remember?' He didn't wait for a reply. 'Back then, the playground was pretty basic. None of these fancy wooden things you see now. But what you don't know you don't miss. We used to put hours in with you when you were a nipper.'

Adam thought he could feel a memory tickling the back of his mind. But then it disappeared.

'I used to watch you running up and down the steps of the slides. I was in awe at your energy. It was endless. I couldn't keep up with you! But the swings were always your first choice. You would swing so high, I thought you'd touch the clouds. And you'd shout at me, over and over, 'Push me, Daddy, push me higher!' ' Bill smiled, lost in his memory. 'I think of those days a lot.'

Adam didn't answer. He wished he shared these memories with his father, but they were gone, or perhaps buried too deep to recollect.

'You don't remember, do you?' Bill sighed.

Adam shook his head, and saw the disappointment flash across his father's face. He took no joy in that.

'I'm sorry, Dad,' Adam said, and he was.

'Ah, you were young, I suppose. I never forgot, though. Everyone has their happy place, where they go to when they need to escape. And that's mine. Those memories of you on that swing. Back before it all went wrong.' He patted Adam's shoulder, squeezing it for a second, as if he was going to say something else.

But Matthew's squeals of delight as they reached the Lagan towpath put a halt to any more trips down memory lane. They walked down to the water's edge and laughed as the ducks became startled by Matthew's noisy shouts. But they also knew they were on to a good thing, so they started to swim lazily towards the river's edge, anticipating their reward.

Bill pulled out the bag of bread and passed some to Matthew who threw it, about a foot in front of them. Adam grabbed it and pegged it into the water and they all oohed and aahed when the ducks attacked it with glee. To prevent a bloodbath between two particularly rapacious birds, Bill threw in some more bread.

'Come on, son, let's get you out of that,' Adam said, unbuckling the straps of the stroller. Matthew reached up his arms and Adam hoisted him high in the sky.

'Come to granddaddy,' Bill said, his arms outstretched. 'I haven't had a proper cuddle all morning.' He pulled him in tight and breathed in his smell.

It was unfathomable to Bill that only a few months ago he'd not seen his son in twenty years. An unhealable rift between them both, or so it seemed, for such a long time. But somehow or other, now he not only had his son back, but his grandson too.

Late at night, when the lads were asleep upstairs, he'd sit with a mug of tea and think about it all. Mary. Their marriage. When he and his young bride left Coleraine together, to go live in Manchester, finally finding their way to the quiet suburb of Didsbury. Their utter joy when Adam came along. They had it all.

They lost it all.

Bill lectured at Manchester University. Mary stayed at home with Adam, by choice. She was besotted with her son. And it was idyllic. By the nature of Bill's job, he had lots of holidays, so they'd come home to Coleraine months at a time, staying either with Bill's or Mary's parents.

For the longest time it was good. But they managed to screw it all up. They threw away what they had. Like it was nothing. How could they have done that? To each other? To Adam?

Mary had been so determined to remove Bill from their life. She succeeded. She got to keep Adam all to herself. The irony that she lost Adam anyway, wasn't lost on him.

She was a hard woman.

But she hadn't always been that way and he knew he had to take responsibility for his part in that metamorphosis.

Matthew's cries of Dada and Gaga, the name he'd given Bill, filled the air and he shook his head to rid his mind of memories. If it wasn't for this child, there was a good chance that he'd not have found his way back into Adam's life. Having a child changed Adam. Made him open to look at his own relationship with Bill.

He felt emotion well up inside him and he reached out to clasp Adam's shoulder again. 'I'm glad you're here, son.'

Adam nodded at his father. 'I'm glad too, Daddy.' He had no idea what or where he would go next, but for now, he would have to be content to get to know his father again, properly as an adult, to just take each day as it came.

The pounding of feet running down the

towpath made Adam start. He was about to look behind him when the air shifted. Rachel was back. He always felt her before he saw her. His sixth sense.

She smiled at him and his heart stopped for a beat. He smiled back and she said, 'Prepare yourself.'

'For what?' he said to her in his mind.

She pointed to the towpath behind him, and he heard a voice shouting as its owner ran towards them. He leaned over to take Matthew from Bill. There was nowhere for them to run, but if danger was coming their way he'd die protecting his son. He knew that sounded dramatic. But things changed when he became a father. He looked at the world differently now. And when Rachel's young life was cut short, for no reason he would ever come to terms with, he also knew how vulnerable they all were.

'He doesn't look too happy,' Adam said. The guy in question was doubled over, panting as he tried to catch his breath a few feet from them.

The man who was accosting them was about fifty, Adam guessed, his face red with the exertion of running or, he supposed, from his temper. Adam relaxed, this guy was no threat.

'Is he saying your name?' Adam asked, cocking his ear.

'I think it's highly likely he is,' Bill replied.

Adam relaxed further. His father didn't look concerned in the slightest. He knew this guy, whoever he was.

'Hello,' Bill said, waving at him.

'How could you? What kind of man are you, to

26

blatantly lie to my face? I knew it . . . and you made me feel like I was being ridiculous when I questioned you. You . . . you charlatan!' He spat the words out at Bill, in a torrent of emotion.

'What in the name of God is he on about?' Adam asked. 'What have you been up to?'

'I've done nothing wrong. You are mistaken,' Bill replied, not taking his eyes from the man. He held his hands up and smiled as if he'd not a care in the world.

'You know this eejit then?' Adam asked.

Bill nodded. 'Adam, I'd like you to meet George. George meet Adam and Matthew.'

George stepped back, looking Adam up and down. Is he sneering at me? Adam thought. The barefaced cheek of the fecker. That was definitely a look bordering on contempt.

'I knew you were hiding something!' George said. 'Every instinct told me that you were cheating on me. I'm never wrong. All the signs were there. But even in my wildest dreams, I never suspected that you have a family . . . it's despicable.' He looked at Adam with sympathy. 'I feel sorry for you!'

Adam burst out laughing. It was the most ludicrous situation he'd ever been in. This eejit thought he was dating his father.

'Would you be wise! I'm not his boyfriend. Sure, I'm young enough to be his son!' Adam said.

'As am I.' George puffed out his chest and flicked his long brown wavy hair off his shoulders.

Yeah right, Adam thought. The only way that fella would see thirty again was on the back of a bus! As for the hair, dyed off his head . . .

'One big difference. I *am* his son, you doughnut,' Adam said.

George's face went through several emotions, one after the other. Disbelief. Recognition of the truth. Horror. It stayed on that one, with his mouth forming a round O of surprise.

'George, relax. It's true,' Bill said mildly.

'He's your son?' George spluttered.

'Aye. And this handsome fella is my grandson,' Bill replied.

'Oh.' George looked stricken as he looked from one to the other.

'I got it really wrong, didn't I? You must have thought I was crazy, running at you like that. I am officially mortified.'

Adam's annoyance disappeared at once. He felt sorry for the fella. 'Ah, you're all right. Easy mistake. And no harm done. You're lucky you didn't do yourself a mischief, the way you ran down that path.' He glanced at his father. 'And you weren't the only one kept in the dark. I didn't know about you either.'

Bill mouthed, 'Sorry.'

'So how long have you two lovebirds been dating?' Adam asked.

George brightened up at the opportunity to talk about his favourite subject — his romance. 'Well, we were at a single and mingle in the George in Dublin a few months back.'

'George at the George,' Adam said, laughing. 'I like it.' The George was an iconic gay bar in Dublin.

'That's what your father said too, when we

28

met! Like father like son. Anyhow, I arrived there early, to support my pal Alan who was taking part in the Dolly Parton singathon competition. No one does 'Nine to Five' like my Alan. And there was Bill standing at the bar, and he just looked at me in the way he does, you know?'

'Oh, I know,' Adam replied with a laugh.

'I. Felt. Weak.' George punctuated each word. 'Weak from my toes to my nose.' He pointed to both.

'Sounds like it was love at first wobble,' Adam said.

'You're funny,' George replied. 'I think I'm going to like you.'

'So I've been told. And aside from nearly giving me a heart attack when you came charging at us, it's nice to meet you.' Adam offered his hand and George shook it.

Adam then turned to his father. 'Dad, were you wearing a blond wig and taking part too, in this Dolly Parton singathon?' He shivered as the image of Bill donning a pair of fake enormous boobs took centre stage in his mind's eye.

'It was pure coincidence that I was there at all. Was at a loose end in Dublin, having been at a conference in Trinity earlier that day. I wandered in a for a pint. As for the Dollys being there, well they were an added bonus,' Bill said.

'Did your mate win?' Adam asked.

George shook his head sadly. 'No one could compete with Fergal O'Doherty. He did a duet with himself. 'Islands in the Stream', singing the parts of both Kenny and Dolly. It was something else.'

'Fair play.' Adam took a quick look around him, in case this was in fact an MTV prank show.

George clasped one of Bill's hands between his own. 'I'm not normally like this. It's just, I don't know, my radar for cheating is pretty much spot on. And I was convinced you were hiding something, or rather, someone from me. I'm sorry. I shouldn't have doubted you.'

Bill brushed away his apologies, giving him a warm hug. They looked good together, Adam thought. He realised that this was the first time that he'd ever seen his father with a man. He waited to see if he was weirded out in any way. Nope. Not in the slightest.

Bill grazed Matthew's cheek softly, saying to George, 'Well, you were right in some ways. My head has been turned by another man. This little fella has stolen my heart.'

'Aw. And I can see why,' George replied. 'He's gorgeous, a wee dote. Right, I better get back to work and I'll leave you all to the ducks. I sincerely apologise, Adam, once again. It was lovely to meet you both. Honestly, I'm not normally like this. A couple of unreliable ex-boyfriends have obviously messed up my radar. My bad.'

Leaving a trail of blown kisses in the air, he walked away, with Bill promising him that he'd ring him later on.

'Nice guy,' Adam said. 'I like him.'

'When he's not all paranoid about me cheating on him, he's a really decent bloke.' Bill agreed. 'Clever guy. What he doesn't know about quantum physics . . . '

'When you were going to 'meetings' about the housing estate last week, that's who you've been sneaking off to see, I take it,' Adam said. Bill nodded and gave an apologetic shrug. 'You could have told me. You didn't have to hide it.'

'I know.'

'Did you think I'd not approve? If I haven't reassured you that I don't care what sex you date, I'm sorry. Because it doesn't matter to me whether it's Georgina or George. Honestly, Dad,' Adam said.

'I know that too.'

'Then why didn't you tell me?'

'Ah, you have enough to be dealing with. Talking about my love life didn't seem appropriate. I would have got around to it soon,' Bill said.

'There's to be no more tiptoeing around me. I'm happy for you. If I've learned anything since Rachel died, it's that life is for living. So no more secrets.'

★   ★   ★

Bill grabbed the bread, throwing a handful of crusts at the ducks.

Adam looked at his father sharply. That was the face of a guilty man if ever he saw one. He *was* hiding something. 'Dad!'

'Well, George wasn't entirely wrong when he said he thought I might be seeing someone else,' Bill admitted.

'You auld dog. Go on.' There was a lot about

his father he had to learn, it seemed.

'Well, in my defence, we never said our relationship was exclusive. In fact, at first it started very casually. The thing is, there is someone else who I see every now and then. From before I met George. Nothing heavy. I think the term people use is a 'friend with benefits',' Bill said.

'You've got a shag buddy! I always wanted one of those, but never could quite make it work. Whenever I tried it, before I knew it, we'd be in a relationship and I'd be looking for a way out,' Adam said.

Bill nodded. 'I get how that could happen. But in this case, it's only sex.'

'First of all, respect,' Adam said, and laughed when Bill took a bow. 'But maybe it's time you had a conversation with George. Let him know you're not exclusive. He's suspicious and now feels guilty for that. You're messing with his head. Besides, in my experience lies always have a way of being found out.'

3

The on-hold-hell and the friend with benefits

Maggie May's Bistro, Queen's Quarter, Belfast

'Basically, they had you imprisoned in what I like to call on-hold hell,' George said.

'Yes!' Adam shouted, jangling the car keys in front of Matthew, a surefire way to keep him happy for a few minutes while they chatted. 'I mean, I'm a patient man, but how many times can you hear, 'Your call is important to us, but all our operators are busy right now, please stay on the line.''

'Don't forget the elevator music that always follows that demonic message,' George said.

'Mandatory!' Adam replied with a laugh. 'I wouldn't mind so much if they played something decent, like 'Teenage Kicks'.'

'Ah, an Undertones man.' George said, tipping an imaginary cap to him. 'Respect.' And he started to hum the song, Adam joining in too.

* * *

Bill watched them both with a big grin on his face, delighted they were getting on so well.

Song finished, Adam got straight back to his rant. He still wasn't over the hour he had been

33

on hold for earlier, as he waited to speak to someone about his TV satellite account. Trying to cancel it was proving trickier than escaping from Fort Knox. 'I might have lost my temper with that poor gobshite of a call-centre operator but for the fact that by the time he'd gotten to my 'important' call, I'd lost the will to live!'

'Nothing like a robot voice to make you feel anything but important.' George shook his head sadly. 'Last week I lasted twenty-two minutes on hold with the electricity board, only to hit the number two instead of one, with my stupid pudgy fingers. Ended up in the wrong division altogether and there was no way to navigate back. Sure I had to hang up and start all over again!'

'And why in God's name do they insist you have to key in your account number at the beginning of the call?' Adam said. 'Because — '

' — when you do get to speak to a living and breathing person — ' George jumped in.

' — they'll ask you to do it all over again!' Adam finished with glee.

George thumped the table, making his glass rattle, in appreciation of Adam's point. 'Yes! The more I think about it, those automated systems are just a way to piss off customers. Give us the run around long enough and we'll soon give up.'

Bill leaned in and said, 'As entertaining as it is listening to you two, did you get sorted in the end? Or are you still paying for a satellite service in a house that you don't even live in any more?'

'Did I heck. Matthew was due a feed and he started to holler. I had to hang up to sort him out,' Adam said.

George said, 'Horrendous. I say we riot.'

'Down with robots,' Adam joked.

'And big businesses,' George threw in.

'Before you both head off to make placards,' Bill laughed, 'have you time for dessert?'

'I could be tempted.' George leaned in to squeeze Bill's hand. 'Back in a minute.' He jumped up, heading to the toilets.

'I like him,' Adam said.

'So do I,' Bill replied.

'You'd do well to hold on to him,' Adam said. 'A good guy. Can't think why he's with you!'

'Funny. I'm beginning to come around to that idea too,' Bill admitted.

'Have you decided what to do about your 'friend'?' Adam asked, making quotation marks with his two fingers.

'As it happens I have. It's time I gave dating George a proper go. He's the first person since Christian, that's made me think about settling down again . . . ' He paused for a moment, then continued, 'I've arranged to meet my friend tomorrow. I'm going to finish things with her, but I need to talk to you about that first of all.' Bill said.

'You want some advice on how to let her down gently?' Adam teased.

'No, it's not that. The thing is, you know who my friend — ' The door to the bistro slammed shut, interrupting their conversation and making father and son look up. A woman stood at the door, looking towards them. Tall, slim, blond, wearing impossible high heels and a navy dress that clung to her small breasts and tiny waist.

35

She strutted with purpose towards them, well aware that all eyes were on her as she passed.

'Shite.' Adam and Bill said, at the same time.

Adam nudged his father in the ribs, 'It's Jane Fitzpatrick. From Coleraine.' Adam hadn't thought about her in months, not since that onerous incident in this kitchen with Rachel. He shuddered at the memory. He supposed it was only a matter of time before they bumped into each other, now that he was back in Ireland. Maybe with any luck she'd ignore him. Shite, she was headed in their direction, waving as she came.

He braced himself for a scene. They had history and, in his experience, when Jane was around, things always got complicated. She was his childhood sweetheart, a summer romance from his holidays in his parents' hometown of Coleraine. There was a time when he thought he'd love her for ever.

They grew up and apart, as is often the way. He stopped visiting Coleraine in his late teens. His life became all about partying in Manchester with Pete and Jenny. To his surprise, on his stag night he bumped into her again. He almost screwed his life up that night. He got so drunk he collapsed on her bed. His drunken moment of madness was no more than a kiss, but it still nearly put paid to his marriage to Rachel. Jane followed him over to Manchester and had gone all stalkery on him. She'd pretended that her bumping into him in Didsbury was an accident, rather than on purpose. Her sole aim was to lure him away from Rachel. At first, he'd enjoyed her

36

attention, thought it was harmless. His ego lauded. But when it began to get too serious, he told her that he didn't love her. For him, it was always Rachel. Jane didn't stand a chance. He shuddered again as he remembered their argument. He'd seen a different side to Jane, one that he'd rather not see again. Things went from bad to worse when she had gone all *Fatal Attraction* on him, threatening to tell Rachel about their kiss on his stag weekend in Coleraine.

It was Adam himself who let the cat out of the bag. When he walked into his kitchen and saw Jane sitting beside his wife at their dining room table, he thought it was game over. If he'd seen a rabbit boiling away on the cooker, he wouldn't have blinked twice. He'd blurted out in a shameful rush that the kiss hadn't meant a thing, only to come to the crashing realisation that Jane hadn't said a word, despite her threats. She'd come to say goodbye.

'Brace yourself. This is going to be awkward,' he hissed to Bill. He straightened himself up, ready for a row.

'Tell me about it,' Bill answered and before Adam could consider that statement, to his astonishment Jane barely glanced at him but instead slid into the seat beside his dad.

'Hello, Bill,' she breathed huskily, and then she leaned in to kiss him. Not in a you-are-the-father-of-my-old-boyfriend-and-it's-good-to-see-you way, but in a full-on-passionate-with-tongues-I'm-getting-stuck-in-there way!

By the time Bill had extracted himself from the embrace, scanning the room to make sure

George hadn't seen anything, the penny dropped for Adam.

Of course. Jane was Bill's 'friend with benefits'. Disbelief, followed by indignation on it's heels winded Adam for a moment.

'You've got to be kidding me,' Adam spluttered when he found his voice. '*She's* your shag buddy? Are you wise?'

Jane looked at Adam, then to Bill, then back to Adam again, a smile lighting up her face. She was clearly delighted with the unfolding drama. Adam couldn't help but notice that there was more than a touch of the cat who got the cream about her. If Bill was enjoying this situation too, he'd not be held responsible for his actions. He was mollified to see a sheepish Bill watching the corridor to the toilets.

Remembering the park the other day and the hysterics of George, Adam could see why he might be apprehensive. He felt irked that his father was placing him in this situation. He pushed the thought of his mother away. What was it with her lately, invading his every thought?

'Jane, go grab a coffee for yourself, I need to have a quick word with Adam,' Bill said, his voice firm. To Adam's surprise, Jane went to the counter to make her order. She was never that obedient when he dated her.

'How could you?' Adam hissed at him. 'That's my ex. There's a code about this sort of thing . . . ' He looked down at his now sleeping son, and vowed that he'd never do anything so crass as this.

'She's a passionate woman. It was hard to say

no. And I didn't know she was your ex at first,' Bill said. 'Honestly. She only told me that later on. I haven't seen her, since you came back. I wouldn't do that.'

Fair enough, Adam thought, slightly appeased. But even so. He was aggrieved by this turn of events. He didn't want to date Jane, but he didn't want his dad to either!

'Look son, we can talk about this later, but right now I need you to get her out of here,' Bill said. 'George'll be back any second. He doesn't need to see this.'

'Your mess. You sort it out,' Adam, petulance lacing every word. 'I thought you liked George,' Bill said. 'It will hurt him if he realises I've been sleeping with Jane. Please, if you won't help me out, do it for him.'

Adam glanced towards the corridor and saw a smiling George on his way back towards them. He'd be gutted if he knew about this. 'If I do this, then the next ten poonami nappies are yours. Regular ones don't count.'

'That's outrageous. Five,' Bill countered.

'Seven!' Adam said. 'Take it or leave it.'

'Done!' Bill said and shoved Adam out of the seat. 'Go on. I'll keep Matthew with me, he's asleep anyhow, just go buy me some time with herself. Tell her I'll see her tomorrow as already arranged.'

Adam said to George as he passed him, 'Something's come up. I've to head away. But I'll see you soon.' Then he walked over to the counter, grabbing Jane by her hand.

'Hey!' she yelped in surprise.

'Let's go for a stroll. Dad's got Matthew. I think it's time you and I had a catch up.' Adam started tugging her towards the door.

'I need to say goodbye to Bill,' Jane said, grinning in delight. Father and son fighting over her. She loved it.

'I've said your goodbyes for you. Come on.'

'Oh, I get it,' Jane said. 'I was expecting this.'

And then she gave him a look that made Adam shudder. As he told Bill later that night, it was as if she was about to open her mouth and swallow him whole.

4

Tom, Dick and Jane and the angry son

Bill's house, Malone Road, Stranmillis, Belfast

Adam had been watching the road, waiting for Bill to arrive home for over an hour. He'd been gone a long time and, with Matthew asleep, he found himself at a loss. There was a time when he'd love nothing better than to slob in front of the couch and throw on some *This Morning*. But he'd fallen out of the habit of doing nothing. He was never a big reader. Rachel was the one for the books. And he couldn't even leave the house, not with the wee man asleep.

He closed his eyes and whispered her name, hoping he could conjure her up. Nope. Nowhere to be seen.

Finally, he heard his father's Nissan Primera pull into the drive. He opened the front door and impatiently beckoned his father in.

'Hold your horses, let me get in the door!' Bill complained, shrugging his jacket off.

'What happened? Did she lose her shit?'

Bill threw his eyes up to the ceiling. 'She did not do anything of the kind. I simply told her that it was fun while it lasted and let me tell you, it was fun. The things she could do with a pair of jump leads and — '

'Dad!' Adam exclaimed. 'I don't want to hear

41

it.' But then he grinned and whispered, 'Did she do that thing, you know, with her toe?'

Bill nodded, with a big grin.

'I'm sure her carry on is outlawed in a lot of countries,' Adam said. 'But enough of that, go on . . .'

'Well, I just said that I thought it was time for us to call it quits. No more benefits, shall we say. We'd have to stick with just the friends bit.'

'And how did she take that?' Adam was sure something had been broken. A glass or a plate. And there had to be tears.

'She was a lady. An absolute lady,' Bill replied. Sometimes his son was so over-the-top dramatic.

'She took it well?' Adam couldn't believe it. 'Jane Fitzpatrick?'

'Yep. Just smiled and gave me a hug, and agreed that our relationship had come to a natural end. Said it was inevitable, she'd been expecting it even.'

'No dramatics, no shouting nor crying?' Adam asked.

'Nothing. I've told you. Would you relax? It's all sorted. I think she's a lot more together than you ever gave her credit for, son. A fine young woman.'

Adam shrugged. None of that sounded like the Jane he knew. And the way she'd looked at him yesterday, well, there was something odd about it. He shuddered again.

A cry from Matthew came over the baby monitor. 'Oi oi, someone's awake and will need changing,' Adam said.

'This one makes four down, three to go. I

swear you are adding something weird into his feed, to make the nappies extra smelly. Mother of God, the one this morning nearly had me throwing up my porridge.' Bill blanched at the memory, then walked out the door like he was walking the green mile.

Adam laughed, delighted. Good enough for him. A little bit of penance for his father, the player.

The landline rang and Bill shouted down the stairs, that he should answer it. 'Williams house of madness,' he said when he picked up the phone.

★ ★ ★

'Hello, you,' Jane said. Her voice was husky and low. Oh fuck.

Did she want a shoulder to cry on? No bloody way was he getting roped down that rabbit hole.

'Dad's upstairs. Will I get him for you?' Adam said.

'I didn't ring looking for Bill. I rang for you.'

'Everything okay?' He crossed his fingers behind his back in the way he used to do as a child.

'It's okay, Adam, you don't have to be coy. And I'm not going to make you work hard for it, although goodness knows I should. I'll be the grown up here and say it first.' She paused. 'I feel the same way.'

Oh fuckity fuckity fuck. 'About your break-up with Dad?' he chanced.

'No, silly. About getting back together with

43

you.' She paused again. Please don't say it, please . . . Adam thought. But Jane had never been good at reading his thoughts. She paused for a moment and then blurted out. 'I've never stopped loving you.'

I'm going to kill him. Adam thought, looking up the stairs. I'll fucking kill him.

'When Bill finished with me, I knew what was really going on. He was stepping aside so that you and I can get back together,' Jane said.

This wasn't good.

'Er, Jane, I think you've got the wrong end of the stick there,' Adam said.

Silence at the end of the phone.

Adam took a deep breath. 'I didn't ask Dad to finish with you. I've no problem with your relationship with him at all, at least not from a jealousy point of view. It's just weird.'

Silence again. Then a sigh, which built up to a groan. Then the sound of something smashing. A cup or a glass.

'Did you drop something?' Adam asked. 'Are you okay?'

Bloody typical. His dad got nothing but lovely understanding.

The sound of tears and hysterical sobbing began to get louder.

'Aw, Jane. I'm sorry,' Adam said. But in truth he wasn't even sure what he was supposed to be sorry for.

'You still love me, I know it.' But her voice didn't sound as certain as her words.

Adam felt his irritation grow with every sob she made. He didn't need this. It felt disloyal to

Rachel to be even talking to his ex-girlfriend. Jane had nearly broken them up, had caused them both a lot of pain. He looked around the room, hoping for once that Rachel wasn't there, a silent witness to this.

'We can be together. Jane and Adam, like we carved on that bench when we were kids. I still go up there to look at it. You know you never stopped loving me. Just admit it!' Jane ended on a scream.

And that's when Adam's thoughts all began to fold in over each other, each turning his irritation to anger. How bloody dare she tell him that he'd always loved her. Was she insinuating that he'd never loved Rachel?

'My wife is hardly cold in the grave. The woman I loved more than any other woman in this world. The woman I still love. I will always love. What the fuck do you expect me to do? Run off with you and live happily ever after? For fuck's sake.' The red mist has descended now. Anger at Jane, anger at his father, and anger with the fact that Rachel was gone and he was on his own.

'So you don't want to go out with me?' Jane asked in a small voice.

He slammed the phone down in disgust.

He was still shaking when Bill walked down the stairs, oblivious to what had just transpired. 'His lordship had no sooner had me wipe his bum than he was flaked out asleep again. Good lad. Hey what's with the face?'

'Jane rang.' Adam had the urge to punch his father. He stomped into the living room.

'Looking for me?' Bill asked, following him in.

'No, looking for me. Had it all worked out. She rang to tell me she loved me too. Wanted us both to pick up where we left off.' Adam's voice was low and cold.

'No.'

'Oh yes. Said you had finished with her to step aside for us two to get back together again.'

Bill started to laugh. He had never been good at reading an audience.

'I'm not laughing,' Adam said. 'You might think it's okay to live a life where you willy nilly go around sleeping with every Tom, Dick and *Jane*, but in my world, it's not acceptable.'

Bill raised an eyebrow and took a seat. He remained silent and waited for Adam to continue. In his experience, it was wiser to let someone have their say when they were this wound up.

'Is this what you did with my ma? Shagged everything that had a pulse?' Adam shouted at him. He knew he was being unreasonable and unfair, but he didn't care.

'No, that's not what happened and you know it,' Bill said.

'I know nothing,' Adam shouted. His anger towards his dad grew wilder. He felt it fire its way around his body, and he started to pace the room. 'I don't know anything about your life together. All I know is that you left her! But you didn't just leave her. You *left me* too!'

Bill stood up. 'Son — '

'I don't want to hear it. Today, because of you, I have sullied my wife's name by having to even talk to that woman.' He pointed in the direction of the hall phone.

'You've done nothing wrong.' Bill desperately tried to think of ways to calm Adam down.

'I know that! But Jane thought that my feelings for my wife were so shallow that I'd move on to her, weeks after Rachel's death. That's what she thought. Like father, like son, eh? Anything with a pulse!' He spat the words out.

'Watch your tone, Adam. I know you're upset, so I'm giving you some leeway here, but don't let this get out of all proportion. I won't be spoken to like that,' Bill said.

'Does the truth hurt? Am I getting close to the bone here? The fact that you can't be trusted or relied upon? That?' Adam couldn't stop himself. The hurt and pain he'd felt as a teen when Bill disappeared came bounding back at him, at a speed that sent him into a spin.

He wanted to hurt Bill. He wanted Bill to feel just some of the pain he'd lived with back then. *That he still lived with now, it appeared.*

The hurt in Bill's eyes, the way his shoulders sagged in sadness and the colour that drained from his face, gave Adam pause. But he shoved any guilt he felt to one side.

'I'm going out for a walk,' Adam shouted.

As he slammed the door behind him, he also closed his mind to the last words he father uttered.

'I didn't leave you, son.'

5

The granola and the mistaken identity

Jenny and Pete's House, Didsbury, Manchester

Jenny was lying in bed alone, for the fourth night in a row, waiting for Pete to join her. He'd promised tonight he'd be up in five minutes, but that was an hour ago. She turned, trying to heave her body upright, but her back groaned in protest. She called liar, bloody liar, to whichever genius said that the second pregnancy was easier. Ha! It was probably a man, she thought, thumping the pillow in frustration. Her maligned pelvis felt like it was being split in two.

She looked at the clock and decided she'd stay put and wait it out, rather than go back downstairs to look for Pete. Her eyes stung, gritty with tiredness. If she closed them, just for a moment, she'd be okay. She sighed in relief, as the pain eased, when she gave in to her fatigue.

Pete's car leaving the next morning was the next sound she heard. Had he come to bed at all? She couldn't tell. The other side of their kingsize was a tangled mess, but she could have done that as she moved about in the night. She picked up her mobile to ring him. She wasn't surprised that it went to voicemail. Even so, disappointment hit her.

'You never said goodbye when you left this

morning,' she said after the beep. 'So . . . good-bye!' She hit end. That was such a lame message. Did she sound like a nagging wife? Probably. She didn't want to be like that. She was beginning to feel that she was trapped in some sort of ground-hog day. Only yesterday she'd rung him to say much the same thing when he'd disappeared while she slept.

And to be fair, his response seemed reasonable, considerate even. 'I didn't like to wake you, love.'

It also was a crock of shit and they both knew it.

'I waited up for you,' Jenny had replied.

'Did you? Oh, sorry love. I started to watch the Sunday game and before I knew it, it was two in the morning. You were snoring away when I came up.'

'Let's go to bed together tonight. Promise me.' She tried to make her voice sound bouncy and light.

'Sure thing, love.'

Only he hadn't sounded sure. And she was pretty certain, he'd slept on the couch. Again.

Jenny was worried. When she'd told Pete she was staying in Manchester, he had appeared over the moon. He had in fact hollered with delight. New York had lost its appeal to her. She was a Mancunian through and through. In New York, her ability to mock was not appreciated, as it was at home. And she missed the camaraderie of the city that always had a kind word or banter to share with its inhabitants. The pace in New York was different and the natives were not as friendly. When Rachel died, her situation, what she must do, became clear to her. She still loved Pete. She missed him and she missed her friends, her beloved Manchester.

But maybe Pete didn't feel the same way after all. Was his excitement at her decision because he wanted to see little Adam more? Had she read the signals wrong, misreading that his elation was for her too?

Damn it, no. When he kissed her that first day, she felt how aroused he was. You can't fake that kind of electricity. Or response. And for the first couple of weeks after she moved back in, it was great. They fell back into being a family again with ease. It had been so long since she felt that happy, secure and safe. New York had been harder than she'd admitted to anyone. And now that she was back, she didn't think she could ever leave again.

Little Adam loved being home too. He blossomed in front of their eyes, each day becoming more settled in his old, new home. He adored his daddy. And the way he lit up when he had both of them together in the same room was a joy to see. He kept calling them to him and shouting, 'Group hug!' as he wrapped his little arms around their necks. She had done the right thing. She brought him home to his daddy.

His daddy. That was the issue though, right there. She was sure of it. She rubbed her tummy gently and said, 'Will he adore you too, my little one?'

Tears welled up in her eyes. She couldn't ignore it any longer. Something wasn't right and she had a feeling it was to do with this baby. She wished that it was his baby she was carrying, not Grant's. She wished she'd never taken that job in New York and left him in the first place.

Should have, could have, would have . . . she sighed, the magnitude of her regret overwhelmed her.

She could no longer ignore that in the past week, every time she spoke about life as a family of four, Pete's face changed. And his body, his face, his demeanour shut down, as he changed the subject abruptly or walked away.

She tried everything to get him to talk to her, open up and be honest. He kept saying everything was fine. Yep. Things were just ticketyboo.

Then last night, things had taken a new turn when she'd suggested they order a Chinese takeaway. He'd given her a look and muttered something about high sugar content. That wasn't her Pete. Then again, maybe he wasn't her Pete any more.

She edged her bum across the bed, then rolled on her side so that she could get up. She was parched and was gasping for a cup of tea. When she was pregnant with Adam, Pete used to bring her tea in bed every single morning. He had this knack of timing it, so that when she woke up it was the perfect temperature.

'Can't have my princess scalding her little lips, can we?' he'd say, and she felt like the most precious thing in the world to him.

Maybe she didn't deserve tea in bed now. Maybe this indifference is what you get when you disappear across the Atlantic, taking up a flash job as a PA, then come home with your tail between your legs. Or a baby in your tummy, as was the case for her.

She sighed and made her way downstairs opening cupboards and shutting them with a bang again, as she searched for tea bags. Where the flaming hell were they? Bloody pregnancy brain, she couldn't retain a single thought. Not to mention the fact that everything in her kitchen was upside down. Bloody Oz woman, Jo, had changed everything. Okay, maybe it hadn't been her kitchen for a few years — she had left, after all — but it had been for a decade before Pete had married *her*.

She located the tea and coffee in the cupboard, that used to hold her drinking glasses. It was all wrong, and made no sense as far as she was concerned. Everything was topsy-turvy, upside down in here. And that made her laugh. Jo was from down under and she had turned her house upside down. Ha!

She peered through the cupboards, looking for her box of Special K with cranberries. When she picked it up and shook it, it was empty, save for one lone flake. Was that flake symbolic? Was she that flake? Alone without even a cranberry to keep her company?

Damn it. She could make some porridge, she supposed, but the rumble from her tummy ruled that one out. This baby needed feeding now! Her only other choice was health Nazi Jo's blasted granola mix. A large batch was still uneaten, sitting in the cupboard in a plastic cereal box.

Pete had told her how every month Jo toasted

her own nuts and weighed out her sunflower seeds one by one and her coconut flakes too, making up her own sugar-free breakfast crunch. Jenny yawned loudly. Just thinking about all that effort made her tired. She bet Jo was a diet bore. Ha! How the hell poor Pete ever ended up with someone like her, Jenny would never work out. He must have been starving the entire time they were together.

She pushed aside the image of a gorgeous-looking Jo from her mind. She didn't need that picture taunting her, not while she was nearly nine months pregnant.

Another rumble from her tummy, quickly followed by a kick from the baby for good measure, and Jenny had no choice but to shove her 'I-will-not-touch-a-single-thing-placed-here-by-health-Nazi-Jo' principles to one side. She pulled open the lid to the Tupperware container and the most intoxicating smell hit her. Nuts, honey, maple syrup, oats and apricots, which God damn it, was her second favourite fruit after the cranberry. She loved those little bites of golden sunshine.

She'd have one little bowl, just to keep the baby happy, then she'd make some porridge.

Sweet mother of all things crunchy! She'd never tasted anything so delicious in her entire life. The nutty texture, the apricots, the coconut, the cinnamon, the raisins and, glory be, the almonds too, were all covered with the hint of maple syrup. What kind of a witch was Jo? No wonder Pete had fallen for her. If she could make granola taste so bloody good, what other hidden talents did she have?

She had to have one more bowl. For the baby, not for her. The phone rang and she was tempted to ignore it, so she could continue gorging, but the thought that it might be Pete ringing on the landline made her answer it. She had him trained to only use the mobile so she didn't have to get up, but he might have forgotten.

'Hello,' she muttered, mouth half full.

'Hello, Jo dear,' a voice said.

It was Audrey, Pete's mother, the old witch. She knew full well she was speaking to Jenny, that Jo had left Pete weeks ago. She had all her marbles and that 'slip' was intentional, its aim only to wind her up. She wouldn't give her the satisfaction.

'Hello, Audrey. It's Jenny. JENNY!' She shouted loudly, just to annoy her. 'I know how forgetful you get, now that you're getting so OLD.' Ha! Take that.

'No need to shout, dear,' Audrey sniffed. 'You'll have to forgive me, but it's hard for me to keep up with *all* of Pete's women.'

Her comment hit home and hurt. But Jenny knew that from years of going head to head with Audrey, she was better off keeping her sweet rather than taking her on. She'd do her best to win her over with humour. That used to work years ago. 'Oh well, never mind. I'm happy to report that it's the original and the best here.' Jenny joked.

Her joke was met with silence. Jenny was sure she could see tumbleweeds fly across her kitchen floor. She waited for Audrey to speak, but she

54

was much better at this game than her. Jenny couldn't bear the silence. Plus she wanted to get back to that damn bowl of granola. Like a drug addict, she needed the crunch.

'What can I do for you Audrey?' Jenny asked, trying her hardest to be pleasant. 'Pete's gone to work already.'

'I've tried ringing him, but his phone is switched off. Will you ask him to bring some of my special medicine with him when he comes to visit tomorrow?'

'Yeah, will do.' Jenny shoved another spoon of granola into her mouth, unable to stop herself. She mumbled, 'What medicine is that?'

'Never you mind. Goodbye, Jo love.' Audrey said. And Jenny could have sworn she heard her laughing before she put the phone down. The old witch was good, she'd give her that.

The phone rang again almost immediately and she grabbed it, assuming it was Audrey once more. This time, she'd give her a piece of her mind. 'What?' she snapped.

'And hello to you too.' It was Adam's soft Irish lilt. 'Who put your knickers in a twist so early in the morning?'

'Sorry, thought you were Audrey again!' Jenny answered, delighted to hear her friend Adam's voice.

'Say no more.' Adam knew only too well how much those two loved to bicker. They were too alike, that was the problem. The only saving grace was that they both loved Pete. Speaking of which . . . 'Pete's not answering his phone. Is he home?'

'He's very popular this morning. Nobody can get him. Me included,' Jenny said. 'Is everything okay?'

'Yeah. Kind of. I just fancied a chat, that's all. I miss all of you,' Adam replied. 'I woke up early. Dad's gone to work.'

'Are Belfast's charms already wearing thin?' Jenny was gladdened by that thought. They all wanted Adam to come home to Manchester.

'Belfast is grand. But it doesn't have you all.'

Jenny put her bowl down as inspiration hit her. 'Book a flight. Come on over to visit, you can stay here with us. For a few weeks. You and Matthew.'

'Ah, I can't do that. Sure, I've only just left you all a few weeks back. And you've just moved back in with Pete. Not to mention that you're due the baby soon. You don't want us cluttering up the place.'

'We do. I do. Anyhow, if this baby is like the last one, it won't be in any rush to come out. I've weeks to go yet! Please come,' Jenny begged. Now the thought was in her head, she wanted nothing more than to see him. Nobody knew Pete better than Adam. Maybe he could work out what was going on in his head.

'But you're having a baby soon . . . ' Adam said again.

'Er, I hadn't forgotten about that, thanks very much, Adam Williams. You'd be doing me a favour by coming. If I'm honest, I'm worried about Pete. There's something wrong with him. But he won't say what.' Jenny paused and her voice cracked with emotion. 'He needs you,

56

Adam . . . I need you.'

'Ah, Jen pet.' Adam hated hearing her so distressed. Could he go back this soon? Then he thought about his row with his dad the day before. They'd barely spoken at breakfast and while he knew that they'd have to deal with it at some point, there was a merit to dodging that bullet by jumping on a flight. Not to mention the fact that he'd had six voicemails in a row from Jane, wanting to meet up. Maybe this was the perfect get-out-of-deep-and-meaningfuls that he was looking for.

'I'll even babysit little Adam and Matthew. You and Pete can go for pints. Like the old days,' Jenny threw in for good measure, determined to get a yes from him.

'Why didn't you just start with that! I'm on my way!' Adam joked. 'You know what, in all seriousness, I'd love to come over. Give me a few days to sort out flights.'

6

The mermaid and the beached whale

Audrey's Retirement Home

Jenny was pleasantly surprised. Audrey's residential care home looked bright and welcoming. She had envisioned her in a dreary grey building, with no soul and a Nurse Ratched type roaming the corridors with a clipboard in hand. And that wouldn't suit Audrey one little bit. But it was contrary to every pre-conceived idea she had. Sitting behind the large reception desk was a young Scottish lad called Rick, who welcomed them warmly as they signed the registrar. He gave little Adam a lollipop.

'So that's why he likes coming here,' Jenny joked. Pete had brought little Adam here a few times since they'd been back, without her. She'd been avoiding this day, the unavoidable confrontation with her ex-mother-in-law.

The grounds surrounding each apartment were pretty, filled with flowers and trees to provide shade, to the wooden benches that sat underneath them. There was a big communal room where the residents could watch movies, play cards or sing songs. And Pete told her that most weeks, special guests were brought in to entertain them all. Magicians, singers and even a comedian, on occasion.

58

Little Adam loved visiting his nana Audrey. There were always chocolate treats by the dozen. She always whispered in his ear, 'What your mum doesn't know can't harm her.' Oh yes, he loved his nana.

Jenny took a deep breath, steeling herself for the visit. On the drive over, Pete had made it clear that he wanted them to get on. He banged on about how close Jo and Audrey had become, and that hadn't helped one little bit. She felt pressure coming at her from all directions.

'I used to get on with Audrey too,' Jenny had replied and he'd just raised one of his eyebrows.

Memories of dozens of battles fought with her mother-in-law over the years flooded her mind. She'd gone head to head with her on more than one occasion. But their relationship was complicated and had many layers. They'd also been friends. She liked her. Most of the time. And she felt Audrey liked her too.

'Just be nice. She's got a bit, well, frail, with her arthritis,' Pete said.

'I can do nice!' Jenny replied. And she could. She'd walk in there and be nothing but charm itself.

'Nana!' Little Adam screamed, running into her arms. She pulled him in tight, wrapping her green cardigan around him in a blanket of grandmotherly love.

'You're looking well,' Jenny said. And she meant it. Audrey's vibrant red hair was set in soft waves, as she had always worn it, as long as she'd known her. There were a few more lines on her face, Jenny supposed, but she still looked bloody good for her age. Her hazel eyes twinkled with joy as she cuddled her grandson.

Audrey nodded, just once, then her eyes dropped to Jenny's stomach. Without comment, she raised her cheek for a kiss from Pete, finally saying to him, 'Hello, son.'

As Jenny waddled in after Audrey, who walked between her two big loves, Pete and little Adam, she felt like an outsider. She came here knowing that Audrey most likely hadn't forgiven her for leaving Pete, nor for taking her grandson to the other side of the Atlantic. But when she made that decision a few years ago, she had her reasons and she had hoped Audrey would understand that.

If she could go back in time, she would. Audrey was going to have to find a way to understand and accept their past. Or they'd never move on.

A mix of lemon and bleach aromas filled her nostrils as she walked into Audrey's small square sitting room. 'Some things never change. Mr Sheen has been busy again,' Jenny whispered to Pete, sniffing the air. And he laughed in response. If Aggie and Kim — from the show *How Clean is Your House?* — came in here this minute, Jenny doubted that they could find a spot that had even a smidgen of dust on it. Audrey would give them two a run for their money any day.

Jenny shuddered thinking of all the times Audrey had surprised them at their home over the years. She did it deliberately, Jenny was sure of it, arriving without any warning, just so she

60

could catch her dirty knickers on the bedroom floor, or last night's spaghetti Bolognese congealing on unwashed plates.

Maybe Pete was right. They were all older and wiser. It was time to bury the hatchet. That's what he said. She giggled as she imagined a hatchet buried in Audrey's head.

As if reading her mind, Pete frowned. She stifled her giggle and made a decision. If she wanted to be back in Pete's life, both she and Audrey needed to find a way to get on again. There was nothing else to it, Jenny would have to be . . . nice.

'Place looks great, Audrey,' Jenny said, waving her arms around. 'You could eat your dinner off that floor, eh!'

Audrey sniffed, loudly, just to make sure she had the room's attention. Then she delivered the epitome of snide mother-in-law remarks. 'Well, *Jo* dear, it's just how I like to do things. Your house always plays such havoc with my allergies. The dust isn't my friend you know . . . '

Oh you're good, you old witch, Jenny thought. She felt Pete's hand on her arm and realised that she was on her tippy toes, ready to pounce. Think of your blood pressure, she told herself, dropping back down on to her heels. Last week, her GP said her BP was dangerously high and right now, if he placed the machine on her wrist, she reckoned new levels would be recorded.

Audrey threw a defiant look at her, as if to say, go on, come at me.

Then Pete did this thing with his eyes that she could never resist. Puppy dog eyes, she called them. Big and wet and slushy. He just wanted everyone to get on. Her resolve to be pleasant strengthened. She could do this, for him. And for little Adam. She smiled to reassure him that she was fine. But then added a whispered warning, 'If she calls me Jo one more time . . . '

'Mum, it's Jenny. Remember? Jenny,' Pete said firmly and slowly. Jenny squeezed his hand in gratitude.

'Did I say Jo again?' Audrey tinkled laughter like it was the silliest gaff she'd made. 'Oh I am forgetful. I'm so sorry, Pete. I do try my best to keep up with all these changes. But it's not easy, at my age . . . '

'You're doing great, Mum,' Pete said adoringly, moving closer to give her a quick squeeze.

She beamed up at him. Then urged them to sit down, but not before grabbing a huge bar of Dairy Milk and passing it to her grandson. 'And here's a little treat for you.'

'He's not even got his coat off and she's shoving chocolate down his throat,' Jenny whispered to Pete.

'I know,' Pete replied, smiling, missing the point. 'Isn't she great? Best nana ever, eh Adam?' he shouted over to his son, who already had a full row of chocolate squares shoved in his tiny mouth.

Jenny decided to let it go. Just this once. But Pete better take him for a run outside when the sugar high kicked in. If not, the drive home would be fun.

They took a seat on the brown sofa, in front of a coffee table already laden with homemade scones, jam and cream, and a large pot of tea. It

62

had a tea cosy on it, knitted by Audrey herself, no doubt. When Jenny looked closely at the tea cosy she realised it was actually a chicken. With its feathers covering the handle of the pot and its red beak covering the spout.

Jenny pictured picking up that chicken. If she half closed her eyes, the head looked a lot like Audrey. She imagined grabbing its scrawny neck and wringing it. She felt better almost immediately.

'I like that, Audrey.' She pointed to the tea cosy.

'Thank you, dear,' Audrey replied.

Dear was an improvement at least. Maybe they'd get through the day with no casualties after all.

And then she saw it.

Sitting on top of the mantelpiece was a large framed portrait of Pete and Jo on their wedding day. Jenny's heart sank. Pete looked so happy and in love. And Jo was looking up at him, with adoration too.

This whole part of her husband's life, she wasn't part of it. She had no right to it, because she walked out. And he'd married Jo. But Pete was hers . . . everyone knew that. Since high school. Pete and Jenny, not Pete and Jo. Pete and Jo was a blip, a mistake and one that he was going to divorce.

It was and would always be Pete and Jenny.

Yet somehow or other, there was another woman, another wife, standing with her husband on her mother-in-law's mantelpiece.

Jenny couldn't help it. Big tears began to well

up in her eyes. Damn it, damn it, she wouldn't give Audrey the satisfaction of seeing her upset. She brushed them away angrily with her hand.

Pete was about to take a mouthful of scone, piled high with strawberry jam and clotted cream, when he saw Jenny's tears. He followed her gaze to the photograph. His stomach plummeted, as did the scone, that fell to the floor with a dull plop.

'Sorry, Mum,' he said, scooping up the mess on to his side plate.

'That's all right son. I'll have that out in a jiffy,' Audrey said.

He looked at Jenny's face. Now she looked angry as well as sad. What the hell was his mum thinking? She knew he was in the process of divorcing Jo. He understood that she'd been upset by the news, of their separation, because she'd grown fond of Jo. But he thought she'd accepted it.

'You need to take that down, Mum,' he said, nodding towards the photograph. Then he turned to Jenny, 'I'm sorry.'

Jenny couldn't speak. She was afraid that if she did, a sob might escape in place of words.

'I forgot that was even there,' Audrey said, going back to her seat and delicately taking a sip of her tea. Her innocent act wasn't fooling Jenny. This was deliberate. And in a few minutes' time, Jenny would find out that Audrey was only warming up. She had a lot more 'Jo' treats in store for her.

'You have to take that down, Mum,' Pete repeated firmly.

64

'Of course, son. I only have it there because you do look so handsome in that photograph. So in love with your beautiful bride. And what a beauty she was too. The most radiant of brides I've ever seen.' Audrey stood up again and actually stroked the picture.

Pete replied, 'I liked that suit. Got it in the Trafford Centre. It was on sale, in Mr Best. They threw in the tie for free.'

'You look very handsome,' Jenny managed to say. She wondered how she'd got herself into a situation where she had to compliment her ex-husband on his attire for his second marriage.

'You've put a few pounds on, son, since this picture was taken,' Audrey teased, poking him in his side.

'Hey, you can't say that!' Jenny shouted, seeing the look of hurt on Pete's face. He was sensitive about his weight.

'I'll say what I want, when I want, to *my* son,' Audrey shouted back, moving closer towards Jenny.

Pete's head started to pound. Shit, he'd forgotten what these two were like when they went for it. Once they got their horns locked, Kofi Annan himself would find it difficult to broker peace.

'Mum, you're right. I have put on a few pounds. And I'm going to lose them soon,' Pete said, trying to calm the waters. 'But thanks, love,' he whispered to Jenny.

Audrey patted his hand, mollified. 'Good boy. I'm just thinking of your heart. You know we've a long history of heart disease in our family.' She looked at Jenny pointedly. In that stare she managed to convey that somehow or other Jenny was failing miserably at being her darling son's wife again. Somehow or other, Pete's weight gain was her fault. Saintly Jo and her bloody gorgeous granola would never have allowed that gut to spill out over his jeans, as Jenny had.

Jenny watched Pete pick up the wedding photograph and look at it in silence, deep in thought. What was going through his mind? Regret? Heartache? The unease she'd been feeling for days, began to strengthen and then it grew wings and manifested itself into full-on panic.

What if Pete still loved Jo?

Oh shit, she thought. There was no doubt about it. Pete was standing there, looking . . . wistful!

The effects of the chocolate were beginning to kick in for Adam and he'd started to run around the small apartment, slamming doors open and shut as he went. 'He's spirited,' Audrey said, catching a piece of Lladró before it came to an untimely demise.

'Only when he's been force-fed a shedload of sugar,' Jenny said through gritted teeth.

'Oh, speaking of Jo,' Audrey said, batting her next grenade back at her, quick as a flash.

'I didn't realise we still were,' Jenny replied, but she was ignored. The master was at play. When would she learn?

'She wrote to me this week. What a gorgeous surprise when the postman arrived. I never get anything nice other than bills and flyers about funeral homes. And this was on the most gorgeous notepaper too. She has such lovely handwriting, you know. I always think it says a lot about a person, their penmanship.' Audrey looked at Jenny.

Everyone knew that Jenny's handwriting could have been a doctor's.

'I read somewhere that bad handwriting is a sign of great intelligence. The brain working faster than the hand can,' Jenny said.

Audrey ignored this and continued, 'Anyhow, she's having a lovely time back home. Now where did I put it?' She opened a book that was sitting on the coffee table and pulled out the letter.

'How convenient. You had it right by your side all along,' Jenny remarked.

'Look, Pete. Here's a picture of your Jo on the beach. Such a stunning figure. Not like us two, eh Jenny?' Audrey patted her tummy.

The cheek of this woman knew no bounds. She was comparing Jenny's pregnancy weight to her own old woman's tummy that was clearly made up of homemade buns.

The photograph of Jo was the last straw for Jenny. All fight fizzled out of her, like one of little Adam's helium balloons that had been popped.

Jo was on white sands, with blue sea and even bluer skies behind her, which provided the perfect backdrop for her yoga pose. She was wearing a pair of red hot pants and a teeny bikini top in white that strained to keep her small perky boobs in place. And what the hell was she doing smiling for the camera, with one leg up in the

67

air, parallel to her body? She remembered Rachel emailing her once, joking that it was ridiculous how bendy that woman was.

She looked down at her own body, starting with her two swollen feet, wedged into her flip-flops. Her two pinky toes looked like two pigs. Angry red pigs. She pushed them under the couch. And then hanging over her legs, defying all laws of gravity was her large abdomen, with its belly button sticking out.

Her T-shirt that said, 'Does this baby make me look fat?' had seemed so clever and witty when she had put it on this morning. But now it seemed like a cruel jibe. She attempted to stretch her cardigan across her boobs in an effort to hide the insult. Thank goodness she couldn't see her bum. She felt sorry for everyone else though, because it had seemed to grow two sizes in the past month. Her size ten jeans were a distant memory and the only thing she could squeeze into now was a pair of stretch leggings.

Jo was a mermaid on white sands, and she was a beached whale. Beached, with no hope to be saved.

She felt eyes on her and looked up, expecting it to be Pete with his big worried head on him. But his eyes were still firmly on the photograph of Jo. And who could blame him? Ms-Sex-on-bendy-legs Jo.

But it was Audrey's gaze she felt.

'Jenny,' Audrey's voice repeated.

'Please,' Jenny whispered, tears stinging her eyes. 'No more.'

And to her surprise, Audrey looked at her

kindly and said, 'I was just going to say to you that I thought you looked so pretty today. Your skin is so . . . radiant. And your bump is so neat. You're a tiny little thing. Pregnancy suits you, dear.'

And with that, Jenny burst into tears.

7

The unidentifiable squelch and the voulez-vous

Karen's Publishing House, Manchester

Karen looked at her watch. She was going to miss her metro train home if she wasn't careful. She waved goodbye to the security guard in reception and made a dash for it. She pulled off her heels and in her stockinged feet ran down the concrete stairwell to the platform, weaving in and out of fellow commuters. Her Spanish nanny Ramona would have a fit if she missed this train. Tonight Ramona was beginning a new endeavour — French conversation lessons for beginners — down at the local comprehensive. She was determined to do everything to ensure her new relationship with her French boyfriend flourished. She was in love and Jean-Luc was 'the one.' And Ramona in love, was a tour-de-force, pun intended!

The gods were kind to her, because the metro pulled into the station just as she pushed her way through the last of the commuting throngs to the platform. She ran through the open doors in front of her. But her delight at making it, was short-lived when she stood in something wet and sticky. She lifted her foot, which was now covered in some kind of pink goo. She was afraid to look down, to investigate the nature of the squelch,

70

feeling her stomach heave as it ran through the possibilities. No. Some things are better left undiscovered. So she took a step to the side, trying unsuccessfully to scrape the offending matter on to the train floor. With no other option, she slipped her shoes back on, trying to close her imagination to the sensation, as the squelch moved its way between foot and shoe.

She was happy to be back at work — in fact, it felt good to be out of the house, back doing something that she knew she was good at. But this commute was going to kill her! In future, she would have to make sure she left the office on time. She pushed aside the image of her colleagues, heads bent over their computers, when she left. Most of them would be there until late this evening. Karen didn't have that luxury. She had obligations, commitments and the weight of the juggle struggle fell squarely on her shoulders. She looked down at her feet again and vowed that from tomorrow, she'd start wearing flats. No more running in heels or barefoot.

When she slammed the door shut to her house at seven o'clock this morning, she'd promised herself she wouldn't lose track of the time and be late home. But that was before the events of the day happened.

Her PA was sick. Karen suspected she'd overdone it at a launch party for a new book they'd published. Rumour had it that she'd been the last to leave and had drunk over a third of the warm wine on offer. She couldn't prove that, of course, and she was prepared to turn a blind eye. This once. She tried to avoid events like those now. Books and booze seemed to go hand in hand and she no longer swam in those shark-infested waters.

She'd also had the mother of all negotiations with a particularly picky author this afternoon. He didn't care for her suggested edits. Karen knew she was right. She knew that if the author ignored her they could kiss goodbye to any commercial success with the book. But sometimes authors thought they knew best. In addition to all that, she had a debut author's manuscript to finish reading. It was her second read through and they needed to make a decision as to whether they would publish or not. It was in great shape already, but with some tweaks, it could be magnificent. Karen liked it when she found something raw and great, like this one. She looked forward to working on it.

Her day had flown by, and in truth if Ramona hadn't sent her a text saying, 'You on train now, okay?' she would probably be at her desk, oblivious to the hour. For the umpteenth time, she asked herself if she was selfish trying to have it all. She wanted to be the best possible parent to Josh, Ellie and Olivia and continue her successful role as a publisher. She had coupled her passion for books with a vision and ability to work with both creative and commercial intuition. But guilt and self-doubt were worthy adversaries to her ambitions. She spent part of her days feeling like a failure. Her juggle struggle seemed to result in a large number of dropped balls.

As the train trundled on, she closed her eyes

and tried to find a happy place, somewhere to forget how busy her life was, for a few minutes. Her mind wandered to the Valencian coast. She loved it there. Karen imagined the warmth of the Spanish sun tickle its way over her body. *Spain*. Her mother lived there and while she missed seeing her on a more regular basis, it was wonderful having a bolt-hole to escape to every now and then. She had brought Ramona and the children there after Rachel died. That trip had been a lifesaver. But it had also left her lagging behind on her many deadlines.

Rachel. Just thinking her friend's name sent a sharp pain shoot across her ribcage. She pictured her heart broken in two inside her, hanging together by a thin thread that could snap in an instant.

Wouldn't it be so much easier if one could forget the things that cause us so much pain?

She pictured her children's faces: Josh, Ellie, Olivia. She tried to remain focused on them. Because, if not, she'd jump off the train at the next stop and hightail it as quickly as she could to the nearest bar. She'd order herself a vodka cocktail of forgetfulness.

It was just so horrendously hard to get her head around the fact that she'd never see Rachel again. Their lives had been linked together through so many highs and lows it was unfathomable to her that Rachel wasn't here any more to help her through this next difficult stage.

She put her headphones on to listen to an audio book she'd managed to snag from a friend in US. By immersing herself into the world of *Pompeii* by Robert Harris she tried to forget how sad she was, how scared. And it worked, because before she had another thought, she was walking through her front door at home. Ramona was standing in the kitchen waiting for her, tapping her foot impatiently, arms folded across her chest.

'Hello, darling,' Karen said, when Josh flung himself into her arms. He smelled of Play-Doh, markers and raspberry Petits Filous yoghurt.

'I missed you, Mama.'

'I missed you too.' Karen replied, kissing his forehead. He was six years old, blond and the sweetest little boy. He loved life and more than anything else he loved *her*. While there was much in her life that could be described as shitty, she could never quite get her head around the fact that she was so charmed with her children. Because not only did she have Josh, to her joy, her heart had expanded to love tri-fold when the twins came along. She walked over to the play pen, with Josh clinging on to her leg, dragging him behind her as she went. He squealed with delight at his game.

'Hello, double trouble.' She said, scooping up Ellie, whom she placed on one hip, then Olivia whom she placed on the other. 'How are Mummy's girls?'

'I here, still waiting for you.' Ramona shouted over to her.

'One moment. I know you are rushing out, I've not forgotten. But these little monkeys come first,' Karen said, her voice tight.

The tut that exploded from Ramona's mouth let her know that this sentiment wasn't appreciated. There was never enough time. Karen's life had become one long, exhausting rush of running to and fro, back and forth, all the while dropping those bloody balls, one by one, with a loud crash to the ground.

Karen placed the girls back in their playpen and left them fighting over a teething ring. Ramona now had her coat on and was hovering at the door.

'One moment, before you leave. How did it go today?' Karen asked. 'Anything I need to know?'

'All fine,' Ramona said. 'I feed, I wash them. I get them ready for bed. Anyways, I go now, Karen.'

'You are a wonder.' Karen decided to push her luck. 'Have you got five minutes? I need to jump in the shower because I've managed to step in something on the train that is making my skin crawl.' Her body involuntarily shivered in response.

'I no time for showers. I need to go. My Jean-Luc, he no speak no English or Spanish, and I no speak no French. How we talk? How we communicate? You answer me that?'

Karen giggled.

'What so funny?' Ramona asked.

Karen put a hand over her mouth and bit back the laughter. 'Nothing. Honestly.'

'Anyways. I go now,' Ramona said.

'*Bon chance*,' Karen said.

'What?'

'*Bon chance* — it's French for good luck.'

Ramona nodded her head and repeated the words. '*Bon chance*. I like it. *Au revoir*. That's goodbye. I learn that myself.'

Karen waved her off and tried to remember when she last felt the flush of first love like that.

With Mark, her last boyfriend? No. That was lust, pure and simple, and he was never right for her. Or her children. She shuddered when she thought about how he'd been so tough on Josh. Why did things have to be so bloody difficult?

She realised that a shower was out of the question until the children went to sleep. So for now, she'd have to do the best she could with the mess on her foot with good old baby wipes. It wasn't the first time they'd come to the rescue. Honestly, over the past six years, she reckoned she had single-handedly been responsible for keeping the baby wipes industry going here in Manchester. They'd gone through thousands of them. This morning when Ellie had spat up on top of her jacket, just before she was due to leave for work, she'd used half a dozen of them cleaning herself up. Little moist miracle workers.

When her foot was finally back to its usual dry condition, she put the kettle on. She knew she should eat something, but she found her interest in food was at an all-time low these days. She'd had a takeaway salad from Pret A Manger earlier at lunchtime, and even that, she struggled to finish.

A craving for a drink snuck up on her once more, creeping its way around her body. A glass of red wine. A Spanish Rioja perhaps. Or a large Grey Goose vodka, with tonic and a splash of lime. She licked her lips, the thirst for alcohol so intense she shivered. Her sobriety hung in the balance. She knew it and she felt powerless to take back control.

In the past, when on the odd occasion she'd

felt a speed wobble, as she and Rachel always called them, she'd have just picked up the phone and rung her best friend. Rachel could always talk her down, whatever trouble she found herself in. She'd have got into her beat-up red car and driven over here, her arms full with doughnuts and lattes.

She imagined herself telling Rachel all about her day, right up to the unmentionable sticky goo she'd brought home with her and her conversation with Ramona. And she could almost hear Rachel's laughter ring out in the empty kitchen. She'd have loved hearing about Ramona and her new French lover. They could have got at least an hour out of the double entendres on that one. And she knew that by the time Rachel left to go home to Adam, everything would have been okay again. Thirst quenched by the love of a best friend.

Loneliness overwhelmed her.

She could imagine Rachel right now, urging her to ring Jenny. When she'd left for America, Karen had started off well, sending emails to her on a regular basis. And Jenny had always answered them. Her stories of settling into the Big Apple were witty and always funny. But then one day, one of them didn't answer the email straight away. Was it her or Jenny? It didn't matter. Either ways, it started a new pattern of not responding for a few days, then a week — and before long their emails trickled out.

The truth of it was this, pure and simple: they'd become lazy. Rachel had been the buffer in between them both. She kept in touch and was always filling Karen in on Jenny's adventures. And she assumed Rachel did the same with Jenny too, on Karen's life.

But now that Rachel was gone, the bridge between the two of them was gone too, leaving another gaping hole in her life.

Rachel would say to her, call Jenny, build that bridge. After all, she had been genuinely happy to see Jenny back. She looked wonderful. New York had suited her. Okay Rachel, I'll ring her tonight.

Once she'd put the children to bed, she settled herself on her couch and dialled Jenny's number.

'Hello, Jenny. It's Karen. Is it a good time?' Karen said.

'Oh hi.' Jenny sounded distracted.

'How are you? How's the pregnancy going?' Karen asked.

'Right now, it's bloody horrendous. I've only gone and got piles. Bloody horrible painful piles. Pete's disappeared off the face of the earth, nowhere to be seen. He's like the flaming scarlet pimpernel these days. I seek him here, I seek him there ....' Jenny complained.

'Is something wrong?' Karen asked, mildly alarmed. 'Are you okay?'

Jenny sighed. 'I'm fine. It's Pete I'm worried about. I don't know what's going on with him this week. He's not talking to me, not properly.'

'Oh, I'm sorry to hear that. I was so happy when you two decided to give it another go,' Karen replied.

'So was I. But since I've moved back in, I seem to spend a lot of time here on my tod,' Jenny admitted.

'I know what that feels like. My kids are fast asleep and the house is so quiet,' Karen said.

'Lucky you,' Jenny replied. 'Little Adam is still running around the house. Bloody Audrey gave him this huge bar of chocolate yesterday, he's still not come down from that high, twenty-four hours later!'

'Grandmothers, tell me about it. When we were at Mum's a few weeks back, she changed every routine I've established with the twins, within hours of me arriving. I swore I wouldn't let her, but . . . ' Karen said.

Jenny laughed. 'How is Heather?'

'She's good. Still living it large on the Valencian coast. She keeps threatening to come home to the UK, but she couldn't give up her lifestyle there,' Karen said.

'Where's the sultry Ramona then?' Jenny asked, sarcasm laced her words.

'Learning to speak French, would you believe. She's met this guy while we were in Spain. Jean-Luc, who lives in Normandy. They had a brief fling, but it appears love has struck them both. It's like that movie *You've Got Mail* right now, emails flying back and forth every day, Ramona with her translator dictionary, trying to work out what he's saying,' Karen said.

'And Ramona wants to learn how to speak French for this bloke? In fairness, that's romantic,' Jenny said. 'Do you think she'll go live over there?' Jenny would be delighted to see the back of Ramona. She was convinced she still had her eye on Pete.

'Gosh, I hope not. I'd be lost without her. But

79

right now, he doesn't speak English nor Spanish. And Ramona doesn't speak French. So I think it's essential one of them learns a new language!' Karen said.

'Some might say that Ramona doesn't have much English . . . ' Jenny interrupted.

'Oh, she's improved over the years. And trust me, when she wants to get her message across, she does just fine. But you know Ramona, she's always been ruled by that heart of hers,' Karen said.

'Haven't we all,' Jenny replied. 'Good luck to her. I hope she manages to 'voulez-vous coucher avec Jean-Luc, ce soir!''

'Ooh la la!' Karen joked back and then they both giggled for a minute.

'How are you coping, what with David and his new bit, the divorce Rottweiler?' Jenny asked.

Karen felt her bottom lip begin to wobble. She had so many conflicted emotions about all of that. It would be a relief to talk through how she felt with Jenny. 'Well, to be honest I have been struggling — '

She was cut off by what sounded like a window smashing down the phone line.

'Jenny?' Karen stood up, not knowing what to do. She sagged with relief when she heard her friend's voice back on the line.

'Gotta go, sorry . . . Adam, you little — '

And the line went dead, leaving Karen, sitting by the phone totally alone.

She felt panic begin to bubble up inside of her. She was five seconds away from waking up the children, putting them in the car, to drive to the twenty-four-hour Tesco's. She could practically taste the vodka.

No, she couldn't be alone. She looked at her phone and did the one thing that still felt like the most natural thing in the world for her.

She called David.

He answered the phone after the first ring, his modulated, kind voice unleashing a dam of tears.

'Oh David,' Karen sobbed.

'I'm on my way.'

8

Stepping up a level and the fear

Robyn's Apartment, Didsbury, Manchester

David turned to Robyn, his face contrite. 'Can we put that wine on hold for an hour. Perhaps two hours, tops?'

'What's wrong this time?' Robyn sighed. She was beginning to get really sick of Karen's constant texts. When would that woman realise that her marriage was over?

'I'm not sure. But she's terribly upset. I've simply got to go. You understand, don't you?' He kissed the top of her head.

Robyn nodded silently. One look at her face and David knew that despite her affirmation, she really didn't.

'I know it's been difficult this past month. I've not been here much, going back and forth to Karen's. It's been a bit of a struggle getting used to sharing custody. Not to mention with all of us dealing with Rachel's death. I'm sorry you've borne the brunt of that,' David said.

'I do understand. I'm not a monster, you know. I just miss you when you're not here with me. And this weekend, you've got the children, so I won't see you then either. Sometimes it feels like I see more of my porter downstairs, than I do of you,' Robyn said.

82

'Hey, don't be getting any ideas about him. I've seen the way he looks at you, all puppy-dog eyes,' David joked.

'Stop.' Robyn shuddered. Things would never be that bad.

'Who could blame him for fancying you? I adore you,' David stated firmly.

She smiled, already forgiving him for leaving and leaned in to kiss him hard on the lips. That would give him something to think about. 'Don't be too long. I'll wait up, and that way we can still retrieve something of the evening.'

Not for the first time, David thought how lucky he was to have found Robyn. She was smart and sexy and it was always fun being with her. Despite her austere appearance in court, and sometimes curt and stern demeanour out of it, she was soft and enchanting when you got to know her. Maybe it was time to bring things to a new level. 'I have an idea. Why don't you come and stay with me and the children tomorrow, for the weekend? I know you've met them a few times, but you've not spent any real time with them. We can do lots of fun things and let them see for themselves how amazing you are.'

'Are you sure? That's a big step,' Robyn said.

'I think we're ready for it. I, for one, am anyhow.'

Robyn looked at him for a moment before answering. She knew that by saying yes, she would be taking their relationship into a new phase. She quite liked being David's girlfriend. Did she want to start playing stepmummy in their precious free time at the weekend? She wasn't sure she did.

David could see the doubt in his girlfriend's eyes. 'You get the added bonus of sleeping with me every night.'

'That's a strong selling point,' Robyn said, smiling.

David grabbed her hands between his. 'I wouldn't ask if I didn't think we were at that stage. I don't want your relationship with the kids to just be a quick half-hour in the park, with an ice cream. You are too important to me for it to be just that.'

'I do like ice cream.'

'Well then, I promise to always have a freezer full of every flavour you desire,' David said.

'How could I say no to that? You've got yourself a date,' Robyn replied.

He grinned like a kid with his first crush as he walked from Robyn's apartment to his car. She made him happy. He was determined not to blow this relationship.

As it was late evening, the traffic was in his favour and he got to Karen's within ten minutes. The front door opened before he had switched off his ignition. Standing in the doorway, with just the dim light of the porch shining behind her, Karen looked small and delicate. She'd lost weight, he was sure of it. Despite everything, the affairs, the break-ups, the makeups and the eventual messy divorce, his heart exploded with love for this woman. He wanted to protect her, save her from whatever heartache she was going through. He had always wanted to slay demons for her, and he doubted that would ever change.

Decades of loving Karen, it appeared, was impossible to give up.

Every time he thought he had a handle on it, he found himself getting caught unawares by her. She'd smile, or make a face, say something funny, nudge his shoulder and confusion would cloud his judgement.

He firmly believed that they shouldn't be together any more. They stopped working as a couple some time ago. Karen felt the same. He was in no doubt that he wanted to be with Robyn. He was *in* love with her.

But still, standing there before him, looking vulnerable, was a tremulous Karen. *His Karen*. And he wondered, if he only had five minutes more on this earth, which woman would he want to hold in his arms.

He decided it would be safer not to answer that question.

He walked over to her and wordlessly pulled her into his embrace. Her head rested on to his chest and he wrapped his arms around her, trying to stop her shivering.

'Come inside.' He led her by the hand into their family room, guiding her to their couch.

'Shall I make a pot of coffee?' David asked, then answered the question himself. 'Yes, I think that would be nice. I'll do that.'

Karen looked at the large clock hanging above the mantelpiece. 'I bet you were about to have a large glass of red when I called, weren't you?'

'You know me too well.' He was, if nothing else, a creature of habit.

'I don't have any drink in the house,' Karen

said sorrowfully, feeling fresh tears begin to creep up on her.

'Of course you don't,' David said. Something about the way she'd said that made him wary. He'd do a quick check through all the cupboards while he was here, just in case she'd hidden a secret stash. And maybe he could find an excuse to check in her bedroom too. 'I am more than happy to have a coffee. Have you got the good stuff in?'

'Of course,' Karen answered. Decades of buying his favourite brands were instilled in her, and she found herself still putting things he loved more than she did into her trolley each weekend when she shopped. And in fairness, their tastes had become entwined with each other's too. She liked much the same things as he did.

When the coffee was made, he sat beside her on the big soft grey couch and they sipped in silence for a few moments.

'I wasn't lying when I said there was no alcohol,' Karen said.

'What?' He put on his best innocent face.

'I heard you out there, opening presses,' Karen replied.

'Oh gosh, I'm sorry for doubting you,' David said. But he had to be sure. If Karen started to drink again, he needed to know. If not for her sake, for their children's.

'Don't be sorry. I'm glad you still care enough to check.'

'I'll always care. Now, let's forget about all that. What's up with you?'

Karen thought about all of the things that were upsetting her right now, but all that came out of her mouth was, 'I miss her.'

He nodded and they let that statement sit between them for a moment.

Karen loved that he didn't try to talk her out of that, or tell her that it would be okay, because he knew that it wouldn't. Not right now, leastways.

'Things keep happening, you see, and I think, I'll ring Rachel. Because she was always the one I'd call, you know? Like this evening, I had to take my shoes off to run for the train,' Karen said.

'That's dicing with danger a bit. Could be anything on the street,' David said with a shudder. He couldn't remember the last time he went barefoot anywhere, other than in the shower!

'Well, it wasn't the street that caused my problem. I stood in something gooey and awful and unidentifiable on the train.'

'Crikey,' David made a face of disgust.

'Quite. And I just wanted to tell someone. I just wanted someone to say . . . I don't know, to say to me, eewwww . . . ' Karen said.

He nodded. Righto. He had imagined all sorts of problems, but goo on the train was not one of them. He turned to her and said, a little shyly at first, but when she laughed, more forcefully, 'Ewwwwww.'

And with that ewww, she started to feel infinitely better. 'Oh, David,' she sighed on a smile.

He liked the way she said that. For so long, for years in fact, she'd say his name, but it was always in a reproachful, disappointed kind of way. He seemed to always muck things up, say the wrong thing, *do* the wrong thing. He never meant to. But his brain and his mouth didn't always align in time with each other.

Right now, she was looking at him like she liked him again. Like she used to look at him, before he messed things up. To be fair, he knew it wasn't just him. She did her own share of messing up also.

'I miss Rachel too, you know. I knew her as long as I've known you.'

She nodded. 'You used to joke when we started to date that you got one free when you got me.'

'I did. My very own BOGOF!' He laughed. 'She was a top woman, though.'

Karen nodded and the tears started again. She leaned in against his shoulder and he held her until the tears subsided.

'I thought about having a drink today,' Karen whispered into his jacket collar. She couldn't look at him. She felt shame at her weakness.

David pulled back and held her shoulders. 'Tell me you didn't have one.'

She shook her head. 'Of course I didn't.' She felt annoyance that he looked sceptical. 'I promise.'

'Okay, okay. I'm not judging you, Karen, I just want to help.'

She nodded. She knew that. He'd proven to her over and over that he was on her side, even if now and then he spectacularly let her down. 'I could almost taste it. I've never wanted anything so much.' She licked her lips.

'You need to go to a meeting.' David was alarmed all over again.

She shrugged. He was right and she knew that, but her life was so crammed right now, she couldn't fit a single more element into it. 'There's no time.'

'Don't be so ridiculous,' David said, annoyance laced into every word. 'Of course there's time. You make time when it's a matter of this importance. I have the children this weekend. That's when you must find a meeting. That's an order.'

Karen raised an eyebrow. 'An order?'

'Well, maybe a firm suggestion.'

'I promise I'll go to one. I know I need to. Believe me when I say I don't want to go back to who I was, when I drank,' Karen said.

'I'm glad you can talk to me,' he said. 'Don't ever be afraid of telling me how you feel.'

'I know that.' She paused. 'Everything is such a struggle right now. This feeling in my stomach, like I'm ill-prepared for an important meeting — all the time.'

David nodded and something niggled at the back of his brain. He read something once, it stayed with him, because it seemed so poignantly true at the time. What was it. Yes. It came to him.

'No one ever told me that grief felt so like fear,' David said.

Karen nodded at the truth in the words. 'That's beautiful.'

'CS Lewis wrote it. But it feels strangely appropriate,' David said.

'Yes, it does,' Karen said. Because that's exactly what she'd been feeling. Fear.

David kissed her on her forehead and glanced at the clock over her head as he did. Crikey, he'd been here nearly two hours.

'I have to go,' David said. 'Will you be okay?'

She nodded, but the tears were back in her eyes.

'How about one more cup of coffee, then?' David said, and Karen jumped up to put the kettle back on.

He took the opportunity to quickly text Robyn.

Not long. Leaving soon. Promise.

He waited for an answer, but none came. Damn it, she'd be pissed off with him, he knew she would. And who could blame her? He'd missed more dates with her lately than most women would ever accept.

I really am sorry. Can't wait for the weekend. You'll have my full attention, I promise. The children will love you.

This time his phone buzzed back.

If you leave now, we can open that wine. In bed.

'You've got to go,' Karen said, seeing him on his phone when she walked in.

He nodded. 'Would you mind frightfully if I

skipped that second pot of coffee? Apart from anything else, it would have me up all night.'

'Not at all,' Karen replied. The idea of him up all night, in bed with Robyn jumped into her head and she felt suddenly queasy. 'I really appreciate you coming over like that. I'd be lost without you. But you must go now. Don't ever keep a lady waiting.'

She stood on her tippy toes and kissed his cheek, pushing a lock of his fringe away from his eyes.

'See you on Friday,' David said. 'I'll collect the children around four.'

'Sounds perfect.' Karen's voice was stretched tight with false bravado.

As he pulled away from the house, he had the weirdest sensation that he was pulling away from something precious.

He braked the car slightly for just a fraction of a second, but then he continued on his way.

9

The evil stepmother and the offensive green bits

David's apartment, Didsbury, Manchester

When David collected the children from Karen's for their weekend with him, he was relieved to see her looking so well. She had managed to swing it that she worked from home, so that she could say goodbye to the children, before they left. One of his custody agreement issues he refused to budge on was that weekend visits start at 4 p.m. He only had them every second weekend, so this time was precious. He didn't want to be that dad, that just collected and put the children straight to bed.

Robyn was due to arrive in an hour or so. As yet, he hadn't told the children that she was staying with them. His earlier conversation with Karen about this issue played on repeat in his head. He was irked that she had placed nuggets of doubt in his mind about the weekend. He'd only mentioned the fact that Robyn planned to stay as a courtesy to Karen. Her reaction took him by surprise.

'Where will she sleep?' she'd asked.

'Er . . . with me,' he answered. 'Don't worry, she won't be sleeping with the children.'

He wrongly assumed that's what was bothering her.

'I should hope not,' she said and the expression on her face, let him know exactly what she thought of that notion. 'The girls are small, they won't notice anything. But Josh is an impressionable age. He loves *you*, David. He associates his time in your house as *his*. He might not want to share this with Robyn.'

He'd not thought about it in those terms before. But he couldn't un-invite Robyn now. David promised he'd talk to Josh and almost convinced himself that Karen was doing what she did best — unduly stressing.

His girls were crawling around the floor, with the toys he'd bought from the Early Learning Centre going down a treat. They were ready for bed, dressed in matching pink babygros, clutching their bunny rabbit toys in their hands. He felt a familiar flood of emotion hit him as he looked at their innocent, beautiful faces. I'll always protect you, he thought. All of you. He turned to look at Josh, who was sitting at the dining room table, drawing pictures of the Ninja Turtles. They all looked the same to him but each was very different, Josh had assured his daddy earlier.

He looked so content, lost in his creative world. David considered talking to him about Robyn, but didn't want to disturb him.

They'd just wing it. What could go wrong?

When she walked in the door, arms laden with shopping bags, she looked every bit as jittery about the weekend as he felt.

'Hello, Josh.' She walked over to the table, leaning in to kiss his blond head. He ignored her.

'Say hello, Josh, don't be rude.' David chastised his son, when he saw the hurt on Robyn's face.

Josh didn't look up, but mumbled an unenthusiastic hello.

'They are wonderful drawings,' Robyn enthused. 'Is that Leonardo?' What David didn't know was that she had spent the afternoon researching children's action characters, in preparation for the weekend. She was relieved she'd thought to include the Ninjas.

'No,' Josh replied, making a face. 'That's Michelangelo.'

'I can't tell one from the other either,' David said.

'I'll get the hang of them soon,' she replied, reaching out to touch his hair. He pulled away like she had electrocuted him.

'Come meet the girls,' David said, leading her towards the living room. Karen tutted in his head.

Robyn kneeled on to the floor beside the two girls, who were happily bashing the living daylights out of two soft toy rabbits. David sat down beside her and lifted Ellie into his lap. She happily snuggled into him, reaching out to pull the collar on his shirt. Robyn didn't know what to do at first. Should she pick up Olivia? Her confidence had faltered following the lukewarm reception she'd received from Josh. David nodded towards her, encouragingly, so she reached down to pick Olivia up. There were no snuggles from this twin though. She swapped the floor for Robyn's head as the new means to bash her poor rabbit.

David's alarm turned to pride, as he watched

Robyn take every soft blow without a single flinch. She made over the top ouchy noises that soon had both girls giggling.

David began to relax. It was going swimmingly well.

Only, of course, it wasn't. Josh walked into the room and was watching the four of them playing on the ground. He didn't like this new scenario one bit. He began to wail. With ferocious intent.

'What's the matter?' David asked.

'My feelings are hurt,' Josh sobbed. 'I'm sad.'

'Come sit here beside me,' Robyn coaxed, noting that there wasn't a single tear coming from the boy's eyes.

'I don't want you, I just want my daddy. And my mummy,' he wailed.

'Give me Ellie too,' Robyn said. 'I think my head can just about take a dual bashing from these two girls. You take care of Josh.'

David jumped up, pulling his little boy into his arms. 'Daddy's here,' he said soothingly, sitting down with his son on the couch. 'What's all this about?'

Robyn noted that Josh's sobs stopped as soon as his daddy's eyes were only on him. She decided it was time to divert the girls' attention from her head, so she placed them on their backs on the floor and started to tickle them. They rolled over, bums in the air, squealing with delight as her fingers found their tickle spots. The more they laughed, the more she did.

'Tickle me, Daddy,' Josh said, deciding he wanted to be part of that fun. He jumped down beside the girls, and began to squeal, before

David even touched him.

'You're doing great,' David whispered to her. And Robyn thought, I am you know. I'm doing great.

'I'm enjoying myself,' she replied truthfully.

An hour later, while David got the girls ready for bed, Robyn was in the kitchen, getting their supper ready. She had called into the local deli and bought pizza bases on her way to David's. As she wasn't sure what Josh's tastes were, she had chopped up a smorgasbord of items, catering to their every possible whim — salami, cheddar, tomatoes, pepperoni, olives, onions, goat's cheese, spinach leaves and a homemade tomato and basil sauce for the base.

Her plan was to ask Josh to help her make the pizzas. She felt like she was making progress with the girls. They accepted her into their lives with smiles and snuggles, given with abandon. Josh, understandably, was trickier and more wary. He was older. He remembered a time, in the not so distant past, where he had his mummy and daddy both at home with him. She caught him looking at her at regular intervals from under his long lashes. Robyn's parents had divorced when she was a kid and she knew only too well how confusing that time could be. She wanted to make this transition with her in his life as easy as possible for him.

She laid all the toppings out, ready for each of them to assemble on their own bases.

'Would you like to help make your own pizza?' Robyn called out to Josh.

'That sounds like super fun,' David said. 'We

96

love pizza, don't we?' He picked up Josh and lifted him up on to one of the chairs.

'Look at this,' David said enthusiastically. He clutched Robyn's arm. 'You've thought of everything. Well done, darling. Say thank you to Robyn, Josh.'

Josh mumbled his thanks and David pushed a pizza base towards him.

'Far nicer than getting a takeaway,' David said to her.

'I remembered you telling me that Josh loved pizzas. I thought he might think it was fun to make his own. I don't know about you, Josh, but I like to make funny faces on my pizza!'

She smeared the sauce on to the base, then added pepperoni slices on top, followed by cheese. She then used a combination of tomatoes and olives to make a smiley face. 'Ta da!'

'That's stupid,' Josh replied, determined to be unimpressed.

'Josh!' David reprimanded him. 'Don't be rude. I've already warned you about that.'

'It's okay,' Robyn said. She felt hurt and silly. She'd spent the day surfing the net, looking for inspiration on fun things to do with children. She should have been preparing for the Dunne Richards divorce. What an idiot she was. It was going to take more than a silly pizza face to make Josh accept her.

'What do you want on your pizza?' David asked. 'Start with this sauce. Oh, it smells delicious.'

Josh pulled a face. 'It has green bits in it. I don't like green bits. Mummy doesn't make me eat green bits.'

'I can take them out,' Robyn said, and she found herself, fingers deep into the sauce, trying to catch the tiniest bits of basil, extracting them and placing them on a side plate. She managed to get one spoon of sauce without any offending bits in and she held it out to Josh. He looked at it with suspicion like she was handing him a poisoned chalice.

'What toppings do you fancy?' David asked, holding up the salami and pepperoni.

Josh shrugged.

'Tell you what, why don't I make you one, with the things you normally have,' David said. The tickle-laughter was now a distant memory as the room filled with tension. He began to assemble a pizza for Josh.

'I want sweetcorn,' Josh said, scanning the toppings to make sure he asked for something that wasn't available.

Course you do, Robyn thought. That child is good.

David walked over to the press and prayed to the gods of the larder, that he had sweetcorn in there somewhere. Jubilant, he held up a small can of Jolly Green Giant when he found it.

'Here! I've got some.' He opened the can and poured the contents into a bowl.

'It's got green bits in it.' Josh complained, pointing to the chopped up mixed peppers that were scattered throughout the yellow corn.

'Oh for goodness' sake, Josh,' David said, scooping them out. His patience was wearing thin.

By the time they put the pizzas into the oven,

it was Olivia and Ellie's bedtime. Their eyes were heavy with sleep, exhausted from the fun earlier on. David and Robyn gave them a bottle each, side by side on the couch. Then they crept into the children's room, placing them gently on to their backs. David turned on their large mobile that hung between their matching cots and, as it circled lazily, it cast animal shadows on the wall. The lullaby it played was 'Clair de Lune'.

'They are so sweet,' Robyn said, gently touching Ellie and Olivia's cheek, one by one.

'Unlike my little monster next door,' David whispered.

'I was a fussy eater too, when I was his age. It's no big deal,' Robyn said.

'The pizzas!' David said.

'They'll be burnt to a crisp!' Robyn cried.

And with perfect timing, the smoke alarm started to blare, filling the apartment, bouncing off the walls. Ellie and Olivia opened their eyes in unison and screamed, their faces red with frustration at being woken up so abruptly. Seconds later they could hear the wails of Josh joining in.

'I'll take care of the girls. You go sort out the pizza and Josh,' Robyn said, ushering David out the door.

He reassured Josh that all was okay and opened the oven, which spat out black smoke into the room. It was obvious that the blackened pizzas were beyond saving.

'I'm hungry,' Josh complained.

David stuck on two frozen pizzas from the freezer and gave Josh a rice cake to keep him happy while they waited for these to cook.

Meanwhile, Robyn managed to get the girls asleep again. She walked into the living room, her face flushed and red. She didn't look like her usual coiffed self and David marvelled how his kids could unravel a person in only a few hours. That took skill.

They ate their pizza with little enthusiasm.

'Let me get Josh ready for bed. You open a bottle of wine and put your feet up,' David whispered. What if Robyn lost interest in him and his children?

'That would be nice,' Robyn admitted. She'd never wanted a drink more in her life. She was exhausted.

'Say goodnight to Robyn,' David said to Josh.

'When are you going home?' Josh asked, ignoring his father.

Fuck, David thought. His winging it plan was coming back to bite him. Robyn looked helplessly at David. She didn't know how to answer that. She shouldn't have to.

'We thought it would be really nice for Robyn to have a sleepover here tonight,' David said. His voice was high, with forced jollity.

'Where will she sleep?' Josh demanded. 'There's only two bedrooms.'

Robyn looked at the kitchen longingly. She needed that wine. Now.

'Well, we thought she might sleep in with Daddy,' David said.

Josh looked at them both and shook his head. 'Mummy sleeps with Daddy. Not her.'

Oh fuck. He took a steadying breath and said,

'We don't call people 'her'. That's rude. And you know that Mummy sleeps in her house and I sleep here in my apartment. And tonight, Daddy's special friend is staying over.'

'I don't like *her*,' Josh said. He emphasised the word with venom.

'Josh!' David exclaimed. 'I'm so sorry,' he apologised to Robyn.

'It's fine.' Robyn brushed aside his apologies. Her heart went out to this little boy, who looked confused, sad and angry. She hated that she was in any way part of that. She turned to Josh and said, 'It's okay. You don't have to like me. But maybe when you get to know me a little better, you might change your mind. Because I like you an awful lot.'

Josh looked sceptical at that statement.

'It's been a long day. You get Josh to bed,' Robyn said to David. 'Don't push him,' she whispered. 'He'll come round in his own good time.'

David took Josh by the hand and helped him into his pyjamas before supervising his teeth-brushing. Somehow tonight, he'd managed to let both Josh and Robyn down. The sound of Karen's tutting got louder in his head.

'I want to sleep with you tonight, Daddy,' Josh said, when he tucked him into his single bed, beside the girls' cots.

'No, Josh. Robyn is sleeping with Daddy tonight. This is your bed, with your Ninja Turtle duvet. Be a good boy now. Go to sleep,' David urged. He leaned in and kissed an unimpressed Josh goodnight.

A few minutes later, he walked into the sitting room and found Robyn sitting on the couch, legs curled up under her bum. She hit pause on the TV screen.

'What are you watching?' David asked.

'*Pretty Woman*,' Robyn replied. She needed some light relief after the stressful evening they'd just been through.

'I don't think I've ever seen this movie,' David said.

'Well, sit down sir and let's remedy that straight away. It's the perfect movie to lose yourself into and forget about the stresses of the day.'

'Was it awful for you this evening?' David asked, accepting the glass of wine Robyn had poured for him.

'Let's just say I've had less taxing days in court!' Robyn joked. Seeing how David's face fell, she added, 'It wasn't all bad and we were naive to think it would be plain sailing.'

'It will get easier,' David promised. 'Josh just needs to see how amazing you are.'

'We've all the time in the world. But for now, I'm so tired, I just want to sip this wine and watch this movie. Can we talk about the children again tomorrow?'

'Absolutely,' David said. He nodded to the screen, where Julia Roberts's face was frozen, laughing, as she watched a black and white movie. 'You know, I never had you down as a romantic weepie type of lady.'

'There's a lot about me you don't know yet. I love everything about this movie. It's basically the modern-day Cinderella. You've only missed

102

the first few minutes. Vivian — that's Julia Roberts's character, got into Edward's car — that's Richard Gere. She's a prostitute. They're in his room now.'

David leaned forward with interest. 'Why didn't you start with that sentence first of all?' Robyn threw her cushion at him.

David snuck glances at Robyn several times in the movie. She was right, he was enjoying it. As it happened, he could see a lot of Edward's character in him. They were both debonair, sophisticated, clever and knew how to wear a good suit. He loved the sound of Robyn's giggle and she had to clamp her hand across her mouth when Vivian said in one scene, 'Fifty bucks, Grandpa, and for seventy-five the wife can watch.' He wondered if Robyn had a pair of long black boots like Vivian's.

When the movie came to the scene where Vivian walked into the lobby of the Bel Air hotel, wearing a red evening gown, he saw Robyn's face change. It became wistful and softer somehow. Her eyes filled with tears alongside Vivian's as she watched the opera *La Traviata* performed on screen. David's eyes, much like Edward's, were firmly on the lady beside him. He was profoundly moved and filled with love for this woman. He gently nudged her shoulder. 'How about we skip the rest and go to bed.'

She smiled. 'I'd like that.'

They walked into the bedroom, pausing to kiss in the hallway before they opened the door. David ran his hands down her spine, and pulled her in close. Her two hands pulled at his shirt, opening buttons and they stumbled into the bedroom.

'I've been thinking about taking your clothes off all day,' David said, pulling her top up over her head. 'God, you're beautiful.'

And she pushed him back towards the bed, falling on top of him.

'Daddy, what are you doing to that lady?' A voice said from under the covers.

They broke apart and looked behind them. There, sitting in the centre of the bed, was Josh.

Robyn disentangled herself from David and put her arms across her almost naked body. David sat up and said, 'Josh, what are you doing in here?'

'I had a nightmare,' he said, shrugging. He didn't look the least bit scared.

'A nightmare?' David asked.

'I fell asleep straight away and it was a really bad dream.' Josh looked at them both and then decided that it was time to throw in a few tears. He squeezed his eyes closed and willed water to spill down his cheeks. He'd become quite good at crying on spec.

'It's all right,' David said, cradling him in his arms. 'Don't cry.'

'I'm too scared to sleep in my bed. There's a monster under it,' Josh continued.

'There's no such thing as monsters,' David said. 'It's perfectly safe in there. I mean, do you think I'd leave my two girls and you in a room where anything might harm you all?'

Josh replied, 'The monster doesn't like girls, just boys like me.'

David rocked him in his arms again. He was so tiny, only a baby really. The poor little thing was shivering with fright.

Robyn walked out of his en suite bathroom, wearing a pair of pyjamas. David looked over to her and whispered, 'He's in quite a state. Not like him at all.'

'Shall I read you a bedtime story?' Robyn asked Josh, reaching over to stroke his hair.

'I want my mummy!' He screamed, recoiling from her touch.

'It's okay, Daddy's here,' David soothed again. 'I'm sorry, Robyn, I think I'm going to have to let him sleep with me tonight.'

'Where do you suggest I should sleep?' Robyn asked.

'Josh's bed or the couch?' David suggested.

Robyn looked unsure and said, 'Maybe we should just call it a night. I'm tired, David. I had a long day at work and just need to close my eyes. I think I'll go home.'

'Please don't do that. Stay. We can go to the park tomorrow and eat lots of ice cream. Tomorrow night will be better, you wait and see,' David said.

Robyn didn't look convinced. 'I'll tell you what. I'll go home and then tomorrow I can meet you guys in the park. You can get me a double scoop of ice cream.'

'Are you sure?' David asked. He was both disappointed and relieved at her decision. Karen had been right, he'd done this too quickly, with not enough thought.

'I'm sure,' Robyn said. 'And we have Sunday

too.' She saw David pull a face.

'What?' She asked.

'I was going to tell you tomorrow darling. Adam and Matthew are coming home. And Karen is making Sunday lunch for all the gang . . . ' David's voice stopped, as he saw the look of disappointment on Robyn's face.

'And I'm not invited, as I'm not one of the gang,' Robyn said.

David thought she might cry, but then her face and voice hardened when she said, 'I'm not quite sure how I'll ever become part of your precious gang, when I am constantly excluded.'

'It's not like that, it's just, Adam has been through so much,' David said. 'Say you understand.'

Robyn couldn't bring herself to say any such thing. She replied, 'Goodnight. I'll see you all at the park tomorrow.' Then she walked out the door, turning back one last time to look at them. David blew her a kiss and Josh stuck his tongue out at her.

Poor little darling.

10

The asparagus starter and the slimy scum sucker

Karen's house, Didsbury, Manchester

'Is he here yet?' Jenny said, looking over Karen's shoulder as she walked into her house.

'No, not yet. Adam insisted he'd make his own way here from the airport,' Karen answered. 'David has arrived though.'

'With the Rottweiler?' Jenny whispered.

Karen giggled and shushed her friend. 'He's on his own.'

Little Adam ran around Jenny's legs, shouting, 'Josh! Josh!'

'Everyone's out the back, go on through,' Karen said. Little Adam had already worked that out and by the time they'd got to the garden, Josh was pulling him up on to his trampoline. They bounced up and down, arms and legs flailing, big grins on their faces. Ellie and Olivia were in the shade, in their playpen, Ramona close by. She glanced up from her book, and took her sunglasses off to take a look at the new arrivals.

'Ramona,' Jenny said curtly, nodding at her. She would always be wary of her, since she had that brief fling with Pete.

'*Bonjour*,' Ramona replied, equally cool.

The sound of a French greeting, with

Ramona's Spanish accent made Jenny snigger. But the snigger stopped abruptly when Pete walked over towards her and she jumped up to kiss him, once on each cheek.

'Very continental,' Pete remarked. 'I likey!'

'*Je suis* speaky *la français* now,' Ramona said.

'I think roughly translated that means she only speaks French now,' Jenny threw her eyes up to the skies. Silly cow.

'*Petit pois, bonjour, bonjour*,' Pete replied, in his best Del Boy accent.

'Ha!' Jenny snorted out loud. She gave Pete a double thumbs up. 'Lovely jubbly!'

Pete laughed back. Jenny always got his jokes. He moved a little closer to her.

Karen and David looked lost at the exchange.

'Not fans of *Only Fools and Horses*, I take it,' Pete said.

'Must have missed that episode,' David replied.

'Oh of course! Now I get it. Sorry, I'm running a bit slow today!' Karen added.

Karen looked at Jenny's arms, still holding on to a bunch of flowers. 'Shall I take them for you?'

Jenny exclaimed. 'What am I like! Should have given these to you when I walked in! Baby brain in full force here.'

'You shouldn't have,' Karen said, walking back into the kitchen with the flowers to find a vase. The house was beginning to look like a bloody florist's. If Adam arrived with another bunch, she might scream.

When you throw a dinner party as a recovering alcoholic, no one knows what to bring you. They don't want to bring booze, so flowers become the norm. A business opportunity there, she reckoned. A shop with thoughtful gifts for the alcoholic in your life.

Speaking of, Karen fretted for the tenth time that day about wine. She'd gone to an AA meeting yesterday. And she'd brought up the issue of the lunch she'd offered to throw, in honour of Adam's return to Manchester. Everyone decided she should forgo offering alcohol, after all it was a lunch, with children present. Better not to tempt fate and buy a few bottles, even if they were for others.

Now she fretted, thinking that it wasn't fair that everyone else suffered because of her frailties.

'Oh. You've got flowers already,' Jenny said, when she followed her into the dining room. The sideboard was covered in colourful blooms.

'I adore fresh flowers,' Karen replied. 'You can never have too many, can you?'

She checked on the roast, taking it out to baste the beef with its own juices. Then placed the par-boiled potatoes into the oven to roast. Her creamy parsnip and carrot mash was ready to serve, as were the Puy lentils. Assuming Adam arrived in the next half hour, her timings should be perfect.

She turned around to chat to Jenny again, but she'd moved out to the garden. Things felt strange between them still. A distance that never used to be there. Maybe she was imagining it, but she didn't think so.

The doorbell rang and she smiled in

anticipation of seeing Adam and Matthew. She'd only made it halfway down the hall to open it when Pete overtook her.

'Someone's eager,' Karen remarked. She understood how he felt. And judging by the crowd that had gathered behind her, they all felt exactly the same.

Pete opened the door, his face as excited as a child on Christmas morning. Standing there, with Matthew in a car seat, was Adam.

'What about you?' Adam asked, raising one dark eyebrow, with a big smile on his face. 'Have you missed me?'

'Mate. Come here,' Pete said, pulling Adam in for a hug. Karen grabbed Matthew and quickly extracted him from his seat to give him a big cuddle.

'He's so big,' Karen said to Adam, as she squeezed him tight. Her throat contracted with emotion, because when Matthew looked at her, all she could see was Rachel's eyes. 'He's so like her,' she whispered and pulled him in closer, breathing in his scent, wishing it was Rachel standing here with him, not Adam. Then she felt shame that she would have that thought. She loved Adam. She wanted both her friends, alive and present, not one or the other.

They all took turns hugging Adam and Matthew, the air full of excited chatter as they bounced dozens of questions at each other.

Karen had set up a coffee table for the children to eat at, and Josh and little Adam sat cross-legged in front of it, munching their pasta. The girls were in their high chairs, bashing the tables in front of them with their two little bunnies, delighted with the captivated audience they had. And Matthew, well, he was happily being passed from adult to adult as they all wanted turns holding him.

'Adam I made your favourite starter, in honour of your home-coming,' Karen said. She placed a plate in front of each of them, with a warm roasted asparagus salad nestled on top. 'It's served with a balsamic shallot dressing and parmesan, exactly as you love it.'

Adam grinned as he took the dish in. 'I've not had one of these . . . well not since . . . it's been a while.' He didn't want to finish the sentence, because he knew if he did, they'd all have to talk about how he was coping since Rachel's death and, for now, he just wanted to enjoy being back with his friends, catching up on their news.

Before anyone had a chance to speak, Adam took a bite. 'Karen, you'd give Nigella a run for her money any day of the week.'

She smiled as she replied, 'I hope I made it the right way. I was working off memory from how Rachel said she used to make it for you.'

'She made this for me every single time we were celebrating something special,' Adam said. He looked at Karen and asked, 'Out of interest, what did Rach tell you about this wee starter here?'

Karen replied, 'Oh, gosh, it was years ago, way back when you first met. Rachel was cooking for you. She was all in a dither, worried about what to make. I can remember her saying she'd never cooked for an Irishman before.'

'Give him bacon and cabbage!' Pete said, in his best Irish accent.

'With potatoes!' Jenny added in hers.

'Tom Cruise and Nicole Kidman had nothing on you two,' Adam joked, referring to the actors' awful accents in the movie *Far and Away*. 'Go on, Karen, ignore these two eejits.'

'Well, she really was stumped on the starter. She looked online at lots of different Irish celebrity chefs. And that's where she spotted this dish,' Karen said.

Adam remembered that first dinner like it was yesterday. They'd both been nervous, realising that her cooking dinner for him was a shift in their relationship. Things were getting serious. Her hand shook as she placed the starter in front of him.

'She'd not really done much cooking for anybody before that,' Karen said. 'I can remember telling David that I thought you might be 'the one'.'

David smiled as the memory came back to him too. 'I'd forgotten about that day. I came home from work and the kitchen was full of cookbooks.'

'She was so chuffed when you loved it. She came over the next day and stood over there . . . ' Karen pointed to the kitchen worktop, and her eyes glistened as she continued ' . . . she told us all about the meal and . . . '

'And about the night that followed?' Adam asked, eyebrow raised again.

'Yes, I do believe she did!' Karen laughed.

'Say no more. There's children present,' Adam

replied, winking. 'Suffice to say, it was a memorable night.'

'Hang on a minute,' Pete said. 'If I remember this story correctly, you called over to us the next day too.'

'He did,' Jenny said to the table. 'And you told us you hated that starter!'

'No!' Karen said.

Adam started to laugh, 'Yes! But I couldn't tell her that. I've always hated asparagus. Besides, I would have said anything to her that night. It was the third date and . . .'

'Say no more,' Pete said, mimicking Adam's earlier statement.

'You took one for the team,' David added. 'Admirable.'

'All these years you've pretended it's your favourite,' Karen said.

'Rach was forever making it for me. Birthdays, anniversaries, Christmas. If it was a special occasion, I'd know one thing for sure, I'd be peeing green the next day,' Adam said, grinning.

Laughter filled the dining room and Pete added, 'The smell of an asparagus pee. That's nasty.'

'Er, hate to break this to you,' Karen said, a big grin on her face, 'Rachel grew to hate asparagus too. She only made it because she thought it was your favourite. I can remember her saying to me that if she never saw another green tip again, it would be too soon!'

Adam put his head back and roared. You old fraud Rach! Once the laughter in the room petered out, silence descended. They were all

113

lost in thought of Rachel.

Adam looked around, wondering if she would come.

Sensing a mood shift, David asked, 'So, come on, what's it like being back in Ireland with your dad?'

'Good,' Adam replied, grateful for the change in conversation.

''Good', that's all you have to say?' Jenny said. 'You can do better than that! We want details!'

'Well, Dad's been great with Matthew. He kitted out the spare room for him, transforming it into a very cool nursery. You know, he marched into Mothercare and told them to box up the window display for him,' Adam said.

'He did not,' Pete chuckled.

'He did. He took one look at it and figured he'd not be able to recreate a better one, so he told them he wanted it. Down to the last soft toy. They saw him coming; by the time he'd left, he'd half the shop with him. High chair, stroller, which I already had, not to mention half a dozen outfits.'

'I bet he has him spoiled rotten,' David said.

'Proper order,' Karen added, looking at her godson with adoration. 'He deserves all that love and more.' She leaned in to Adam and touched his hand lightly, 'Stay here with me. I've got a spare room. I could have it ready for you both in minutes.'

'He's staying with us!' Jenny snapped. 'Hands off.'

'No need to shout,' David jumped in to Karen's defence. 'She was only offering.'

114

'I just thought we'd have more room here and you being pregnant, you might not want — ' Karen apologised.

'He's our oldest friend and we'll never be too busy or full to have him stay,' Jenny said, an edge to her voice now. 'No. We want Adam and Matthew at our house and that's the end of it.'

'Ladies, ladies, there's more than enough of me to go around,' Adam joked, trying his best to deflect the tension that had filled the table and they both half-heartedly laughed. 'Look, I'm going to stay with Pete and Jenny first of all, because it's all arranged. But how about we come over here for a few nights too? I bet they'll get sick of me soon enough and be grateful for a break.'

'Yeah, two or three nights of your farts and we'll be pushing you out the door,' Pete said.

'You said farts!' Josh shrieked with delight, and squealed loudly when Pete pretended to do one, placing his hand under his arm.

'Perfect,' Karen said. 'I really wasn't trying to cause any trouble.' She jumped up to get the main courses so nobody could see her disappointment. She felt foolish now. Of course, he'd prefer to stay with his oldest friends. It was just that seeing him and Matthew made her feel a little closer to Rachel.

Jenny walked up behind her, watching Karen lay the finished starter plates on the counter top. 'I was a bit snappy back there. Out of order.'

'It's okay,' Karen said, but she didn't disagree. 'It makes perfect sense that he'd stay with you guys. Best friends and all that.'

'So are you,' Jenny said, feeling awful now. She could see how upset Karen was. 'He loves you. We all do.'

Karen smiled, but somehow or other, right now, she wasn't sure she believed that. Jenny's words felt flat and insincere.

As she placed the roast beef in the centre of a large oval dish, she asked, 'How is Pete? You said you were a bit worried about him the other day.'

'To be honest, that's why I want Adam to stay over. I *am* worried about him. He's stressed. Muttering in his sleep all the time. That's when he does sleep in our room. He's never at home. I'm not sure if it's me, or work, or the prospect of a new baby, but he's definitely not happy,' Jenny admitted.

'Maybe you need to find a way to alleviate his stress,' Karen said.

'Oh, I've tried that, but he's not interested in sex whatsoever,' Jenny replied. 'Probably just as well, cos my lady bits are in bits!'

Karen giggled, and said, 'I wasn't talking about that, but ouch on that score. I meant how about suggesting he try something, like say, Pilates? It's a great way to get some calm back into your life. I go every week and it's a godsend.'

Jenny took a look at Karen, who right now looked the very opposite of relaxed. She shrugged non-committally. 'I'm not sure it would be Pete's cup of tea, a bit too way out for him.'

'In my class, there are all sorts who go. And I'm pretty sure there's a male-only class over in the community centre each week. You could surprise him by booking a session for him. And if you get Adam and David to go too, he might be less reluctant to give it a go,' Karen said.

'That's not a bad idea. I might just do that.'

Karen placed the crispy golden roast potatoes around the beef, pleased with how the dish had turned out. She scattered some chopped parsley on top of the parsnip and carrot mash and Puy lentils. A final stir of gravy, then she was ready to bring it through.

'Now this meal *is* my favourite,' Adam said. 'I miss a good roast. Dad and I, well we're not exactly Jamie Oliver.'

★ ★ ★

'Do you think you'll stay in Belfast?' Karen asked as she carved the meat.

Adam shrugged. 'I really don't know. It's been good getting to know Dad properly. But it's not without its . . . issues.'

They all looked at him expectantly.

'Well, he's only been double-dating. He's got this lovely boyfriend — a chap called George — and a friend with benefits,' Adam said.

'Good for him!' Karen said. She'd always liked Bill.

'I hope I have as active a love life when I'm his age,' David said.

'Well, you won't believe who his 'friend' is,' Adam said.

They all paused eating and looked at him in anticipation.

'Remember Jane?'

'The bunny boiler?' Jenny asked.

117

'The very one,' Adam replied.

The gasps from all made him chuckle and he filled them all in on the past weeks' drama.

'No wonder you were delighted to get the hell out of Dodge!' Pete laughed.

'Ah, Jane is all right, I suppose. She just needs to move on. I feel bad because I gave her a right mouthful last time we spoke. I'll talk to her when I go back. If I go back,' Adam said.

'Sounds like your dad might be disappointed if you don't. He must have spent a pretty penny putting in the nursery and all that,' David said.

Adam nodded. 'He has. But ah, I don't know. I'll just have to see. Not sure I want to be there in the middle of all his romantic triangles, for the foreseeable. I love Belfast, it's a cool city, but it doesn't feel like home to me.'

Adam wanted to change the subject, always feeling jittery when he had to think about a future that right now was hazy and unplanned. He turned to David and thumped him on his arm. 'How's Robyn?'

David beamed. 'She's lovely. I mean, she's good, thanks.'

'I think you're blushing,' Adam teased. 'I'm glad it's going well.'

'What's the difference between a divorce lawyer and a catfish?' Jenny asked the room. She paused for a beat, then said, 'One's a slimy, scum sucker and the other one's a fish.'

They all giggled, except David.

Jenny, catching the look on his face, said, 'Sorry. Couldn't resist it. It's just, well, normally in a divorce case, the lawyer gets what, one third

118

of the assets in fees? It doesn't usually include the husband in the settlement too.'

'Jenny,' Pete warned.

'Joke!' Jenny said, holding her hands up. 'Come on, lighten up everyone.'

David smiled weakly at her, but he didn't find it one bit funny. 'You might refrain from those kind of jokes whenever Robyn is around.'

'Course,' Jenny said, winking at Karen.

He'd seen the hurt on Robyn's face when he'd told her about this lunch. To his shame, when Karen called him to tell him about it, the thought didn't cross his mind to ask if Robyn could come along. Somehow or other, he'd managed to separate his life into two halves. One side with these friends, which still included his ex-wife Karen. And the other, with Robyn, that none of them were part of. And it hadn't really bothered him up until this point.

As his friends all laughed at the divorce lawyer jokes, he felt like he was betraying the woman he loved. He wasn't sure how he was going to change the friendship dynamics, but somehow or other he had to try.

11

The melon and the terrified lady bits

Didsbury Leisure Centre, Manchester

Adam arrived at the leisure centre a few minutes early. He walked into the locker room and looked at the long timber bench that ran across the back of the empty room.

Sleep.

The word sneaked into his mind and once it was there, his body responded greedily. His eyes watered, stung, and when he yawned, every muscle in his body screamed out in protest. He threw his gym bag on to the hard wooden surface of the bench and lay down, using it as a pillow.

Sleep.

Just ten minutes would get him through the exercise class Jenny had booked for him, Pete and David. Since he returned to Didsbury, he'd only managed to snatch a few hours each night. And before that, he'd struggled to get more than four hours in a row. It was catching up on him.

He closed his eyes, but then his mind opened, letting in random thoughts at galloping speed.

Rachel.

Is that the sound of a baby crying? Matthew? No. Sure he's with Karen. He's safe. But is he? I don't think I'm feeding him enough. And what in God's name was I doing, letting him have a lick of that Cornetto ice cream? Rachel wouldn't like that. And what was up with the shit in his nappy this morning? Pea-green shite. Ha! Maybe he was eating asparagus!

Pete. Something's not right with him. That face he made when Jenny placed his hand on her tummy when the baby kicked earlier. What was that? Disinterest? Annoyance? Yep. There's definitely something off there.

Perhaps there's an alien inside Jenny! I mean, now that I think of it, she has a look of yer man. Adam chuckled as Jenny's face morphed into that of John Hurt.

He should tell Rachel that one.

Adam sat up. It was no use. His tiredness wasn't curable with a quick nap on a hard bench. He suspected even going to bed early for a good night's sleep wouldn't cure it. Last night, as he rocked Matthew back to sleep, he'd worked out that the last time he'd slept through the night, without bad dreams, or insomnia, was the night before Rachel died. They were both exhausted because Matthew had been colicky all day, crying and making sure that both of them felt his pain. And boy, did they feel his pain. When he finally closed his eyes, they fell into bed, her sticking her bum into him, the way she did, him pulling her head under his chin, the way he did, wrapping his arms around her. Spoon to spoon. And Matthew, the wee angel, had slept through the night. Eight glorious hours of uninterrupted sleep.

But that was then. Sometimes, when he

remembered his old life, he felt like he was watching scenes from a beloved movie. Had it really happened? If Matthew wasn't here, he suspected that he might not believe any of it had.

To be fair, this insomnia was nothing to do with their little man who still slept through the night. It was his brain that just wouldn't shut down no matter how hard he tried. The weight of decisions he had to make each day as a single parent overwhelmed him. He missed the guidance of his wife. Like, right now, Matthew could do with a haircut. But it would be his first one. And Adam knew he couldn't screw that up. Photographs would have to be taken, a single lock kept in a silver box. They'd received one as a gift for his naming ceremony and Rachel had been so excited for the day that they'd fill it with a treasured memento.

Yesterday, after he caught Jenny trying to pull Matthew's dark curls into two pigtails, he knew he couldn't put off the haircut any longer. So he took him for a walk around Didsbury, looking for a potential salon. But he'd no sooner walk in the door of one, that he'd walk right out again. The music was too loud in one, and in another, he'd put money there was someone smoking weed in it. Then the way that young wan was waving her scissors around in Curl Up n' Dye, it was tantamount to a blood-bath disaster.

Rachel would have known where he should bring him. He'd bet that she'd already chosen the right salon, ready for the moment that Matthew needed his first cut.

'Rach?' He whispered to the empty locker

room. Nothing. She'd been so quiet lately. His loneliness felt like it was going to swallow him whole.

'You all right, mate?' Pete shouted, running into the room, tossing his bag at Adam's feet. 'Looking a bit glum there.'

Adam shrugged. 'Just knackered.'

'Well, that's fatherhood for you,' Pete replied, satisfied with Adam's answer. 'We better get ready. The class starts in five minutes.'

'We could just head to the pub. She'd be none the wiser,' Adam said as he tied up the laces on his trainers.

The thought of a cold pint of lager made Pete lick his lips, but he shook his head, banishing the thought with a regretful groan. 'We have to do this. There's no arguing with a hormonal Jenny. You've seen what's she's like.'

They both paused as they remembered the scene at breakfast that morning.

They had walked into the kitchen and found her standing in front of a melon, with a large carving knife. Her eyes flared, her nostrils flared, even her hair flared. She then began to stab the melon, roaring as she plunged the knife into its red flesh.

Adam had pushed a reluctant Pete forward towards her.

'Why does it have to be me?' Pete said, in a feeble attempt to dodge a hormonal bullet.

'She's your wife,' Adam replied. 'Plus, the way she's waving that knife around, it would be irresponsible of me to go over. I mean, Matthew's already lost one parent, he can't lose another.'

'A low blow, Adam Williams, using that old overused chestnut, my wife is dead,' Pete said.

'Grow a pair.' Adam gave him a hard shove.

Pete stumbled towards Jenny, who was looking at the poor dismembered melon with satisfaction. As he inched his way towards her, he asked, 'Everything all right, love?'

The look she gave him in response left him in no doubt of the answer. He took a step backwards.

'All right? Me? Oh yeah, I've never been better.' Jenny's face had gone a funny colour. Red, with two large splotches of purple above each cheek.

'That's good, love.' Pete was about to turn away, make a run for it, when a whimper stopped him in his tracks. 'Ah love,' he said, moving back towards her, arms outstretched. Two big fat tears rolled down Jenny's face.

Jenny pointed to the pulpy remains of the fruit and wailed, 'This melon, well, that's the size of what I'm expected to squeeze out of . . . ' her voice dropped to a whisper and she pointed down below ' . . . my lady bits!'

Pete winced. To be fair, that had to hurt. She started to wave the knife again, gesturing to her stomach. 'And look at the size of me. I'm just one big disgusting lump. With a melon inside me that's so big, so bloody enormous, I know it's going to rip me apart.'

Pete looked at Adam, who was now a funny shade of green. He mouthed silently to Adam, 'I've got this.'

Adam gave him the thumbs-up, but stayed

back, just to be safe. Jenny was a passionate woman, and you never knew with her how she might react to any given situation. Throw in the hormones, they might need to make a run for it.

'You see, love, it might not be all baby melon inside you, making you look so fat,' Pete continued.

Jenny looked confused by his words, but his tone was kind and knowing, so she tried a brave smile.

'Just think about all the rubbish you've been chucking down your throat, love. Chocolates, crisps, fried-egg sandwiches. You had two of those last night for a snack, remember?'

Adam looked at his best friend in horror. What in the name of God was he saying? Had he lost his tiny mind?

Pete was on a roll. 'I'd say there's a good chance a lot of that big 'melon' in there . . . ' he patted her protruding belly, 'isn't all baby at all . . . '

Don't say it, you gobshite, Adam thought. Walk the fuck away.

But Pete wasn't on his wavelength and finished the sentence, ' . . . you've just got really fat.'

There was silence for about thirty seconds. Nobody spoke or moved. Adam never took his eyes off the knife in Jenny's hand and wondered if those words would be the last that his gobshite friend ever uttered. Then with a loud clatter, Jenny dropped her knife to the counter top and started to wail.

'It took me nearly an hour to calm her down,'

Pete said, leaning back against the gym locker door. 'She cried a river. I think if I live to be a hundred, I'll never understand women.'

'Tip to the wise: never tell a woman they're fat, you numpty!' Adam threw his towel at him.

But instead of laughing, irritation flashed across Pete's face. 'That's me all right. Getting it wrong all the time. I mean, melon baby isn't even mine. Yet somehow or other, I'm still getting it in the neck morning noon and night. I can't do right for doing wrong.'

Adam watched the pain on his friend's face. Jenny was right. That's what's going on.

He walked over to Pete and sat down beside him. 'Hold on there a minute. The baby is yours, or will be in every way that matters.'

But Pete wasn't in the mood to discuss this. He ignored Adam and stood up, yanking his sweat pants out of the crack of his arse.

'Snug fit.' Adam joked in automatic reflex to a jibe that was laid open, ready for the taking. But Pete didn't bite. There was none of the usual banter thrown back at him.

Instead, Pete took a deep breath and pulled in his belly, which was hanging over the top of the sweat pants. Sighing, he said, 'These fit perfectly the last time I wore them.'

'When was that, back in 1981?' Adam laughed, trying to lighten up the oppressive air that had suddenly clouded the locker room.

'There's that razor-sharp humour we all love to hate. You'll cut yourself one of these days, if you're not careful,' Pete replied.

'All right mate, relax would ya? I'm sorry.

What's really going on here?' Adam asked.

'You know, Jo only cooked organic healthy food. Six months ago, I was fit, slim . . . ish . . . ' Pete sounded nostalgic.

'Hang on here a minute, you hated Jo's cooking. You were always sneaking off to Kentucky Fried Chicken for a snack box,' Adam replied.

'That's not the point. Jenny's idea of healthy eating is to cook the chips in the oven, as opposed to the deep fat fryer! It's no wonder I've piled on this much weight.'

'So what are you saying here? That you miss Jo? That you regret breaking up with her and getting back with Jen?' Adam asked.

'No! Yes . . . no, of course not,' Pete said.

'That clears up that, so,' Adam replied.

Pete fell down on to the bench again, his shoulders hunched in defeat. 'I can't go into the class looking like this. It's probably full of Jo types, all sexy in their tight Lycra. And men who look like Will Smith, with their muscles bursting out of vests.'

'Ah, would you give over. You're way too hard on yourself. I was only saying to Jenny the other night that you reminded me of a movie star,' Adam said.

'Do I?' Pete's face lit up with expectation. 'Jenny did say that I looked like Bruce Willis in *Die Hard 3* once.'

'No, that's not who I was thinking of. But I reckon there's more than a passing resemblance to yer man Samwise from *Lord of the Rings*.' He nudged Pete with his shoulder, to show him he was just joking, in the way he'd done with him for decades. Only problem was, this time Pete wasn't laughing.

'A hobbit. I look like a fucking hobbit. That's about right,' Pete said.

Shite. They'd been best friends since sixth form, and part of their routine, part of who they were, was this banter. Jenny wasn't wrong when she said that something was up with him. 'Ah look-it, if you're Samwise, then I'm Frodo. We're both hobbits. I'll even be the big hairy one.'

Pete smiled, but it was forced and the air crackled with tension.

A creak signalled the opening of the door to the locker room and they both jumped at the noise.

'Now, *that* on the other hand is a sight to behold,' Adam waved his hand towards the door.

David swaggered in, wearing a pale pink tracksuit, with the collar upturned and a sweatband on both his wrists and under his mop of wavy blond hair.

'Bet you feel better now,' Adam said under his breath to Pete.

'You've no idea.' Pete jumped up to stand beside Adam.

'So what exactly is this class Jenny booked us into?' David asked. 'She was most mysterious when she rang. Just said I had to be here, or there would be trouble. Then Karen rang and insisted I come too. I wouldn't mind, but I could be on the golf course right now. It's most inconvenient.'

'Pilates,' Adam and Pete said together.

'Apparently, it can balance your life,' Pete said. 'Helps with stresses. All the craze now. It was your Karen that told Jenny all about it.'

'She's not my Karen any more. But I should have known she was behind it all. She can't do without her weekly class of Pilates, it's the only thing that keeps her sane. Apparently. And of course I'm the one paying through the nose for it every month! A load of mumbo-jumbo nonsense.' David stuffed his gym bag into a locker, then took his tracksuit jacket off, revealing a bright green polo shirt underneath.

'Nice colour. No chance we'll lose you in that.' Pete stuffed his hand in his mouth to stop laughing.

'It is rather nice, isn't it? Robyn bought one for each of us,' David said.

'His-and-hers clothes. Must be getting serious,' Adam said. Teasing aside, he was happy for David. He'd had a rough year. 'Listen, we might as well get it over and done with. I, for one, am not going to take on Jenny. As I told young Pete earlier, as a single parent, I can't be taking any risks with my life.'

'Quite right. And Karen would kill me if I back out,' David replied. He wondered how she was today. She'd seemed quiet at lunch on Saturday. So much sadness behind her eyes. He'd text her later on, check in on her. Maybe he'd call in.

'Hold on here a minute, I thought divorcing someone meant that you didn't have to answer to them any more,' Adam remarked.

'No.'

'Not a bit of it.'

David and Pete replied at the same time, shaking their heads sorrowfully.

'Divorcing Karen just means that now I have two women to answer to. It's pretty tricky at times, I don't mind telling you.'

Adam slapped his shoulder and said, 'Could be worse. You could have no woman to answer to.' He meant it as a joke, but somehow or other it came out sounding all pathetic. And he felt tears sting his eyes again. What the hell was wrong with him?

David's smile disappeared instantly and he grabbed Adam's arm. 'Oh goodness, I'm ever so sorry. I didn't mean to . . . I never meant . . . you know I'd never say anything . . . ' David, his face flushed red, bumbled his way through an apology.

'Would you be wise. I know that. Blame my perverted sense of humour. Come on, lads, let's brace ourselves. On the other side of that wall, fit women in Lycra await us.'

Shoulders back, they marched side by side to the hall and opened the double doors.

12

The achy breaky heart and a gin-soaked Peggy

Didsbury Leisure Centre, Manchester

'Shite,' Adam said as he took in the big hall.

'I don't see any Lycra in here,' Pete said.

'This doesn't look like any Pilates class I've ever seen,' David added.

They looked around the room, which was packed with about fifty or so pensioners. Grannies and granddads, all wearing jeans with a sharp crease down their centre, bright red, green and blue plaid shirts, with cowboy hats perched on top of their greying hair. From a large stereo system at the top of the hall, Patsy Cline's voice was crooning about falling to pieces.

'Well, howdy there, folks. Ruth's the name, line-dancing is the game.' A woman's voice boomed out from the other side of the hall.

Where the hell did she spring from? Adam thought. She was wearing one of those headpiece microphones and she bounced over towards them, tipping her hat in greeting.

'We're looking for the Pilates class,' Pete said. 'I think we might be in the wrong room. Is there another hall?'

'No, just this one. You're in the right place, but you've got the wrong day. Pilates is on Tuesdays,

131

today's it's seniors line-dancing. But I can assure you, it's much more fun with us than with all that find your inner core malarkey.'

She started to laugh and the room joined in. Adam, Pete and David found themselves laughing along too. Laugh and the whole room laughs with you.

'Sure, we'll come back next Tuesday.' Adam turned to the lads, whispering, 'Let's get out of here!'

'To the pub!' Pete declared, delighted at this twist of fate.

But then Ruth's voice filled the hall again, 'Let's give our three youngsters a warm how y'all doing welcome.' She raised her hat and waved it in the air. 'Yee-haw!'

A loud cheer rang out, some even started to clap, and suddenly they were surrounded by a sea of check and plaid. Like a magician, Ruth had somehow found three hats and she quickly shoved them on to their heads, saying, 'I always keep spares for newbies. There, now you don't look quite so stupid.'

She ushered them to the front of the class, and next thing they knew, they were in a line, with Ruth facing them.

'Jenny did this on purpose,' David hissed. 'I knew she was still pissed off with me about the divorce with Karen. The way she looks at me sometimes, it's most unsettling.'

'She is, mate. Sorry. But I've not done anything to piss her off!' Pete said.

Before Adam could respond, he felt a pinch on his arse. He jumped and turned around to see a small lady, with snow white hair and a twinkle in her grey-blue eyes, peering up at him.

'I'm Peggy.' She winked. 'Don't fret, I promise to keep a good eye on you.'

'It's not your eyes I'm worried about, missus,' Adam said, rubbing his arse cheek. He moved a step closer to Pete. 'She has some grip for a pensioner,' he whispered.

'It's 'Achy Breaky Heart' time folks!' Ruth said, 'Doris, hit it!'

Doris pressed play on the CD player and as the music filled the hall, a murmur of approval rippled through the room. Billy Ray Cyrus's voice started to sing and despite themselves, the lads could feel themselves beginning to sway to the music, their feet tapping along.

'Just follow my lead, gentlemen, and one, two three, we're off! Left to right, step together, shuffle, shuffle.' Ruth bellowed out over Billy Ray's voice, her legs moving side to side, back and forth on the floor with ease.

Adam looked at Pete and David, and realised that they looked exactly how he felt. They had become three rabbits frozen in the glare of headlights. Wearing cowboy hats. And despite Ruth's calls of heel, toe and shuffle, none of them moved. Adam felt a trickle of sweat make its way down the small of his back. Then Peggy, with a force that belied her small frame, shuffled sideways hard into Adam. It took him by surprise, and sent him flying into Pete, who in turn hit David. Like trees felled, they crashed to the floor in an undignified heap.

Billy Ray Cyrus continued to croon about his achy breaky heart, oblivious to their pain.

'More like my achy breaky arse!' Adam shouted and the three friends looked at each other for a moment before breaking into loud laughter. David was the first up and he helped to pull them back on to their feet. The class giggled good-naturedly along with them and Ruth said, 'Don't let that worry you one little bit. It happens to the best of us. Now, let's start again from the top! Just watch me closely boys, you'll get the hang of it, I promise!' She nodded at Doris, the DJ, and once again, they were off.

Adam concentrated on Ruth's legs, and to his surprise, his own started to move in time to the beat. When he shuffled to his left, he spied Pete and David also shuffling with big goofy smiles on their face. Pete actually looked quite good. Fecker, he must have done this before.

'Now, march it back. Clap, clap, roll those hips, shuffle, shuffle, step together,' Ruth shouted at them all.

'Sorry!' Adam apologised, when Peggy bumped into him again. But she didn't seem in the least bit worried, having another sneaky pinch of his arse before she moved away.

'Cross and heel, and behind and front and heel and turn,' Ruth continued, and Adam realised that now he was beginning to understand the lingo.

The next twenty minutes passed by in a blur, and to their astonishment Adam, Pete and David were actually line-dancing in a pretty reasonable way.

'Give yourselves a clap. You've moved and you've grooved with attitude!' Ruth declared and everyone cheered 'Yee-haw', waving their hats in the air. 'Now go catch your breath with some well-earned refreshments.'

Doris, it turned out was also in charge of drinks. She had jugs of lemon barley water on the table with a stack of white plastic cups lined beside them. Slices of lemon and oranges were on a large platter and several plates of biscuits. They grabbed a plastic cup of juice, threw a few slices of fruit in and sat down on one of the benches, side by side.

'Bloody hell, I'm sweating like a pig here,' Pete said, wiping his face with a towel. David and Adam nodded in agreement.

Ruth walked over and explained, 'It's low-impact exercise, but it sure gets your heart rate going, doesn't it? A great way to lose weight and tone up while having fun, I always say.'

'I haven't laughed like that in a long time,' Pete admitted. 'I must tell my mum about this class. I think she'd love it here, she was always a lovely dancer. Dad and her used to waltz all the time. The proper way, mind. The kind where you do all the fancy moves.'

'You've got great rhythm. Maybe you get that from her,' Ruth said.

Adam looked around at the pensioners, all laughing and chatting, catching up on each other's weeks, and he tried to picture his own mother with them all. And no matter how hard he tried, the image of Mary Williams wearing a cowboy hat and blue jeans jarred. He didn't think she'd ever done anything as fun as this in her life. But then, another memory niggled him. His mum and dad jiving, in the kitchen, one Christmas when he was a kid. She was laughing, happy, his dad was singing as he swung her around the room. What was up with him? He'd spent most of the past ten years doing a very good job of not thinking about his mother, but now she kept jumping into his head. It didn't matter what she had been like, once upon another time. His mother had cast him away like a bad smell, ten years ago. She left Didsbury and she never once looked back. There was a reason that the bad memories stuck, whilst the good ones floated away, almost forgotten. His mother's face, flushed with anger and accusations took residence again, in his head and heart. All this revisiting of his past was doing him no good. He was better off without her. He'd told her that on the last day they spoke.

Pete stood up, moving closer to Ruth. He was chuffed with her praise of his rythmn. 'You know, I did play the drums years ago. I used to be in a band. The *Didsbury Tribune* once compared us to the Smiths.'

'How nice for you,' Ruth said politely, but without any real interest. 'Well, I must say, you are all good sports. I hope you've forgiven me for pushing you into staying for our class. I know you hadn't signed up for this.'

'Not at all. Sure, it was a bit of craic,' Adam said.

'I did rather enjoy myself,' David admitted.

'That's the great thing about line-dancing, it doesn't matter if you have two left feet.' Ruth glanced at David's feet before she turned to walk away.

'Bloody cheek,' he replied, stung by the inference.

Peggy sat down beside Adam. 'I thought she'd never go.'

Pete whispered to David, 'Aye aye, his new girlfriend's back.'

Peggy placed a large black handbag on to her lap and opened it, peering into it. Muttering to herself, she pulled out a headscarf, a pair of brown leather gloves, a phone, a packet of Maltesers and then with a satisfied 'There you are!', she retrieved a silver hip flask.

Adam nudged Pete, who nudged David, and they sat watching her, mouths agape, as she took a sip from the flask, then poured a good drop into her lemon barley water.

She turned to face them. 'Oh I'm being rude, aren't I?' Peggy said, smiling. 'Pass me your cups, and I'll give you a snifter. But don't tell Ruth! I'm on my last warning here. She doesn't approve. Something about invalidating the insurance or some such nonsense.'

'Mum's the word,' David said, the first with his plastic cup outstretched.

'Rules are made to be broken, I always say.' Pete held his cup out.

'This your own home brew, Peggy?' Adam asked, taking a sniff.

'It's just gin. A little snifter to help loosen up

the joints. Bottoms up, guys,' Peggy said, taking a long swig again.

'Cheers.' They all clinked plastic with her and happily sat sipping their cocktails while Garth Brooks crooned about going down to the River.

And then, all at once, she was back.

Rachel.

His Rachel. Leaning against the wall, opposite him, watching Adam, smiling. The sun peeked through the hall's windows, and danced on her auburn hair. Adam felt something give inside him, as it always did, when she appeared.

'Have I got competition?' Rachel asked, pretending to be cross, but failing miserably, because her lips curved upwards. She'd never make a poker player.

'You just might,' Adam said, smiling back at her. 'She's my kind of gal, this Peggy.'

Rachel moved closer towards him. 'I've got moves too.' Then she did a little shuffle to the right and a toe, heel, click. 'Ta da!'

Adam laughed and said, 'That's it, Peggy is blown out.' His face softened and he said, 'You know that it's only ever been you Rach.'

Her smile made him want to weep.

'The hat suits you,' she said.

'I'll have to buy one, so,' Adam replied.

His couldn't take his eyes off her. He wanted to hold her, to touch her. He wanted to feel the warmth of her lips kissing his. He wanted . . .

'How you doing, love?' she interrupted.

'All the better for seeing you. You look beautiful, Rach.' He felt a golf-ball-sized lump take up residence in his throat.

Adam was brought back to the gym with a sharp nudge to his ribs. Irritated, he turned to Peggy, who was holding up the silver flask again. He smiled his thanks with distraction as she poured another drop into his cup and turned back to Rachel.

But he was on his own again.

For the one millionth time since she died, he felt her loss. The sun retreated from the window in solidarity and darkness descended over the hall.

'Where did you go to just then?' Peggy asked, her voice quiet and gentle.

Adam turned to her, raising one dark eyebrow.

'I've been here all along.' He wasn't in the mood for chit-chat or line-dancing any more. He wanted to go and get Matthew from Karen's house, then go home. But he didn't have a home. He wanted to feel his son's soft head in the nape of his neck. And he wanted to cry. Damn it, damn it, *damn it!*

Peggy wasn't to be deterred. 'You might have been sitting here quietly, but your mind was somewhere else. Somewhere that made you happy. Or maybe you were with *someone* that made you happy. Either ways, you were gone there for a while.'

'I was thinking about my wife. Rachel.' He looked around the hall again, hoping to catch a glimpse of her.

Come back, Rach. Please.

'Well, I don't need to ask if it's a happy marriage. I know the look of love when I see it. Your face was filled with it,' Peggy said.

139

'We were in love.' Adam looked down and felt that familiar ache that rarely left him. It gathered speed as it raced around his body.

Peggy didn't say anything, she just added some more gin to their plastic cups. Pete and David were back on their feet and they were practising the toe, heel, click move.

'She died,' Adam whispered.

They both took another sip of their drinks in silence, his words hanging between them. Then, she put her head back into her bag and pulled out a purse. She opened the flap and showed him a photograph encased in a plastic frame, of a young couple, about his age. The woman was smiling and so was the man, whose eyes were firmly on the lady by his side.

'That was taken on my wedding day. That there is my Terry,' Peggy said.

'Look at you, you were movie-star beautiful,' Adam told her.

'I had my moments,' she replied, touching the photograph. 'But I was most beautiful when I was with my husband. I lost a lot of my shine the day he died.'

Adam touched her hand, and felt her weathered skin beneath his fingertips. She placed her other hand over his. 'He died forty-two years ago, in September.'

'Does it get easier?' Adam asked.

'No. But you can learn to live with it, live a good life, even a happy one. Our children helped with that. And now I've got grandchildren too.'

Adam said, 'We have a son. It was Rachel's gift to me before she died. He's coming up to a year old now. When I feel the grief attacking me, threatening to undo me, I just have to look at him. It helps.'

She nodded in understanding. They sat listening to the music for a few minutes, then Adam turned to her and asked, 'Can I ask you something?'

'Yes.'

'Do you ever see your husband?' Adam asked. Was he the only one who had visits from a dead spouse? Sometimes he worried that he was losing his mind. Other times he knew that these visits from Rachel were the only thing that kept him sane. And allowed him to put one foot in front of the other.

'Well, let me see. I see him in the eyes of my daughter and in the walk of my son. And when my grandson laughs, it's him, every nuance of him, in that joyful sound.' She looked up at Adam. 'But you didn't mean like that, did you?'

He shook his head.

'Do you see your wife?' Peggy asked.

Adam nodded.

'And do you talk to each other?' Peggy asked.

'Yes. She was teasing me about you as it happens. She thinks my head has been turned by your sass.'

Peggy's giggle made Adam smile. 'Oh, it's been a long time since I ever made a young woman jealous! In my day, I was quite the head-turner.'

'I don't doubt that for one moment,' Adam said.

'Well, in answer to your question, I don't see

141

Terry any more. I still talk to him a lot. When I'm up at his grave,' Peggy said.

'Rachel was cremated. We scattered her ashes up in Portmeirion. But she's never left me. Not really. She comes back every now and then, sometimes for a quick chat, other times for longer,' Adam admitted.

'You're not ready to say goodbye to her yet,' Peggy said.

'I don't think I ever will be,' Adam whispered.

Then Ruth's voice called out. 'Put down your cups, it's time to 'Turbo Hustle'!'

Peggy said, 'Your friends are eager!' David and Pete were already in position, ready to begin.

She put her flask back into her bag, then closed the clasp. 'You're wrong, you know. You will be ready one day. When the time is right, you'll find that you don't need her to visit you. In the meantime, how about we give your lovely Rachel something to be really worried about? Would you dance with me?' She held her hand out towards him.

Adam laughed out loud and bowed towards her. He offered her his arm and said, 'I'd be delighted. And by the way, Peggy. You were wrong about something too.'

She stopped and looked up at him. 'What's that?'

'You didn't lose it,' Adam said.

'Lose what?' Peggy asked, puzzlement creasing her face.

'When Terry died, you didn't lose your shine.'

13

The accidental porn star and the thing called love

Pete and Jenny's house, Didsbury, Manchester

'Shove over,' Pete said, plonking himself in the middle of the couch in between Adam and David. The two lads inched themselves to either side and he threw a can of lager at each of them. Jenny was at her sister's, which gave them the perfect excuse for a lads' night in.

'All's quiet upstairs,' Adam said. He double checked the baby monitor was on and relaxed when he saw the green light. Little Adam and Matthew were both out for the count.

'Do you think we've got enough to eat?' David asked, sarcasm loaded on to each word.

They looked down at the mountain of food in front of them. Three large pizzas, a bag of chips, a bag of onion rings, dough balls, three dips and garlic bread.

'I may have over-ordered,' Adam said, licking his lips, not one bit sorry.

Pete rubbed his stomach in anticipation and it responded by growling in approval. 'This here, is not for the faint-hearted. But I, for one, am ready for the challenge.' He pinged the elastic in his tracksuit bottoms. He'd changed into them an hour earlier.

'Amateur. I'll take your tracksuit, sir, and raise you commando style,' Adam replied, nodding to his own tracksuit bottoms.

'What, you're not wearing any jocks?' David asked.

'Nope. Nil by arse. Naked as the day I was born underneath this,' Adam said.

'That's hardly necessary for a pizza and lager, is it?' David glanced down at his suit and tie.

'Many would think that,' Adam said, shaking his head at the naivety of his friend. 'But you see, I've fallen foul before at evenings such as these. You think you're sorted. Elasticated waistband at the ready. But then as you move on to round two . . .'

'The dough balls . . . ' Pete interrupted.

Adam nodded in agreement, then continued, ' . . . things begin to feel a bit tight. Restricted, shall we say. But you still have chips and garlic dip to tackle.'

'Not to mention the onion rings,' Pete added sorrowfully, thinking of his M&S boxer shorts that were beginning to feel more uncomfortable with every word Adam stated. He *was* an amateur.

'So you're saying jocks impede your eating? What utter nonsense,' David replied, laughing. They were taking the rise out of him again.

'Oh, you poor, innocent young man. I'm telling you. Try it. Let it all hang out and you'll find you can get all the way to round three,' Adam said.

'The garlic bread,' Pete said.

'What surprises me is how much time you've put into thinking about all of this. Some of us have lives!' David sneered.

Adam turned to them both and bowed his head, placing his two hands together, as if in prayer. 'Success depends upon previous preparation, and without such preparation there is sure to be failure.'

'Oooh, get you . . . ' Pete jeered.

'Well, if Confucius said so . . . ' David winked, recognising the quote. He loosened the knot on his tie, then pulled it up over his head, opening his top button on his white chambray shirt.

Pete nodded towards his crotch.

'That's as far as it goes for me. The jocks stay on,' David replied firmly.

Laughing, delighted with themselves, they moved forward to grab a slice of pizza each.

'Five minutes to kick off,' Pete said, nodding towards the TV. Manchester United were playing Liverpool on their home ground at Old Trafford.

'It's like old times,' David said, smiling at his two buddies. He'd missed this. Not the football, of course. He never watched that. But if it meant spending time with Adam and Pete, he was happy to endure it. Over the past few months, things had been so stressful, they'd not had time to just sit down and be silly. And in his world, there weren't that many times where he got to just kick back and be a less uptight version of the man he normally had to be.

'Hey, Confucius. Remember that time you failed to prepare for your presentation to that company? What was it called, Tyrone something or other?' Pete said, mid-mouthful of pepperoni pizza.

'Not one of my finest moments. 'Twas Tyrone Communications you're thinking about,' Adam replied.

'Please tell me you were wearing underwear for the presentation,' David said and looked up in surprise when this question was met with snorts of laughter from Pete.

'No!' David said. 'You didn't go into the office commando.'

'Did I heck! I was wearing underwear during the presentation, but . . . ' Adam said.

'You still managed to show the boardroom your arse!' Pete snorted with laughter.

'You have a habit of doing that,' David said. 'Flashing in public.'

Pete started to sing, 'I've got you under my skin . . . ' with David joining in.

'It got me the girl, didn't it?' Adam said. Years ago, in the early days of dating Rachel, he almost lost her to her ex-boyfriend Simon. Simon had returned from Hong Kong and decided he wanted to rekindle his romance with her. And he nearly won too. But Adam had fought back and turned up at Rachel's house, singing, naked, with a red rose stuck between the cheeks of his arse.

'I had to bring out the big guns that day,' Adam said.

'Don't boast,' David replied, but he was smiling. Had Adam not stripped, responding to a dare Rachel had given him earlier, maybe she would have stayed with Simon. And that would have been so wrong.

Pete and David watched Adam's face change

as he remembered that day with Rachel. Pete jumped in quickly and said, 'You're not getting out of this story, mate. Back to the presentation with Tyrone what's its name!'

Adam shook his head, and laughed as he continued. 'There I was, ready to impress the boss with this killer presentation I'd pulled together. I held nothing back. I had histograms, scatter graphs, bar graphs, frequency distributions.'

'Impressive,' David said.

'I have my moments. It was, if I do say so myself, pretty slick. But unfortunately for me, as well as all of those, I had a certain home video made by Wendy, from the Dragon Heen Chinese takeaway, down the high street, sitting on my computer.'

'They do a mean satay down there,' Pete said.

'Never mind the satay!' David exclaimed, his attention firmly on the story. 'When you say 'home video', I'm assuming you mean of the Pamela Anderson, Tommy Lee variety?'

'He does,' Pete confirmed. 'By the way, that was a classic.'

'Great lighting,' David agreed.

'Well, unlike Pamela and Tommy, mine wasn't a planned leak! And it wouldn't have even been made if I hadn't been going through an Asian cuisine stage. I used to go the Dragon Heen at least once a week,' Adam said.

'And that had nothing to do with the fit blonde at reception, with the big . . . ' Pete looked at the dough balls he had in his hand.

'Nothing at all,' Adam laughed. 'Well, how

could Wendy fail to fall for the charms of this wee Irishman? I asked her for a drink and she said yes. One thing led to another and before I knew it things started to get interesting.'

'And that's when you made a video?' David asked.

'I had no idea she was filming me. I was a reluctant porn star, you could say,' Adam replied.

'You jammy bastard!' David said. 'Why doesn't stuff like that ever happen to me?'

'Robyn not into home movies?' Pete asked. 'Jenny isn't either.' His face dropped in disappointment.

'I'm not into home movies!' Adam exclaimed. 'I don't see the point of them,' Adam said. 'I should have guessed she was up to something, because she kept ordering me around, saying 'move your arse this way, turn that way, make more noise, make less noise'. And there was an awful whiff of sweet and sour off her. A strange night, won't lie.'

The lads laughed along with Adam, then all reached down to stuff more pizza into their mouths.

'Anyhow, I'd kind of forgotten all about it. I lost my yin for Chinese food for a while after that. Then a few weeks later, I got an email from her, with a copy of a video she said she thought I might like.'

Pete and David sniggered.

'I saved it on my computer, planning to look at it later on. I was in the middle of making a slide show for Tyrone Communications.' Adam paused for a moment. 'The plan was that the grand finale of my presentation would, with just one click, bring me to an animated graphic, which summarised the analytical data I'd compiled for them earlier.'

'You're losing me. Get to the good bits,' Pete said, stifling a yawn.

'Well, somehow or other, I put the wrong link in and when I clicked that icon, you can guess, right?' Adam said.

'No!' David exclaimed.

'Oh yeah. I'd attached the wrong video. Wendy's . . . ' Adam looked down at the dough balls in front of him, winking, ' . . . assets were resplendent for all to see on the screen!'

'Oh my God,' David said, mouth wide open.

'It gets better,' Pete said, grabbing the garlic dip for his fries.

'Pandemonium broke out. Cue lots of confused looks from my team. But I swear, a few from that room were fast asleep for half my presentation, but all of a sudden they were all eyes!'

'What did you do?' David asked.

'The only thing I could do. I threw myself at the laptop, hitting escape, delete, every button I could find. I had no idea what was coming up next though,' Adam said, shaking his head.

'What?' David asked, watching Pete hold his belly as tears of laughter spilled out of his eyes.

'I managed to hit pause on the video, right at the moment when my hairy arse came up on the screen. Frozen, in all my glory, for all to see, me, a reluctant porn star!'

David clutched his side, he was laughing so much. 'Stop, can't, not able.'

'Don't mind telling you, I was lucky to keep my job that day. Gas thing was, Tyrone Communications signed the contract within the hour. They told my boss they'd not had such an entertaining presentation in their lives.'

'Have you still got it?' David asked.

'Absolutely not. Deleted it years ago,' Adam said. 'I'd rather take part than watch. End of.

Pete turned up the television. 'Aye aye, here we go!'

Adam jumped up to grab some more beer, walking backwards so he didn't miss a moment. He realised, as he moved back to the couch that he was having a good time.

He was having the craic with his mates.

He'd watched a match with his dad the previous week, but it wasn't the same. Bill didn't have the same interest. He was more of a hurling supporter than football.

Guilt hit him again, when he thought about his dad. He'd called a few times to check in on him and Matthew. They both were ignoring the row they'd had before he left, skirting around it. His father told him how much he missed them both.

Before he had a chance to give any more thought to that, Ruud van Nistelrooy grabbed possession of the ball. He dribbled through the Liverpool defence and made his way towards the goal. Adam sat back down and passed a couple of beers to Pete and David, who accepted the cans wordlessly, their eyes firmly on the TV.

Then Van Nistelrooy looked to his left and passed the ball to Giggs, who used his head to shoot towards the goal. They all held their breaths as they watched the ball fly through the air, towards Jerzy Dudek. He dived to his right and the ball soared by him, landing in the back of the net. The three lads jumped up, roaring their appreciation.

'Did you see that?' David exclaimed. He picked up a dough ball and shouted, 'He passes to his left.' He threw the dough ball to Pete, who leaned forward and headed it with ease.

'The crowd goes wild . . . ' Adam made a cheering sound.

'Pizza, pints, good friends and Manchester United . . . that's the perfect night right here,' Pete said, mouth full again.

'If Carlsberg did . . . ' Adam added and they all raised their cans, cheering each other on. 'Half-time and one up. How bad?'

'It's a bit different from the old days though,' Pete said, throwing his eyes upwards towards where little Adam and Matthew were asleep. 'Few years ago, we'd have been down the pub, doing tequila shots to celebrate that goal.'

They were silent for a moment as they remembered the many nights they had sat propping up the bar over the years.

'Have you seen much of each other while I was gone?' Adam asked. He tried his best to keep a whine out of his voice.

David and Pete looked at each other and shrugged. 'It's been busy, what with Jenny moving back in,' Pete said.

'And I've had my hands full with Robyn,' David added.

Adam held his hands up and pretending he was juggling. 'Don't be boasting now, David.'

'Look he's gone all red!' Pete said, poking David in his side. 'Lucky bastard is at it night and day.'

'A gentleman never shares details, but let's just say that Robyn is a passionate woman,' David replied, chuffed with himself.

'Good for you, mate,' Adam said. 'Meanwhile, for me, I'm reverting back to my teenage years. Living with my parent, albeit this time it's at my dad's, not my mam's, playing the one-hand wonder.'

'I locked myself in the bathroom this morning,' Pete said. 'You know, to . . . ' He gestured with his hands.

David sniggered like a fourteen-year-old school-boy.

'Jenny not up to it now?' Adam asked. 'Fair enough. Rachel was the same when she was pregnant towards the end.'

'Karen and I had sex right up to the last week,' David boasted.

'It's not Jenny that's the problem . . . ' Pete admitted. 'I just feel a bit weirded out. I was grand at first, but then one night Jenny was talking about little Adam and how much he looked like me.'

'He is the image of you,' Adam said.

'Mini you,' David agreed. 'By the way, am I the only one who gets weirded out every time you call him little Adam?'

'You're just jealous he's not called little David,' Adam joked.

'I could never have done what you did, helping Jenny when she delivered him,' David said. 'I found it hard enough to cope with Karen's labours.'

Pete hated that he'd missed Adam's birth. He was grateful his best friend had stepped in for him. But he wasn't sure he'd be able to be there for this one either. He felt cold when he thought about it.

Pete loved that his son looked like him. They had the same eyes. The same hair. The same round face. The same smile. When Pete looked at little Adam he saw himself. One version of himself, that is. And he could lose hours looking at the little fella, sitting down at the table, drawing his little stick men pictures, tongue sticking out, completely immersed in the activity. Little Adam made him happy. Made him feel complete. Made him feel hopeful for the future. But this baby . . .

'What's going on, mate?' Adam asked.

'The thing is . . . well, the thing is . . . ' He paused and looked down. He felt ashamed for even thinking negative thoughts about an innocent little child.

'Go on,' Adam urged.

'The thing is that it's made me think about what it will be like when this baby is born. It's not going to look like me, is it?' Pete said.

'I don't know. Sure all babies are small and round,' David joked.

Nobody laughed.

'Know your audience, mate,' Adam said, shaking his head.

'Sorry,' David muttered.

Pete waved away his apology.

'Well, lots of dads have children who don't look a bit like them,' Adam said. 'Sure my Matthew is nearly all Rachel.'

'Exactly!' David exclaimed. 'And Josh isn't a bit like me. Image of Karen, everyone says so, when they meet him.'

'Thank fuck for that,' Pete said, getting his own back for the earlier jibe.

'Yes. Quite,' David agreed, happy to take it.

'It's not just how the baby looks . . . ' Pete paused.

'What else then?' Adam said.

'You'll laugh,' Pete said.

'No we won't,' Adam assured him.

'Absolutely not,' David agreed.

Pete took a deep breath. 'Every time I go near Jenny, I swear I can hear the baby shouting at me through her tummy, 'You're not my daddy.' I feel judged.'

Neither Adam nor David were quite sure what to say to that.

'Has that ever happened to you?' Pete looked at each of them.

'What? As in an unborn child talking through its mother's tummy to her ex-husband, who's not the baby's daddy and who is unsure if he wants to be?' Adam asked.

'Yeah. That.' Pete looked hopeful.

'No,' Adam said.

David shook his head too.

'But, in the spirit of honesty, I did used to imagine Matthew could talk to me when he was a newborn. And whenever he did, he looked a lot like my dead granddad. Narky old sod he was too,' Adam admitted.

'What did he say to you?' Pete asked.

'Mostly he took the piss, winding me up that Rachel loved him more than she did me,' Adam said.

'Is that around the time you got all weird at the naming ceremony?' David asked.

Adam nodded. 'I was a complete fecking eejit. No other words for it.'

'I've never had a talking newborn,' David said to Pete. 'Or a talking baby in womb. I'm a bit boring though. Not sure I have the same imagination that you guys have. More's the pity, many would say.'

'How did you get Matthew to stop talking to you?' Pete asked. 'Because Jenny has worked out that I'm avoiding her now. She keeps making all these attempts to get me into bed and there's only so many times I can claim a headache!'

'I suspect Jenny is not the kind of woman to be sidelined,' David said.

'You suspect right, mate,' Pete replied.

'Matthew kind of stopped changing into my granddad when I copped on to myself that I was acting like a gobshite,' Adam said. 'In my defence, we weren't getting much sleep then, so sleep-deprivation had something to do with my hallucinations.'

He felt foolish remembering how jealous he had felt of his son when he first arrived. Rachel was besotted, quite rightly, with her new baby, but became a bit over-protective. And his stupid ego couldn't take it. He felt sidelined. It all seemed so juvenile now, looking back. What had he been so scared of? He'd sit forever on that same sideline now, to see Rachel holding Matthew in her arms again.

'You think I'm acting like a gobshite too,' Pete stated.

'No, as it happens. I think you're trying to get your mind wrapped around a tough situation. And it's wrecking your head. You need to talk to Jenny about all of this,' Adam said.

'I can't. She's had it rough by all accounts these past few months. She needs me to be strong for her. I can't let her down,' Pete said.

'So what? You're going to spend the rest of your marriage in the toilet wanking off, rather than have a conversation with her?' Adam asked.

'Just your average marriage, so . . . ' David joked, and they all laughed.

'Talk to your missus,' Adam said firmly. 'Am I right, David?'

'I don't know if I'm the right person to ask that. You see, talking to my missus, or rather my ex-missus, is causing me a few problems right now,' David said.

The two lads turned their attention to him now.

'Karen's been having a rough time. She misses Rachel. They were such good friends, more like sisters, really. Karen always said that they grew up together. They each knew where all the skeletons were buried, so to speak. So I've been calling over there a bit. Offering a shoulder for her to cry on,' David said.

'You're a good man,' Pete said.

'Hang on a minute. You've not . . . ' Adam said, pretending he was shagging someone.

'No! Of course not. We're friends now. Good friends. The best of friends,' David protested.

'But . . . ' Pete said. 'There's always a but.'

'Sometimes, when I'm back in my old home, I wonder if I made the wrong choice. It doesn't matter how much I love the apartment, I still think of that house as my home. And I miss the kids. It's not the same being a part-time dad. You should see their faces, well, Josh's in particular, when I call over. He loves having us all together under one roof,' David said.

'I get it,' Pete replied. 'Little Adam lights up when it's the three of us together too. He does this thing, where he grabs us both and says, group hug! Some grip on him for a little fella.'

They all smiled at this.

'Do you think Karen would want to get back together?' Adam asked. In many ways that wouldn't surprise him. A few weeks back, he thought that's exactly what was going to happen.

'No!' David declared. But his face said something different. He looked doubtful.

Adam raised one dark eyebrow at him and David shrugged. 'I have to admit that sometimes she looks at me, and it's like it was back in the early days, before things got all messed up.'

'Where does Robyn come into all this?' Pete asked.

'I love her. I'm in love with her. We're good together,' David said. 'I don't want to lose her.'

'Sounds like you have your answer then,' Adam told him.

'It's just Robyn is a bit pissed off, with all my running back and forth to Karen. And to top it all, the other weekend I asked her to stay with me and the kids, and it was a bloody disaster.'

'What went wrong?' Adam asked.

'Josh was upset. He had a terrible nightmare. He sobbed. His little heart was hammering so fast. So of course, he needed to sleep with me. And he was frightful to Robyn. She couldn't do enough for him, but he kept throwing it back at her,' David said.

'And Robyn is annoyed by that?' Pete thought that was a bit much.

'Oh gosh no. She was gracious and understanding. She was wonderful, really. Planned lots of treats and fun things for the children. But Josh just can't seem to take to her.'

'Sounds like you have your hands full, mate. Keeping two women happy is a fate I wouldn't wish on any man!' Adam said. 'Listen, I'll call over to see Karen tomorrow night. We'll stay the night. I've been meaning to do that, to check in.'

'She'd like that,' David said. 'I think she feels the loneliness most in the evenings. And I'm worried she might have a drink.'

They all picked up their cans and took a swig as they thought about the disaster it was when Karen was drinking too much a few years back.

Then the baby monitor's light flashed and Matthew's cries filled the living room.

'Make it quick, mate. Five minutes to second half,' Pete said.

Adam ran up the stairs, but before he reached the top one, the smell hit him. Ah Matthew, he thought, your timing is brutal! He thought about going into the nursery to change him. But there was a good chance he'd wake little Adam there. So he scooped up his son, throwing the changing bag over his shoulders as he ran downstairs, trying to soothe him. Matthew, meanwhile, was intent on not just waking up little Adam, but also the whole street.

'Poonami alert,' Adam said.

'We kind of smelled that,' Pete answered, placing his onion ring and curry dip, back on the table. His appetite had suddenly gone.

'Sorry,' Adam laughed, seeing his face. 'I'll change him on the table. I didn't do it upstairs, in case it woke up little Adam.'

'Appreciate that,' Pete said.

Adam pulled his changing towel out of the bag and laid it flat on the dining room table, with one hand. He'd become good at this. He remembered that first month after Matthew was born; two hands weren't enough to do everyday jobs with a baby. Now he could manage with one hand tied behind his back, quite admirably. He placed Matthew gently on top of the towel. He was still screaming his head off and didn't seem ready to stop the tears. There was only one thing for it. He'd discovered that one song could halt tears in moments. They'd been in Bill's car a few weeks back and as soon as this song came on, Matthew ceased crying.

'I'm gonna have to sing to him,' Adam shouted over to the lads.

'Glam rock time?' Pete asked. He'd witnessed this a few times now.

Adam nodded. Pete and David walked up behind him, flanking him on either side.

In his best falsetto, he started to sing the song 'I Believe in a Thing Called Love' by The Darkness. Then Pete and David joined in.

Matthew immediately stopped crying and Adam said, 'Keep going, keep going!' So they all continued singing about a thing called love.

★   ★   ★

By the time they got to the end of the song, Matthew was back to his usual good-natured self and Adam had managed to clean him up and put a new clean babygro on him.

'Thanks, lads,' Adam said. Then, with a glint in his eye, pure devilment on his mind, he turned towards David and Pete, and pegged the closed nappy bag at them both, shouting, 'On the head, son.'

He roared laughing as he watched David and Pete both try to dodge the bag, and in that second, despite having his hand on Matthew's tummy, his attention was diverted. Matthew wiggled in excitement, picking up on the energy in the room and rolled on his side. Adam went to place his hands on his son's tummy, but Matthew was literally on a roll and moved again, this time falling off the table.

Adam's screams bounced between the men as he tried to grab the babygro between his fingertips, but the weight of Matthew and gravity

160

were not on his side. His fingers lost their grip and in one sickening thud, Matthew fell to the ground.

14

The Humpty Dumpty fall and wise Dr Gates

Pete and Jenny's house, Didsbury, Manchester

David and Pete rushed forward at the same time, both with their arms open in an effort to catch Matthew too. But they both had the sickening realisation that, like Adam, they were too late.

For a second, a nanosecond, silence boomed through the room, bouncing off the walls, only shattered by the strangled sobs of Adam.

'Oh Jesus, oh Matthew, my boy . . . ' Terror flooded Adam's body. His knees sagged under the weight of his guilt and he fell to the ground beside his son. He began begging God that Matthew would be okay.

As Adam's pleas filled the room, muddled together with the sound of ragged breaths from Pete and David, as if they'd been running, Matthew lay still on the ground.

Then his eyes opened wide and he emitted a shriek of pain that made them all jump.

'He's crying. That's a good sign,' David said, sounding calmer than he felt.

'It's when they don't cry that you should worry,' Pete added. His mother always said that.

'Should I pick him up? I don't know what to do!' Adam turned to ask them, tears pouring down his face. He lay down, so his head was side by side Matthew's and he softly, gently, caressed his son's cheek.

Matthew instinctively moved towards his father, trying to wriggle on to his side.

David kneeled beside him. 'Let's just have a quick look to see if there is any swelling or bruising on his head.' Adam's sharp intake of breath made him quickly add, 'I'm sure there's nothing wrong.'

David kneeled on the other side of the child and as he gently moved his head side to side, Matthew stopped crying, looking at him with curiosity.

'He's moving without any obvious distress and there's no bleeding that I can see. I think we should bring him to A&E, just to ensure he's okay,' David said.

Adam nodded, grateful that somebody was taking control. He tried to kneel so he could pick up Matthew, but he was still shaking and unsteady.

'Shall I take him?' David asked gently.

'No. I've got this,' Adam said, telling himself to calm down. His son needed him to be strong.

He stood up, with David and Pete's arms steadying him. Pete put his soft cot blanket over Matthew with extreme tenderness.

'If anything happens to him, if he's hurt . . . ' Adam began, then faltered, unable to continue.

'Nothing is going to happen to Matthew,' Pete said.

'I couldn't go on, you see,' Adam ended, his voice broken with emotion.

'You never have to find that out, mate,' Pete said. 'He's fine. He's a strong 'un, like his dad. Look at him!' Matthew was reaching up to honk Adam's nose.

'I'll drive. Why don't you jump in the back with Matthew?' David said.

'I need to stay with little Adam,' Pete said, feeling awful. 'But I'll keep in touch, by phone, promise.'

The drive to the hospital went by in a blur. Matthew whined when Adam placed him in his car seat. He sat beside him and continued to stroke and soothe him, continuously whispering endearments.

'What if he's broken a bone?' Adam asked. 'He's very agitated.'

'Then they'll fix it,' David replied, glancing at him in the rear-view mirror. He just hoped that there was nothing else going on internally that they couldn't see. Babies' heads were so heavy, they tended to fall head first. He kept glancing in the mirror, to double check that he was awake. He remembered hearing or reading at some point, that falling asleep would be bad. As far as he was concerned, the louder the cries, the better.

Traffic was on their side and within ten minutes David was pulling up in front of A&E. 'Go on in. I'll park the car and come find you.'

Adam gently took Matthew out of his car seat and then ran into the hospital, holding him close to his body. He looked around the full waiting room, scanning for a nurse or doctor. People looked up, interested in the latest drama that had

164

just entered the hospital, anything to break up the monotony of waiting for their turn to be seen.

A nurse walked by and Adam ran up to her.

'Can you help me?' Adam asked.

'Who's hurt? You or the baby?'

'My son.'

'What happened?' she asked as Adam followed her into the pre-assessment area.

He babbled out an explanation and she nodded and smiled in sympathy as she took Matthew from him.

'Let's have a look, little man,' she said softly, gently examining him from head to toe.

Adam held his breath the whole way through, once again pleading with God to let everything be okay.

'There doesn't appear to be anything broken,' she said.

The relief at those words made him want to weep.

'But I would like a doctor to see Matthew, just to rule out a head injury,' she continued. 'In the meantime, are you going to collapse on me?'

Adam looked at her in confusion.

'To be honest, I thought it was you who was hurt when I spotted you out there. You're as white as a ghost.'

'It was my fault,' Adam said. 'I let him fall. I should have been more careful. He just rolled off . . . '

'If you knew how many babies come in here every week, for the very same reason. They are stronger than you think. Try not to worry, okay?

You stay here with Matthew for now and I'll be back in a bit, with a doctor,' the nurse said kindly.

She handed Adam back his son and told him to take a seat, pulling the curtain around him as she walked away.

'You didn't half give me a fright, wee man,' Adam said.

Matthew looked up at him, not in the least bit worried about his father's near heart attack. Then he placed his fist in his mouth and sucked noisily on it.

'You're hungry, wee man,' Adam said. He looked down for his changing bag where he always kept formula and a bottle of cooled-down water, ready to make a bottle on the go. But, of course, the bag wasn't with him. Damn it. He never left anywhere without it. On a normal day that was. He'd ring David. He dialled his number and David answered on the second ring.

'I need a bottle for Matthew and I don't have his changing bag,' Adam said.

Then the curtain opened and David walked in, phone to his ear, holding Matthew's changing bag up like a trophy. 'This what you're looking for?'

'You bloody star!' Adam said.

'I grabbed it on the way out. Thought it might come in handy.' David smiled. 'Right, let's get this bottle made.' He opened the bag and rooted around until he found everything he needed.

'A cheeky little cocktail for the young sir,' David said as he shook the bottle vigorously. Matthew gurgled his appreciation, smacking his lips together, the way he always did when he was hungry.

'Here you go,' Adam said, giving the bottle to him. Then he filled David in on what the nurse had just said.

Adam's eyes were firmly on his son, he couldn't pull them away. Waves of terror kept creeping over his body as he remembered the sound of the thud when Matthew hit the floor. Thank God it was carpeted.

'I think I better go move the car. I just kind of dumped it. Will you be okay for a few minutes?' David was reluctant to leave Adam and Matthew, but was worried he'd get clamped, and that would be no good for anyone, when it was time to bring them home.

'I will,' Adam said. He wanted to grab Matthew and run. No. That's a lie. *He* wanted to run. He wanted to run so hard that his feet bled. Who the hell was he kidding, thinking he had any control over what he was doing? He was making it up as he went along and Matthew deserved better.

'Hello,' a woman said as she walked in holding a clipboard in one hand. In her fifties, with dark hair in a bob, she looked efficient and a little bit daunting.

'Hello,' Adam answered nervously. Maybe he'd be in trouble for dropping Matthew. Maybe they'd take him away from him. Fresh worries began to fight for his attention.

'I'm Dr Gates. Looks like he's enjoying that bottle.' She nodded towards Matthew, who was holding his feed in his two little pudgy hands for dear life. He wasn't going to give it up for anyone.

'He was hungry. Can't seem to keep him full at the minute,' Adam said.

'He's what age now?' She looked at the chart. 'Nearly a year old.'

Adam nodded. 'Yes.'

'Well, he's most likely having a growth spurt. My grandson is much the same age. My son said the same to me only last weekend.'

'You don't look old enough to be a grandmother,' Adam said.

She took the compliment. 'I feel every day of my age right now. Have been on my feet nearly twelve hours straight.'

Adam shook his head in amazement. Doctors and nurses were, as far as he was concerned, some of this world's walking angels. The jobs they did every day, often working double shifts, well, it was remarkable.

'Can I take a look at Matthew?' She sat down on a chair beside Adam. 'You keep holding him, and that way he can still have his bottle if he wants it. I'll work around that.'

She gently began feeling his arms and legs, making soothing noises as she did. Matthew became aware that a new possible fan was in town, so he took the bottle from his mouth for a moment and began blowing raspberries at her. Dr Gates began doing the age-old baby talk that adults do. 'Ah the baba, dabba, dabba, doo.'

Matthew showed his appreciation by blowing a kiss to her, to which Dr Gates emitted a laugh of appreciation that made Adam join in too.

'He likes you,' Adam said.

'Well, I like him too. What a gorgeous little boy you have. Can we call anyone for you? Your wife?' she asked.

Adam sighed. He sometimes lied when he was in a situation like this. Where someone didn't know about Rachel. It was difficult to take on other people's reactions when he was such a mess himself. But there was something about Dr Gates that made him speak honestly. 'She died.'

Dr Gates kept one hand on Matthew's head, then turned to Adam and placed her other hand on his arm. 'That must be difficult for you.'

He nodded. 'She died. In here. This hospital. Car accident.'

Dr Gates shook her head, as if doing so it would make the words untrue.

'I'm sure being back here tonight is difficult for you. Can you talk me through exactly what happened to Matthew, so I can do all possible to get you home?'

Adam recounted the events that led to Matthew's fall one by one, leaving nothing out. Except for the bit about the accidental porn star. He figured that was best kept to himself.

'It seems to me that between the carpet and you grabbing Matthew's babygro, his fall was broken. It could have been so much worse,' Dr Gates said.

Adam began to shake once more. Did she think he'd didn't know that?

'You can't take your eyes off them for a split second at this age. They are full of wonder with

169

the world and their new crawling skills. They can't help themselves.'

'You think it was my fault. And you're right. I should have been more careful.'

Dr Gates turned to Adam. She looked him squarely in the eyes. 'I've been doing this job for over thirty years. I've seen all levels of humanity walk through these doors. Good people and bad people. I try not to judge, but sometimes, it's impossible to ignore the undertones between a husband and a wife, who presents herself with a bloodied and bruised face, needing stitches, who says she slipped and fell. Or a child who has fainted in school and is obviously malnourished. I've become a good judge of character.' She paused and leaned in, touching Adam's hand again. 'This baby, your baby, is obviously well cared for. I watched you earlier, feeding him. This child is loved. And one mistake, one slip, doesn't make you a bad parent. You remember that.'

Adam sagged at her words and felt tears begin to bubble up in his eyes.

'You've had a shock. In fact, Shelley our nurse, said that she thought you were the one who needed more medical attention than the baby!' She smiled again.

He had no words.

'I'm so sorry about your wife.'

'So am I.'

His need for Rachel, his ache to see her, pierced and stabbed his arms, his legs, his head, his heart, till he thought he would bleed out.

'Is your mum alive?' she asked, the question

170

taking Adam by surprise.

He nodded.

'Can I call her for you? Right now, I think you could do with some TLC too. And if she's anything like me, there's nothing she likes more than spending time with her boys,' Dr Gates said.

Adam wished that this woman he'd just met a few minutes before, was his mother. He would ask her to bring him home with her. He would climb into a soft bed and wake up to breakfast on a tray. He would feel safe and loved.

'She doesn't know about Matthew,' he replied. 'We fell out years ago. I haven't seen her in a long time.'

If the doctor was surprised, she didn't show it. She just stood up and said, 'Families, we're a complicated thing, aren't we? None of my business, but speaking as a mother and grandmother, there isn't a reason I can think of that would make me turn my child away from my door. But for now, I'm happy to send you home. Come back if anything changes with Matthew, keep an eye on him. Nothing's broken. There's no bruising to his head. He's alert, he's eating, he's happy. So I'm happy.'

Adam was dumbstruck. The relief took his voice clean away.

'But you're not happy, are you?' Dr Gates continued. 'And who could blame you. So much on your plate. Have you someone with you? A friend?'

He nodded once more.

'Good,' Dr Gates said. She kissed Matthew

171

lightly on his forehead. 'You're such a good boy. Take care of your daddy.'

Then she stood up and walked out.

15

Baby stories and the guilty parents club

Didsbury Hospital, Manchester

Pete, Jenny and Karen joined about a dozen or so other people in the waiting room of the hospital.

They sat side by side on grey plastic chairs, waiting for some news from Adam or David.

'Tell me, exactly how did it happen again?' Jenny asked. She shifted on her seat to try to find a more comfortable position. As each day progressed, the pain in her lower back intensified and she was struggling now to get around.

'One minute we were singing 'I Believe in Love', the next minute Matthew was on the ground,' Pete said. 'I tried to catch him. But I never was much good at catch in school.'

'Adam must be beside himself,' Karen said.

'He was hysterical,' Pete told them.

'It was good of Ramona to take little Adam,' Jenny said. She'd already said this twice before. But she hated the sound of silence. She needed to fill it anyway she could.

Pete had rung them all after Adam left for the hospital, and Ramona suggested that he bring little Adam to Karen's house. She was looking after Josh, Ellie and Olivia anyway, which meant Pete, Jenny and Karen could go to the hospital to be there for Adam.

173

'Anyone else having the heebeejeebees being here?' Pete asked.

'The what?' Jenny asked.

'Heebeejeebees. As in I'm creeped out here,' Pete answered.

'I am,' Karen whispered. Her eyes were glassy with emotion.

'What am I missing?' Jenny asked when Pete reached out to hold Karen's hand. Karen looked down at a thread that had pulled on her trouser leg. She wondered what would happen if she yanked it. She suspected that with every pull, she might become unravelled too.

'Pete?' Jenny asked again.

'It's just, this is where we were, when Rachel had her accident. We sat here for hours, waiting for news,' Pete answered.

'Oh jeepers, right,' Jenny answered.

'It was so cold that night,' Karen said.

'I don't remember that,' Pete answered.

'You never feel the cold,' Jenny said.

He nodded. He didn't. 'I remember how quiet it was though. Not like this evening.'

And with perfect timing, as sometimes is the way in life, a man jumped up, shouting to a nurse who was passing by, 'A man could die here waiting to be seen! I'm bleeding out!'

They all turned to look and sure enough he was cut on his arm. But it didn't look that serious.

'We'll be with you as soon as we can,' the nurse replied mildly, unruffled by his outburst.

'Were you here long that night?' Jenny asked.

'Hours,' Karen answered. 'We waited with

Adam while they operated on Rachel. Then we waited for her to wake up . . . ' She couldn't finish the thought, never mind say any more. 'I have to get out of here. I need some air. Sorry.' She walked towards the main entrance.

'I'd go after her, but I don't think my legs would put up with it,' Jenny said. She looked down at the two swollen limbs that had replaced her normally thin legs. She'd overdone it today. She'd put her feet up tomorrow and they'd be back to normal again.

'Give her a minute. She'll be back,' Pete said.

'I can't imagine how hard it must have been that night,' Jenny said.

'Be grateful you weren't here,' Pete remarked. 'I'll never forget it to the day I die.'

The thing was, Jenny didn't feel grateful. She bitterly regretted never having the chance to say one last goodbye to Rachel. She'd loved her. And she missed her every day. Why the hell did she ever go to New York? It all went wrong after that. She should have stayed here, then maybe this baby would be Pete's, not that moron Grant's.

'Where are they?' Pete asked, irritated that they were still clueless as to what was going on.

Then Karen walked back towards them, with David by her side.

'I was moving the car,' David explained. 'And look who I bumped into.'

'How is he?' Jenny asked.

'Waiting to see the doctor. But when I left, he was having a bottle. I think he's okay. Gosh I hope so.' And suddenly, David felt his calm quietness disappear and panic begin to bubble

175

up inside him for his friend and son.

They all fell silent again for a moment and Karen closed her eyes, praying once again that all would be okay.

She felt a hand pat her shoulder, but it was an awkward gesture. She turned to see who it was. Jenny. She smiled weakly in response.

They sat in silence for half an hour, watching the doors of the A&E swing back and forth, until finally they opened and Adam walked out, holding Matthew in his arms. Adam was pale, sweat patches staining his underarms. But Matthew was smiling at them all, as if he hadn't a care in the world.

'He's okay?' Karen asked, moving towards him, kissing his forehead over and over.

'He's got a head like his father. Titanium,' Adam answered. 'I didn't know you were all here!'

'Where else would we be, mate?' Pete said.

'Course we came. You daft ha'p'orth,' Jenny added.

And then Adam couldn't stop the tears.

He wasn't on his own.

He had his friends.

They formed a circle around him, and then wordlessly, placed their arms around each other, in one big group hug.

Adam wiped his eyes, feeling embarrassed by his tears. He was surprised to see the normally calm David doing the same. 'You were fucking amazing,' Adam said to him.

'He was, you know,' Pete said. 'Dead calm.'

Everyone turned to look at David and he

shook his head in denial at the compliments. 'I did what anyone would do.'

'I went to pieces, but you were there to pick me up,' Adam said. 'I owe you.'

'You owe me nothing,' David replied. Then clapped Adam's shoulder. 'That's what friends are for, right?'

'The best of friends,' Adam replied.

Jenny was crying now and Pete pulled her in for a hug, blinking back tears of his own. 'It's the hormones,' he told everyone.

'Listen, as Jenny and Pete need to come to my house to get little Adam, why don't we all meet back there and have a coffee. I have cake,' Karen said.

Half an hour later, they were all sitting in Karen's kitchen. Matthew was fast asleep in his car seat, oblivious to all the earlier drama.

'How are you feeling now?' Jenny asked Adam. She was worried about him. He looked so lost and alone when he walked through those hospital doors. Trying to be brave, trying to be funny. But it was obvious he was deeply shaken.

'Truthfully? I'm pissed off at myself. I fucked up. I took my eye off him and if anything had happened . . . ' He stood up and walked over to check on Matthew for the third time in five minutes.

'He's still asleep, mate,' Pete said. 'And welcome to the not very exclusive parenting club of 'we've all fucked up'.'

Adam looked doubtfully at him. 'You're just saying that to make me feel better.'

'I lost Josh once,' Karen blurted out. They all

177

turned to her and David patted her hand, remembering when it happened. 'We were in the Trafford Centre — David, Josh and me. Shopping for a Mother's Day present. David had promised me a new handbag and I wanted to choose it myself.'

David said, 'I've shocking taste in handbags.'

'Anyhow, David went off in one direction and Josh was with me. One moment he was at my legs, the next he was gone,' Karen said. 'The panic I felt when I realised he wasn't there, I will never in my life forget it.'

'What did you do?' Jenny asked.

'I ran to the security guard at the door of the shop and screamed at him to lock the doors! Raise the alarm. I kept thinking what if someone took him, what if he was being led out of the store right that minute by someone . . . ' Karen's face flushed at the memory.

'Ever since James Bulger, that's been my worse fear. I hate bringing little Adam with me to shopping centres,' Jenny said. They all nodded in agreement, thinking about the little two-year-old who was brutally murdered by two young boys in Merseyside, ten years previously.

'Where was Josh in the end?' Pete asked.

'He was exactly where I had been standing, looking at those handbags all along. He'd hidden in between two rails of clothing, thinking it would be fun to start playing hide and seek with me. He just forgot to tell me that I was it!' Karen said.

'He loved playing that game. Still does. The little monkey,' David said.

'So I understand how terrified you felt. And how guilty. I could have lost our son, for what? A handbag?' Karen said. 'And actually, now that I think of it, I never did get that present!'

David threw his eyes upwards and laughed. 'I knew this day would come. Noted. One handbag owed!'

'You were great that day too,' Karen said to David. 'So calm. I never forgot that. Did I say thank you?'

David shrugged. 'No thank yous were needed. And I'm not always calm. I was terrified today, I was terrified that day, and I've never told any of you about this, but Josh nearly died once because of me.'

Karen turned in shock towards him. 'What?'

'At his school. I was talking to Natalie, my old boss. She'd come to offer me a job in her new firm. One moment Josh was beside me, next he was running out on to the road. I got to him and pulled him out of harm's way. But only just in the nick of time.' David kept his eyes on his lap. He still felt guilt and shame that he could have inadvertently caused Josh's death.

'Oh, David. You should have told me,' Karen said. 'It was an accident.'

'It made me realise what was important in life. I'll never forget that.'

Pete then turned to Jenny and said, 'Well, we both have lifetime membership of the parents-who-have-fucked-up club.'

'Damn straight,' Jenny replied.

'Remember that day in the supermarket down the main street with little Adam?' Pete asked.

179

'With the wine and gin?' Jenny said, becoming pale at the memory.

They all sat forward. 'This sounds like a good story,' Adam said.

'Well, we brought little Adam shopping and he'd just started to walk. He wanted to push the trolley,' Jenny said.

'It was so cute. His fat little bum sticking out as he pushed that trolley like a drunken sailor from side to side,' Pete added.

'And I was trying to get my camera out to take a picture . . .'

'She never left home without that camera! Always snapping pictures of him. We've got thousands,' Pete said.

'As I was saying, I took my camera out. But it had the tiniest memory on it and I had to delete some pictures, so I could take the snaps. It was a rubbish camera,' Jenny said.

'It's so hard to delete pictures of the children, isn't it?' Karen said.

'Impossible,' Jenny agreed. 'Even the ugly ones.'

'And then we were in the snack aisle and I had a real urge for chilli nuts,' Pete went on. 'So I went off to look for them.'

'I looked up, finally ready to take the photograph, but little Adam was gone,' Jenny said.

'He's fast,' Pete said with pride. 'Turned that corner to the next aisle on two wheels like a pro.'

'We ran after him. And as we turned the corner ourselves, we heard the crash.' Jenny covered her face in her hands. The memory still made her ashamed.

'He was in the alcohol aisle,' Pete said, his voice dropped an octave, to show how serious it was.

'It was carnage,' Jenny continued. 'Little Adam crashed the trolley right into a huge pyramid of gin that was on special offer. Like a game of bowls, the bottles fell and rolled towards another display, this time all New World wines.'

'From Argentina,' Pete added.

'And the trolley, meanwhile, carried on its merry way, ending up into the prosecco,' Jenny said.

'What about little Adam?' Adam asked.

'Unharmed. Glass was in broken shards all around him and he stood there in the middle of it all, with not even a scratch on him,' Pete replied. 'Then he just toddled off, looking for his trolley.'

'What did you do?' Karen asked, laughing.

'I picked him up and said to Pete, run, and don't look back,' Jenny said.

'A month's wages in that carnage,' Pete agreed.

'That's why you never go to that supermarket any more!' Adam said.

Karen refilled everyone's cup and said, 'So I think what we've learned here is that we're all doing the best we can. And none of us are perfect.'

Adam still wasn't convinced. He wondered what Rachel would make of all this. He felt like he'd let her down. Again.

'No you haven't,' Rachel said.

She was back. Sitting cross-legged beside a still-sleeping Matthew. Watching over him.

He stood up and walked over to her, leaving the others to chat.

'I'm so sorry,' Adam said to her. He sat on the other side of Matthew and looked at his wife, hoping to see forgiveness in her eyes.

'You don't have to apologise to me, Adam,' Rachel said.

'But I do. I messed up.'

'Would you get over yourself? You'll never make it to his eighteenth in one piece if you keep doing this. You need to stop beating yourself up every time you make a mistake.'

'But I let him fall,' Adam said.

'Yes, love. And you'll let him fall again, I've no doubt. He'll climb a wall and you'll watch him, proud of how fearless he is, then beat yourself up when he comes crashing down like Humpty Dumpty. You'll cheer him on at football matches and then beat yourself up again when he has a clash with a bigger lad and gets a sore head. All part and parcel of being a parent. You need to toughen up.'

Adam looked at Rachel in amazement. Even in death, she knew exactly what to say, how to reassure him, make him feel better.

'Don't forget I dropped Matthew once too,' Rachel added. 'And you can't let yourself become overly obsessive about him now, like I did that time.'

'I had forgotten that!' Adam replied.

One afternoon, while on maternity leave, Rachel had placed Matthew on the kitchen table in his car seat and he'd rocked it so much, it fell off. Rachel and he went through an awful time, because Adam felt so excluded by her, as she obsessed about every detail regarding Matthew's care.

'So basically what you're saying is, I need to cop on,' Adam said smiling.

'Bingo. You've got it,' Rachel said.

'Thanks for being here.'

'You know I'm always in your head and heart, whenever you need me,' Rachel replied. 'Besides, a mother never leaves her son. No matter what. Maybe you should think about that fact too.'

And then she was gone again.

16

The hypnotist and the ladies
of the night

Karen's Publishers, Manchester

The things her publisher got her involved in. A new client had written a book about hypnosis and Karen's boss thought it would be 'fun' if they all had a session with him, in their lunch hour.

So instead of her usual salad at her desk, herself and twenty or so of her colleagues all marched with little enthusiasm into their boardroom. The large desk had been pushed against the wall and they were all instructed to lie down on the floor. Karen had never been a fan of communal dorms, and she moved to the far corner of the room. She pushed herself against the wall, away from Cassie, the new intern who seemed to have taken a shine to her and wouldn't leave her side.

Roberto Moore, the author and hypnotist walked in, all long hair swishing, tanned and wearing a brilliant white T-shirt that matched his brilliant white toothy smile.

'I know what you are all thinking,' he said.

Bloody telepathic too, Karen thought.

'You think that hypnotism is all Svengali and mind control.' He waved his hands up and down maniacally and most in the room laughed nervously.

'Or else you're worried I'll make you do something that you are not comfortable with. Like snog your colleague.' He smiled at one of the lads near the front.

More nervous laughter.

'And of course, I'm not going to make that happen. Unless you want me to.' He gave a theatrical wink.

Karen reckoned this guy had done this exact performance more than once before.

'Today, I just want you to relax, let the possibility of the unknown into your imagination. And if you do that, I promise you, you will be able to tap into some amazing abilities that you did not know you possessed.'

Tom from Accounting shouted to him, 'So what are you going to do? Click your fingers and we'll all nod off?'

Claire, the receptionist chimed in. 'I could do with a sleep. My husband snored all night long. He'd wake the dead.'

The room laughed, relaxing a little.

'There will be no circus tricks here. No stopwatches swinging from side to side, or clicking of fingers to make you sleep, I promise,' Roberto said. 'I just want to get you all into a state of relaxation. Then I can suggest some things to you all that might help you in your day-to-day lives.'

'Like what?' Tom asked.

'Like anything. But for today, your management team want me to keep it simple. So we've decided that I'm going to suggest to you all the power of matching and mirroring. Lots of you do it anyhow. But this will perhaps fine-tune your technique. Basically, it will help you create rapport with others,' Roberto said.

He walked around the room, moving between prone bodies on the floor as he continued to explain. 'Think about it like this. If you mirror the person you're talking to — in speech patterns, body language, volume and pitch — you are making that person feel more comfortable. We all like people who are like ourselves. So, this is a great life tool to learn.'

'Will it help me get a date?' A guy shouted from the front.

'Use it and people will subconsciously admire you more. It can't hurt,' Roberto said.

He did give people the chance to leave, but Karen stayed, more out of curiosity than anything else. Roberto told them all to focus on a beach that made them happy. Karen thought about the Valencian coast, where her mum Heather lived. The blue skies, azure water and white sands were as close to paradise as you could get. And as Roberto suggested that they walk barefoot in the sand, to feel the grains between her toes, hear the sounds of the birds in the sky, the waves crashing to the shore, she felt her eyes get heavier and heavier.

Twenty minutes later, she woke up alongside her colleagues who all looked as dazed as she did.

'Did you fall asleep?' she hissed at Cassie.

'Yes!' Cassie wiped some dribble from the side of her mouth. And Karen found herself doing the same.

Which made her giggle. What on earth had just gone on in here?

He had a hypnotic voice, she'd give him that. And she felt energised after it. Maybe the management team should introduce it into their working week to get everyone over hump day Wednesday. Because today she was struggling. Her phone buzzed, alerting her to a text from Ramona.

Bonjour. I need go out early today. You here by 6 latest, non?

She was taking these French conversation classes so seriously. She was determined to surprise Jean-Luc when he came to visit with everything she'd learned. He did seem as enamoured with Ramona as she was with him.

Maybe she should give Ramona the details of the hypnotist, to help her with her French. She quickly typed a text message back to Ramona, smiling as she imagined her face, trying to work it out.

Je suis tout à toi à six heures

She looked at her watch and felt the ever increasing tide of panic, when she saw it was 5 p.m. She'd need to leave in fifteen minutes to get home. And she had so much more to do. She'd have to bring work home with her to tackle once the children were asleep. She groaned as she remembered that she had to make something for the cake sale at Josh's school the next day too. She'd promised him she'd do it herself, not just buy cakes.

★ ★ ★

Without opening her diary she realised that she was going to miss her AA support group tonight. She'd promised herself she'd find the time to go back this week. Time. There was never enough. Karen texted her AA sponsor, Alex, to let her know she'd miss tonight's group.

She shook off Alex's nagging voice in her head, who had warned her about getting complacent. What does she know anyhow? Karen told herself that she'd not really thought about pouring a drink this week. She'd been too busy.

Liar!

She flushed red, thinking about what happened, after everyone left the other night following Matthew's fall. She'd searched the house, looking for alcohol. She didn't care what. Ramona found her with her head in the laundry basket, a spot she'd often used to hide a bottle or two.

Maybe she wasn't as in control as she might like to think.

Next week she'd 100 per cent make sure she got there.

She quickly answered a few emails, then changed into her Skechers, ready to dash to the metro.

To her surprise, when she arrived home with five minutes to spare, Adam was sitting at her kitchen table, doing a decent job of spoon-feeding three babies at once.

'Surprise!' he said when she walked in.

'Hello, you.' She walked over and kissed his cheek.

'I let love's young dream off to get a grip on her *petit pois* and *tout le mondes*!' Adam said.

Karen laughed, opening her arms wide, to embrace Josh, who said, 'Hey, Mama.'

She pulled him in tight. 'You smell like tomato sauce!'

'Uncle Adam made me dinner,' Josh said.

'Nuggets, chips and a dollop of sauce for the sir. My speciality,' Adam said.

'He made a face out of the nuggets and the ketchup was blood coming out of its nose. It was gross,' Josh said, clearly delighted with it all.

'Thank you for that,' Karen said to Adam, taking over spoon-feeding Olivia and Ellie, while he continued doing aeroplane deliveries of mashed potatoes and vegetables to Matthew.

'Rough day at the office?' Adam asked.

'It was unusual,' Karen said. 'But I've had worse.' She leaned on to the back of the chair, placing her elbow on its back. And to her astonishment, she watched Adam do the same.

'What's so funny?' Adam asked when she started to laugh.

She told him about Roberto while they finished feeding the children.

'You could have some fun with that,' Adam said.

'Watch it, or I might have you doing all sorts!' Karen joked.

Once the children were fed, they placed the three babies into the big playpen so that they could play safely together.

'Look at him. Sure he's delighted with himself, right in the middle of the two ladies,' Adam said.

Matthew sat between Olivia and Ellie who were taking it in turns to kiss him.

'Do you think we're seeing a flash into their future?' Karen asked.

'David would kill him!' Adam laughed. 'But look at it this way. At least they'll have each other to ask as dates for their graduations. Not that I think your girls will ever be stuck. Little beauties, both of them.'

'Thank you,' Karen replied. 'Gosh, I remember my graduation. What a palaver! I invited this guy, who was totally gorgeous — '

'Natch,' Adam replied.

'But a total flake. He did warn me when I asked him to be my date, that he didn't do formal. I told him I didn't care,' Karen said.

'Don't tell me he didn't turn up?'

'No. He came all right,' Karen said and put her hand up when Adam sniggered. 'Stop! It was very innocent I'll have you know! He *arrived* an hour late, missing the pre-graduation drinks reception Mummy had organised.'

'That was deliberate, I'd say.' Adam remembered going to a fair few graduations in his day and the meeting of overly doting parents was the most horrendous part of it all.

'There he was, long, curly hair, wet from the shower, in his stockinged feet . . . '

'Where were his shoes?' Adam asked.

'Oh, he had them with him, but he was running late, so was kind of getting ready in the car, when he beeped the horn outside my parents' house.'

'The chancer!'

'He was wearing a long, thin, black leather tie. And black jeans,' Karen said.

'Well, he was technically wearing a black tie.'

'I thought he looked incredible.'

'So did you have a good time?'

'The best!' Karen said. 'We snuck in some drinks under my dress.' They'd got quite drunk that night. Was that the start of her reliance on alcohol? Maybe.

'I remember going to this girl's graduation when I was seventeen. And it was only when I called to her house to collect her, that I realised I'd shagged her older sister too,' Adam said.

Karen gasped. 'You're making that up!'

'Afraid I'm not. It was only when I saw them together, I realised why I thought my date looked so familiar.' Adam laughed. 'Neither sister was impressed when they worked it out.'

'Oh, those were the days,' Karen said.

'They were. Sit down and relax. I've dinner sorted for us too,' Adam said.

'Nuggets and chips?'

'In a way. But we have the most glorious of all nuggets, the biggest nugget of them all, the mighty chicken Kiev!' Adam said. 'I called into the supermarket and grabbed a stick-it-in-the-oven-dinner. But I'm sure it will be grand. Ready in twenty.'

'It's a treat having someone cook for me. Right, seeing as you've got this all in hand, I'm going to have a quick shower. That's if you are okay to watch over the kids?'

He shooed her away to the stairs.

Adam cleared away the kids' plates and laid the table. The Kievs, roasted vegetables and potatoes au gratin, were all in the oven, heating through.

He persuaded Josh to go up to his bedroom to retrieve his jammies, then he helped him get ready for bed. 'Will we have a go at changing your sisters, to give your mum a little break?' Josh ran away, having none of it.

Twenty minutes later, Karen came down to find the children ready for bed and in the playpen. He was plating up their food.

'This smells delicious,' Karen said. 'You've been busy!'

'It's all about how you place it in the oven. Great skill needed to get it in the most optimum spot, you know.'

As they ate, he filled in Karen in on the goings on at Pete and Jenny's. They were still dancing around each other, polite but distant. A disaster about to happen.

He noticed Karen kept glazing over, every now and then, as he spoke. Wherever she was, it wasn't with him.

'So I said to Pete, let's head to Wales, find a cult, wrap sheets around ourselves and sing folk songs,' Adam threw in.

Karen looked up at him. 'What did you say?'

'Just checking you were paying attention. You looked like you were fading out on me a bit there.'

She apologised, blaming tiredness, avoiding

192

eye contact with him.

Adam could tell she was lying. She'd been thinking of something else. Rachel? Could it be possible that she was getting visits from Rachel too, just like him?

'Karen?' He leaned in, touched her hand lightly. 'Was that Rachel you were talking to, just then?'

She looked at him in horror. 'What do you mean?'

'I mean, does Rachel ever visit you here?'

'As in her ghost?'

'Yeah,' Adam answered, then felt stupid for asking the question. It was obvious by the look on Karen's face that she thought he was losing it.

'Do you see Rachel's ghost?' Karen asked.

Adam nodded slowly.

'Often?'

'Every few days, I suppose,' Adam said.

'And what happens when you see her?'

'We chat. Mostly about Matthew, or us. It's nice.'.

'I'm sure it is.' Karen wished with all her might that she could have the same experience. If only Rachel would rock up here in her ghostly magnificence and ask her about her battle to avoid alcohol. Ask her about David and how confused she felt right now about him. Ask her about Robyn and how jealous she felt about her right now. Ask her about work and how stupid she felt during the hypnotism session.

'Do you think I'm mad?' Adam asked in a voice so quiet she almost didn't hear him.

She shook her head. She didn't think he was

193

any more mad than the rest of them. 'I think you're grieving.'

'Do you believe that she's visiting me?' Adam asked.

'I believe that you think so.'

'I don't want to analyse it. If I do and then she disappears, I've got nothing.'

'You've got Matthew. And us.'

He nodded. 'But I want her too.'

They sat in silence, neither of them able to find words.

'I don't know all her stories you see,' Adam said. 'I never got to learn everything about her. There wasn't enough time.'

That Karen understood. How many times had she said that phrase lately. Maybe she could help Adam. She scoured her brain, trying to remember a Rachel story that she felt he might not know. Something from their distant past.

'Did Rachel ever tell you about the time we were in Los Angeles?' Karen asked.

'I knew you went on the big West tour. Didn't you go to Vegas and do the Grand Canyon and all that too?' Adam said.

'We did. But did she tell you about the night we went looking for Brad Pitt?' Karen asked.

'No!' Adam brightened up. 'She always did have a glint in her eye whenever he came on the screen.'

'Okay, well you have to remember that we were young. Twenty-four or five. We got cheap flights to Los Angeles and booked an even cheaper hotel. We weren't having a good time, really, because we were in the middle of nowhere, with no car. So we decided to get the bus into Los Angeles, to the Sunset Strip. I wanted to go to the Viper Rooms. Johnny Depp was my particular crush,' Karen said, with a wink.

A yelp from Matthew halted the story for a moment. Adam played referee to Olivia and Ellie who were both fighting over a toy that he firmly held in his hand.

He returned to the table once peace was resumed. 'Go on.'

'We spent ages getting ready to go out. Chose our favourite outfits. We both had on these ridiculously short denim minis with cut-off biker tops. You know the kind?'

Adam nodded and smiled. 'I'm picturing it now. Very nice.'

Karen laughed. 'Well, we thought so anyway. I'm sure we looked like a right state. Off we went, on a bus, because we had hardly any money and with our little tourist map in hand, we rocked up to the Viper Rooms, cocky as you like.'

'Did you get in?' Adam said.

'We might have, if we'd remembered to bring our ID. Over there, you'd don't get served alcohol without it.'

'Oh, you naive fools.' Adam said.

'I know. We never thought of bringing them with us. So off we had to walk, disgusted with our bad luck to look so young that ID was needed. Oh to have that problem now. We decided to walk for a bit down Sunset Strip. We hadn't a clue really, what or where we were going.'

'The innocence of the young.'

'The stupidity you mean!' Karen laughed. 'Next thing we knew we heard the whoosh of blades coming behind us. And we were surrounded by these guys on roller blades, with hockey sticks in their arms.'

'What?' Adam exclaimed. And even though it was a story that had happened to the girls long before he knew them, his heart started to race, worried about what Karen was going to say next.

'They were vigilantes.'

'Roller blading vigilantes?' Adam asked, looking doubtful.

'Yes. As mad as that sounds, they were out and about to protect the citizens of Los Angeles. They warned us that we had wandered into a rough neighbourhood. Told us to grab a cab and get off the streets. Fast.'

'No!' Adam exclaimed.

'Yes!' Karen said. 'Terrified, we clung to each other, tottering in our heels, which by then were cutting the feet off us, and we hailed the first yellow cab that went by. That's how we met Sonny. We gave him the name of the hotel we were staying in and off we went.'

'Thank goodness for that. All's well that ends well,' Adam said.

'Oh, that wasn't the end of the story. We were in the cab for ages and I was getting a bit worried. We should have been at our hotel by then. And we seemed to be in an area that didn't look that good. Prostitutes were lined up on all corners of the street, in twos, looking for their next john. Next minute, Sonny, our cab driver pulls up outside this hotel. It was called the same

196

as ours, but most definitely wasn't the one we were booked into. We told Sonny that, and he turned around to look at us, before saying, 'So you girls are not ladies of the night?''

'Ladies of the night?' Adam repeated.

Karen nodded, giggling. 'We had strolled into hooker central on Sunset Strip. So he assumed we were hookers too, or, as he politely put it, ladies of the night! The hotel he brought us to was a regular place, renting out rooms by the hour.'

'No way!' Adam laughed.

'Yep!' Karen went on to tell him how Sonny was so mortified that he got their story wrong, he brought them on a tour of the city, even found them a really cool bar near their hotel that would serve them, without IDs.

'You know, he refused to charge us a cent.'

'What a gent,' Adam said.

'He was,' Karen replied. 'Only Rachel and I could end up getting mistaken for two hookers.'

She started to laugh and Adam joined in and then the laughter changed, and Karen was crying so hard, snot was streaming from her nose.

They sat at the table, chicken Kiev going cold and congealed on their plates.

'It's pretty shit, isn't it?' Adam said.

'Yes, it is, rather.'

'I'm glad you told me that story.'

'I've loads more. I'll help you learn all her stories, I promise you,' Karen said.

'When does the easier start, do you think?' Adam asked.

Karen had no idea.

17

Anthony Worrall Thompson and the silent witness in the park

Karen's house, Didsbury, Manchester

The house was quiet. It gave Karen the creeps. She ran to the living room and turned on the TV just to have sound fill the deafening silence.

It had been a long time since Karen was on her own, completely, for a weekend. When she'd left her mother's house all those years ago, she'd shared with friends, including Rachel at one point.

Then she'd moved in with David before eventually marrying him. If he or the children weren't here with her, Ramona usually was. But right now, Ramona was on the Eurostar, whizzing her way towards Paris for a weekend of romance with Jean-Luc. She had packed and repacked her suitcase three times, determined to have just the right capsule wardrobe for her romantic weekend.

'He won't care what you wear,' Karen had said to her this morning before she left. 'It's what you won't be wearing that will interest him more.'

Ramona pretended to look shocked and said, 'I a good girl. Who says I will show him what's under clothes?'

'You go enjoy yourself. Stay in bed for the

weekend and only get up for croissant and coffee,' Karen advised. 'Life is too short, don't waste it.'

Ramona's big brown eyes had filled up. 'I know. I live life, I promise you.'

She wondered how David and Robyn were getting on with the children. It hadn't been a huge success the last time they were all at David's. Piecing together comments from Josh, she understood that Robyn had struggled a bit.

And that had cheered her right up. She wasn't proud of the fact that this pleased her. But it did.

Things had become complicated. She went from desperately missing David to celebrating his absence at the turn of the hour. And while she may or may not want to have him at home again, the thought of Robyn with her children didn't sit well with her.

Flicking through the TV channels, she did a whistle-stop tour of the seventy-odd stations on her TV. Nothing caught her interest. She'd never really been a TV person.

It had been so good having Adam to stay for a few nights. They'd spent evenings chatting about Rachel, swapping stories. He understood her pain, because he was feeling it too, only tenfold. She would have loved him to stay on this weekend as the children and Ramona were away. But he had promised to help Pete put together the nursery for the new baby. She'd even offered to keep Matthew with her for a few days, but he wouldn't hear of it.

'You enjoy some me time,' Adam advised.

As she made herself another cup of coffee, she

noticed the Post-it note on the fridge from Ramona.

Heather ring. *Again*. Call your mama.

She knew she couldn't put it off any longer. She'd used the children and work as an excuse for not talking to her mother for over a week now.

Karen punched in the long Spanish number, reading it from the pad that sat beside the phone. One of these days she'd get around to learning how this new phone worked and she'd save all the numbers on to its digital memory card.

'Ola!' A bright cheery voice said.

'Hello, Mum.' Karen tried to match her tone, but failed miserably.

'At last! I thought you'd emigrated to a kibbutz, darling. I've been ringing you for days now.'

'I know, Mum. I'm sorry.'.

'It's just, it's very hard for me. Over here. Worried about you and the children. I don't think you give me a moment's thought, do you?' Heather was determined to have her say.

'That's not true. It's just I'm back working — ' Karen said.

Heather cut her off. 'I mean, is it too much to ask for a daughter to call her mother the odd time? Let her know she's alive and well? Let her talk to her grandchildren?'

'No, it's not and — '

'I said to Esther last night — you know my

200

bridge partner? The one with the unfortunate lisp. Well I said to her, how selfish can one child be? We bring them up and do our best, then they fly from the nest, never to look back.'

Karen sighed and tried to tune out her mother. Best to let her get it off her chest. She'd let it drop then and they could move on. She glanced down at her nails. All but two nails had chips on them. That's what she could do. She'd take advantage of having the house to herself, strip naked, and have some spa treatments.

'Darling, are you going to bother speaking to me at all? Why did you call me if you had nothing to say!' Heather's voice interrupted her thoughts.

'Sorry, Mum. I was trying to speak, but you kept interrupting me,' Karen said, trying very hard to keep the edge out of her tone.

'Oh, excuse me for caring,' Heather sniffed her disappointment.

Please don't let it be true, that we all turn into our mothers, Karen thought. 'I know you care. And I do too.' Karen tried to get the conversation back on to solid ground. With her mother, things sometimes derailed at the rate of knots. 'How are *you*, Mum?'

'Busy, busy, busy. We had the most wonderful regatta fund-raiser last week. Simply everyone was there. And guess who turned up! Antony Worrall Thompson!' Heather exclaimed.

'The TV chef?' Karen asked.

'Yes! And he's such a gentleman. I took quite a shine to him, I don't mind telling you. So did Esther, but she was rather over the top, the way she kept placing her hands on his chest and leaning in so he could see her cleavage. If you asked me, well, it smacked of desperation. And I don't think he had a clue what she was withering on about,' Heather said.

Karen giggled at the image. She'd met Esther before and she was single-minded in her goal to meet and marry well. The fact that she had reached the age of sixty with, so far, no likely candidate coming forward, didn't seem to bother her in the slightest.

'I'm glad you're well, Mum,' Karen said, and she felt her earlier irritation dissipate. She loved her really, and when they saw each other, it was great. The trick she'd learned was to keep their visits short and that way they remained sweet!

'How are the children?' Heather asked.

'They are with David this weekend. And Robyn.' The phone went silent for a moment and Karen thought they'd been cut off at first. 'Mum?'

'I'm here, darling. I just didn't want to say the wrong thing. I know I irritate you at times.'

'No, you don't!' Karen objected, flushing at how close her mother was to reading her mind a few seconds ago.

'Yes I do. And I think that's perhaps the role all parents fall into the older they get. Or maybe it's just me.'

'You can say anything you want to me, Mum.' If she could have found a way to reach into the phone, she would have hugged her mother and not let her go.

'Well in that case, can I just say that I think

you are incredibly brave? I know you and David had your problems. And I know you said you were happy with the separation and the divorce. But it must be hard waving your children goodbye, especially with that woman in the picture. There must be some ethical grounds we could lodge a complaint, on that one.' Heather's voice was now laced with anger.

Karen laughed, her mother's outrage at David and Robyn's relationship showing no signs of abating.

'I don't think Josh likes her very much,' Karen said.

'He always was a good judge of character. Gets that from you, darling.'

'Oh, Mum . . . ' Karen couldn't finish the sentence. Her throat was weighted with the biggest lump.

'I can come over, you know,' Heather said. 'I just need to juggle a few things around over here, get someone to manage the end-of-season barbecue, and I'm sure Esther could find someone else for the bridge charity marathon.'

For a moment, Karen thought about saying yes to her mum, do all of that. Come here and look after me. Cook me dinner and make sure I eat it. Help me take care of the children, and sit with me in the evenings while Ramona is Skyping her boyfriend.

Distract me from my thoughts. My grief. My sorrow. My jealousy. My need for a glass of wine.

But instead she said, 'There's no need. You've got an awful lot on over there. And I've got all of this under control. You're coming for Christmas.

We shall all look forward to that.'

'Darling, you need to know that I'd drop everything in a heart-beat for you.'

'I know, Mum.' Karen pinched herself to stop tears falling. She had to get a grip. 'I promise you. I'm fine!'

'What are you going to do for the weekend? Don't just sit at home dwelling on things. Get out and go for a walk. Feel some fresh air on your skin.'

'Will do. You go on and I promise to call you next week,' Karen replied.

They said their goodbyes and Karen stood looking at the phone for a few moments, unable to move away. She always gave her mother such a hard time. In her head, leastways. Heather irritated her and frustrated her on a regular basis. But she adored her too and couldn't imagine a world without her in it. When Rachel died, she'd brought Ramona and the children to Spain to stay with her for a few weeks. And Heather had taken one look at Karen, pulled her into her arms and held her while she cried. Then she organised Ramona and the children, and put Karen into her bed, insisting she take the big king size. That fortnight she'd rarely left her daughter's side. She was a force to be reckoned with, with boundless energy.

Maybe it was time to listen to her mother. Mother *does* know best. She went upstairs and changed into a pair of jeans, with Converse and a sweatshirt. While it was now early November, it was still dry. She'd go to the park.

Twenty minutes later, she joined the dog

walkers, the mums and dads pushing buggies and the sweaty joggers, in Didsbury Park. It was a lovely day, with only a slight chill in the air. The wind whipped through her blond bob and she relished it.

How often did she get a chance to do something like this? Normally, when she came here to this park, it was with the kids. She would spend her time trying to slow Josh down for the first half of the walk, then speed him up for the second! Always fun, but it was a different experience from this gentle ramble. She looked around her, determined to take in every detail of the blue skies, the perfect backdrop for the large oak trees whose leaves were beginning to turn golden brown.

A little cockadoodle puppy galloped towards her, its lead trailing behind him on the leafy path. And running behind the puppy was its owner, shouting, 'Lulu, come on, girl!'

Lulu was adorable and jumped up to lick and sniff Karen's legs. She quickly grabbed its leash and gave the thumbs-up to its owner who shouted her thanks, slowing down her frantic dash to a more manageable jog.

Karen kneeled down and let Lulu lick her face and she laughed in delight as the little puppy tickled her. 'Oh, I'd run away with her!' She said to the owner.

'Thank you!' The owner replied, looking alarmed as she snatched control of Lulu's lead again.

And then she was gone. Karen felt a bit silly. She had been ready to start a chat with the owner. But to that woman, of course she was a stranger.

Karen walked on, feeling idiotic for letting the dog upset her. She needed to get a grip. It was just every emotion seemed heightened. She couldn't bear it.

And then she saw them.

Whatever joy she'd just felt in that slobbery wet kiss from Lulu the dog vanished as she watched the scene unfold in front of her.

David and Robyn were swinging Josh between them, and his squeals as they lifted his little feet off the ground made her want to reach out and pull her son to her.

They were obviously having a picnic. The double buggy had the hood up and she suspected the girls were having their mid-afternoon sleep. The fresh air always conked them out. A large wicker picnic basket sat on top of one of the wooden benches. It looked picture perfect.

She turned around quickly and began to run back the way she'd come, passing Lulu and its owner on the way. She didn't stop running till she got to the car, then she jumped in and howled. Like a crazy woman, she screamed until the windows of her car steamed up and she pounded the dashboard so hard her hands turned red.

Suddenly she was spent. Her body sagged from the emotional assault and she lay her head on the steering wheel until her breathing quietened.

She switched on the engine and drove, knowing exactly where her destination was. She felt calm and resolute.

She walked through the heavy double doors, a bell ringing to let the shopkeeper know she had arrived. Karen walked straight to the back wall, knowing exactly what she wanted.

She picked up a bottle of Grey Goose vodka and paid for it without saying a word to the young man who served her.

18

The reckless email and the YR
and ketchup sauce-off

Pete and Jenny's house, Didsbury, Manchester

As soon as Pete hit send, he regretted it. He ran downstairs and asked Adam if it was possible to retrieve and delete a sent email.

'What have you done, you numpty?' Adam replied.

It pissed Pete off that Adam assumed that he'd done something wrong. He might have had a legitimate reason for asking that question. To do with work, maybe.

It was his mum's fault anyhow, showing him that photograph of Jo. She looked so brown and fit and healthy. And non-judgemental. And, more than anything, not pregnant with some faceless bastard's baby.

He'd thought about what he would say to her for weeks now. Planned it in his head, and when it was just a thought it seemed like a really sensible thing to do. He'd just send over a bright and cheery email, checking in. Nothing too serious. Test the lie of the land.

But instead of that, he found himself saying to her that he missed her and wondered if she missed him too.

Adam was right. He was a numpty. He

trudged back upstairs to see what he could do about retrieving, and deleting, the email he had sent to Jo.

'Pete,' Jenny's voice called out. He heard her shuffling her way towards him, so he quickly signed out of his email account. He tried to rearrange his face, so that he didn't look as guilty as he felt.

'What you doing?' She asked when she saw him at the computer.

'Work, love. Deadlines and stuff. Sorry,' Pete said.

'Don't be sorry. You must be exhausted. Having to work at the weekend.' Jenny walked over to him and manoeuvred her bump sideways so she could kiss his forehead. 'I'm going to make you a Jenny special. One sausage sandwich coming up.'

'You don't have to do that, love. You sit down and I'll make it,' Pete said, his guilt trebling now, making his face flush.

'No!' Jenny said. 'Look at you, all red from the stress. You're working too hard. Let me take care of you. Okay?' Jenny touched his cheek gently and shuffled out the door.

He wondered what his mum would make of it all. Maybe he'd go and visit her next week to ask her opinion about it all. The good thing about Audrey was that she was a straight talker. And she knew her son.

Then two minutes later, Adam's head appeared around the door. 'You're a bollix.'

'I beg your pardon!'

'Don't think I don't know what you're up to,'

Adam told him. 'You've emailed Jo, haven't you?'

'Keep your voice down!' Pete hissed. 'And close that door! I take great offence that you would suggest such a thing.'

'Your wife is downstairs, telling me how worried she is about you working so hard at the weekend. Her two feet are so swollen she's wearing your bloody sandals, yet she's standing at that cooker, frying up a storm for you. And you're up here, doing what?'

'Don't. I feel bad enough as it is,' Pete said. 'Am I really a bollix?'

'A dickhead of the highest order,' Adam said, but the anger had abated from his voice. 'Right, spill. What exactly did you do?'

'I did email Jo,' Pete admitted.

'I fucking knew it!' Adam said. 'I told you not to. What did you say?'

'Just said hello. That's all.' Pete suddenly became very interested in the wallpaper that was beginning to peel on the wall.

'And what else?'

'Just that,' Pete lied.

When you are friends for over twenty years, your lying radar becomes fine-tuned to deceit. 'I call bullshit,' Adam said.

Pete started to shift in his chair. It had become uncomfortable all of a sudden. 'I kind of told her I missed her,' he blurted out.

Adam sat down on the seat beside him and sighed. 'Listen, mate, you need to get your shit together. If you want Jo, then go get her. But are you even sure that's what you want?'

Pete shrugged.

'From where I was watching, you two had fallen out of love long before the issue of her visa came into question and she was sent packing home to Australia,' Adam said.

Pete knew Adam was right. For the last few months they had been together, their initial spark had long fizzled out.

'I saw first-hand how hard it is to be a single mother,' Adam said. 'My mum had it tough and she had no choice but in turn to become tough herself. That girl downstairs is hurting and she needs looking after. If you plan on letting her down, you do it now, before this wee baby comes along and things get even more complicated.'

'I shouldn't have sent that email.'

'Fire up that computer and let me see if I can delete it,' Adam said, his tone softening.

Pete switched it back on and logged into his hotmail account.

You have one new mail, flashed up on to the screen.

'Shite,' Adam said.

Pete hit enter, scanning quickly to see who the sender was.

It was from Jo.

'Shite,' Adam repeated.

'What will I do?' Pete said, panicked.

'Open it,' Adam said.

Hi Pete. Good to hear from you. Of course I miss you. I feel bad that we ended things the way we did. But I am glad that I'm home again. I didn't realise how much I missed Sydney, until I got back. Fancy coming over? Jo x

211

'Shite.'

'Is that all you can say?' Pete said.

'It appears so,' Adam replied. 'But it doesn't matter what I have to say on all this. It matters what you do.'

Jenny's voice called up the stairs. 'Pete, Adam, get your arses down here. Sambos are ready.'

Pete quickly closed down the computer and they went downstairs. Did he want to go to Australia to be with Jo?

Jenny ushered them to the kitchen table and held up the Heinz ketchup and the YR brown sauce. 'Which one do you want, Pete?'

Adam turned to Pete. 'Yes, what *do* you want, Pete? You need to make a choice. But make it carefully. Chose the wrong sauce and your sandwich is ruined. For ever. You won't get a second sandwich. Oh no. You just get the one.'

'You all right there?' Jenny said to Adam, making a face to Pete.

'He's talking shite again.'

Pete threw Adam a dirty look. 'I'll have my sandwich plain, love. I don't feel like making a choice right now.'

'You were never a plain sandwich man. You couldn't live without sauce.' Adam wagged his sandwich at Pete. 'I'm a YR man. Have been my whole life. But every now and then I've strayed and had ketchup. And while it might taste delicious for a short while, afterwards, I'm left feeling a little bit let down.' He grabbed the YR bottle and squirted a dollop on top of his sausages. He picked up the sandwich and took a bite.

'You're weird,' Jenny said.

212

'That may be the case. But I know which sauce I like,' Adam replied.

Jenny sat down and then jumped. 'The baby just kicked me, the little monkey. Nearly broke a rib! Quick, have a feel, Pete.'

She grabbed Pete's hand and placed it over her tummy. They waited for a few moments, but the baby was quiet again.

Pete sighed and pulled his hand away.

Jenny said, 'Remember how you used to sing to little Adam? Louis Armstrong's 'What a Wonderful World'.'

Pete nodded. He used to love snuggling up beside Jenny on the couch, leaning his head low to her tummy and singing to the baby.

'He used to go berserk when you started. Jumping up and down to the sound of your voice,' Jenny continued.

Pete smiled at the memory. He did a good Louis Armstrong, there was no denying it.

'Maybe if you sing to my bump, then maybe this little one would like it too,' Jenny said.

Adam watched his two best friends look at each other, both in pain, both unsure, both desperately unhappy.

'Go on, Pete,' Adam encouraged.

And for a minute Adam thought that Pete would do it, but instead he picked up his sandwich and took a large bite.

Adam couldn't bear it. They were going to destroy whatever chance they had to be a family again before they even gave it a proper go. He needed to get Pete on his own, talk some sense into him.

'Pete and I are going to work on the nursery once we've eaten. Give it a bit of a makeover,' Adam said.

Jenny kept her head down low and didn't respond.

'It might be noisy, so why don't you go out for a bit? Go visit Karen. She's on her own this weekend. I think she could do with the company,' Adam urged. 'She even offered to take Matthew, rather than be on her own.'

Jenny looked doubtful.

'Leave little Adam here with us, he can help look after Matthew,' Adam continued.

'That's a great idea, love,' Pete said. 'By the time you come back, we'll have the nursery looking like a little palace, fit for royalty, you'll see.'

And I'll work out what sauce I like more, Pete thought.

19

401 days and the Grey Goose in the room

Karen's house, Didsbury, Manchester

When the doorbell rang, Karen didn't move.

She didn't know who it was or what they wanted, but she did know that she was not in the mood for company.

The irony of that thought wasn't lost on her. It was her loneliness that had driven her to buy the alcohol in the first place.

Her landline started to ring. She let it go to the answer machine. And then she heard Jenny's voice boom into the hallway.

'Karen? Are you there? I need a wee. But more than that, I need a friend. I need you — ' Then the phone clicked dead.

To Karen's shame, this plea from Jenny didn't make her get up at once. Her eyes were fixed on the bottle of Grey Goose vodka.

She had been staring at it for over two hours now.

Her mobile rang then and she looked down, to see who it was.

Jenny. Of course.

Sighing, she stood up. She knew her friend. She would stand on the doorstep, ringing the phone for hours if she had to. Her car out the front gave her away. She knew Karen was in here hiding.

She opened the door and Jenny said, 'I'm sorry, gotta use the bathroom. The baby is pressing on my bladder and I'm about to piss myself!'

'Charming,' Karen said, and moved aside to let Jenny run into the loo under the stairs.

She walked into the kitchen and put the kettle on.

'What's all this then?' Jenny asked when she walked in. 'You expecting company?'

She nodded towards the Grey Goose in the room.

Karen shook her head.

Jenny shrugged off her jacket and sat down at the dining room table.

Beside the bottle was one glass, empty, and a notepad and pencil. She hoped that meant she'd not had a drink. Jenny peered at the page and it was filled with numbers.

Karen took a seat opposite her and pointed to the notebook. '401 days; 9624 hours; 577,440 seconds.'

Jenny couldn't work out what Karen was on about. Maybe she'd been drinking after all.

Karen pushed the bottle of vodka towards Jenny. 'Those are my numbers. In the beginning when I stopped drinking, I used to mark off the days in my diary. Keep track of my running total of days sober. But I stopped doing that a few months ago.'

Jenny whispered. 'I'm nearly afraid to ask. Are those *still* your numbers?'

216

Karen looked at her, and made a grimace. 'Just. If you hadn't arrived, I might be back to zero again.'

Jenny moved to stand up, and Karen put her hand up to halt her. 'Don't. I can't cope with kindness. Not right now.'

Jenny sat back down. 'I probably couldn't have stood for long anyhow. Just as well. What do you need?'

'Distraction,' Karen answered. 'I know I can't drink this. But my body is betraying me. My head and heart don't agree. It's quite the contentious issue right now.'

Jenny looked at Karen and blurted out, 'I think Pete and I are over.'

Karen looked up with a start. For goodness' sake, they'd only just got back together.

'He doesn't want the baby. I can see it in his eyes. He's like a rabbit in headlights whenever I mention it.' Jenny rubbed her tummy tenderly.

She told Karen about her humiliation at attempting to seduce Pete a few weeks back, about his refusal to talk about their future and, worryingly, his reluctance to touch the baby bump.

'Do you think I'm imagining it?' Jenny asked.

Karen thought about that for a moment before answering. She wanted to reassure Jenny, but she'd noticed a distance between the two of them when they were here at the lunch. And again at the hospital. There was a forced jolliness about Pete. It didn't ring true.

'I don't think you're imagining it,' Karen said sadly.

217

'Maybe I was naive to think that I could expect him to take on another man's child,' Jenny said.

Karen felt a stab of pain at the image of Robyn's face laughing joyfully as she swung *her* son in the park.

'I might not be the most unbiased about that subject right now,' Karen admitted.

'What happened?'

'Robyn did.'

'Rottweiler lawyer bitch,' Jenny said.

'Yes! That's exactly what she is,' Karen replied, laughing. 'She's with my children right this second. Kissing them, holding them, nurturing them. And I don't like it. I know that's not very nice of me. But it's true.'

'I think it's a fair reaction, considering the way she tried to stitch you up over the divorce, bringing up your drinking and all. I mean, the cheek of her, you've stopped all that ages ago,' Jenny said.

Both their eyes turned to look at the big fat grey elephant or Grey Goose as it was in this case, in the room. And then they started to laugh, so hard till they both clung to each other, holding their sides.

When they calmed themselves down, Jenny nodded to the bottle and asked, 'Are you going to have a drink?'

Karen shook her head. 'Not today.'

'One day at a time, isn't that what they recommend?'

Karen nodded. 'Yes it is. Right now, I'm working on one hour at a time. So more distraction please. What about the baby's father? Is he out of the picture altogether?'

'He's a tosser. Even if Pete and I don't make it, there's no future for me and Grant. I'm ashamed that I ever let him touch me. You should see the state of him, Karen. He's a total knobhead.'

'Why did you let him in the first place?' Karen asked, genuinely curious.

'I was lonely,' Jenny admitted.

'We all do stupid things when we're desolate,' Karen acknowledged, looking at the bottle again.

'Shall I take that home with me when I go?' Jenny asked.

'You could do. But if I really want a drink, all I have to do is go to the off-licence and buy another,' Karen replied.

'Best not add temptation though,' Jenny said, and swiped the bottle, putting it into her handbag.

'You have to talk to Pete, you know,' Karen said.

Jenny nodded. The problem was she was scared of what he might say if she pushed him.

'If things don't work out, will you go back to the States?' Karen asked. To her surprise, the very thought of that made her feel emotional again. She didn't want to lose Jenny, not now that she'd just got her back.

'I can't take little Adam away from his dad again. They adore each other. I'll move out and find somewhere close by and we can share custody.'

'How did it ever come to this?' Karen asked.

Jenny shrugged. 'That's life for you, I suppose. You fall in love, you fall out of love. And somewhere along the way, you try not to screw your children up too much.'

Karen leaned over and held Jenny's hand. That gap that had formed between them suddenly felt much smaller.

20

Pete the worrier and an old wound

Audrey's Residential Home, Didsbury

Audrey knew her son better than he knew himself. The moment he came into the world thirty-six years ago he'd worn a frown on his face. Like he had the weight of the world on his broad shoulders.

He had always been such a complex child — on the one hand he was gentle and empathetic; on the other, he was funny and a masterful mimic. He used to put on shows, in their good sitting room. He'd write invitations for her and his father, then push them under their bedroom door early in the morning, before they'd even awoke.

They'd sit side by side on the couch, and try to find the stomach to eat the breakfast that he would have made to accompany his show. He used to put food together based on how colourful it looked. There was the time he did a peanut butter and ketchup sandwich. Nibbling that before you'd had your first cup of tea tested even the most doting of mothers.

He'd strut into the room, introduce himself formally, saying something like, 'Ladies and gentlemen, prepare to be amazed by the incredible, the talented, the wonderful Pete Gifford!'

And they'd clap and cheer and whistle. Then he'd go out of the room and walk back in. And his face would look different, as he became Tom Jones and started to sing, 'It's not Unusual!' As soon as the last note was over, he'd switch and become Hilda Ogden from *Coronation Street*, singing 'Feelings'. Then lastly, he'd go into Bruce Forsyth, saying 'You get nothing for a pair, not in this game. Didn't she do well?'

His comedic timing was always on point. And Audrey and his father adored him.

But despite this, he could lapse into a fit of anxiety for no apparent reason.

She remembered his first day of school. He was excited to start, but worried that the lunch they'd planned and painstakingly plotted, was all wrong. When his grandparents' house in Kendal flooded, he'd worried for months that they would drown in their sleep if it were to happen again.

Then there was the time that he came home from school on library day. He hadn't chosen a new book. Audrey had been puzzled and questioned him. He confessed that he'd forgotten to return the previous week's book and couldn't get another out. Audrey had called his teacher, annoyed that she'd been so strict, over a genuine mistake. Pete was a good boy, he never forgot to return his books. Surely he should be allowed one week's grace? The teacher told her that she had tried everything to get Pete to pick a book, saying kids forgot to return books all the time. But he had been insistent he shouldn't.

When he came home and told her he had

made a new best friend — a young kid called Adam — she'd been overjoyed. And then when she met him, she'd rejoiced, because Adam's happy-go-lucky attitude was the perfect antidote to Pete's anxieties. He laughed in the face of worry. And Pete began to flourish. They were inseparable as kids and that hadn't changed now as adults.

Watching Pete now, picking at one of his hangnails as she made them a sandwich, she saw that same frown he'd worn for three decades. She knew that something big was amiss. He'd not been himself for a long time. He'd had a lot to cope with. Rachel's death. His imminent divorce from Jo. But Jenny and little Adam were back now and she had hoped that their presence would help bring back the old Pete.

Placing a cheese and pickle sandwich down in front of him, she poured the tea and decided it was time to get to the bottom of his worries. That was her job. As his mother, she had to soothe away his fears just as she'd been doing for decades.

She waited until he finished eating, then she asked, as she had done thousands of times before, 'What's up, son?'

He looked at her with such sadness that she felt her stomach sink in fear.

'Nobody is ill, are they?' she whispered, not sure she had the strength to hear the answer. Her biggest worry was that something would happen to Pete or his family. She did not want to outlive any of them.

He shook his head, then apologised for scaring her.

'Then what is it that has you so worried? And don't tell me it's nothing. I know you.'

'I don't think I can love this baby,' Pete blurted out.

'And how on earth have you come to that realisation? You've not met the little thing yet! Unless you've got some news for me?'

'The baby won't be mine. It will be . . . his!' Pete said.

'This ex-boyfriend of Jenny's. I thought he was off the scene.'

'He says he doesn't want anything to do with the baby.'

'That's what I thought. Are you worried that Jenny still loves him?' If her daughter-in-law was messing her son around again, she'd swing for her. Bad enough when she disappeared off the face of the earth, going to America, with *her* grandson, she better not be —

Pete put his hand up, as if waving off her thoughts. 'Jenny and Grant are over. He doesn't want the baby, he made that clear.'

'And does Jenny want you?' Audrey asked gently.

Pete nodded without hesitation. While he was flooded with doubt, he knew Jenny. They'd been childhood sweethearts. Best friends. And she was honest, always had been. When she told him she loved him, he believed her. And more than that, she had showed him that time and time again since she had returned.

'And do you love Jenny?' Audrey was

determined to get to the bottom of this.

Pete paused before answering. He'd thought of little else since Adam had told him to cop on and make a choice.

'I never stopped loving her, Mum. Even when I was with Jo, it was always her.' As Pete said it out loud, he knew it was true.

Audrey nodded in satisfaction. While she had some issues with Jenny and the things she'd done to her son, she knew that she was the only woman who could make him happy.

'Why do you think you'll not love the baby?' Audrey asked.

Pete shrugged.

Audrey sucked in her breath and said, 'Not good enough, son. I brought you up better than that. Spit it out.'

'What if I can't love this baby as much as I love little Adam?' There, he said it.

Audrey thought about this for a moment, before replying, 'I can see how that might be an issue. If you let it. The way I see it, you have to make a decision to love both children equally. Balance the love you have in your heart equally between the two children.'

Pete didn't look convinced. 'And what if Grant comes back one day and wants to get to know the child?'

'Ah here, would you give over! What if the sun falls down and lands on your head?' Audrey said.

Pete laughed at his mother's words. He wished he could just snap his fingers and make his worries disappear.

'I have something to tell you,' Audrey said seriously. 'Something that I wasn't sure I'd ever share.'

She folded her napkin on her lap and opened up a wound almost as old as she was.

21

The beached whale and the gushing waters

Pete and Jenny's house, Didsbury, Manchester

Jenny was irritated. Her feet were so swollen she couldn't fit into a single pair of her own shoes. So she was reduced to wearing a pair of Pete's ugly Jesus sandals.

The small of her back was in competition with her shoulders and neck. Both wanted the award for most aches in a pregnant woman's body. The baby was attempting to turn around in a space that was so cramped it had no choice but to crash into her ribcage and pelvis in alternate jabs of tortuous pain.

And speaking of her pelvis, it felt like it had split in two. Every time she walked she felt it click, clack, bone against bone. When she visited her doctor earlier today, he'd cheerfully told her that she had a condition called pelvic girdle pain. Her hormones were making her joints and muscles relax and separate. It all sounded rather jolly, the way he described it, but in fact it was anything but.

Relax, he told her. She'd like to see him relax with this pain. Her doctor assured her that it was a good thing and would help her pass the baby through the pelvis bone.

227

She'd left his office in a rush, knowing it would not bode well for future vaginal inspections if she told him what she really thought about his condescending and quite frankly bullshit explanation.

She'd been irritated all day. She wasn't stupid, she knew the end result of being pregnant involved pain and huge discomfort. But she'd done a good job of ignoring that fact until he'd — quite frankly — gleefully recounted what was heading her way.

Now it was all she could think about.

She kept looking at little Adam in horror. How she'd ever managed to fit him inside her, she couldn't fathom. Her imagination began to ramp up. When she thought about going into labour, she could only see a toddler-sized baby trying to push his or her way out. And the baby in question was singing a song — Frankie Goes to Hollywood's 'Relax'!

Maybe a bath would help, she thought. Little Adam was at nursery. Pete was at work. Her midwife had suggested warm baths as a means to help ease the pain. It was worth a shot.

She heaved her body up out of the sofa, wobbling for a moment, almost toppling back. She felt weak today. And tearful. The phone rang, making her start and she moved slowly to the hall to answer it. 'Hello? Pete?'

'Jenny,' David's voice replied. 'Good. I'm glad you're in!'

'So it would appear,' she snapped. 'What do you want?'

He didn't answer straight away, for a moment

she thought he'd hung up.

'It's okay. I'll call later,' he said, sounding wary.

She felt lousy. She knew she'd been giving him a hard time lately. Pete had been cross about her lawyer jokes. 'Sorry, David. I'm just irritable with this baby. How can I help you?'

'I left a bag at your house last week and I really need to get it back. I forgot it, with all the hullabaloo after Matthew's fall.'

'I'm looking at it right now. It's in the hall.'

'Can I call over for it? I'm not far away.'

'I'm going up for a bath, but there's a key under the plant pot on the right. Let yourself in. I'll make us a cuppa when I come down,' Jenny said.

'Great stuff,' David replied. 'Enjoy your splash.'

Jenny climbed the stairs slowly, muttering under her breath about splashes. She started to run the bath then searched for a gift she'd received a few Christmases ago. A gift set from Boots, full of bath bombs and bubbles. Ah, there it was. She poured the bath gel into the running water and breathed in the scent, reading the label out loud to herself. 'Jasmine and rose bath crème! Very nice! Thank you, oh sister of mine.'

She undressed, taking a peek at her body in the bathroom mirror. Jenny tried to recreate the famous Demi Moore pose, holding one hand across her breasts, the other under her bump. She twisted her body sideways, and pouted at the mirror.

Oh, for fuck's sake. She was more Dudley

229

Moore than Demi. She looked ridiculous.

Laughing at herself, she turned the tap off, then tested the water. Satisfied it wasn't going to scald her, she lifted her legs into the water, wincing as another dart shot up into her groin and buttocks.

She gingerly managed to lower herself into the water and lay back, placing her head on the back of the tub. Now this was the life. Why was it that she never had a bath? She'd always been a shower-and-go type of gal. She'd envied those girls who could luxuriate in lovely foamy baths. This would be the start of a new her. She'd learn to appreciate the beauty of a long soak. No more would she have to regift all those bath sets she always seemed to get at the office Christmas Secret Santa.

She closed her eyes, feeling the water lap around her. She would need to be a contortionist though to get the water to cover her body up. The house was silent. Remembering her midwife's instructions, she willed herself to relax. Nope. She was bored already. She wondered how long she'd been in the water for. It felt like hours. She quickly peered over to the shelf beside the bath where she'd placed her watch. Damn it. It had been less than three minutes since she'd sank her ass into the water!

She closed her eyes again, trying to remember the breathing exercises the midwife had told her about. The Scottish woman's voice rang into her ear. 'Slowly inhale through your nose and exhale through your mouth, allowing all your air to flow out with a sigh . . . '

Jenny tried that, ending with a loud 'Aarggh-hhh . . .'

She felt ridiculous. She tried it a second time, but gave up halfway through.

What else had the midwife suggested? Oh yeah, she said that with each exhale, she should focus on relaxing different part of her body. And with that, bloody Frankie Goes to Hollywood's 'Relax' started buzzing around her head again.

'I don't think your mama is very good at this,' Jenny said to her bump. She glanced at the watch again. She'd been in the bath six whole minutes. If she got up now she could catch *Loose Women*, which would be just starting. Oooh, that would be far more beneficial to me than lying here in my own filth, she thought. Time to get up.

And that's when it all went wrong.

Jenny held on to the sides of the tub, and attempted to pull herself up. But her arms weren't strong enough and she only managed to lift her arse a few inches from the bottom of the bath.

Hmm, she thought. This could be tricky. She tried to move sideways, wriggling her bum so that her bump fell to the right. If she could just turn herself so she could get on her knees, she knew she could push herself up. But once again, she fell back in an undignified splash.

'Hello!' David's voice called out, downstairs. Shit, she'd forgotten all about him. He'd let himself in, as instructed. She hated when people did that.

Fan-bloody-tastic! Jenny thought.

'I'm still in the bath,' she shouted down. 'You

go ahead. The bag is in the hall.'

'Nonsense,' David replied. 'You take your time, I'll put the kettle on and have a nice cup of tea ready for you, when you come down.'

Damn it, Jenny thought.

She took a deep breath and used all her strength to heave herself up. And she nearly made it too. She managed to raise her bottom high enough that she got one leg to tuck under her. Then the pain hit her again, shooting up through her pelvis and she screamed out in pain as she flopped back into the water again.

She heard David running up the stairs, calling her name.

'I'm okay,' she said, but her voice was brittle with pain.

'Clearly you're not,' David said outside the bathroom. 'I'm coming in.'

'I'm naked,' she screamed as he walked in, but she was too late. She started to scoop up bubbles, placing them strategically over her breasts and bloody painful vagina!

'Oh good Lord. You're naked,' he exclaimed, averting his eyes.

'What did you expect? I'm in a flaming bath.'

'Of course. Sorry. What's wrong? Are you in labour?'

'No!' Jenny exclaimed. Then she added, in a small voice, 'I'm stuck.'

He started to laugh. 'Oh, thank goodness for that. Crikey, for a minute I thought I was going to have to deliver that baby here and now!'

'I'm glad you find it so funny!' Jenny said. 'Meanwhile . . . '

'Quite,' David said. 'Right, let's get you up. Heave ho and I'll have you up in a jiffy.'

'No!' Jenny said. 'There will be no heave hoing. Have you forgotten I'm naked under these bubbles?'

David didn't like to point out that that particular cat jumped out of the bag when he'd walked in and seen everything.

'Turn around,' Jenny demanded. 'I'm going to let the water out of the bath, then you can pass me a towel and I'll drape that over myself while you help me up.'

'Great idea,' David said. He turned his back to her, then realised he was facing the mirror with an unimpeded view of Jenny's breasts as she leaned forward to take the plug out.

He quickly looked down and turned his eyes towards the door instead. He'd only come to collect a bag, he'd not expected all this palaver!

There was an awkward silence as they listened to the water drain out of the tub; occasionally they asked a banal question or two of each other. When they had exhausted small talk, mercifully the drain gulped the last lot of water down.

David passed a towel to Jenny. 'I'm a beached whale,' she said forlornly. 'About to suffocate under the weight of its own bulk.'

David turned around and said gently, 'More like a beautiful ladybird who's fallen on to its back with its little legs in the air, trying so hard to right itself.'

'My legs *are* little,' Jenny said, much preferring the ladybird analogy.

'Tiny,' David agreed, then calling out, one,

two, three, he pulled her up and lifted her out of the bath.

'You're strong,' Jenny said, in admiration. She would never have thought that about him before.

'I have been working out a lot. Bench pressing about two hundred pounds these days. Which I'd say is about . . . ' David stopped when Jenny flashed him a warning look.

' . . . Which I was about to say was at least double your weight.' She smiled, pleased at that remark. 'Right, I'll leave you to get dressed and tea will be ready when you come down.'

'Thanks, David,' Jenny said. 'I appreciate your help.'

'I'm not all that bad, you know,' David said. 'I can be a nice guy.'

When Jenny came downstairs, she found him sitting at their kitchen table with tea and biscuits laid out waiting for her.

'I don't think you're a bad guy,' Jenny said before she bit into a Jaffa Cake.

'You do a good impression of someone who does think that,' David replied.

'Have I been a right bitch?'

'Well, you've been a bit . . . difficult,' David finished.

Jenny laughed at that word. She accepted that she could be difficult.

'It's just all this stuff with Karen and the divorce. I've been worried about her . . . ' Jenny said.

He nodded. 'I get that. I want you to take her side. I'm glad she has you. But for the record, she wanted to get divorced, she pushed for it. I

234

wasn't the only one who met someone else.'

'Mark.'

He nodded. Mark was the man that Karen had an affair with before their own marriage ended. She had tried to have a relationship with him for a while, but they broke up within a few weeks.

'He wanted Karen, not our children. Arsehole.'

'Arsehole,' Jenny agreed and she clinked mugs with him. Then she frowned as a thought struck her. 'Do you think that it's the norm, rather than the exception, that men don't want to take on someone else's child?'

David shook his head quickly. 'No. Not in the least. I think if you love someone, you love all parts of them. Children and all. Or at least I hope that's the case.'

David thought about Robyn and how hard she'd been trying to bond with the children. Josh was being difficult, he knew that. But it sometimes felt like an impossible situation. He wanted to support all of them — his girlfriend, his ex-wife and his son — but sometimes he felt like he was being torn into three different directions.

'Are you and Robyn serious?' Jenny asked.

'I think so. I love her. She says she loves me. And when that happens, you have to grab it, don't you?'

'Yes. I suppose you do.'

'It's been a tricky time for Robyn. But she's stuck around. I mean, just as we get together, Rachel dies. I've been spending huge amounts of time with Karen. And Josh and the children are trying so hard to adjust to their new normal.' He paused for a moment, then thought, in for a penny, in for a pound. 'And, of course, there's the fact that none of my friends have made any attempts to befriend her. She feels quite isolated.'

Jenny interrupted, irritated at the inference that she had done something wrong. 'Now, wait a minute. I'm Karen's friend, you can't expect me to be all chummy-chummy with your new girlfriend!'

'No, I don't for one moment expect that. But I have to admit, I thought *you* of all people would have been a little bit nicer to her.'

'Why me?' Jenny snapped.

'It's just you went through all this when you dated Robert. Remember?' David said.

Jenny felt embarrassment wash over her. To her shame, she'd forgotten all about that. When she'd dated Robert, a friend of David's, after she split up with Pete, she had been really angry with her friends because they wouldn't give him a chance. They'd made it so hard for someone new to enter their clique. 'Oh shit, David. I'm a bitch. I really am. I'm so sorry.'

'It's okay. But it would mean the world to me, if you would just try to get to know her. You might be surprised at how much you like her. You have quite a lot in common, you know.'

Jenny looked up at him in disbelief. Then they both looked down at the floor as he felt a splash of water hit his leg.

'*Shit!* David, brace yourself, mate. My waters have just broken!'

236

22

The missing father and the flows and the rides

Pete and Jenny's house, Didsbury, Manchester

David looked in horror at the water that had trickled from Jenny on to the floor.

'And I just had a bath!' she wailed. 'What a waste.'

'You're not getting back into another one of those again!' David said. He didn't think his back could take it. 'Right, let's get you to the hospital!'

'I want Pete, but I don't know if he wants me. Or us,' Jenny said pointing to her tummy. 'I'm scared.'

'I know you are. But you must trust me,' David said. 'I'm here and it's all going to be fine.' He felt sweat begin to trickle down his spine. Time to find that calm they all congratulated him on recently. He tried to remember all he'd learned for Karen's labours. But it seemed like such a long time ago now.

First things first. He needed to find her bag! There has to be a labour bag. It was all Karen talked about for weeks, in fact months, for each of their pregnancies.

'Where's your bag?' David asked. 'Upstairs?'

'I don't have it packed yet!' Jenny wailed

again. 'I was going to do it tomorrow.'

'That's fine. I'll pack one for you, no problem at all.' He ran upstairs to her bedroom, then ran back downstairs again, two steps at a time, 'What do you want me to put in it?'

'Er, my nightdress, it's in the top drawer, I'll need my big knickers, same drawer, you'll find toiletries in the bathroom, and there's a bag on the top shelf, with all the babygros in it,' Jenny said.

'Not a problem,' David replied, smiling while inside he was panicking, thinking he'd never remember all that. When she mentioned big knickers his mind kind of wandered.

'Ring Pete!' Jenny said. 'And the hospital, to tell them we're on our way. The numbers on the pad by the phone in the hall.'

'Yes. Of course,' David replied, pulling his mobile phone out as he went upstairs. He dialled Pete's number. Answer the bloody phone, he thought. Voice message! He tried to sound cheery as he left him a message. He didn't want to get him in a state.

'Put my scrunchie in,' Jenny shouted, as he started to punch in the number for the hospital.

What the fuck was a scrunchie? David thought. He scanned the room looking for a likely suspect. Then spotted a small teddy bear on the bedside locker that looked like it had all its stuffing flattened out of it. Its face was kind of scrunched-up-looking. Probably a favourite teddy bear of Jenny's from childhood or something. Yes, that had to be it. He stuffed it in the small bag he'd found at the foot of the bed, along with the other items.

He ran downstairs again just as the door opened.

'Pete!' Both Jenny and David said at once.

'No, just me!' Adam said, walking in with Matthew in his car seat.

'I'm in labour,' Jenny lamented.

'Oh, sweet Jesus. Are you all right?' He ran over to her.

'Oh, I'm just peachy,' she replied, but smiled as she said it. 'Find Pete for me, will ya?'

'On it,' Adam said. Then he turned to David. 'Where is he?'

'No idea. He's not answering the phone. Look, I'll bring Jenny into the hospital, I'll call Karen too. And you go find Pete,' David suggested.

'Perfect.' Adam ran towards the door, then back in again as he remembered Matthew. 'Where's little Adam? I'll drop him and Matthew off at Karen's.'

'In nursery.' Jenny said. Then she made a face as a contraction started. Oh boy, she'd forgotten what they were like. It was like her hooha was being electrocuted! She leaned over the back of the kitchen chair and held on.

'Ride with the pain,' Adam said, remembering Rachel's labour.

'Flow with the tide,' David added.

She looked at both of them as she breathed in and out quickly. Were they for real? If she wasn't in so much pain, she would have told them what they could do with their flows and rides.

David checked his watch and announced, 'Eight minutes, thirty seconds since the last one.'

He clicked a button on his watch and smiled in satisfaction.

'Karen bought me this for Father's Day a few years ago,' he said to Adam, who leaned in to take a look.

'Nice,' Adam said. He held up his wrist and showed David his. 'Now, this one shows the time in three different continents.'

'Nice,' David agreed.

'Hello!' Jenny shouted. 'Woman in labour, about to have a baby over here!'

Adam ran over to her and kissed her cheek. 'I'll get Pete for you. And I'll collect little Adam from nursery. You just worry about bringing this little one into the world, okay?'

Jenny clasped Adam's hand. 'What if he doesn't want us?'

Adam looked at David, who looked as helpless as he felt.

'Course he does,' Adam said.

'I need the loo,' Jenny screamed.

Adam helped her to the loo under the stairs and opened the door for her.

He ran back to David. 'What if that numpty has gone to Australia?'

'He wouldn't,' David gasped.

'He would, you know. Jo sent him an email, asking him to go over,' Adam said. 'She's throwing herself at him, all bendy and sexy. Sure his head is turned with it all!'

'I'll kill him,' David felt anger bubble up inside him on behalf of Jenny. 'She's very vulnerable right now. She doesn't need this.'

'Look, if he's in the country, I'll get him back

240

here and I'll drag him by his short and curlies if I have to!'

'What are you whispering about?' Jenny said. 'Have you heard from Pete?'

'No answer yet,' Adam said. 'I'm going to ring around a few likely suspects. Remember what I said now. You just worry about yourself and that little one.'

Her brown eyes filled with tears and she looked so scared that both men wanted to strangle Pete.

'He missed little Adam's birth,' Jenny whispered.

'It's going to be fine,' Adam reassured her. 'He won't miss this one.'

'You promise?' Jenny said.

'We both do,' David said, holding his hand out. 'Now, come on, you. Let's get you to the hospital. They are expecting us.'

23

Audrey's secret past and the saucy ketchup

Audrey's Residential Home, Didsbury, Manchester

'When I was fifteen, I fell pregnant,' Audrey closed her eyes so she didn't have to look at the shock that must be all over her son's face. 'Your father never knew. It is a secret that I've carried for decades.'

Pete's mouth fell open. His mother had a child when she was a child herself? It couldn't be true. She was a devout Catholic. Surely there were rules against that?

'I didn't know I was pregnant for certain, until the night I felt the baby kick for the first time. It squirmed its way around my tummy and I felt both terror and wonder at the life that was growing inside me.

'I told Mammy the next morning. It was a Saturday, and Daddy was out milking the cows. She cried. She begged me to tell her it wasn't true. I don't think she really believed me, until I lifted my top and showed her my already swollen belly.'

Pete could not get his head around what Audrey was saying. He knew that she had no reason to make this up, but part of him wished

242

that perhaps she was going a little doolally and forgetful. That perhaps this was a story she'd seen on TV and was now taking it on as her own. But one look at the profound sadness on his mother's face as she recounted this hidden past, wiped that silly notion from his mind.

'Mammy told Daddy that afternoon. She brought him into the parlour, closed the door behind her and they stayed in there for hours. I didn't know what to do. Eventually I started to make dinner, peeling spuds and carrots, grilling chops. I had no clue what they would say when they came out. But I was relieved that I'd told them. I loved them and I'd only ever been shown love from them too. I figured they'd know what to do.'

Pete moved closer to his mother, captivated and horrified by her story. He held her hand as she spoke, in an effort to let her know that he was on her side. His heart splintered as he witnessed the raw pain on her face.

'When they came out of the parlour, I told them that dinner was ready. Daddy looked at me with such disgust that I felt winded. That look he gave me was the very last image I have of my father. I never saw him again.' A single tear fell down Audrey's cheek.

Pete shook his head. He couldn't bear to hear this. 'What did they do?' His voice croaked out the question.

'It was arranged that I go into St Patrick's in Dublin. A mother-and-baby home. A goddamn hell on earth. On Monday morning, Mammy brought me there on the train. I had a small

243

brown suitcase packed with a few bits and she gave me a tiny yellow babygro, that I had worn myself as a newborn.' Audrey started to pleat and un-pleat the folds of her green skirt. Over and over she continued this ritual, as she told her son her secret. 'They told me that I was six months pregnant. I had at least three to four months to stay in that home, which was filled with other girls, from all over the country, in the same predicament as me.'

'And your mother left you there?'

Audrey nodded, the pain of watching her mother walk down the long driveway was as fresh today as it was over fifty years ago.

'All of the girls went to Mass every morning, where the priest spoke about fire and damnation for each of us sinners. We worked in the kitchens, in the laundry rooms, in the gardens. We all had a job to do. Clean, clean, clean. Always keep the home clean.'

Understanding of his mother's need to have a clean home came with these words. He wished he'd known. He would have helped. He would have been less messy.

'The nuns told us every day we were sinners, dirty, used, unworthy of bearing the title of mother. They told us that no man would ever want to marry us, if they knew our truths. Our dirty secrets. Soon, I began to believe them.'

'That's disgraceful.' Pete stood up, pacing the room. He wanted to find those bloody nuns and tell them how wrong they were, how lucky he was to have a mother like her.

'You have to understand that for most there,

our own families had rejected us. So we had no reason to doubt their taunts. We took our penance. We had brought it all on ourselves.'

They sat silently for a moment. Audrey took a deep breath and said, 'It was a boy.'

'I have a brother,' Pete replied. He felt wonder at saying that statement.

'You have a brother,' Audrey confirmed.

Silence again.

'He was almost eight pounds. Healthy, strong, beautiful.' Audrey closed her eyes and he was back in her arms again.

'I was only allowed keep him for three days. Then they took him from me. A family had been found in America, who were on their way to adopt him.'

Pete's mind reeled as each piece of information was passed to him.

Audrey grabbed his hands and cried out in agitation, 'I had no choice. They wouldn't let me keep him. They took him from me.'

'Oh, Mum,' Pete said, putting his arms around her. 'How could they get away with that?'

'It was a different time in Ireland back then. Just the way things were done — single mothers didn't get to keep their children. They were almost always separated from them in some way. Our babies were sold to rich Americans. Hundreds and hundreds of them, snatched from the arms of mothers like me.'

'What happened after they took him?' Pete asked.

'My mother came to get me. I packed my small brown suitcase, scrubbed my face clean and waited at the front door for her to arrive. She came alone. Without my father. I cried when I saw her, and for a moment she held me in her arms. I whispered to her that it had been a boy, a beautiful boy. Then she took me to the port in Dun Laoghaire.' Audrey's face hardened at the memory.

'She didn't take you home?' Pete was aghast.

'I wasn't welcome there ever again. My parents had arranged for me to go to my cousin Elsie's, here in Manchester. Elsie managed to organise work for me as a kitchen maid in Manchester Hospital. Goodness knows I had enough practice at St Patrick's.'

'So that's why you came to Manchester. I always thought you were older though,' Pete said.

'Fifteen. But I was old. I aged years with every day I spent in that home,' Audrey said. 'I met your father not long after I arrived here. And we fell in love. And married. You didn't come for a long time. I believed I was being punished. But then, eventually, you arrived and I felt joy, because I got to keep you.' She stretched out her two hands and held his head in between them, looking at his face, taking in every line and frown and kissed his forehead. 'I've loved you every day of your life.'

'I know, Mum,' Pete said. 'You are the best mother anyone could ever hope for. Why are you telling me all this now?'

'I've written to John, that's what I called him, every year on his birthday. At first, I kept them at home, hidden at the bottom of a drawer. Then after I had you, I found an agency in Ireland that helps reunite adopted children with their birth parents. I sent all my letters to them and they made contact with your brother. He sent me a letter back. Just the once. He told me that he had a wonderful life, he was loved by his adoptive parents and he wished me well. But he didn't want to meet me.' The pain of that letter laced every word Audrey uttered.

'That's good, that he's happy though,' Pete said, trying to reassure her.

'It's the only thing that's kept me going all these years. And that's why I'm telling you this. Don't you see, son? I have to believe that it's possible to love another person's child. If that's not true, then what's the alternative? You have to love that baby as if he or she were your own. You simply have to. For me, for your brother and for that little baby's sake. *You have to, son.*' Audrey broke down in tears and Pete pulled her close to him.

'I will, Mum. I swear.'

The doubts he'd been plagued with disappeared. He would love this child, and he would balance his love between little Adam and the baby, exactly as his mother had advised.

Pete, the worrier, was no longer worried.

'What's that fecking eejit doing?' Audrey said, looking over his shoulder.

Pete followed her gaze and watched Adam outside his window, jumping and down like a crazy man.

'Has he been stung by a bee?' Audrey wondered, wiping the tears from her face with her two hands. 'You never quite know with Adam. He's a card, isn't he? Buzz him in, son.'

Audrey refilled the kettle, ready to make tea. And Adam came running into the room, out of breath, red in the face, gesticulating towards the door.

'Hello, love,' Audrey said, walking over to give him a hug. 'How's that adorable lad of yours?'

'He's good, Mrs G. But I don't have time . . .' Adam began.

'To spare two minutes to talk to your best friend's mother? Ah here now.' Audrey replied. 'I've the kettle on, we'll have a nice cup of tea. I could do with one, I don't mind telling you. What a day we've had.'

'Are you okay, Mum?' Pete asked.

'I'm grand.' She squeezed his hand. 'He's a good boy,' she said to Adam. 'Always worried about his mother. How's Mary by the way?'

Adam shook his head and gritted his teeth. Always with a little jibe, this one. 'You know I haven't seen my mother in years.'

'Well, shame on you,' Audrey said. 'She adored the bones of you. I know the look of love when I see it on a mother's face. And you know it too.'

Adam looked down at his arm and remembered her touch, as she soothed away his pain, from the belt of his old school teacher. She had loved him. He knew that.

'Tea or coffee?' Audrey asked, smiling at the two boys. 'It's like the old days, isn't it!'

'We don't have time for coffee!' Adam said. 'Listen Pete — '

'No time for a drink?' Audrey interrupted

again. 'You youngsters, always in a rush.'

'I'll have a coffee, I think,' Pete said. 'Maybe some of that nice carrot cake you made too.'

'Two sugars, son?' Audrey asked.

Adam looked at them both in exasperation and screamed, 'Jenny's gone into labour. David's with her but she needs you!'

They turned towards him, mouths open in shock.

'Then why in God's name didn't you say something, Adam Williams! You always were a dreamer.' Audrey shook her head and tutted loudly.

Adam thought it was no wonder that Jenny wanted to strangle Audrey sometimes.

'Mrs G, see you soon. Pete, move your arse,' Adam said. 'Because if we don't make it and it's a boy you'll have to call the baby little David.'

'No way it that happening,' Pete shouted, picking up speed. History was not going to repeat itself again.

As they reached the car, Pete shouted to him, 'I've chosen, you know. I want tomato ketchup. Lovely saucy tomato ketchup.'

Jenny? Adam thought, then broke into a huge grin. Yeah, that's definitely Jenny.

24

The wonky womb and Dr Doug Ross in his scrubs

North Manchester Hospital, Manchester

While Adam drove Pete to the hospital, Karen was at home trying to keep the peace between Ramona and the children. She had collected little Adam from nursery earlier and Adam dropped Matthew off, before he went on his search for Pete. The noise levels were at decibels.

Ramona complained, 'Anyways, I no Mary Poppins. I no sign up for this . . . crèche!'

Josh and little Adam fired their water pistols at her, with perfect aim.

'I know it's difficult but our friends need us,' Karen said, trying her best to calm Ramona down.

'They no my friends,' Ramona replied, sulking. Karen knew the real reason for her bad mood was the fact that Jean-Luc had not called in two nights running. She was nervous that he was fast losing interest in their long-distance romance.

'You can have an extra day's holiday at Christmas,' Karen offered as a bribe.

'I need a holiday now,' Ramona muttered, as she ducked from another dart from Josh.

Karen called David for an update.

'We're in the pre-labour ward now. Just

250

waiting to see the midwife,' David whispered.

'Any sign of Pete?' Karen asked.

'No. And she won't let me leave her. She's become quite attached to me!' David said. 'Robyn will have my guts for garters. We're supposed to be going to the symphony.'

'I can't leave the children here with Ramona, she's in one of her moods,' Karen said. 'If not for that, I'd have gone to let you go.'

'If Pete gets here soon, I might just make it in time anyhow,' David said. 'Right, I better go, Jenny is waving at me to go back in.'

David walked into the room to see a doctor with his head peering into Jenny's vagina. She had her two feet up in stirrups.

'Gosh I'm sorry,' David said, looking away from the business end of things. He'd seen far too much of his friend today.

'Don't worry, half the hospital has been in for a look at this stage!' Jenny said. 'Apparently I have a wonky womb!'

'Ouch, that sounds painful.' David's buttocks clenched in fear at the words. Sounded pretty awful to him.

'Your wife's womb is tilted, and the baby is also in breech, so all in all, I'm thinking we need to look at a C-section,' the doctor said.

'She's not my — '

'I'm not his — '

Jenny and David spoke at the same time, pausing as they both realised what the doctor had said.

'C-section?' Jenny whispered.

'Yes. I think it's the best course of action. Safest for you and for baby.'

251

Jenny blanched. She'd gone through so many scenarios in her head about the birth, but never had she given any real credence to the fact that she might have to have a section. She'd had little Adam naturally, surely that counted for something.

'My husband isn't here yet,' Jenny said.

The doctor looked at David and smirked.

'I'm her friend!' David said indignantly.

'We'll bring you down in thirty minutes,' the doctor said. 'If your husband gets here in time, great. If not, your friend can come with you.'

Jenny started to cry as soon as the doctor walked away. 'I don't want surgery.'

David patted her hand and murmured what he hoped were appropriate comforting sounds, as best he could.

'Where's Pete?' Jenny wailed. 'Adam promised he'd find him.'

'I'll call again to get an update, don't worry,' David said.

'I'm so scared. And I'm all alone.' Jenny cried once more.

'Oh no you're not. I'm here and I'll go down to surgery with you. If you want me to, that is,' David said. 'I always fancied myself in a set of scrubs.'

'I don't know what I would have done without you,' Jenny sobbed, tears streaming down her face.

David handed her a tissue and kissed her head. 'I'll be back in a mo.'

He walked out of hearing distance and rang Adam. 'Any luck?'

'No. He never went to work today. He's not answering his phone. I'm seriously worried he's halfway to bloody Sydney by now!' Adam said.

'Well, things have taken a new twist here,' David said. He filled Adam in on the C-section news.

'I'm on my way to Audrey's now,' Adam said. 'I'm five minutes from there. It's my last chance. I can't think of anywhere else he might be. After this, I'm out of options.'

'Come here if you don't have any luck. She's going to need all the support she can get,' David said.

'I'll call you in a bit,' Adam promised.

David went back into Jenny's room.

'Can I have my scrunchie?' Jenny asked.

'Yes of course,' David said. He rummaged through her bag and gently placed the soft toy on her chest.

She looked down at it and said, 'Why on earth are you giving me that old thing?'

'Your scrunchie,' David said.

'That's Adam's toy!' She said laughing. When a nurse joined them shortly afterwards, they were both still laughing at David's mistake. But the laughter stopped when reality kicked in as the nurse began preparing Jenny for surgery, gowning her up and putting surgical stockings on her legs.

'Sexy,' she joked, holding one leg up to David to inspect.

'Epically,' David agreed.

'We need to bring you down, Jenny,' the nurse said. 'We'll get you your epidural and anaesthetic.' She turned to David. 'And are you coming too?'

David looked at Jenny. 'What do you want, Jen?'

'I've already had one of Pete's friends hold my hand during labour. This is getting ridiculous,' Jenny said.

David remained silent as she made up her mind.

'I'd be very grateful if you would come with me,' she said, her voice low.

He nodded. 'I would be honoured.'

'Someone will come and get you, to gown you up too,' the nurse said. 'Then you can meet Jenny in the theatre once we've got her prepped.'

David leaned in and kissed Jenny's head. 'I'll be with you in a jiffy.'

Ten minutes later, Jenny was wheeled into the theatre and the nurses lifted her on to the operating table. The anaesthetic began to take hold and they placed a screen over her tummy so she couldn't see a thing.

She closed her eyes and tried to focus on the fact that soon she'd be meeting her baby. Soon, she'd get to hold her or him in her arms.

Soon.

What if she had to do this on her own?

Well, if she was going to have to be a mother of two on her own, she might as well get used to it, from here on. She'd manage. She always did.

The nurse said, 'Oh look, here's your very own Dr Doug Ross.'

Jenny thought, David will love that. He's probably swaggering in, tossing his long blond hair, pretending he's George Clooney in ER. She could already picture the smirk on his face. He'd fancy himself something rotten in doctor's scrubs.

'Hello, love,' a voice said.

That wasn't David!

She looked up and saw her Pete.

Jenny started to cry again. Pete came. He was here.

'I thought you weren't coming,' she sobbed.

'I missed the birth of little Adam, I sure as hell wasn't going to miss the birth of my second child,' Pete said, his voice breaking at the end with swelled emotion.

'Your second child?' Jenny whispered.

'Yes,' he whispered back, kissing her forehead.

'Does that mean?' Jenny asked.

'Yes it does.' Pete replied, his eyes glistening with tears too.

'Are you ready to meet your new baby?' the doctor said, over the screen.

'Yes!' Jenny and Pete cried in unison.

The sound of a baby's first whimper filled the room and Pete held his Jenny, his love, as they both saw their daughter for the very first time.

25

Marilyn, Elvis and Audrey's choice

Pete and Jenny's house, Didsbury, Manchester

Pete had forgotten how much chaos came with a newborn. Bags of nappies were scattered in every room. Baby wipes, unused and, in some cases, used, were on the coffee table, the kitchen table, the floor. The whistle of a kettle about to reach boiling point, ready to make bottles, filled the room.

Audrey was standing at the ironing board with a mountain of newborn babygros freshly laundered and ironed.

'You don't have to do that, Mum,' he said, feeling both guilty and relieved all at once.

'I like to be useful, son.' Audrey's smile on her face, warm and true, right up to her eyes, paid credence to that fact.

Pete wandered into the living room where Jenny was cradling their little girl in her arms, their eyes fixed on each other, equally besotted.

'What do you think about the name Davina?' Pete suggested. Nearly two weeks in and they still hadn't agreed a name for the baby. If they didn't choose one soon, she would be answering to Little One for the rest of her life.

Jenny turned to Pete, making a face. 'No. We are not calling our daughter after your celebrity crush!'

Pete had had a thing for Davina McCall for over a decade now. He'd never missed an episode of *Streetmate* in the nineties and only watched *Big Brother* because it meant he could ogle her on a Friday night.

'I think it's a pretty name,' Pete said. 'And it's not like you have anything better to suggest!'

'It has to be perfect,' Jenny said.

'I know, love. We'll think of the right name. Promise.'

'How about Bluebell?'

'No.'

'Or Daisy?' Jenny said hopefully.

'No!' Pete said.

'Violet?' Jenny threw in, not really serious but putting it out there as it was the only other flower she could think of.

'No! And it's a no to Daffodil and Hyacinth too!' Pete said. 'No flower names. You know how pollen plays havoc with my sinuses!'

'What's that got to do with choosing a baby's name?' Jenny asked, laughing.

'I'm not taking any chances, jinxing things,' Pete replied with a wink.

Jenny called him over. 'See this little one? She's going to love you. You'll be her first hero, you know.'

Pete leaned in and kissed Jenny, breathing in her scent, that was all milk, Sudocrem and Jaffa Cakes. 'And I'm going to love you both. For ever.'

'I don't think I'll ever get tired of hearing that,' Jenny replied. 'Can you hear that little one, Mama and Dada love you.'

257

They leaned in close to the baby, smiling at her adorable cherub nose and lips, her cornflower-blue eyes and her milky white skin. She was perfect.

Pete picked her up in his arms and cradled her close. He'd never understand how he ever doubted if he could love her. She was the most precious gift he could have received. He didn't need to work on balancing out his love between little Adam and her. His heart just exploded in size when she came along. And if Grant came back, so be it. He'd deal with that. He wasn't going to waste any more time worrying about a possible issue, that might never rear its head.

'She needs a change,' Jenny said, half-heartedly moving to get up.

Pete put a hand out to stop her. 'You stay there, love. Put your feet up. I've got this.'

He walked out, humming 'What a Wonderful World' to his little one and Jenny lay back on the couch, feeling content. She'd not been this happy in months.

'Cup of tea?' Audrey asked, holding the pot up.

'Only if you sit and have one with me.'

Audrey poured two cups and sat down beside Jenny.

'She's a little dote,' Audrey said.

'I know. And so quiet. Compared to little Adam, who cried constantly those first few weeks!'

'I'd forgotten that,' Audrey said.

Jenny looked at her mother-in-law. She looked tired. The lines etched deep into her face seemed more pronounced today. 'Are you okay?'

Audrey didn't speak for a moment. 'Did Pete tell you? I don't mind if he did.'

Jenny nodded. She'd been afraid to mention it to Audrey in case she caused offence.

'Sometimes, when I'm with newborns like your little one, memories, long subdued, come back demanding attention. Today, my mind is filled with my first born. I only had him for a few days. I've had to make do with those memories for a long time. Days like today, they feel meagre and mean.'

Jenny clasped Audrey's hand. 'I'm so sorry you had to go through that. It was barbaric.'

Tears crammed their way into Jenny's eyes and her mouth tightened with emotion. She could not bring herself to imagine what it would be like to give up either of her children. How on earth had Audrey survived the pain all these years?

'Hearing you and Pete talk about baby names. It brought back a memory I'd forgotten about,' Audrey said.

'Can you tell me about it?' Jenny asked.

Audrey shrugged. 'In St Patrick's, the mother and baby home I was in, the other girls and I used to talk about baby names all the time. I had a friend there. Fiona was her name. She was from Limerick and a farmer's daughter like me. We were the same age. We had a lot in common. She made me laugh.'

If Audrey closed her eyes she could hear the faint echo of their laughter in that cold, dreary dormitory room now.

'Do you know, Fiona wanted to call her baby Elvis if it was a boy and Marilyn if it was a girl?' Audrey said.

'Go away,' Jenny laughed. 'And did she?'

'She did. She had a little girl and for a few days, that baby was Marilyn and we'd go visit her, and dream about a future, which only had pretty pink dresses and love for her,' Audrey whispered.

'Did you stay in touch with Fiona?' Jenny asked.

'I did, for a while. Until she died. But I'd rather not talk about that.' Audrey's voice turned cold and Jenny nodded quickly, not wanting to cause her any further upset.

'And what name did you choose for your baby?' Jenny asked, gently.

'John,' Audrey replied. 'It was my father's name and my grandfather's, and his father's too before that. I wanted to continue the family tradition.'

'That's a lovely idea.'

'It suited him. Or at least I thought it did. Of course, his new parents changed his name when they adopted him, but they did keep John as his second name, which was kind of them.'

Upstairs they heard the dull murmur of Pete chattering to the little one. Audrey nodded towards the sound. 'I know I smother Pete sometimes.'

'No you don't,' Jenny protested, blinking away tears as she envisioned the scene that must have taken place when Audrey said goodbye to her son.

Audrey patted her hand. 'It's okay. You don't have to lie, but I appreciate the gesture. I know I'm over-protective. And I know I interfere when I shouldn't. I try to do too much for him. It's just . . . I suppose I have all this love inside me for two children, but I only get to share it with one. Sometimes I go a little overboard.'

Jenny couldn't stop a sob escaping.

'I'm sorry. Don't be upsetting yourself. I'm an old fool.' Audrey leaned in and wiped tears from Jenny's face.

'You have *nothing* to apologise for,' Jenny declared. 'You are a lovely woman and Pete is very lucky to have you in his corner. You've been an amazing mother and if I can be half as good with my two, then I'll be very proud.'

Audrey put her two hands to her face and cried at the words, so Jenny leaned in and took her in her arms. They rocked back and forth for a long time. 'You're a good mother already, you have nothing to worry about,' Audrey said.

Pete walked back in, stunned to see his mother and wife in each other's arms, both in tears. 'I was only gone ten minutes.'

Which made both Jenny and Audrey giggle.

'Is everything okay?'

'Just fine, son,' Audrey said.

Jenny pulled out a tissue and blew her nose noisily, handing one to Audrey, who followed suit.

'I think she's ready for a nap, love,' Pete said.

'Give her to your mum,' Jenny said. 'She's brilliant at getting her to sleep.'

Audrey beamed as Pete placed her into her arms.

261

An idea began to nibble at Jenny's brain. She turned to Audrey and said, 'When you spoke about baby names with your friend Fiona in the mother and baby home . . .'

'Yes?' Audrey replied.

'You chose John for a boy. What girl's name did you choose?' Jenny asked.

Audrey's eyes glistened as she looked down at the now sleeping baby that she was rocking in her arms. 'I always wanted a little girl as it happens. We tried for a long time to give Pete a little sister or brother, but it wasn't to be. But if I had been blessed with a little girl, I would have called her Chloe.'

Jenny looked at Pete, her eyes wide with an unspoken question. He walked over to her side and kneeled down on the floor in front of the three women that he loved more than life itself. He nodded his answer.

'Chloe,' Jenny whispered.

Pete whispered back, 'Chloe.'

Jenny clasped Audrey's hand as she spoke, 'I knew we'd get the right name, if we just waited. Hello, Chloe. Welcome to the Gifford family.'

26

Suds and a damn good massage

Karen's house, Didsbury, Manchester

The washing machine started to shake so violently that Karen imagined the house was under attack from gunfire. As it rattled against the tile floor, an avalanche of white foam escaped, leaving a watery trail down the kitchen floor. Trust the washing machine to go to pieces when Ramona had a night off.

Josh squealed with delight at the excitement of possible body slides in their own kitchen. Ellie and Olivia started to crawl towards the white bubbles.

Karen picked up her phone and rang David to ask for help. The phone went to message, so she hung up. She texted him instead, with one hand, trying to hold back the kids with the other.

Washing machine flooding floor. Help!

Several minutes passed, then a message pinged back.

Plumber's number in phone book on table.
Can't come over. Sorry.

Karen pictured him telling Robyn that she'd been in touch and she flushed red. She could

263

guess the conversation that must have ensued. David apologetic; Robyn unimpressed. If she was Robyn, she'd be pissed off with her too. She shouldn't have called him. She'd have to stop doing that.

She looked down and saw Ellie laughing, as she placed bubbles on Olivia's head, which she then made into a shape like a Smurf hat. Josh made a beard on his face and said in a put on deep voice, 'I'm Papa Smurf.'

Oh, sod it, Karen thought. She kneeled down beside them, and picked up a large handful of suds, making them into a beard for herself too.

Soon all four of them had beards on and were talking in Smurf language at each other, laughing their socks off.

Then the doorbell rang.

Trying to wipe the suds away, Karen ran to open the door.

'Bill!' she said in surprise. Adam's father stood in front of her.

'A bad time?' he asked, his face, breaking into a grin when he spied the three children behind Karen, all wet and sudsy too.

'Any good with temperamental washing machines?' Karen asked.

'Haven't had one beat me yet,' he boasted.

'Then your timing is impeccable. Please come in.'

She left Bill to the mess in the kitchen, taking the kids upstairs for a bath. Once she'd got them all warm and dry and in their PJs, she took a quick shower, throwing on some yoga pants and a T-shirt.

By the time they came back downstairs, Bill had mopped the floor and the machine was reloaded, with the washing spinning happily again.

Karen felt herself flush, remembering that her knickers had been in that wash. Oh well, too late to worry now.

'I decided to surprise Adam. He won't give me a straight answer as to when or if he's coming back to Belfast, so I thought . . . ' Bill said.

'If the mountain will not come to Muhammad, then Muhammad must go to the mountain,' Karen said.

'Exactly.'

Karen didn't want to get involved. Adam was her friend, and while she liked Bill, she had to remain neutral.

'Did you go to Jenny and Pete's? You know, that's where Adam is staying at the minute?' Karen said.

Bill nodded. 'No answer over there. They must all be out. I figured I'd come here. I hope that was all right?'

She nodded towards the washing machine. 'I'd say your arrival was most serendipitous for me.'

'You look tired,' he said suddenly. 'Sorry, I hope that wasn't rude.'

She shrugged. 'I've not been sleeping terribly well.'

He didn't make a trite comment, and Karen appreciated that. He just accepted her statement. So she found herself continuing. 'I've been struggling a bit since Rachel died, if I'm honest.'

Again he didn't say anything, but looked at her

with such intensity that she found herself continuing her confession. 'Not sure you know this, but I'm an alcoholic.'

She looked away, embarrassed to say any more. Perhaps she'd said too much.

Bill touched her hand. 'You told me the last time I stayed with you.'

Karen shook her head. 'My memory . . . Sorry, I'd forgotten that.'

Bill said, 'I've always thought that an addict alone is in bad company.'

And, to Karen's horror, she felt tears well up into her eyes once more.

'I'm sorry,' she said as she brushed away the tears. 'It's just . . . exactly that. I am in very bad company.'

'Don't be sorry.' He looked at her then into the living room where the children were playing Lego together. 'Have you all eaten yet?'

Karen shook her head. 'It was probably going to be a chicken nugget and oven chips kind of night.' She'd been having too many of those lately. She'd worry about that another day.

'How about you go in and watch a movie with your gorgeous children. Soak up some of their magic in a big snuggle on that couch. And I'll cook dinner. Afterwards I can head to the Giffords to find Adam,' Bill said.

'That sounds like the best offer I've had in a long time,' Karen said, wiping the tears away. 'Have you booked a hotel yet?'

He shook his head.

'Well then, you're welcome to stay here again, you know. It will be tight over at the Giffords' with the new baby. Pete's mother Audrey is visiting too.'

'I remember her. She was the stereotypical Irish mammy. Doted on her son!' Bill said.

'I don't think that's changed,' Karen said, remembering the various things Jenny had complained about over the years.

'If I stay here, it wouldn't be putting you out?'

'Not in the slightest. As you said, an addict alone . . . ' Karen shrugged.

'I'll text Adam and tell him this is where I'll be.'

Bill was right, Karen thought. Snuggling on the couch with the children as they watched *Finding Nemo* on DVD *was* magic. Josh's head rested on her shoulder and the two girls shared her lap. She wasn't sure what she'd do when they got older. She needed life to slow down. Right now, all she seemed to do was rush from one task to another. She seemed to be the only person in her job who needed to leave work by 5 p.m. each evening. But that didn't mean it was the end of her working day. She often stayed up late, reading manuscripts. Could she really have it all — work and at home? Josh reached up and put his arm around her neck, sighing with contentment. These three children were her greatest accomplishment. And her work was also something to be proud of. She was good at it. She had to find a way to make the juggle less of a struggle. And she had to lose the guilt. She would go mad otherwise. She was doing the best that she could.

Halfway through the movie, Bill brought in

plates of steaming pasta with arrabiata sauce. Glasses of cold milk accompanied the meal, and it was delicious.

When the movie was over, she carried the children upstairs, one at a time, and put them to bed. Each of them had their own favourite bedtime story, so the whole process took an hour. But she treasured this time each evening and, on those days when she missed it because she had to work late, she felt off-kilter for hours afterwards.

Once they were settled, she came downstairs again to find a clean kitchen.

'You'll make someone a good wife one day,' she joked and he laughed alongside her.

'I've made coffee and I texted Adam, told him I was here. But there's been no answer yet.'

'He'll be in touch.'

'How long since you've had a drink?' Bill asked. 'If that's not being too intrusive.'

'I can answer to the exact day. I worked it out only recently. I've too much time on my hands.'

'I doubt that very much,' Bill replied, looking upwards. 'Three children . . . '

'And a full-time job. But I do have help. David. Ramona. She is with her boyfriend tonight. He's visiting from France, so I've given her time off.'

'I remember her. Your Spanish nanny.' Bill smiled. 'I've not forgotten that you haven't answered my question.'

She smiled again. 'Four hundred and seventeen days.'

'Good for you.'

'I've been contemplating drinking again for at least sixty of those,' Karen admitted. 'I long for the escape it would give me.'

'Would it be an escape do you think, or a trap?'

'That, sir, is a very good question.'

'I'd a good friend who drank. Years ago. But he used to say that the trick was to not to let your guard down. Alcohol is a patient bugger and can bide its time to bite you.'

'He was right. It is pretty sneaky,' Karen said. 'It's like I have two voices in my head. One is all woe is you if you drink and the other is saying, everyone preferred drunk Karen. She was a lot more fun.'

'I think sober Karen is plenty fun,' Bill said. 'And unless I'm remembering things wrong, when I stayed here the last time, you told me that you didn't like yourself when you drank. That your self-esteem hit record lows, back then.'

'You've a good memory.' She decided to change the subject and found herself getting involved, by asking, 'What's going on with you and Adam?'

'It's frustrating. Things were going so well, but I fucked it up. Excuse my language.'

'You go ahead. I'm a dab hand at fucking things up myself.'

'You heard about Jane?' When she nodded, he continued, 'He started off being pissed off at me for that. But pretty soon it was apparent that we have a lot of unresolved issues to sort through. I don't think he knew how much anger he had inside him.'

'For sleeping with his ex?'

'No. For leaving him and his mum. He doesn't understand how hard it was for me back then.'

'What happened? I'm a good listener if you want to talk about it.'

'I loved Mary when we married. But then I fell in love with Christian, a colleague in the university in Manchester I lectured at. It was such a mess. I don't blame Mary for hating me for what I did to our marriage. I hated me. She couldn't get beyond her vitriol for what I did. And for what I am. Her revenge was that she made sure she had Adam all for herself.'

From what Karen remembered from conversations with Rachel over the years, Adam's mother's revenge backfired. Because she didn't end up with Adam either. What a mess.

'What?' Bill asked.

'It's just Adam ended up without both of you in the end, didn't he? He was the innocent party in all of this, but still he has no mother and he's only just reconnected with you. His head must be all over the place, trying to process it all.'

'He won't talk about his mother to me. But I know he's in a world of pain right now.'

'You are going to have to find a way to get him to open up. And maybe the only way that can happen is if you tell him the truth about what you went through back then.'

Bill looked at Karen and said, 'If I promise to talk to Adam, really talk, will you promise to go to an AA meeting tomorrow? I'll go with you if you like. Or I can watch the kids if that helps more.'

Karen reached over and took his hand to

shake it, to seal the deal. And a spark of electricity made them both start.

'Rubber soles!' Karen said, pointing to her runners. 'I'm wearing my yoga gear!'

'Ah. That explains it,' Bill said, raising one eyebrow. 'Do you go much?'

'Not enough. But I find it relaxes me when I do and I need to find ways to relieve stress that don't include a bottle of Grey Goose.'

Bill laughed and said, 'There are other ways you know.'

Karen felt herself blush, as her mind went to places she was sure it shouldn't, with her friend's dad.

'I could give you a massage. I've been told I'm quite good.' And the way he looked at her left Karen in no doubt that his mind had also gone to similar places.

She raised her eyebrows at him this time and for a second imagined herself lying naked on the floor with him leaning over her . . .

'Turn around. Let me work on your neck and shoulders.'.

Sod it, she thought for the second time today. She swivelled her body around on the couch and shivered when she felt his hands begin to move, side to side, easing the muscles out, loosening them up. He then began to work on her two shoulder blades, nudging his fingertips around their circumference, working the muscles into compliance.

'How does that feel?'

'Glorious.' She turned to thank him, but ended up bumping noses instead. She'd felt

271

chemistry with him from the first moment they'd met earlier that year. Their eyes locked and she wondered what his lips would feel like on hers.

'Adam,' Bill whispered.

'Adam.' Karen agreed. She felt a connection with Bill, a friendship, a mutual respect. She would not risk that, or indeed hurting Adam, for the sake of a one-night stand.

The moment passed. The tension in the air relaxed and Bill continued working on her shoulders.

'Thank you,' Karen said, trying to stifle a yawn. She was exhausted and her eyes felt heavy with tiredness. 'I think I'll call it a night. The spare room is ready for you upstairs.'

Bill kissed her forehead and she went upstairs. That night Karen slept for eight solid hours, only waking when she heard Josh's voice calling her the next morning.

'One moment, darling,' Karen shouted. 'Go downstairs and I'll be right with you to make you breakfast.'

Placing a bowl of cornflakes in front of Josh, she chopped up some bananas to go over the girls' preferred cereal, Weetabix.

Once they were all eating their breakfast, she put the kettle on to make coffee. She realised that she felt completely rested. A full night's sleep and she felt ready to take on anything this world might decide to throw at her. It was a welcome feeling.

Bill walked in, smiling at the children. 'Good morning.'

'Hi, Bill,' Josh said, his mouth full of cereal.

Bill stood beside Karen at the kettle.

Josh shouted, 'I've done my cereal, can I watch cartoons?'

'Sure, darling,' Karen replied. The children moved into the living room.

'You need to go to an AA meeting,' Bill reminded her.

'And you need to find Adam.'

Then he leaned in and whispered, 'Last night . . .'

'Yes?'

'For a moment, I thought we were going to . . .'

'I know.' Karen answered truthfully. 'It was . . .'

'Unexpected.' Bill finished and she nodded in agreement. 'But can I say something?'

'You can say anything,' Karen replied.

'I think you are quite magnificent. And if you weren't Adam's friend, not to mention vulnerable right now, I might have kissed you.'

'And if it wasn't for all of those things too, I might have kissed you back.'

Bill reached over to touch her cheek, then said, 'You are a good woman. You need to start taking care of yourself. Will you promise me that you'll go to your AA meetings?'

'I promise,' Karen said. 'Friends?'

'Friends.' He nodded.

'But without the benefits!' she teased and they both smiled. 'Thanks Bill. I mean that.' She stood on her tippy toes, to thank him with a gentle kiss on his lips.

'Is there no man nor woman safe around you!' A voice shouted.

They broke apart and turned to see Adam

standing in the kitchen, Matthew in his baby sling, watching them with his mouth open.

'Son,' Bill said, his face stricken.

'It's not what it looks like.' Karen had the urge to laugh. She knew that wouldn't be a good idea.

'Are you wise?' Adam hissed at her. 'You had my father's lips locked on yours! Tell me how that wasn't what it looked like.'

Karen couldn't help it. She gave in to the giggles.

'It's not funny,' Adam said.

'It kind of is,' Karen insisted. 'Your face.'

'I have the right to be annoyed!' Adam said.

'You are jumping to all the wrong conclusions. We're just friends,' Karen insisted.

'I've only been back in his life a wet weekend and I've seen more than any son should have to! I can't keep up with him.'

Karen shrugged and put a hand to her face again, when another bout of giggles threatened to attack her.

'Son . . . ' Bill said again.

'Dad, go home to Belfast.'

'I'm going nowhere till we talk.'

'This is ridiculous. Adam, leave Matthew here. And you two go for a walk, or a coffee,' Karen told them. 'That's not a request. It's an order. Listen to what your father has to say.'

27

The free spirit in a yellow dress and a wasted life

Bistro West 156, Didsbury, Manchester

They walked to the bistro in silence, shoulder to shoulder yet miles apart. Each stealing a glance at the other, reluctant to be the one to start a conversation that they knew had to be painful.

Father and son sat facing each other, stirring their cappuccinos until their chocolate swirls disappeared into the milk froth. If only the unspoken words of anger that hung in the air between them could dissolve as quick, Adam thought.

'Karen was lonely. I was just trying to help,' Bill said, when their first cup of coffee was almost gone. He realised as soon as he spoke, that it had come out all wrong.

Adam wanted to reach over the table and grab his father by his throat. He pushed his chair back an inch and took a steadying breath. 'I know Karen is lonely. She's *my* friend. I spent the night there myself the other day, trying to help out. But here's the thing, Dad, despite her loneliness I didn't bloody well sleep with her!'

'Neither did I.'

'First Jane and now Karen.' Adam shook his head in disappointment.

'When you say it like that, it sounds bad.'

'What other way should I say it? You slept with them both, didn't you?' Adam tried his best to keep his voice down but he felt so bloody angry.

'I didn't sleep with Karen. But if I had, it would be my business. Both women are single.'

'You swear you didn't sleep with Karen.'

'I swear. But son, we are going to fall out a lot if you can't handle who I am. There will be other women and men. I like sex,' Bill said.

'Well, that's evident,' Adam replied.

'I told George we weren't exclusive a few weeks ago, in case that's what you are concerned about,' Bill threw in, determined to find a way to make his behaviour better in Adam's eyes.

'What did he say about that?'

'It was okay. We had an honest chat. I told him that I wasn't sure I'd ever be ready for a serious relationship. After Christian . . . ' Bill paused. 'Listen, I won't have you thinking I did something underhand. I didn't take advantage of Karen. As she told you, we're friends, that's all.'

'Good,' Adam said, finally satisfied. 'So are you and George finished now?'

'No. Nothing as dramatic as that. I like him. We both said we'd like to see each other again. We've just been busy lately, so haven't managed to get together.'

'He's a good-looking man. He's busy dating other men,' Adam retorted and was delighted to see jealousy flash across his father's face. What's good for the goose is good for the gander, as his mother used to say.

His mother. There she was again, invading his

thoughts. He moved her aside for the minute and turned his attention back to his father. But he couldn't do that, because she was mixed up in it all.

'You said Mum made you leave. And I accepted that. But you were married for years before then. Help me understand, Dad. Cos my head is reeling with it all.'

'Ask me anything,' Bill said. 'I've nothing to hide.'

'Did you think about men as a young fella?'

'Truthfully? Yes. But I thought it was just part and parcel of being a young man with raging hormones. Because the sight of a good-looking woman was just as likely to make me horny as a good-looking man.' When Adam made a face, Bill laughed. 'You asked!'

'Did you date any man before my mother then?'

'No. My first girlfriend, my first anything, was your mother. She was working the cafe, down on main street in Coleraine. It's gone now, but it used to be *the* main place to hang out when we were kids.'

Bill remembered the day when he saw Mary for the first time. She was wearing a bright yellow sundress, with short sleeves and blue buttons down the front. Her skin was so olive-coloured, she looked almost Mediterranean. Certainly different from the other girls in the town, with her raven-dark hair. He watched her for hours on that first day, shyly working up the courage to speak to her.

'I fell in love with your mother the first time I

saw her,' Bill continued. 'She made me work for her love for a bit. Took me three attempts to persuade her to date me. But when we did ... let's just say there were fireworks. We couldn't get enough of each other.'

Adam tried to picture his mother as a young girl in love, carefree. It didn't match up with the dour-faced person she became, when he fought with her ten years ago.

'We left Coleraine at the same time. First of all, we went to Queen's University in Belfast. I studied Economics and History. Mary studied Art and Literature. She's an accomplished artist.' Bill said.

A memory, long forgotten nipped at Adam's brain. He closed his eyes to search for it and saw his mother and him, sitting at their long kitchen table, painting together.

'She used to draw stories for me,' Adam said.

Bill nodded. 'She was forever making up tales with you, the more fantastical the better. And then she'd paint them for you. My job was to staple them together when I came home from work. That way they were fashioned into a book. I'd love to see those again now.'

Adam remembered those books. One in particular with a dragon on the front with fire bursting out of its mouth. He'd loved that story, he was so proud of it. He wished he had it to show Matthew. Where did it go? He felt shame tug at his conscience now. Somehow or other over the past few years, he'd allowed himself to forget all the good times he'd shared with his parents.

He needed to understand exactly what happened between them. Maybe then he could understand his place in it all.

'Before you got married, did you ever cheat on my mother? And just to be clear, I mean with either a woman or a man.'

Bill felt more hopeful, when he heard the glimmer of humour lacing Adam's words again. 'I swear that until Christian, I never looked at any one else. I loved your mother with all my heart and she was more than enough for me. For a long time too. We left Belfast after we graduated. But not before we got married in Coleraine. Your grandparents and aunts and uncles were all there. It was a celebration. A happy one.'

All of Adam's early childhood memories were linked with Coleraine and their families there. Every year, for the summer, Easter and Christmas holidays, the three of them would travel home to Coleraine. 'Home' was what they always called it there, despite the fact that they'd lived in Manchester for years. But after his dad left, those holidays stopped too. He and his mother had gone back a few times, but it wasn't the same without Bill. Then Mary's parents had both died and they had less reason to go back, he supposed. So one year, they just hadn't gone.

'The lads brought me to Coleraine for my stag. Did I ever tell you that?' Adam asked.

Bill shook his head. 'Did you see any family when you were there?'

'No, I didn't. It wasn't that kind of trip.' Adam took another slug of his coffee and said, 'Tell me a bit more about when you got to Manchester.'

'Life was good there. We bought a house in Didsbury, you came along and Mary and I were besotted with you. Couldn't believe how lucky we were to have a son. Mary became a full-time mother by choice and I got a job in Manchester University, lecturing.' He stopped for a moment and closed his eyes. 'That's where I met Christian.'

So that's where he met him, Adam thought.

'The attraction was instant. For both of us. I tried to stay away. So did he. But I couldn't. One day, he came to my office and closed the door behind him. He walked over to my desk and I stood up. We kissed, without saying a word. And that was the beginning of the end for me.' Bill's eyes filled with tears. 'Nothing else happened for a long time. Just that kiss to hold on to. But everything changed after that moment. It's hard to explain, but have you ever been on a motorway where you missed the exit?'

Adam nodded. He'd done that only the previous week. 'Pain in the arse, especially if the next exit isn't for miles.'

'Well, for me it felt like my life was a constant road trip on the M6 motorway, with no exits. I just kept on driving, doing my best to stay on the road, hoping that eventually I could find a way off.'

Adam thought that was the saddest thing he'd ever heard. He couldn't imagine what that must have been like, living a lie for years.

'We celebrated your first communion, your confirmation, your first day at high school. And I don't want you think I was unhappy all of the time. Because I loved every day I spent with you, in our family. But each time another year would go by, I felt like I wasn't living. I never forgot that kiss,' Bill said.

'I'm sorry,' Adam said, and he meant it.

'This trip down memory lane is not about that. You've nothing to be sorry about. The only thing that kept me going was you. I loved the bones of you. I suppose it was inevitable, but things between Mary and me started to falter. I fell out of love with her and she saw that in my eyes. So she pulled away from me. I think we both forgot that we used to be best friends, once upon another time. I've always regretted that I didn't walk away after that first kiss. Maybe things would have been different for all of us then. But I was a coward.'

'What were you scared of?' Adam asked.

Bill sighed. 'You have to understand what rural Ireland was like in the sixties and seventies. It wasn't like it is now. There were no gays or lesbians. Out and proud that is. And certainly no bisexuals. It was a taboo subject, whispered behind closed doors. That stays with you. Always at the back of your mind.'

'What changed? You stayed away from Christian for years, what made you go to him?' Adam asked.

'I'd watched him fall in and out of love so many times. Hell, he even cried on my shoulder once or twice over a broken love affair. We became friends. Confidants. I wish I could tell you that there was this big moment in my life, defining, that made me go to him, but it was just an ordinary day. And I thought, it's time. So I drove to his house.'

'You found the right exit at last, Dad,' Adam said, and he swallowed back a lump in his throat.

Bill closed his eyes and nodded, remembering the moment that Christian opened his front door. There was no going back for either of them after that.

'What age was I?' Adam asked.

'Fifteen,' Bill replied. 'There was little time between that day and when I went to your mother and told her about Christian. I did try to do the right thing.'

'It's driving me mad, Dad. So much about that time is hazy,' Adam admitted.

'You spent a lot of time at Pete's then.'

Adam nodded. He got drunk for the first time around then too. 'I remember you both shouting at each other. And I remember the day you left. You said you would be back. But that never happened.' He watched his father's eyes fill with pain. 'I remember Mum telling me that you didn't love either of us any more. That you were never coming back.'

Bill's eyes flashed with anger. 'That's not true. I never left you. Not by choice.'

Adam sighed. He could hear the truth in his father's words. But he could also remember the look on his mother's face. It was a look he recognised. His mother was grieving back then. Bill might as well have died when he told her he was leaving her. She never got over it.

'You said you didn't want to stay away. That

she made you,' Adam said. The fight was gone from him now.

'Mary told me that if I didn't leave Manchester, she would report Christian and me to the university. It was 1982 and although by this time homosexuality had been decriminalised in the UK, it was still rather taboo. She was quite clear that she'd make sure the university knew that we'd started our affair back in 1965, when we first kissed. And back then, it was still illegal to have sex with a man.'

'That's twisted.'

'She was bitter. She was hurt and she was lashing out.'

'Even so . . . ' Adam replied.

'Christian and I resigned. We stayed in Manchester at first. I tried to see you. I sent letters, I sent presents . . . '

'I didn't get any of them,' Adam said. 'As far as I was concerned, one day you just left with no explanation.'

'I should have just told you. But I thought you were too young to understand.'

'I would have understood that better than thinking you stopped loving me overnight.' He and Pete used to skip school so that they could hang around the university, in the hope that Adam would catch a glimpse of Bill. But it was as if his father had vanished off the face of the earth, overnight.

'The summer after you left, we went to Coleraine. And it got really weird over there,' Adam said. 'Every time I'd walk into a room, the adults would all clam up. I knew they were

283

talking about you. I just didn't realise what they were saying.'

'I followed you over there,' Bill said.

Adam looked at him in surprise.

'When I called at my parents' house, they wouldn't let me in,' Bill said.

'No way. Why?'

'My father hissed that no fucking faggot was welcome in the Williams' house. My mother blessed herself like I was pure evil. Tommy and Hugh, your uncles, gave me a good hiding, just to make sure I understood that people like me were not welcome.'

'Your family? I can't believe it.'

'Mary told them about me. She was angry and wanted to hurt me, and she figured my family was my Achilles heel. In that one move, she made sure that I could never go back home to Coleraine again.'

'That's cruel.'

Bill didn't disagree. 'Christian was furious and said, no more. We left Ireland and moved to the south of France.'

Adam had no concept of how bad it was for his dad back then. 'I'm shocked. I really am.'

'I've done a lot of things in my life I'm not proud of, but you need to know one truth: I always loved you. There's a difference between leaving someone and being pushed away,' Bill said. 'I felt I had no choice but to go.'

'It's okay, Dad.' And as Adam said those words, he realised it was. Any anger he'd felt towards his father disappeared. He couldn't say the same about his mother, though.

'After you left, Mum changed. It was as if all the light in her got extinguished. She kind of collapsed inside herself. And she got all weird with me. Forever saying I was just like you.'

'Would that be such a bad thing?'

'Rachel always said I was like you. A flirt. A charmer.'

'You come from a long line of Williams flirts,' Bill told him proudly.

Bill motioned for the waitress to send over two more coffees. Then he asked, 'Why don't you see Mary any more? What happened?'

'Things had been bad for years at home. A steady decline. Looking back on it now, I recognise that she was grieving for the loss of her marriage. Overnight, I seemed to become a disappointment to her. I could see it in her eyes. I stayed away as much as I could, staying at Pete's most nights. Then, she found out that I was dating two women at the same time. And she flipped. As in went nuts. We had an awful row. And we both said some terrible things.'

'She'd a temper on her.' Bill remembered.

'She went off to find each of them, and told them, publicly, in front of their friends, that I was making a fool of them. It was cruel. I was an idiot, I shouldn't have cheated in the first place, but they didn't deserve that humiliation. I had enough of her nagging. I packed my bags that night and I walked away.'

'Life changed Mary, made her bitter. And it twisted everything up. But she wasn't always like that. The Mary I choose to remember is the free spirit, painting, laughing, loving, wearing a pretty yellow dress,' Bill told him.

'I'd forgotten about that side of her. But it's so weird, these past couple of months she keeps invading my thoughts. I genuinely had given her no more than a passing thought for years before that.'

Once again, he felt a niggle of shame. He should have tried harder to build a bridge with her, make amends. In nearly ten years, there was only one time that he made any attempt to see her. He told his dad about that.

'Rachel persuaded me to go see her, after I proposed. I went home, walked up to the front door, with a stupid bunch of flowers in my hand, and my heart in my mouth. I wanted her to meet Rachel. To know her. But Mum had gone, sold up our home and left Didsbury. Imagine that. She didn't even think to tell me she was leaving.'

Bill didn't know what to say to that. His head and his heart were heavy with the waste of their family life.

'Mary and I, we had so many dreams of a life growing old together with children and grand-children. A life filled with love and craic and laughter. And instead, we both managed to miss out on so much,' Bill said.

Adam reached over and clasped his father's hand. 'You're here now. That's what matters.'

Bill nodded and knew one truth. There wasn't a thing in this world that would ever remove him from his son's life again.

28

The wetting of the baby's head and the photograph

The Old Nag's Head, Didsbury, Manchester

The three friends sat side by side at the bar. Elbows on the counter top, they watched in appreciation as the barman placed three bronzed pints in a line in front of them. Nodding, they reached and picked up their glasses and raised them to their lips, in unison, like a synchronised swim team.

'To Chloe,' Adam said, smacking his lips in appreciation.

'To Chloe,' David and Pete cheered.

They held their pints up in the air and clinked glasses, before downing them in one last long satisfied drink.

Adam nodded at the barman, for three more. Then said, 'I've decided to go back to Belfast next week.'

'Do you think you'll stay there?' David asked.

Adam shrugged. 'No idea. But I'd like to spend some more time with Dad. It's as good a place to be as anywhere for a while.'

He'd spent most of his adult life ignoring the history of his parents, of his childhood. But since Rachel's death, he'd been faced with ghosts from his past. Having Bill back in his life was both welcome and confusing. But they'd cleared the air a lot with their chat. Some time together, just living and enjoying Matthew, would be good for them both.

Pete placed a brown envelope on the bar in front of them.

Three pairs of eyes looked down at the padded envelope.

'That's divorce papers, anyhow,' David said.

'How did you know that?' Pete asked, annoyed that David had stolen his big dramatic reveal. He'd planned a joke and everything.

'One never forgets what divorce papers look like. There's something about the envelope, official and menacing. A4, about two inches thick. Unmistakable,' David said.

They looked down for another moment at the envelope that was indeed about two inches thick.

'Can I assume that I don't have to knock sense into you? That you're gonna sign them?' Adam enquired, taking another drink.

Pete leaned over him to retrieve an ashtray. He pulled it close to him. 'Can I borrow your lighter, mate?' He asked the barman, who handed him a box of matches.

'You fucking numpty,' Adam said. 'Jenny is the best thing that ever happened to you. I thought you said she was your ketchup.'

'I quite agree,' David said, albeit looking puzzled by the word ketchup. 'She loves you. And that little baby needs a father. I think it's quite callous to just walk away — '

Adam scrapped back his bar stool and stood, David following suit. They were both aggrieved and ready to go into battle for their friend Jenny.

Pete ignored them both, just reached in and retrieved a photograph out of the envelope.

He placed that on top and they all leaned in to take a close look.

Jo smiled up at them, leg in the air, doing yoga on the golden sands of a beach in Sydney.

'She does have remarkable flexibility,' David said, his eyes locked on her leg which was at a ninety-degree angle to her body.

'I don't think I could even get my leg up as far as my elbow,' Adam said, sitting down to try. 'Nope. Not even close.'

Pete picked up the photograph, then placed it in the ashtray. He struck a match and lit the corner of it, watching the paper go up in flames. Jo seemed to dance as the picture flitted from side to side, burning black and amber. And then suddenly, she was gone.

All that was left was a sad miniature mountain of black ash.

Adam and David relaxed and drank their pints. Pete and Jenny were back on track.

Pete then unfolded the papers and taking a pen from the envelope, signed them, twice, with a flourish.

'We'll need three chasers,' Adam said to the barman. 'Your finest Irish whiskey, sir.'

'More than fifty per cent of marriages end in divorce you know,' Pete said, holding back the laughter. 'And then there's the really unhappy ones!'

David and Adam laughed at his joke.

'I stole that from Joan Rivers,' Pete said,

delighted with himself.

'She scares me,' David said. 'Awful tongue on her.'

'Ah but you've no sense of humour, mate,' Pete teased. 'Anyhow, just to reassure you both, I've emailed Jo and told her that Jenny and I are back together.'

'I'll drink to that,' David said and they all picked up their shots and downed them in one.

'How did she take it?' Adam asked, wincing as the alcohol burnt the back of his throat.

'She didn't answer. But her lawyer called my lawyer and ta da!' Pete replied, nodding to the now signed papers.

'You've made the right choice. You and Jenny are perfect for each other,' David said.

'I said the same, back when they first met,' Adam told David.

Pete happily sipped his pint. Everything had fallen back into place and it was as if all the worries of the past month had disappeared.

'How's little Chloe?' David asked.

'Adorable, noisy, gorgeous. Actually, Jenny and I have something we want to ask you,' Pete said to David.

'I'm all ears.'

'We're looking for the right person to be Chloe's godparent. We want someone strong and dependable, who won't let her down. Someone who remains calm in a crisis, for example.'

David felt himself flush in shock at the direction Pete's conversation was going.

'We need someone who could be a good role model for Chloe,' Pete added, then he paused, nudging Adam, before finishing, 'And for the life of us, we can't think of a single person!'

Adam spat his pint out, laughing alongside Pete.

David half laughed, not sure what exactly was happening. But disappointment began to creep up his stomach and he took a slug of beer, to try stifle it down.

'I'm only joking, mate!' Pete said. 'Seriously, Jenny and I would be honoured, if you would be Chloe's godfather. We can't think of another person more suitable.'

David felt his eyes well up, he was genuinely touched. '*Au contraire*, it would be me that is the one honoured. I can't think of anything I'd like more.'

Pete shook David's hand.

'Hug it out,' Adam suggested over his pint.

So they laughed, and embraced quickly, pulling apart when they remembered where they were.

'We're going to set the date next week,' Pete said. 'That way, you and Robyn have loads of notice to keep the weekend free. And Adam, fair warning, you better come back for it too.'

'I'm beginning to rack up some serious frequent-flyer mileage, all this toing and froing. But you know I wouldn't miss it,' Adam said.

'You're gonna have to put down some roots again, one of these days,' Pete said.

'I know,' Adam replied. But he wasn't in any great hurry. Nowhere felt like home to him any more. He assumed when the time was right, he'd know what to do. He had faith in Rachel.

And then, he felt her beside him. He whispered, 'I'm still waiting for that sign.'

'Soon,' she replied. 'Try and behave tonight.'

And then she was gone.

29

The lonely artist and the cliched boss's embrace with a secretary

Ocean View B&B, Coleraine, Northern Ireland

Bill walked through two large stone pillars, that marked the entrance to Mary's B&B. The grandiose Victorian house stood proud against the backdrop of the Irish Sea and shell-strewn beach. Its gravel driveway was framed by lush green grass and raised flowerbeds which were crammed with hydrangeas, roses and peonies.

His heartbeat quickened the closer he got to the imposing yellow front door. He'd not seen his ex-wife in twenty-one years. In truth, he had assumed that he'd never see her again.

But something told him that Adam needed his mother. He was damn sure he'd do all he could to make that happen. Once he put his mind to it, it was quite easy to find her. A couple of phone calls and he learned that she'd set up a B&B not far from her hometown.

A shiver ran down his spine as he lifted the large brass knocker on the door. He let it fall and the sound bounced around him. He waited for the door to open, each second feeling like an eternity, as he tried to imagine the scene that would unfold when she saw him. Would she even let him in? He supposed that this might be a wasted journey, but it was one worth trying.

When she opened the door, time fell away and he was back to another era. Mary hadn't changed. Her dark hair may now be lined with strands of silver grey, but she still wore it long, tied in a loose ponytail at the back. Her face was without make-up and the years had been kinder to her than him. She could have passed for a woman twenty years younger than she was.

Her smile of welcome, warm and open, faltered, then froze as she recognised the man in front of her. Then it disappeared and a frown appeared.

I've done that to her, Bill thought. I'm the maker of frowns.

He watched her face as emotions raced across it, one after the other. She had never been any good at poker.

'Hello, Mary,' he said. He'd been practising his opening speech for hours, editing what he would say, making it perfect. With just the right tone and phrasing. And after all that, all he had was hello.

He'd hazard a guess she would have more to say to him. If she allowed him to cross her threshold.

'We're full.' Mary's voice was firm. She reached up to turn the vacant sign on the porch window. Closed.

'I don't need a room,' Bill said.

'What do you need then?' Mary asked.

'Just to talk,' Bill replied. 'Please don't turn me away.'

She looked at him and then at the door, and

for a moment he thought she would slam it in his face. But instead, she turned on her heels and walked back into the house, leaving the door ajar. He took that as his invitation to follow her. It was as good as he was likely to get.

The hallway was painted a bright yellow, like the dress she'd worn on the first day they met. Walls were lined with paintings of the beach and the causeway, both oil paintings and charcoal pencil.

'These are good. All your work?' Bill asked.

'Some are. Some are from guests who have stayed. I run writers' and artists' retreats here,' Mary said.

Bill pointed to a watercolour painting of the house. 'This one is yours, though.'

'How did you know?'

'You always had a style unlike anyone else I've known. The way you use colour in particular. It's striking.'

Mary walked into the kitchen, and Bill sucked in his breath in surprise at the room. He wasn't expecting the large open space in front of him. Floor-to-ceiling windows framed the spectacular views of the ocean and skyline from every side from the back of the house.

'Wow!' he said in appreciation. It was breathtaking.

'It catches you unawares, doesn't it?' Mary acknowledged. 'I can't believe how lucky I am to live here.'

'Have you been here long?' Bill asked.

'I moved home to Coleraine about five years ago,' Mary said. 'Despite the fact that Mam died,

I still felt the whispers of family ghosts here, pulling me back.'

'I heard your mum passed on. I was sorry to hear it. I liked Esther,' Bill said.

'She used to like you too.'

He smiled without humour at the words 'used to'. They all stopped liking him when they found out his truth. He tucked that to one side. Raking up the past wouldn't accomplish what he had come here for: to reunite a mother and her son. 'Are you happy to be back?' Bill asked, moving to safer ground.

She nodded, turning away to look out to the sea. 'There was nothing left for me in Manchester.'

Bill still could not fathom that this woman, who adored their son, who made him her life, her every thought, could say such a thing.

She turned around and filled the kettle with water. 'You still a tea man, strong and black?'

He nodded. She remembered. But then again, so did he. 'And you prefer coffee, with milk and two sugars.'

She acknowledged this with a slight smile. Then she busied herself making their drinks. She took a lemon drizzle cake out from a pretty rose-covered tin. She sliced four thick pieces and placed them on the huge dining room table that flanked one side of the large open-plan room.

When she sat down beside him, he smelled her perfume, still the same. If he closed his eyes, he could have been back in their kitchen in Didsbury, albeit without the stunning views. He wondered if there was another world, another life where he was doing that.

'You still wear Chloé,' he said.

'Old habits die hard,' Mary replied. Decades of birthdays, Christmasses and Mother's Days, with gift boxes of this perfume bought by him and then Adam, flashed between them.

'I never meant to hurt you,' Bill blurted out. So much for playing it cool and not raking up old hurts. 'I loved you.'

'And yet somehow you still did,' Mary said.

'I couldn't help myself, no more than the sun cannot stop itself rising every morning.'

'There's always a choice,' Mary replied. 'You had a wife and a son, but you chose to ignore that when you took him to your bed.'

Bill thought about all the times he'd pushed Christian away, the years he told himself that he was confused, that he didn't really love him. He knew how much he had to lose. He fought hard to keep it. But in his worst nightmares, he never expected the fallout to be so catastrophic.

'I paid a high price for that love,' Bill said.

She acknowledged this with a blink of her eyes. 'Are you still with him? Christian?' She swallowed, just saying his name out loud was clearly painful to her.

He shook his head, feeling a familiar ache that always stabbed him when he thought of Christian. 'He died when we were in France.'

She didn't look surprised or sorry, just accepting of his fate.

'We were together for nine years. Neither of us knew that he had a heart problem, undetected from childhood. He had a massive heart attack one day while reading *Le Figaro*. One moment he was laughing, then he was gone.' Bill still felt pain at that memory. It never faded.

'And now? Are you with someone? Man or woman?' Mary asked.

Bill laughed and Mary snapped, 'What's so funny?'

'The way you said that. You sound just like Adam.'

'Oh.' Her face clouded when she heard her son's name.

Bill wondered what she would make of his flings with George and Jane. He thought it best to keep all that to himself. 'Let's just say, I date,' he replied.

'I've no doubt you do,' Mary sniffed.

'And what about you? This idyll you have here, is there someone to share it with?' Bill hoped there was.

'I date too,' she answered. He saw pain in her eyes again, despite the defiant tilt of her chin. Shame made him lower his head. He had damaged her all those years ago and there was nothing he could do about it.

'Why are you here, Bill?' Mary asked, sighing softly.

'For Adam.'

Her face instantly crumpled as she asked in a whisper, 'What's wrong?'

He quickly waved her worry away reassuring her that Adam was alive and well. 'But he's not okay. He needs his mother.'

'He hasn't needed me for a long time.' Stubbornness lined her face again. He'd seen

298

that look before. When Mary Williams decided something, it was near impossible to change her course.

'What did he do that was so bad?'

Mary closed her eyes for a moment, before answering, 'He didn't do anything. It was all me. He walked away ten years ago and he made it clear every day since then, that he doesn't need me, by staying away.'

'By God, you're a stubborn woman, Mary Williams.'

'And what if I am?' she shouted back to him.

'You're wrong,' Bill said. 'A child always needs their parents.'

'And I take it from that statement that you and him are as thick as thieves again,' Mary said, her voice acerbic.

'We're getting there. I went looking for him this year. We've a lot of time to make up. And he had a lot of questions and hurt he'd been carrying around for a long time.' Bill had promised himself that he wouldn't dwell on the past with Mary, but he found that once again he surprised himself when he said, 'Why did you do that to me? Did I hurt you that bad that you had to take away everybody I loved?'

She poured herself another cup of coffee and stirred in her sugar and milk. She didn't answer him.

'Not enough that you told your family and mine in Coleraine that I was gay, so that they all cut me out of their lives, you turned my son against me too.' Bill felt his heart quicken as anger nipped at him.

Mary remained silent. He couldn't read her face. He continued, 'You know, my parents both died and went to their graves, having not spoken to me for over a decade. I kept trying to make them understand that I was still *me*. I hadn't changed from their loving son, just because I was in love with Christian.'

Mary stared out to the sea and blinked back tears.

'I begged them to forgive me,' Bill went on, 'but in truth I wasn't even sure what I needed forgiveness for. Our marriage broke up and yes, I fell in love with someone else. But I told you, as soon as it started. I asked for a divorce.'

He looked down at his hands and rubbed the third finger on his left hand. He'd worn a ring there for years and still, all this time later it felt bare. A circle of love they'd said, when she put it on him.

With every part of him he wished it could have ended any other way than it did.

Her roar, her anguished cry, knocked him off his stool. He looked up from the floor to see her standing above him, eyes wild and face flushed. 'You humiliated me!'

'Is that what it was about? You were humiliated?' Bill roared back, picking himself off the ground. 'So you made damn sure that you did the same to me!'

She laughed at that and shouted back, 'Yes! I did. And I'm glad.'

But her laugh rang hollow and the tears that sprang to her eyes made a liar of her.

Pacing the room, he said, 'I wanted to be the

300

one to tell them. On *my* terms. Gently. Give them time to understand. But you took that away from me. You turned something that was beautiful into something that was sordid and dirty.'

Mary grabbed his arm, digging her fingers painfully into his flesh. 'I lost everything because of you! Have you any concept what it was like for me? I had no idea you didn't love me. I thought we had the perfect marriage. I was the stupid bloody idiot who thought we had everything.'

Her body slumped at this and she pulled her hand back from his arm, as if in shock, that she was touching him.

'I loved you Mary, I swear to you, that's true,' Bill said sadly. 'But then, when I met Christian, I realised I wasn't *in* love with you. There's a difference.'

Mary stood up and walked to the sliding doors, pulling them across and letting the sea breeze rush over her. 'I need some air.' She turned to face him. 'Come with me. You still like to walk, I take it?'

She didn't wait for his answer, just strode down her garden path. He ran after her, catching up at the gate at the end, that led to a sandy path to the beach.

'This is breath-taking,' Bill said, taking in the expanse of blue sea, meeting the horizon. The waves rushed on to the beach, white foam bubbling on the sand. And the faint cry of gulls, winging their way overhead, echoed through the air.

'If we have ugly things to say to each other, I

want to say them out here. I don't want them filling my house, tainting it,' Mary said, then she sighed, looking out to the sea. 'Maybe it's time we let some of them go . . . '

Bill smiled. She always was a dreamer, fanciful. Adam was like that too.

'He's his mother's son,' Bill said.

She shook her head. 'No, he's more like you. That's why we argued. I behaved so badly. I don't know what came over me.'

'I understand why you did what you did to me. But I'm at a loss as to why you would behave like that with Adam. You adored him.'

She didn't answer at first. Just kept on walking along the sand, near the water's edge. The wind whipped her hair around her face.

'Did you know my father was unfaithful to my mother for most of their marriage?' Mary asked.

'I didn't. But now that you say it, I'm not surprised.'

★   ★   ★

Bill had once raised his suspicions about her father's wandering eye, but Mary maintained her parents lived in married bliss. It was the confession that she had known about her father, rather than the infidelity itself, that shocked him.

'After you and I broke up, there was a scandal. At home in Coleraine. Did you hear about it?'

He shook his head. 'No. I was in France.'

'He was caught with a young girl half his age. One of his friend's daughters.'

'What happened?' Bill fell into step beside her.

302

Mary pulled her sandals off and caught them in her hand and he did the same with his shoes and socks.

'My mother was humiliated. And once the affair became public knowledge, she couldn't hide the fact that she'd known my dad had cheated on her, pretty much on and off the whole of their married life. Like a badly written soap opera, they fought, she ranted, he apologised, they fought some more, then she took him back,' Mary said.

'That must have been hard,' Bill acknowledged. 'Esther was a proud woman, I would imagine she'd have found gossiping neighbours particularly hard to take.'

Mary picked up a stone from the beach and skimmed it across the sea, three times before it disappeared, with a plop.

She continued skimming pebbles as she spoke. 'When I was eleven, I saw my dad with his secretary. Terribly clichéd I'm afraid.' Mary threw a pebble back to the sand and turned towards the sea, looking out to the vast expanse. 'I called in unexpectedly one day. I needed money for a school tour and Mam had forgotten to give it to me that morning. I was too lazy to walk home at lunchtime, so decided to go to Dad's firm instead. Claire, his secretary wasn't at her desk, I found out why pretty quickly, when I walked in unannounced.'

'And you were only eleven?' Bill was horrified.

'Yes. It was such a shock. I backed out of the room quietly and I never told anyone. I felt I should keep it hidden. And that made me feel guilty, like I was somehow complicit in his infidelity. It was a head wreck.'

Bill's eyes filled with tears for the young child that had to live with a secret that was too big for anyone so young. 'No child should have to see something like that.'

'Up until that moment, I didn't even know what sex was. But I swore, when I got married, I'd not make the same mistakes my mother did. I'd marry a good man. And I really thought I had found that with you.'

Two gulls flew by and swooped down low on the surf of the wave, picking at the water. Then with a loud chorus of caws, flew off into the horizon.

'I fell in love with you on our first date. You made me laugh, you made me question myself and my life, you made me want you,' Mary said.

'I thought you were the most beautiful woman I'd ever met,' Bill said. Then he caught her arm and said, 'And I still do. I mean that sincerely.'

She shrugged. 'But not quite beautiful enough.' She continued walking and he followed her, at a loss as to what to say next. Because she was right and mere words would not change that.

'After you left, things got a bit messed up here.' She pointed to her head. 'You, my father, all became tangled up in a mixture of hatred and disgust. I know I became bitter. I know I was unspeakably horrid to you, destroying your relationship with your family. There is no excuse for that. And I'm sorry. I truly am.'

He was staggered by the apology. He hadn't

expected one. And he wasn't sure what to do with it.

She continued, her words spilling out fast. 'But I thought to myself, I need to save Adam. Keep him away from you and your influence. So I hid your letters, your presents. Told him you didn't want to see either of us any more. That you'd left both of us, not just me. I want you to know that I lie awake at night, feeling guilty about that. I know I was wicked.'

'I've told him the truth of that. I had to, Mary. I didn't want to stick the boot in you, but I could not let him believe that I didn't love him. That I walked away.'

She didn't answer him. He was worried that this would sever whatever small connection they were brokering, with her earlier apology. So he said again, 'I had to tell him, Mary. I had to get him to speak to me, know that I loved him.'

'Any boot you gave, I deserved,' Mary said. 'The crazy thing is, that by cutting you out of his life, I lost him anyway. We fought constantly. Every time he did something that reminded me of you, of my father, I found myself panicking. And the guilt of my actions weighed heavy on me. I stopped painting. I stopped living. It was almost as if I was punishing myself. Then I found out he was seeing two girls at once and I just saw red. We fought, worse than any other fight we'd ever had. I said some terrible things. So did he. And then he walked out, swearing he'd never cross any threshold I was in, ever again.'

'What a waste,' Bill said.

'I made a right old mess of things,' Mary's

voice broke. 'You know, I used to think that I was a non-judgemental person. And I think I am again, now. I live a life, where I pretty much live and let live. I get all sorts here. And I welcome them all. But when it came to my family, I got it so wrong, I became intractable, unyielding, judgemental. I'll never forgive myself for that.'

'There's time for you to sort this out,' Bill replied.

'Adam doesn't want me,' Mary said. 'And who could blame him?'

'He might not know that he wants you, but I can see that he does,' Bill said. 'You needn't have worried about him, because he fell in love with a lass. Rachel. The most beautiful woman, inside and out. The truest of hearts. And they got married. They have a son. Matthew. The love between those two, it was pure.'

Mary sobbed at this news. 'I'm a grandmother?'

Bill pulled out his wallet and took out a photograph of Adam, Rachel and Matthew. He'd taken the shot, in the back garden of their house in Didsbury.

'Oh, they look so happy. What a gorgeous snap,' Mary said. Her hand hovered over Matthew's face.

'They were happy on that day. I watched them from their kitchen window and felt their happiness bounce around the garden and into the house. It was a joy to be around, infectious.'

'Was?' Mary said. Her face blanched and she gripped his arm, as if to prepare herself for bad news that she knew was coming at her with great speed.

Bill placed his hand on hers and said, as gently as he could, 'Rachel was killed in a car accident three months ago.'

Her head buzzed and tears splashed down her cheeks. She was dumbstruck with horror.

'You see, he needs you, Mary. Our boy needs his mother.'

30

The unclean shirt and the return of the prodigal mother

Bill's House, Malone Road, Stranmillis, Belfast

If Adam knew that on this day he would be seeing his mother again for the first time in a decade, he would have changed his shirt. He'd have put something decent on, as his father would say.

Bill had left early this morning, forgoing their usual porridge and song-filled breakfast. He had been shifty for days, in fact. Adam assumed he was up to no good again, stringing some poor fella or lady along.

Adam was in the kitchen, peeling spuds for dinner, when he heard the front door open.

'In here, Dad,' he shouted, not turning around from the sink. 'His lordship is upstairs asleep.'

'Hello, son.' A voice, a ghost, a hidden heartbreak, whispered.

Adam didn't turn around. He didn't trust his ears. His mother's voice? But that was impossible. Wherever she would be, it would not be in his father's house. He looked up from the sink, into the window in front of him. And in the reflection of the glass he saw her, standing a foot behind him. His father hovered behind her, his face unsure, wearing that same frown he adopted when worrying about his son.

Adam dropped the vegetable peeler into the sink with a clatter and wiped his hands slowly on his jeans. He gulped, trying to get rid of the saliva that was choking him.

And then he turned around to face her.

He had spent years blotting her out of his mind, so seeing her here, in three dimension was surreal. Over the years, whenever Rachel questioned him about her, he shut her down. There was nothing to be gained in talking about his relationship with Mary Williams. She was an interfering old witch. She'd never really loved him. She took joy in tearing him down.

Yet looking at her now, all he could think about was how her hand had felt when it caressed away his tears, thousands of times in his youth.

He'd imagined over the years the many things he would say to her, if by some unfortunate twist of fate, he came face to face with his mother. But all those rehearsals were a waste of time, because now he was rendered dumb.

He looked at his father. How could he have brought her to him? Not after all she'd done to them both. And destroying Bill's relationships with his family. And with him. He'd lost years with his father at a time when a boy needs a father most. He felt anger dance around his head, and floaters began to shimmy in front of his eyes.

Yet as he watched her, looking at him, tremulous, all he could think of once again was that day when he was ten and she gently washed away the pain of the belt from bollicky Will, with a cold facecloth.

'Son?' She looked unsure. Scared.

Son.

He thought of Matthew and contemplated a world in the future, where he was not in his life. A world where Matthew would shun him, turn his back on him. A world where he was no longer allowed to be his parent.

Son.

He thought of Rachel, cold in the ground, but haunting his dreams, night and day. A mother, who was ripped from her child with one shuddering crash of a lorry. Rachel had fought so hard to stay with Matthew and with him, but in the end, she had no choice but to go.

His parents had a choice.

But despite all the things that tormented his brain, demanding answers to so many questions, they all disappeared. And instead the only thing that came out, was a quiet, anguished, single word.

'Mam.'

She took a deep breath. 'I have no excuses. After Bill left, I reacted as I did, from a place of great pain. I was wrong to keep you from him. I know that now.'

'Your mother and I have made our peace. We hurt each other and you got caught in the crossfire,' Bill said. 'We're both to blame.'

Mary looked at Bill and nodded her thanks to him. He was helping her. He was shouldering the blame alongside her and she felt lighter for it.

'The guilt of who I became after we split up

changed me. Made me angry and bitter. And when we fought, when you left, I felt like it was what I deserved. I took Bill from you. So therefore it was only right that I lost you too. I'm a stupid, stupid woman. I was wrong.' Mary watched him intently. 'I don't expect you to forgive me. Because I'll never forgive myself for all those wasted years. But I want you to know that I'm here for you and Matthew. If you need me. I won't force myself on you. I don't have that right. But I'll stand, silently, by your side, waiting for you to let me know, when . . . if . . . you want me.'

Adam looked at her, then at his father and back to his mother. He felt tiredness seep through his body again. He couldn't take any more of this. The emotional battering from ghosts from his past and his present were too much. He just wanted it to end.

A mother never stops loving their child. That's what the doctor had said, at the hospital, when Matthew fell.

He thought of Rachel and Matthew, and how his son would never get the chance to fall out and make up with his mother. And he felt pain pierce him, cut him in two. Yes, it was a waste.

No more.

He took the first step towards her, and her eyes were round with surprise. She moved a step towards him and then they ran into each other's arms.

She smelled as she always had done. She felt as she always had done. And as her arms wrapped their way around him, he thought, for the first time in a long time, that this feels like it could be home.

31

Marching creepy crawlies and Nurse Ratched

Josh's School, Didsbury, Manchester

A series of unfortunate incidents resulted in Robyn answering the call from Josh's school principal, which in turn led to one of the most bizarre moments of her life.

Her boyfriend's ex-wife in her kitchen, combing her hair.

Earlier that morning, David had left for work, late, and in his haste, left his mobile phone behind him. The fact that he was leaving late had been her fault. She'd looked at him, standing in her bedroom, towel hung low on his hips, and she'd been struck by something she'd not felt in a long time. She didn't just love this guy, she loved *every* part of him. He made her laugh, he made her feel safe, he made her feel sexy, he made her feel intelligent . . . he made her *feel*.

An hour later when he ran out the door, teasing her that she'd get him fired, neither of them noticed the phone sitting on the kitchen counter top. And by the time she did notice it, David was long gone with no way for her to contact him. So she decided to bring the phone with her to work. She figured she would meet David later that day to pass it on.

313

The first hiccup of that plan was that David was in fact not in his office all day, and incommunicado. He was meeting a new client who needed some TLC. So his plan was to spend the day shadowing him, as he went about his business.

They both played a bit of phone tag for an hour or two, laughingly leaving messages for each other. David finally admitted defeat, suggesting to Robyn that they meet after work for an early supper.

As he said in his last message, 'How much trouble can I get into without a phone for one day!'

Famous last words.

Robyn felt inordinately giddy at the new plan to meet up that evening. They hadn't been supposed to see each other today and she kissed his phone for its part in a much more fun evening for her than the one she'd thought was on the cards.

Later that afternoon, she was knee-deep reading a deposition from the husband of one of her clients — a young woman who had signed a pre-nuptial agreement in the early flushes of love. The silly, naive woman was now paying the price for that. Because if Robyn couldn't find a way to break the pre-nup, she would leave their marriage without a penny. And having spent a few hours in the same room as the husband, hours that she would never get back, she was determined to find a loophole. That girl deserved danger money for having put up with an arrogant buffoon like him as long as she had.

When David's phone rang, mid-afternoon, Robyn answered it, assuming it was him again.

'Hello, darling,' she'd said huskily.

'I'm looking for David Marsden,' a stern voice clipped back at her.

It was Josh's head teacher, a woman without a sense of humour, it seemed, when Robyn apologised, saying she thought it was her boyfriend on the phone. Mrs Joyce demanded to know where David was. David had once jokingly told Robyn that Mrs Joyce made Nurse Ratched look like Mary Poppins. She was beginning to see what he meant.

Robyn gritted her teeth, deciding it was perhaps best if she didn't remind the woman that manners cost nothing. She explained politely that David was temporarily not available and suggested the school call Karen if there was a problem.

'We've tried that. But her phone has gone to voicemail. Everyone is too busy these days for their children. It's not good enough,' Mrs Joyce complained.

That felt harsh and in the case of David and Karen's children, vastly untrue. Robyn was amazed at how much those two did for their kids.

'Have you left a voicemail for him?' Robyn asked, fighting the urge to make a response to her outrageous comment. 'He's ringing in to check his messages throughout the day. I'm sure he'll call you back very soon.'

'Soon is not good enough,' Mrs Joyce snapped. 'I need to speak to someone immediately.'

Robyn ran through her possibilities. Could she suggest one of David and Karen's friends? Pete or Jenny? Adam, perhaps. She didn't think she had their numbers. And besides, was that even allowed in schools? Surely you needed to be a family member?

She sighed, feeling sorry for Josh. To him she was the quintessential evil stepmother. But it appeared that right now, she was also all he'd got.

'I'm David's girlfriend. What do you need?' she asked.

'Well, it's a bit delicate. He needs to go home. Now,' Nurse Ratched said.

'Is he ill?' Robyn asked. 'Does he need to see a doctor?'

'Not a doctor as such. But he does need to go home. I'll explain when somebody comes to collect him.'

'And it can't wait until you hear back from his parents? I'm sure they will call you any minute.' Robyn looked down at the deposition in front of her. She was sure she about to crack this, she just needed a few more hours.

'No, it most certainly cannot wait. Someone needs to come to the school immediately.' Mrs Joyce was firm. 'It's urgent.'

Robyn told her she'd be there in twenty minutes. The pre-nup would have to wait till later on, or the next day. She rang David's secretary and asked her to pass on a message to him, if he happened to call into the office. She also asked his secretary to keep trying Karen's number at work. She smiled as she heard the delicious anticipation of gossip in her secretary's voice as he asked her if all was okay.

'Oh, you wouldn't believe what's going on,' Robyn said to him as she walked out the door. She laughed out loud, knowing he was driving himself mad, trying to work out what the drama was. He was so easy to wind up.

When she arrived at Josh's school, she half expected Karen to be there already, that she'd had a wasted journey. But both parents were still missing in action.

She walked into the head teacher's office and felt a trickle of unease. Funny how certain things can make you feel guilty for no reason. Same whenever she saw a policeman. She immediately felt like she was hiding something and had to fight the urge to run in the opposite direction. She shook her head at how silly she was being. How scary could Nurse Ratched really be?

She heard his tears before she saw him and she quickened her pace. Oh Josh!

He was sitting on a plastic chair, wearing a girl's Barbie-pink hat that looked ridiculous on him. Fat tears splashed down his face.

Despite the fact that they had had a precarious start to their relationship, her heart melted when she saw his chest heave as he sobbed.

'Whatever is the matter, Josh?' she asked, kneeling down beside him. Her irritation toward Mrs Joyce trebled. How dare she sit behind her desk, so cold and remote, when a little boy was in so much distress? And what on earth was he doing with a bloody pink hat on?

'I want my mummy and daddy,' he hiccupped back to her. 'Is Daddy with you?' His little eyes were wide with hope and she wished with all her might that she could take away whatever fear and pain he was in.

She stroked his hand and whispered to him, 'I know you do, buddy, and I've left messages with them both to come get you. In fact, I bet they are on their way. But for now, I'm all you've got. And I'd like to help you. Would that be okay?'

He looked at her, his big blue eyes, filling up with fresh tears and his bottom lip wobbled, as sobs racked his little body again.

She pulled him to her and hugged him tight. His two hands crept up around her neck and he nestled his head under her chin. She rocked him back and forth, wishing she had more practice at this. When his sobs quietened down, she looked up at the head teacher, who was staring at them both with a solemn expression. 'What happened to him?' she demanded.

Mrs Joyce shuddered as she spoke. 'I wouldn't get so close to the child, if I were you. His teacher noticed he has *head lice*. His head is crawling with them.'

She said the words like she was telling her he had the bubonic plague.

Despite herself, Robyn felt herself shudder, then her scalp began to itch at the mere mention of the crawlies. She remembered the pain of her mother yanking a metal comb through her long hair when she was a young girl. She also remembered how scared she'd felt and once again, her heart filled with sympathy for Josh.

His sobs grew louder. 'Mrs Joyce said that my head was disgusting and full of creepy crawlies. Are they going to eat my brains? I don't want

318

them to eat my brains . . . ' he wailed.

Robyn could not believe her ears. 'Mrs Joyce said that to you?' she asked, incredulous.

He nodded then buried his head in her shoulder again.

Robyn turned to face the head teacher, who, for the first time since she walked in, didn't look quite so sure of herself.

'I never said anything about them eating his brains. That's his imagination and I won't be responsible for that. But you have to understand that we cannot allow a child with head lice in the school. We have a reputation to uphold here. The last time an outbreak occurred, we had parents up in arms, threatening to pull their children.'

'You called a child disgusting,' Robyn spat the words out.

Mrs Joyce blanched.

Robyn lifted Josh off her lap and looked him in the eye. 'Nothing is going to eat your brains. It couldn't be further from the truth. I had head lice when I was a little girl and while I know you think I'm a bit of a monster . . . ' she smiled so he knew she was teasing, 'I turned out okay, didn't I?'

He nodded, his eyes round with shock at her words.

Robyn turned towards the head teacher and said loudly, 'In fact, I turned out to be a lawyer. Some would say a rather good one. I do enjoy a good litigation case.'

'I don't think I used the word disgusting . . . ' Mrs Joyce tried to take back her mean words.

'I'd hazard a guess that Mrs Joyce herself had

319

head lice at some point. Am I right?' She turned to the head teacher, who pointedly ignored her question. 'I thought so,' Robyn declared. 'Now, here's what we are going to do. We are going to bring you home to my place and Mrs Joyce is going to ring your mummy and daddy and tell them that you are with me. Don't worry about a thing, we'll get this sorted in no time.'

He smiled tentatively, his sobs reducing every moment, until eventually they ended on one big hiccup.

Robyn gave his hand a little squeeze, then walked towards Mrs Joyce. She looked her squarely in the eye and said, 'Imagine what would happen if this story went into the public domain. Head teacher bullies child. The papers would eat up a story like that.'

'I beg your pardon!' Mrs Joyce blustered.

'Oh no, I beg yours,' Robyn said, raising her voice a fraction. 'I'd go so far as to call it harassment, picking on a poor child over a problem not of his own making — I'm sure a certain court would agree with me.' She looked around the room and waved a hand. 'Where are the other children? If Josh has head lice, then he got it from someone else. Why is he the only child in here?'

Mrs Joyce stood up, opened her mouth, but had no retort for her.

* * *

'It's your responsibility to follow anti-discrimination law, you know. I think I'd enjoy the opportunity to take you on in court.'

320

Mrs Joyce found her voice. 'Hold on a moment.'

'No, you hold on. I suggest you apologise to Josh immediately. And, by the way, I'd like a copy of your school's Behaviour Policy. I assume you have one, as it's a legal requirement? I'd hate to think you were breaking the law, Mrs Joyce, as well as bullying young children.'

'I resent the implication of bullying!'

'Oh, I'm not implying anything. I'm stating facts. And I would hazard a guess that your parents would be quite interested to hear how lovingly and sensitively you deal with issues like these. Head lice is part and parcel of going to school. Not nice, but never the child's fault. And as for your despicable, judgemental comment about David and Karen not answering your call, they are both at work. Juggling ridiculous hours to maintain an income that can pay extortionate fees for a school like this. Supposedly one of the finest schools in Didsbury, isn't that what you boast? I would question that.' Robyn walked back to Josh, who was staring open-mouthed at her. 'Let's go home, buddy.'

He didn't move, his feet seemed locked to the ground.

'What's up, buddy? Is it that you don't want to come with me?' Robyn asked. She should have expected that. To him, she was the horrible person who took his daddy away from his mummy. And even though there was no truth in that, it would always be how he saw things. The poor little fella.

He shook his head at her assumption. 'The

321

other kids will laugh at me if I go out wearing this hat. But Mrs Joyce said I wasn't to take it off, until I got home.' He pointed to the pink woolly monstrosity. Robyn had always hated bubblegum pink and never more so than right now.

Robyn whipped it off his blond curls.

'But the crawlies will jump into your hair. That's what Mrs Joyce said,' Josh whispered.

'I'll take my chances,' Robyn declared.

When he still didn't move, she said to him, 'How about a piggy-back ride?' She'd watched David give him these dozens of times and she knew he loved them. Daddy train, David called it. 'Robyn train?' She winked at him.

He smiled in delight and jumped up on her back, clasping his hands around her neck.

As she walked out the door, she flung the hat back towards Mrs Joyce and snorted with laughter when she saw how the head teacher jumped back in fright.

Half an hour later, they'd made a quick pit stop in the local pharmacy and Josh was now sitting beside her kitchen sink, on one of the breakfast chairs next to the island. She'd placed a towel around his little body and was painstakingly combing through his blond hair, strand by strand, removing the lice one by one. She planned to put the treatment in her own hair, just in case, they had done any moonlit flits during the Robyn train ride!

'Are they moving?' Josh asked.

'No,' Robyn lied. 'The magic potion on your head has stunned them all.' She was appalled

322

and fascinated at how the little things were running for dear life as the lotion began to coat them.

'My brains are really intact?' Josh asked.

'Yep. 'Fraid so, buddy.' Robyn laughed, suspecting correctly that now he was out of Mrs Joyce's judgemental care, he was enjoying the grossness of the situation.

Halfway through the procedure, the intercom buzzed. 'That will be your daddy, I reckon,' she told Josh.

She pressed open on the buzzer, to let David into the apartment. Two minutes later, both David and Karen burst into the room, panting from running up the stairs.

They stopped in shock at the scene they found when they walked in. Josh sucking a lollipop, his hair wet from the cream, and Robyn smiling at them with a metal comb in her hand.

'Hi, Mummy, hi, Daddy. Robyn gave me a lollipop,' Josh said, waving it in the air. 'It's not my favourite colour. It's a green one. But she didn't have red.'

'I'll get them in for next time you're here,' Robyn promised.

'And she gave me a piggyback ride. She's good at them, Daddy. And she didn't mind if the crawlies jumped into her hair, did you, Robyn?' Josh said, grinning widely.

Robyn smiled. 'I don't think I'm quite as good at the train rides as your daddy. But I did my best.'

David looked at Robyn. 'You didn't need to do all this. Thank you.'

She shrugged off the praise.

'You see that?' Josh said, taking another lick, as he pointed at the plastic bottle. 'That's Robyn's magic potion. It stuns the crawlies. She got a family-sized bottle, so there's enough for all of us.'

Karen was standing back listening to the exchange and felt stunned. In a million years she'd never have pictured Robyn in a scenario like this. The woman she'd faced in mediation when she was going through the divorce with David was nothing like the woman who stood before her now. Face bare, with no make-up on, hair scraped back into a bun, metal comb in hand.

Karen felt completely thrown off-balance.

'As I told Josh, both our hair will be silky smooth by the time this treatment is done!' Robyn said, then, as if in realisation of how she looked, she put her hand up to her face self-consciously. 'I must look a state.'

'You look magnificent,' David said.

'You might not say that when you're combing through my hair in a few minutes!' she joked. 'Right, buddy, I think you are just about done. Not a crawly in sight.'

'Yay!' Josh cheered. The he said, 'Robyn told Mrs Joyce off. She was mean to me.' He was delighted to share this news. He ran over to Karen, who picked him up in her arms, his legs wrapping around her waist.

Karen and David turned to her, faces full of questions.

Robyn filled them in on the earlier conversation, stating how she'd found Josh and what she'd said to Mrs Joyce.

Karen and David looked dumbfounded.

David found his voice first of all. 'I've thought about telling Nurse Ratched what I think about her for months. She's a horrible woman. Always making snide comments. When I rang the school, she was overly nice, telling me that she hoped Josh was okay and to send her love to him. I wondered what the hell was going on.'

Karen looked at Robyn, as if seeing her for the first time.

Robyn felt nervous. Karen hadn't spoken since she came in and she was nervous that she'd overstepped the mark. Should she have just sat in the office with Josh and waited for one of them to arrive?

David walked over to give Josh a cuddle, pulling him from Karen's arms. And then Karen moved to Robyn and clasped her hands between hers. 'Thank you.'

Robyn couldn't find her voice for a moment.

'I mean it. I am so grateful Josh had you today, fighting for him.'

Robyn felt herself flush. 'Anyone would have done the same.'

'Not anyone. You,' Karen said firmly, then stared in horror as she saw something march down the side of Robyn's face.

'What?' Robyn said, as she felt something move in her hair. She reached up to scratch her scalp.

Karen picked up the bottle of head lice treatment. 'Take a seat. I think we better get this on you quickly.'

'Don't worry, they won't eat your brains,' Josh said, reassuringly.

'Come with me and I'll get your hair washed,' David said, bringing him into the bathroom.

Robyn took a seat and Karen placed a towel around her shoulders. She suspected there was a time when Karen would have cheered at the thought of her scratching her lice-infested head.

But today, all previous battles were forgotten. Karen squeezed the treatment into her scalp and said, 'Go on, tell me again exactly what you said to her. I wish I'd been there. She's such a frightful woman . . . '

32

The never-ending love and the talisman

Maggie May's Bistro, Belfast, Northern Ireland

Adam looked at the text one more time.

> Meet me in Maggie May's Bistro tomorrow for a
> coffee. 3pm? Please, Adam. I just want to talk.
> Jane. X

He'd been tempted not to come. He wasn't sure he wanted to see her today, or at any time in the foreseeable future. He thought about leaving. But before he could contemplate that any further, she walked in.

This time there was no sexy strut. She looked more like the Jane he'd dated in the summers of 1984 and 1985, wearing blue jeans and a vintage Van Halen T-shirt, her long blond hair in a low pony-tail. She'd not aged a bit.

'I wasn't sure you'd come,' she said.

He shrugged. His plan was to listen to what she had to say, then get the hell out of Dodge.

'How are you?'

'Fine,' he replied.

'And Matthew?'

'Also fine.'

She nodded, as if she'd been expecting this reaction.

'I owe you an apology,' Jane said.

Oh. Okay. That wasn't what he expected.

'I knew that Bill was your father. And I stupidly thought that by sleeping with him, it would make you jealous.'

He'd guessed that much.

'And now that I've had a few weeks to think about it all, I'm mortified.'

'About what part?' he was genuinely curious.

'It all. I don't know what I thought I was doing. But most of all, I'm ashamed that I played games with someone that I care about. Someone who is grieving the loss of the love of his life. I never even stopped to think for a moment about the pain you must be in. I just thought about myself.'

Adam had not been expecting any of that.

'You needed a friend. You deserved better than what you got from me,' Jane said.

Adam held up his hand. No more. If one more person came and apologised to him, his head would explode. 'You're grand. Let's forget about it.'

'Thank you. How are you doing? It must be difficult. You must miss her.'

Adam looked at her and wondered if this was just another mind game. He didn't have the energy for it. He just wanted to go back to his dad's. 'I'm fine.'

Jane nodded. 'Look, I'll head off in a minute, I've said what I wanted to say. But before I go, there's one more thing. Do you remember back when Mam died?'

Adam nodded but in truth it felt like a life

time ago. 'What was it, 1984 or 85? I spent the summer in Coleraine.'

'You've a good memory. It was 1985. I was a mess. Fear makes you do funny things I think,' Jane said.

He remembered a lot of anguish and pain that summer. Bill had just left. His mother was angry and crying all the time. The only good thing in his life was Jane. They'd fallen in love and been inseparable. And then, the unthinkable happened. Cancer. Quick and relentless, until suddenly Jane's mother was no longer there.

He looked at her and thought, you lost your mother too. Just like Matthew. And some of his anger towards her melted away.

'Do you remember the day of the wake?' Jane asked.

He nodded again.

'I ran away. I was terrified, I didn't want to go. But Dad wouldn't listen to me.'

Adam hadn't thought about that time in decades. He remembered walking into her house with his mum. She wore black head to toe and cried a lot for a woman that she'd not known that well.

Jane's father had grabbed him when he walked in, demanding to know where Jane was.

He'd truthfully told him, he didn't know.

He remembered how her father slumped at that news. Adam felt fresh sympathy for Mr Fitzpatrick. He understood his pain now.

While her family all panicked about where she might have run to, Adam instinctively knew where she'd be.

Their bench. Their park. Their place.

He ran out of her house and didn't stop until he reached her, head bent low, shoulders hunched.

She was lost in a world of heartache and Adam had felt ill-equipped to deal with it.

He begged her to come back with him to her house. But Jane refused point blank.

'I can still remember how that fear tasted. Bitter and acrid in my mouth. It filled me up so much, I thought I was going to drown in it,' Jane said.

Adam now knew first-hand what that felt like now.

'Remember the movie *The NeverEnding Story*?' Jane asked.

Adam laughed; he'd not thought about that movie in a long time. 'A cracker! I loved that movie!'

'Me too,' Jane said. 'You went out and bought a leather snake bracelet. You said it reminded you of the talisman that was in the movie.'

Adam shook his head as that memory came back. 'I had forgotten that. Wow.'

'I think we saw that movie half a dozen times that summer,' Jane said.

'I remember one day we watched it three times in a row. We hid in the back of the cinema, waiting for the next show to start,' Adam recalled.

Jane smiled at the memory too. She sometimes wished that they could go back to that time.

'On the day of the wake, when I was too scared to say goodbye to Mam, you took that bracelet off and . . . ' Jane began.

'I said it was your Auryn. Your talisman. Like

in the movie,' Adam finished.

'Yes,' Jane said. 'To protect and guide me. That's what you said it was for. You wrapped it around my wrist and you told me that it would give me the strength I needed to go say my goodbye to Mam.'

She rubbed her wrist as if it were still there.

'You were a brave wee thing that day,' Adam said. He remembered how much she trembled as she walked up to the open casket, in the front room of her family home. But she'd rubbed the bracelet and somehow or other, his talisman worked for her.

'The real reason I wanted to see you, apart from needing to admit how much of an eejit I am, was to give you this.' Jane reached inside her purse and pushed something on the table in front of him.

'No!' He exclaimed. 'It can't be the same one.'

'It's your bracelet. I kept it.' She picked it up, uncoiled the two ends of the snake, and placed it on his wrist. 'Back with its rightful owner now. I thought that maybe you and Matthew might need it, to protect you both wherever you go.'

Adam touched the leather in disbelief.

'It's time for me to let go of the bracelet. And of you too,' she finished on a sigh.

'You deserve the love of a man who adores you. Only you,' Adam said. 'That's not going to be me, Jane.'

She smiled. 'I know that.'

She stood up and kissed him lightly on the cheek. And then she was gone.

33

The godparents and the grazing gazelles

Cineword, Didsbury, Manchester

Karen and Jenny walked out of the cinema smiling.

'Feel-good movie, right?' Jenny asked.

'Yes,' Karen replied, totally satisfied with how *Something's Gotta Give* turned out.

'Diane Keaton looks unreal for her age. You'll be like her in a hundred years or so,' Jenny said.

Karen laughed at that. 'I'm not like that now, never mind in forty years' time!'

'You know who'd be like Jack Nicholson in forty years . . . ' Jenny said, with a glint in her eye.

'Adam!' they both shouted out at the same time.

A movie had seemed like a good choice when they decided to get together. A way to dip their toes back into their friendship, without having the pressure of conversation. But now that they'd spent some time together on their own, without children or men, Karen, didn't want the evening to end.

'Have you time for a coffee?' she asked.

'I'd like nothing more,' Jenny replied. 'But there better be something sweet and sticky on the go too!'

They walked to the nearby Caffè Nero, and sat down with their cappuccinos and skinny raspberry and chocolate muffins.

'How are you?' Karen asked.

'How have you been?' Jenny said at the same time.

'You go first,' Karen urged, smiling.

'Well, I'm hormonal as fuck. Swearing like a fishwife. Fat with leaky boobs that seem to have a mind of their own and my C-section scar itches like crazy, but I'm afraid to scratch it in case I reopen the stitches. But, despite all of that . . . I've never been happier.'

Karen and Jenny laughed.

'You and Pete are back on track then?' Karen speared a piece of muffin with her fork.

'It's like we never split up. All the stuff that happened with Pete and Amy, Pete and Emma, Pete and Jo, me and Robert, me and Grant, well, it seems so trivial and inconsequential.'

'Don't forget Pete and Ramona,' Karen reminded her.

'How could I forget that one!' Jenny said. 'Well, ALL of that, it's like it was a bad dream. It feels like we've wiped the slate clean. Finally. Chloe, believe it or not, has made us closer.'

'I always thought you and Pete were the ones who would make it to end,' Karen said. 'I could see you both, growing old together.'

'There was once or twice, I think we both tested that sentiment. But honestly, it's like all past transgressions are gone. We've forgiven each other.'

'And forgiven yourselves, too.'

Jenny paused for a moment and thought about this. 'You're a wise one, aren't you? Yes, I think we might have.'

Jenny looked at Karen, trying to make up her mind if she could ask something or not. She decided to give it a go. 'Speaking of forgiveness . . . do we still hate Robyn? Just wondering can I invite her to the christening . . . '

Karen laughed and replied, 'No we don't hate Robyn any more. I'm not sure I ever want to have a girly night out with her, but we're okay. She's okay.'

'Phew!' Jenny said. 'And David and you, friends?'

'We are! And a lot like you and Pete, we seem to have forgiven each other too. Although, I'm *not* going to list out both of our indiscretions and flings. I suspect we might be here for some time if I did that!'

'Speaking of flings, have you seen Mark at all?' Jenny asked, referring to Karen's last boyfriend.

'No. And I don't want to either. I'm taking some time away from men. Also, I'm back in AA again,' Karen admitted. Going to regular meetings gave her back some control on what had felt like a life spiralling.

'My sponsor — Jean — says to me that I need to remember that it's usually the gazelle that's grazing on the outside of the herd that gets eaten first of all. The gazelle that stands in the centre, surrounded by other gazelles, lives to fight another day. Or a lion, if you get my drift,' Karen said.

Jenny shook her head in amazement. 'Wow.

334

That's deep. Are gazelles the ones that look like big Bambis with the double horns?'

'The very ones. Well, I suppose, for me, I have to learn not to self-sabotage. Drink became all about that for me. I'd begun to let dark thoughts creep in. I told myself that I didn't need support, I could do it on my own. But the loneliness just compounded my isolation and fear. I came close to blowing it several times.'

'Shit, Karen.'

'I'm getting better at telling that voice in my head that likes to screw with me, to fuck off.'

'Good for you,' Jenny said. 'I'm sorry I've been such a shit friend. I could have, no, I *should* have been a lion, fighting those lions for you. Or another gazelle, guarding you . . . but maybe I'd have got eaten then too by a lion . . . sorry, I'm rambling. The point is, I wish I had been there for you.'

'That's okay,' Karen said. 'You've had a lot on.'

'I have been busy. But I hate to admit this, I was jealous,' Jenny blurted out.

'Of what?' Karen was gobsmacked.

'Of you and Jo. Rachel would send me these messages, telling me how close you and Jo had become. And I know it was me who left Pete, but I never wanted to leave my friends. I missed you all. I missed you.'

'Jo could never replace you, Jenny!' Karen exclaimed. 'We liked her, she was a lot of fun and a really nice girl, but she could never be our Jenny!'

'Really?' Jenny asked.

'Really,' Karen replied.

'But she's all bendy and makes her own granola.'

Karen started to giggle.

Jenny went on, 'I can't even touch my toes. And I normally hate granola but hers is food of the gods.'

'Can't say I've tried it, but I'll take your word for it,' Karen said, smiling.

'And Audrey showed me a photograph of her on the beach in Sydney and even I kind of fancied her!'

'Well, she's not had any children to batter her body yet,' Karen pointed out.

'I don't know about you, but before I had kids, I didn't have a stomach like hers.' Jenny looked down at her mum tum spilling over her jeans.

Karen popped the last of the muffin into her mouth and said, 'But is she happy? Really happy?'

'Ha!' Jenny replied, using her finger to pick up the last of the crumbs off her plate. 'Miserable I'd say!'

Karen leaned in and said, 'You are worth ten of her.'

Jenny felt silly for ever doubting her friend.

'We've set the date for the christening. Adam's coming back for it.'

'I'd hoped he would.'

'He might bring Bill with him.' Jenny winked then made an obscene gesture with her groin.

'I should have known Adam would have told you!' Karen said. 'Oh, I'm mortified now. It was all a misunderstanding . . .'

'I believe you! Not!' Jenny said. 'Spill!'

'Another time, another place, maybe I might have been tempted. But I promise you, we're just friends,' Karen said.

'Pity, because if you married Bill, then you would be Adam's stepmother and Rachel's mother-in-law. Ha! I can just imagine Rachel's face.' Jenny said. Then stopped, realising what she'd said. Sometimes she forgot Rachel was gone. 'It's weird not having her here, isn't it?'

'Nearly every memory in my adult life has her in it,' Karen replied. 'I still can't quite get my head around the fact that she won't be in my future.'

'I feel guilty that I wasn't there at the end. I should have been with you all, in the hospital. I never got to say goodbye.'

'You did that at the funeral. You came back as soon as you heard. There was nothing else you could have done,' Karen reassured her.

They sat in silence as they both thought about their friend.

'I don't want to lose you too,' Karen whispered. 'Promise me that won't happen.'

Jenny reached over and clasped her hand. 'I promise.'

34

The total eclipse of the rat and the caramelised walnuts

Pete and Jenny's House, Didsbury, Manchester

It was a horrid day. The wind howled and rain teemed down. As Audrey kept saying, it was a day for nowt else but the slippers and a hot fire.

But it was also Chloe's christening. And this time, Pete and Jenny wanted the day to be perfect. The sun might have shone for little Adam's christening a few years back but the day ended with dark clouds. Pete's father had died on the way to the ceremony.

Jenny worried that the day might be too difficult for Audrey, but she was her usual unfazed, happy self, busy making salads for the buffet, now that they were home from the service.

'I have walnut, feta and poppy seed salad, devilled eggs, cooked ham, homemade coleslaw and potato salad, pear and blue cheese salad and some smoked salmon. Do you think that's enough?' Audrey fussed in the kitchen.

'Don't forget I've got trays of hors d'oeuvres too,' Jenny replied, silently offering up thanks to Marks and Spencer's catering department.

'The cake is fabulous Mum,' Pete said, admiring the intricate detailing on the white topped fruitcake that Audrey had made and decorated for them.

'I don't know what we'd do without you,' Jenny said.

Audrey beamed at them both. She couldn't be happier, right here in the middle of everything, helping them.

'Wasn't the service wonderful?' Audrey said. 'I do like that priest.'

★ ★ ★

Jenny walked over to Pete and leaned in for a hug. 'It was lovely, wasn't it?'

'David's speech was a bit . . . ' Pete said.

'I know!' Jenny replied. 'He was quoting all sorts. I kind of lost track halfway through. I think I might have nodded off.'

'Me too, love. But the bit at the beginning and end was good,' Pete said.

'Ooh, yes. I liked that. What did he say again?'

'Something about how he'd always be there to inspire Chloe . . . '

'To fill her heart with wonder . . . ' Jenny mimicked his plummy voice.

'And to give her wings to fly!' Pete finished on a snort.

'Stop, he'll hear us,' Jenny said, holding her mouth. 'Aw, he was sweet. He probably spent hours writing it.'

'On that white cloud of his in heaven,' Pete said, quoting another part of the speech. They both collapsed into each other again.

'What's so funny?' David said, walking into

339

the room, a smile on his face, ready to join in the joke.

Pete and Jenny looked at each other in horror.

Audrey stepped in and said not missing a single beat, 'I farted. It's the eggs, you see. Gives me terrible wind.'

Jenny and Pete started to howl with laughter even harder. And David joined in, waving his hand in front of him. 'There is a dreadful whiff now that you mention it!'

'Hey!' Jenny said, taking offence, only stepping back when Pete grabbed her arm.

'Everyone's got a drink. But I'm worried you're in here working and forgetting about yourselves. Shall I pour one for both of you?' David asked, holding up a bottle of prosecco.

Jenny looked at him, and her heart melted again. He was a softie really. 'Aw. David. You are so good.' She leaned up and kissed his cheek, feeling bad for making fun of him. 'Come on, Pete, and you too, Audrey, let's go have a drink with our guests. We'll bring the food out to the dining room in a bit.'

She accepted a glass of prosecco from David and followed him out to the others. The room was full, with the adults standing chatting, sipping their drinks and the children all in the middle of floor, in a mosh pit of cuddly toys and arms and legs.

Chloe was flaked out in her bassinet, looking darling in her white christening robe, the same one that little Adam and Pete had worn.

Ramona and her boyfriend Jean-Luc stood in one corner of the room, chatting to Robyn.

Ramona was wearing a skin-tight white dress, with her two large breasts threatening to spill out if she leaned in any direction. Jean-Luc couldn't keep his eyes off them, which, after all, was her intention. This dress was her good-luck charm. She was yet to find a man who could resist her when she wore it.

'Nice dress . . . ' Jenny said to her, mumbling at the end, 'that you're almost wearing.'

'What you say to me?' Ramona asked.

'I just wondered where you bought your dress,' Jenny improvised, shrugging innocently when Pete shot a warning look at her.

'I buy in store, that Daveed buy dresses for Karen in,' Ramona said. Then she turned to Robyn, 'Sorry. He buy you dresses there now too.'

'It's quite all right,' Robyn said, smiling. She thought Ramona was hilarious.

Ramona turned to Jean-Luc and explained, 'Daveed was married to my Karen. But now he with Robyn. Anyways.' She flicked her hair and Jean-Luc nodded and smiled. He hadn't understood a single word she'd said, so he just stared at her boobs some more and wondered how soon they could leave this strange party and go back to her room.

Robyn looked mortified, so Jenny said to her, 'Come get another drink. You're almost empty.'

Robyn was grateful for the escape. 'I know Karen and David love that woman, but I find her both hilarious and frightful.'

Jenny laughed. 'That just about sums her up. You and I are going to get on just fine. Come on, let's get you that drink.'

She reunited Robyn with David, leaving to find a new bottle of prosecco.

'All okay darling?' David asked. 'I hope it's not too difficult here, I know you don't know everyone.'

'I'm having a great time. Jenny's a hoot.'

David said, 'Yes, she is, quite.' He nodded across the room, pointing out Adam and Pete, who were holding their babies in their arms, measuring them against each other.

'Sometimes, I imagine that one day, these two might get married,' Pete was saying to Adam.

'Aw, the lordship here would be very lucky to win the heart of your wee princess,' Adam replied. 'Looks like grub is up.'

Jenny and Audrey were bringing all the prepared food out into the dining room, lining up the dishes in a row. A pile of plates and cutlery wrapped in pink napkins flanked the food on either end.

Pete handed Chloe to Jenny's sister Sheila, her godmother, and went to help.

'You've done your daughter proud,' Audrey said.

'And you've done your son proud. And me too,' Jenny replied. Their mutual appreciation society was still in full swing.

'All I did was help. This is all you.'

Jenny didn't often feel like a Susie Home-maker, but today she felt all woman. She thought to herself, I've created life, I've dressed that gorgeous life in a cherished white gown that so far she's managed not to get dirty, I've helped create a feast, unlike any that has been in this house before, and to top it all, I am blissfully happy.

She looked at the living room that was full of people she loved and who loved her. Or at least liked her. Mostly.

'Will I call everyone in?' Audrey asked.

Jenny nodded. She couldn't wait for the praise that she hoped would come her way. She'd be gracious, as they all filled their plates and marvelled at how she pulled all this together. She was proud.

And that, of course, is always a mistake, because a fall is never far behind that sentiment.

They all walked in and, as she predicted, they started a chorus of oohs and aahs in appreciation of the feast before them. Little Adam and Josh begin piling cocktail sausages and sausage rolls on to their plates, ignoring the salads.

Pete said, 'Incredible, love.'

Jenny was just about to murmur a modest, 'Oh it's nothing,' when Pete's face turned red. He started to shout, 'Oi, oi, oi!' Then he ran from the dining room, into the kitchen and out the back door, picking up a sweeping brush as he went.

'What in God's name has got into him?' Audrey said. And the room moved closer to the window for a better look.

Pete appeared in the garden with the broom held high in his arms, then began hitting the bushes with ferocious intensity. With each whack he shouted, 'Oi! Oi!'

'Should I go out to him?' Adam asked, not

moving. He'd not seen anything like it before. Was his friend having a breakdown of some kind?

Pete moved back from the bush and began pointing to the ground, shouting into the house, for help. 'Adam, David, quick!'

'Look, Mummy, it's a mouse!' Josh shouted, climbing on to a chair so he could get a better look.

'What?' Jenny gasped, her heart leaping into the back of her throat.

And then they all saw it.

Not a mouse. But a big black rat that appeared to be doing the cha-cha-cha with Pete as he tried to bash its brains in with the broom.

Pete paused for a moment and gestured manically at Adam and David. 'Some help here, please!'

Adam reluctantly passed Matthew to Karen and grabbed David.

'Choose your weapon.' Adam grabbed a mop from the store cupboard. David looked around for something useful, but nothing stood out.

Adam pulled a soup ladle from the kitchen drawer and handed him that. 'Beggars can't be choosers mate.'

Josh and little Adam sat side by side at the window, noses pressed right against the glass, shouting with glee as they looked out for the rat. Every now and then, they'd shout directions to their daddies.

'Over there, Daddy!'

'Not in there, Daddy! Behind you!'

Jenny watched the three men do a dance with

the rat for five more minutes. Then it decided enough was enough and made its escape, scurrying down the front drive, ready to torment their neighbours.

The three men returned, all windswept and muttering about vermin, like they were conquering war heroes back from the battlefield.

Everyone's attention was on them, rather than on the lovely buffet.

'Eat up!' Jenny said, dismayed at how attention had diverted so easily from her feast. She was beginning feel less woman-like with every passing minute.

'I did what anyone would do,' Pete said, as he accepted praise for his bravery.

* * *

Jenny knew she was fighting a losing battle. All eyes were firmly on the window and the possible return of the rat, instead of on the plates they held in their hands. Nobody seemed hungry any more.

Jenny decided to fish for a compliment, to try to get things back on track. 'What do you think of the ham, Pete? I cooked it myself, in a bottle of club orange.' She'd seen Jamie Oliver do that. And was quite proud of the result.

'Nice one,' he answered, one eye looking out the window.

Jenny gasped at the use of the word 'nice'. Audrey patted her arm in sympathy.

'The walnut and feta salad, have you tried that? I even caramelised the walnuts,' Jenny said

345

to the room. She'd normally ignore the part of the recipe that involved anything fiddly like that, but had decided to do it properly. And they were the most delicious walnuts she'd ever tasted.

Pete moved his fork, ready to spear some salad, then shouted, 'Did you see that?', dropping his plate on to the table again with a rattle.

He ran out the door, followed by David and Adam too, who were roaring like they were extras in the movie *Braveheart*.

'Never mind dear,' Audrey said.

'I've been totally eclipsed by a bloody rat!' Jenny said.

35

Wentworth, Anne and the alternate universe

Karen's House, Didsbury, Manchester

'You're early,' Karen said, opening the door in surprise to David. 'Ramona isn't back yet with the children from their walk.'

'I wanted a chat, just the two of us, if that's okay with you?' David asked.

Karen smiled, happy to see him and they walked into the kitchen.

'You look well,' David said to her. She'd put on a little bit of weight, and it suited her, because she'd become so gaunt recently. He thought about saying this to her, but wisely discarded the idea.

'I feel well,' Karen said. 'Or at least better than I have been feeling. I've made some lemonade. Fancy trying some? I made it from scratch with Josh this morning, and I think it's actually quite decent.'

David nodded and began to fidget with his phone while she prepared their drinks.

She could see he was nervous.

'Do you ever think that in another universe, you and I are still happily married?' David blurted out.

Karen placed their drinks on the table silently.

347

She gave the question some thought then replied, 'In work, we get a lot of manuscripts in, about that subject — parallel lives. One I read recently was actually quite good. I think it might just make it into a book one day. In reality, I don't know . . . I haven't made up my mind yet, as to whether I believe in an afterlife, never mind that. What made you ask?'

David took a sip of the lemonade and was surprised at how sweet it was. Ice cold and the thought crossed his mind that a slug of gin with some lime thrown in would make it a perfect cocktail. Once again, he discarded that thought and didn't mention it to Karen.

'On occasion over the years, I've thought about the different stages in my life. When I've come to a crossroads, had I taken a right, instead of a left, where would I be now? In another life, maybe, there's a version of us where I didn't cheat on you and we are still together.'

Karen was a bit taken aback. It wasn't like him to be so deep and reflective. But then again, maybe she didn't know him as well as she thought she did. 'The thing is, David, in that life, the one where you didn't cheat on me, we might be together, but we are probably still deeply unhappy. Plus, you weren't the only one making mistakes. I'd hazard a guess, we are both screwing things up in that life too.'

'So it's inevitable that we end up here,' David said.

'Maybe,' Karen admitted.

They sipped their lemonade again and Karen watched him fidget, as he always did when he had something on his mind.

'What's up?' she asked gently.

He looked at her, and for a moment, she faded away and instead he saw a long, dusty road, with a fork at the end of it. Left or right, he pondered?

'David?' she asked again.

Her voice snapped him back to reality and he took another slug of the bittersweet drink.

'Sorry. Day-dreaming.'

'And I thought I was the dolly day-dreamer,' she said, teasing.

Whatever was on his mind, she figured he'd get to it soon.

'By the way, Josh has elevated Robyn to hero status. Wait till you hear him. She's all he talks about these days. And by all accounts, Mrs Joyce can't do enough for him. He says she's always smiling at him and waving hello.'

David laughed. 'You know, when I dropped him to school the other day, she was all over me too. In all the years I've been going there, I'd be lucky to get a nod from her! Now she's charm personified.'

'Whatever Robyn said to her, it worked! Having a lawyer in the family is perhaps a good thing. She's a keeper,' Karen said.

She's a keeper. David closed his eyes and saw the road again. Left or right?

And he knew which one he not only wanted to take, but the one he needed to take too.

'Her being a keeper, is kind of what I wanted to talk to you about.'

Karen looked at him in surprise. 'Oh?'

'I love her.'

349

'I can tell that,' Karen replied.

'And I'd like to ask her to marry me.'

Karen had suspected that this was coming. She had wondered how she would feel when it did. She supposed you never know, really, how you are going to react until you are in a situation.

She waited a moment to see if crushing disappointment slapped her across the face.

But to her surprise, she felt only happiness for David. She wanted him to be happy too. She really did.

She reached over to touch his hand and said, 'I'm so pleased for you. That's wonderful news.'

David looked at her closely, worried that he might be upsetting her. And he'd hate that. 'And you are okay about it?'

'Yes. I really am,' Karen replied. 'A couple of weeks ago, I might have struggled, but it appears time is a good healer.'

'Do you think the children will be okay with the news?' David asked.

'They will be delighted. They're used to the new set-up, going between the two homes. They like Robyn. In fact, the girls often call me Robyn by mistake, after they've spent time with you both. And I don't mind that in the least. It shows they like her. And they love you. It's all good,' Karen reassured him.

David relaxed for the first time since he arrived. He'd been so nervous.

'I've enjoyed these past few months,' David said. 'Being your friend again.'

Karen's eyes filled with tears and he looked

stricken when he saw them. She quickly reassured him, 'No, I'm fine. Stop worrying. I *am* emotional, but only because I loved spending time with you too. And I want you to know that I'll always be grateful for all the support you gave me. I leaned heavily on you, I know that.'

He nodded. 'I'll always be here for you,' David said. But he needed to say something else too, out of respect for Robyn. It was time to put her first. 'I might need to take a little step back for a while. For Robyn's sake. Can't have been easy for her, me over here so much.'

Karen knew that she was on borrowed time, calling David up to help out with plug changes or to provide a shoulder to cry on. He'd moved on, and so must she. And while she felt nervous about this, she was also excited. It was time for a new chapter in her life. On her own, with the children.

'You have to put Robyn first,' Karen insisted.

'The children will always be my priority though,' David promised.

'I know that.'

'And if you ever need me, all you have to do is call.'

'I know that too,' Karen said, smiling at his use of words. He'd be singing next.

The room fell silent, but it was one of those wonderful companionable ones that only two people who know each other as intimately as they did, could sit in.

'When will you propose?'

'I want to do something special for her. I thought perhaps I could hire a yacht, then

351

maybe . . . ' David paused, when Karen placed a finger over her mouth.

'Don't tell me how. Robyn should be the first person to know about that. And remember, she won't care what or how you propose. She'll just remember what you said.'

For the first time, since David told her of his plans for Robyn, she felt sad. She remembered his proposal to her, all those years ago. They were young, but oh so in love. She'd thought their love could withstand anything. David was her entire world and she would have followed him anywhere, just to be close to him. Her throat tightened and to her surprise, tears fell.

She looked up, ready to apologise to David, but his eyes were damp too.

He whispered, '*I can listen no longer in silence. I must speak to you by such means as are within my reach. You pierce my soul. I am half agony, half hope. Tell me not that I am too late, that such precious feelings are gone for ever. I offer myself to you.*'

'You remembered?' Karen said, completely taken aback. David had just quoted, word for word perfectly, Wentworth's proposal to Anne from the novel *Persuasion*. He had borrowed that quote for his own proposal to her all those years ago. She'd thought it was the single most romantic thing anyone had ever done for anyone.

'Shameless stealing of Austen's words, but at the time, I thought they were appropriate.'

'They were beautiful. And quite perfect. She's always been one of my favourite authors,' Karen said.

They both fell silent again.

Karen thought about the world that David imagined.

If it did exist, she hoped that other version of themselves were happy and still quoting literature to each other. She hoped that they were kinder to each other than they'd been here. And she hoped that they realised how much they had to lose, before it was too late.

36

The pretty woman in red and 007

Robyn's office, Didsbury, Manchester

Robyn's secretary Paul walked in, carrying a large rectangular cream box. It had a large, floppy red velvet bow wrapped around it.

'David has asked me to give you this,' Paul said. He was grinning from ear to ear, obviously in on whatever secrets it held.

Robyn opened the box with shaking hands, wondering what surprise he had in store for her. David was such a romantic. She'd never dated a man before who made such extravagant gestures. Flowers had been delivered to the office on several occasions.

When she lifted the lid of the box, inside was a dress. It was the colour of the bow, pillar-box red, and made of soft velvet. She pulled it out to examine it and realised it was an evening gown. She peeked at the label quickly, to check the size.

'It's the correct size, don't worry,' Paul said. 'David checked that with me.'

She should have known that he would ensure every detail was correct.

She found a small hand-written note in the box.

'*Please be my 'Pretty Woman' tonight and wear this gown. A car will be outside to collect*

354

you, at 5.30 p.m. All my love, David. X'

He'd remembered how much Robyn loved this movie. It had taken them two attempts to finish watching it and he'd teased her relentlessly about it, saying it was a load of sentimental tosh. Yet, here he was, using it as inspiration for whatever romantic evening he had planned for her. She couldn't wait to ring her mother to tell her. She had despaired of ever seeing Robyn settle down and had high hopes for this relationship. She wasn't the only one.

She looked at the gown in her hands, almost identical to the one that Julia Roberts had worn when she went to the opera with Richard Gere. She, however, was no Hollywood actress. She looked at her watch. One hour to make herself look beautiful, if she was going to pull this look off.

'Paul!' she looked up, 'I need a — '

'Appointment to get your hair done in the next ten minutes?' Paul replied smiling.

'Yes!' she breathed.

'I just so happen to have a friend waiting outside, ready to do your hair and make-up,' Paul said. 'By the time he's done, you'll give Julia a run for her money, I promise!'

Robyn knew she'd made the right choice hiring this guy. She stood up to kiss his cheek, but he grabbed her two arms and started bouncing up and down with her, giddy with the excitement of it all. 'Do you think he's going to . . . ? Paul asked, breathless at the romance. He couldn't wait to go tell all the other PAs about it.

'Don't jinx it by saying that out loud!' Robyn declared. But her heart leapt at the thought. What if that's what he was planning? Would she say yes?

'The divorce lawyer finally gets her man,' Paul squealed, winking as he walked out. 'Just saying!' He started to hum 'Here Comes the Bride'.

An hour later, he walked her to the waiting car outside. She had never felt so beautiful in her entire life. Paul's friend had swept her blond hair up into a loose chignon. Her skin was flawless, thanks to his make-up. She did feel like a movie star.

'Go get your man,' Paul said, kissing her cheek.

Robyn had no idea where she was going to and normally she hated surprises. It was unnerving, letting herself be vulnerable. She was going to have to just go along for the ride. She suspected she was going to enjoy every moment.

Twenty minutes later, the car slowed down to a halt as it reached the waterfront. David stood waiting for her, wearing a black tuxedo. He never looked sexier or more handsome.

He opened the door and helped her out, offering her his arm.

'Oh David,' she breathed. 'What have you done?'

'Are you ready for an adventure?'

She nodded, afraid to speak.

David had chartered a yacht, one that had been used in a James Bond movie. And as they stepped on board, Robyn felt like the leading lady for the first time in her life.

As twilight became evening, and lights twinkled on the dark waters of the Irwell, their hired yacht took them on a tour of Manchester.

They passed famous Mancunian landmarks — Spinningfields and the Salford Quays. Their glasses were topped up continuously from a never-ending bottle of rosé Dom Pérignon that their own butler served.

He'd thought of everything. That was her absolute favourite champagne.

A CD played music in the background and, of course, it was from the soundtrack of the movie *Pretty Woman*. 'It Must Have Been Love' by Roxette filled the air around them. She leaned into his arms as they watched beautiful Manchester sail by them.

Then, the song 'Fallen' by Lauren Wood came on.

'Oh you're killing me!' Robyn said. 'You know how much I love that song! The lyrics . . . '

'You might have the world conned that you are a hard-nosed divorce lawyer, but I know your secrets, Robyn,' David whispered into her ear.

Then he said, 'Wouldn't it make the night even more magical, if the music was live, rather than on a CD?'

Robyn protested, 'It's beautiful, no matter how the music is played.'

The butler moved back, as they smooched to the music. David knew her. This man really knew her. And it made Robyn quite breathless.

Then she heard the door opening behind her and a man walked out, singing the Lauren Woods song, 'Fallen'. His voice seamlessly

357

blended in time to the CD. And when he reached their side, the CD was switched off and only his voice filled the deck.

Robyn gasped, looking at David, who was beaming with delight at how well his plans had come together.

As the man's voice sang out, filling the air around him, two men appeared, their arms full with bouquets of flowers. They placed them on the seating on either side of the couple.

The butler stepped up, this time with a tray of tiny, exquisite canapés.

Robyn looked at the door to the galley and laughed as she wondered out loud, 'How many more are hiding down there?'

And as the tenor held the final note, David stood up from their seat and dropped to one knee, pulling a small square box from his pocket.

He opened it and Robyn held her breath, hoping that the ring inside was beautiful, but vowing to herself that if it was horrendous, she'd be gracious. And change it later.

She held her breath as David said, 'I thought you were magnificent the first time I saw you. The way you took control over what was a difficult time for me. And since then, I've fallen deeper and deeper in love with you.'

Robyn looked at him, her heart dancing its way around her chest. Was he really going to do this . . .

'Would you do me the great honour of marrying me?' David finished. He looked unsure as he waited for her answer.

She didn't need a moment to think. Without

hesitation, Robyn shouted in joy, 'Yes, oh yes!'

David sat beside Robyn and placed the ring on her finger, which was a perfect fit.

'It's beautiful.' It was a flawless square cut diamond, surrounded by smaller diamonds. Robyn sighed with relief. She loved it.

★ ★ ★

The water on the Irwell was dark, inky and still.

Lights bounced on to it from offices and apartments that they passed on the water's edge.

David had arranged one more surprise. The tenor returned to sing 'Sempre Libera' from Verdi's *La Traviata*. Robyn thought she might just faint in that moment. This song was the one from the opera scene in *Pretty Woman*, which always made her cry, then snort with laughter, moments later.

When the song ended, they both clapped and cheered. The singer moved back below deck, and the CD came on once more, playing background music courtesy of Roxette.

'I brought the opera to you, my Pretty Woman,' David's voice thickened with emotion. His plans had come off beautifully.

Robyn replied, in a perfect American twang, mimicking the famous scene with Julia Roberts, 'It was so good, I almost peed in my pants!'

David thought he'd never been happier. 'I'm so glad I found you.'

Robyn nodded. 'Me too.'

'I know I come with a lot of responsibility for you — three children . . .'

359

'Don't forget an ex-wife, plus a group of ever so slightly bonkers friends,' Robyn added.

'Yes, all that . . . ' David laughed. 'But I promise to love you and to make your happiness my goal in life. I've spoken to Karen and explained that I can't keep going over there. She understands. She really does.'

'Thank you, David, and I promise to try my best to understand when you are pulled in another direction. I will never become the wicked stepmother to the kids either. I've grown rather fond of them.'

'You're wonderful with them. Josh prefers you to me now when he comes to stay!' David said, one hundred per cent serious.

'He wanted to have a sleepover at my place the other day,' Robyn said. 'It was so cute. He's so cute. And I adore the girls. They are very sweet.'

'You spoil those two. You can't keep spending your money on clothes for them.'

'Well, don't be cross, but I saw the most darling outfits yesterday and I had to buy them. The last ones, honestly!' Robyn turned away from David and looked out to the still water. She would never have thought it possible, how much fun it was when they were all together. 'Being with your children has awoken a part of me that I didn't know existed.'

David was deeply moved by her admission; he pulled her back so that she was facing him again.

'I find myself wondering, more and more, what it would be like to have children,' Robyn whispered. She'd never said that out loud to a living soul before. In fact, she had never said it out loud to herself.

David thought when the girls came along that was it. No more children, three is enough for any family. But that was before he met Robyn. Now, he found himself contemplating a world with his and Robyn's children, too.

'I like to think that any children we had together would be quite spectacular,' David said.

Robyn blinked, her eyes glistening with golden lights reflecting in them. 'Are you saying what I think you're saying . . . ?'

'Yes, I rather think I am.'

'We're going to try for a baby?' Robyn whispered in awe.

She felt like she was about to fall into a glorious rabbit hole. They sealed the deal with a kiss.

37

The Cat in the Hat and the misplaced future

Bill's house, Malone Road, Stranmillis, Belfast, Northern Ireland

Today should be a day filled with excitement. Love. Smiles. Laughter. It was a milestone in any parent's life.

But the thing was, the person who would have had the biggest smile on their face wouldn't be there. And Adam was so pissed off, he couldn't think straight.

Rachel.

Even the clouds were angry. They sulked, dark, heavy over the skyline, in solidarity with Adam's mood.

The wind blustered, looking to have its voice heard too.

* * *

Today, his only child's first birthday, should have nothing but sunshine and light, but instead all Adam could feel was rage.

There's only so much tragedy one person can take and when he should be simply feeling joy, Adam felt like he'd reached a limit. He couldn't take any more. He wanted to shout at the world.

Rachel and he had so few memories as a trio with Matthew. They had planned so much, but had so little time to do any of the things they talked about. They'd never get to watch him do the hotdog dance with Mickey Mouse, or build his own Lego fort. They wanted to snorkel together. Rachel had this romantic notion of holding hands as a family under water. They wanted to become regulars somewhere. With their very own Cheers bar, where everyone would know their name. They'd planned to take a road trip, with no fixed timescale or destination. Perhaps when Matthew was in university, out on his own with less need of them. They had dozens of family traditions to make of their own that Matthew could pass on to his own children one day.

Memories. So many lost memories.

He walked into his father's living room and found his parents, together, kneeling on the rug in front of the fireplace, building blocks with Matthew.

He stood and watched his son laugh and squeal with joy as he pushed another tower to the ground. Matthew had finally had his first haircut, in the end, courtesy of Mary. She'd told Adam that it had been she who'd cut his curly locks for years as a child. He'd forgotten that. He reckoned Rachel would have approved.

Matthew crawled over to his nana and tried to pull himself up, using her for support.

'He's so close to walking,' she said, amazed at the strength in his legs.

'We've have a few false starts,' Adam said. 'I thought last night he had it. But he flopped to the ground with a laugh and waddled on his arse instead.'

Mary and Bill laughed and clapped their hands, delighted with their little havoc maker as he started to fling Lego from one side of the room to the other.

'He's just like his dad,' Bill said. 'Adam was forever breaking things! Do you remember?'

'Of course I do! There wasn't a cup in the house that didn't have a chip on it, courtesy of the laddo!'

Adam felt the ground tremble beneath him. He was on quicksand all of a sudden. Things were changing, evolving around him and he was struggling to keep up. But this time, he didn't feel like he was going to sink without a trace, as he'd dreamt so many times.

He had not seen his parents together in two decades and now, suddenly, they were playing doting grandparents, like they hadn't a care in the world. It was surreal. And pretty cool.

Bill looked up. 'You doing okay, son?'

Adam shrugged.

Bill pulled himself upright, holding on to the arm of one of the sofas. And in that small gesture, Adam became aware of his father's age. He dressed and acted like a man who was twenty years younger than he actually was. He never complained, but he was sure that Matthew and he, must tire him out. His life had been very quiet before they took it over.

He moved forward offering his arm to help Bill steady himself.

'Thanks, son.'

'I know you said no fuss, that you wanted a small birthday tea, but I made a cake. It's finished, if you want to come have a look.' Mary stood up without a single wobble and scooped up Matthew into her arms. Matthew adored her already. He knew he had found another person he could wrap around his finger and he wanted to hold on tight to her.

They walked into the kitchen and Mary lifted the lid on a large cake tin.

Adam gasped at what his mother had created. She had made a Cat in the Hat themed birthday cake.

Dozens of red and white fondant circles, in different sizes, were scattered all over a round turquoise-coloured cake. And on top there was a single candle, with red and white stripes, in the shape of a hat. The cat's hat.

'Dr Seuss was your favourite as a kid. You were always begging me to read one more story for you at bedtime,' Mary said.

Adam nodded. 'I remember that.'

'And *The Cat in the Hat* was your favourite of all his stories,' Bill said.

'It was.' He liked reading it to Matthew now.

'And I know you didn't want to have a fuss today. But we thought it might be nice to have a special cake. Something that Matthew can look at in years to come in a photograph,' Mary said.

Matthew'a little voice said 'Dada' and he held his two arms out, looking to go to his daddy. Adam pulled him in close and breathed in his scent.

'I know you are sad in ways neither your father

365

or I will ever be able to understand. You must be overwhelmed with grief,' Mary touched Matthew's head, wishing she could change the ending of this story.

'We are so proud of you,' Bill said. 'You have stood firm, never faltering, despite all that has been thrown at you. And you should be so proud of yourself too, of the father you are to Matthew. He's a lucky little boy.'

Adam looked back and forth between Bill and Mary. They were there to support him, ready to catch him or Matthew if either of them fell.

Rachel's voice whispered in his ear. 'Make today special for Matthew. You have to do this. For both of us.'

★ ★ ★

Five months ago, things had been perfect. Rachel and he had just bought their first home together, with a little help from Bill and David. And then something horrific happened that blew their life up.

He thought he'd never recover from that. And in many ways he never would. But something new had emerged from the ashes of his life. His world had grown larger — with his parents back in it.

Had Rachel not died, would that have ever happened? He couldn't help thinking that the tragedy had changed more than the obvious.

He knew that he had to find a way to say goodbye to a future that only wanted memories made by all three of them. Now, it was up to him to ensure that Matthew and he built their own future, together.

'Adam?' Bill said, his face twisted in a frown, as it often was these days, when he spoke his son's name.

His anger started to fade and he felt energy surge through him. This was his boy's birthday. What the hell had he been thinking of, letting it go without notice? He was an eejit. A big fecking eejit.

Adam looked at his father and his face broke into a huge grin. He raised an eyebrow and said, 'We're gonna need balloons. Red, blue and white. We'll need jelly and ice cream, you can't have a party without that. Oh, and silly hats. Cat in the Hat, big silly hats. Who's with me?'

Mary and Bill laughed in delight, she clapping her hands together. 'We're having a party!' she said to Matthew, who squealed in delight.

Rachel looked on, her eyes shining bright with approval.

38

The sign and the drunken sailor's first steps

Bill's House, Malone Road, Stranmillis, Belfast, Northern Ireland

Adam, Bill and Mary collapsed on to the sofas, stomachs full. Matthew was asleep, conked out with excitement and the comedown from his first sugar hit, as he'd eaten a huge chunk of cake and frosting.

Mary had created a feast fit for any one-year-old and his family. They'd eaten three courses and sang 'Happy Birthday' at least a dozen times, because Matthew kept saying 'more, more' and clapping his hands, each time they finished the last 'to you!'

He'd then happily played with all the wrapping paper that had been pulled off each gift he'd received. Presents had come from all over the globe. Pete and Jenny had sent him his first guitar. Karen, a first-edition set of Winnie the Pooh books. David and Robyn sent a beautiful Ralph Lauren jacket. Jo had even sent a stuffed kangaroo toy from Sydney that said, 'G'day mate' when you squeezed its front paw. And the last present had been from Lucy, Rachel's sister. She'd, weirdly enough, sent an envelope with 100 US dollars in it.

'I thought she lived in Australia,' Bill remarked.

'She does,' Adam said, shrugging.

Bill and Mary had outdone themselves as grandparents with a sack full of presents each. Adam had been overwhelmed by their generosity.

'I've two more things,' Mary said. 'First of all, I thought you might like to see these again.'

'No!' Adam exclaimed when he saw the books that his mother had made for him as a child. They looked smaller than he remembered, but they were just as fantastic.

'I have a huge box of things I've kept from your childhood. I thought maybe you could read some of these to Matthew.'

'I have a friend who works in publishing. She'd love to see these,' Adam said. 'Thanks mum.'

Mary said, 'I've one more.' She reached behind her and passed a large rectangular parcel wrapped in brown paper and tied with a string.

'It's for both of you, not just Matthew,' Mary said. 'But if you don't like it . . . ' she shrugged, shyly.

'You've already got us enough,' Adam protested. 'I'm sure no matter what it is, we'll love it.' He pulled open the paper, which revealed a painting inside.

'Did you do this?' he asked, his voice tight with emotion. Mary nodded.

She used the picture of Rachel and Adam in their garden at home in Didsbury, laughing, with a newborn Matthew held between their arms as her inspiration. Bill had given it to her, that first day he called to her B&B, to tell her that Adam needed her.

'How did you . . . when did you even have time to do this . . . ?' Adam spluttered out the words.

'When your dad came to see me, he gave me a photograph, a snap he took when you and Rachel weren't looking. I kept it and used that and a couple of other pictures that I got your dad to give me. It's just such a natural photograph, you both look so happy.'

'It's your best work I've ever seen,' Bill said. 'I've missed seeing your paintings Mary. I truly have.'

She took the compliment and smiled her thanks, but her eyes remained on Adam.

'Is it okay? Did I get Rachel right? I know I hadn't met her in person . . . ' Mary said.

'You've captured her exactly as she is . . . was . . . '

He couldn't take his eyes off his wife's face. The curve of her neck as it reached her collarbone, the way her chin dipped as she laughed in delight at Matthew. He had just opened his eyes and looked at them both. He remembered that moment clearly. It hadn't seemed especially noteworthy at the time. But back then he thought he had a lifetime to make more moments.

Adam turned to his mother and nodded at her.

Just once, but in that nod he said a thousand words. And she understood every one of them.

All the hurt, pain, the misunderstandings and the wrongs were finally laid to rest.

When the doorbell rang, breaking the profound silence, they all started at the sound.

Bill jumped up to answer it.

'Who is it?' Mary asked, straining to listen.

Adam heard the unmistakable lilt of George's voice.

'That's dad's ex-boyfriend. Who I happen to think should drop the word ex and just come back into his life.' Adam looked at his mother closely as he said the words. 'Life is too short, Mum. If you love someone, does it really matter who or what sex they are? Surely all that matters is that there's love.'

Mary leaned forward and said, 'I couldn't agree more. I've long since got over your father.'

Adam breathed a sigh of relief.

'I've even had a few flings myself along the way,' Mary said.

Adam laughed. 'Good for you. Can I go get George? I'd like to invite him in.'

'Tell you what, why don't you let me do that?' Mary said.

She walked out to the hall and found Bill and George whispering at the entrance.

'Hello,' she said, moving towards them.

Bill looked like a rabbit caught in headlights.

'I'm Adam's mother,' Mary said, holding her hand out to shake George's.

'I just called with a present for Matthew,' George said. 'I'm not stopping.'

'Well, that's a shame. I was about to put the kettle on, and there's talk of cake if you could manage some,' Mary said, smiling warmly.

George looked at Bill, waiting to take his lead.

'I'd like you to stay, if you could spare the time,' Bill said. 'Wait till you see the picture

371

Mary painted, of Adam, Rachel and Matthew. It's quite something.'

Ten minutes later, Adam watched Bill and George sitting side by side across from Mary who had a now-awake Matthew in her lap. They were all eating cake and drinking tea like it was the most normal scenario in the world. He shook his head in amazement.

'Would you look at us. Just one big, happy, dysfunctional family,' Adam said.

'I'd say we are perfectly imperfect, at least that's what I like to think,' Bill replied.

'Hey, keep me out of this. I only agreed to cake, nothing more!' George joked.

But the way Bill and he looked at each other, Adam had a feeling that things could change in the not-too-distant future.

'Are you planning on sticking here in Belfast then?' George asked.

Adam laughed.

'What's so funny?' George asked.

'If I had a pound for every time someone has asked me that very same question . . . I don't know what I'm doing yet. I suppose you could say, that I am waiting for a sign.'

'Oh, how mysterious and exciting,' George said. 'What kind of sign?'

'I think Rachel will find a way to let me know what we should do next,' Adam said.

When his mobile phone rang out loud in the room, George shouted, 'Shut the front door!'

'Now that's freaky,' Bill said.

'Hello, Adam? It's Lucy,' an Australian accent said.

Adam smiled, hearing his sister-in-law's voice. 'Hey, Lucy. The wee fella loved his money. Thanks for that.'

'Have been thinking of him all day. And you. How was it?'

'Started off rough, but ended well. We're eating cake now.'

'Yum! Well, I've got some news for you,' Lucy said.

'Go on. I love a bit of gossip!' Adam walked out of the kitchen into the sitting room.

'I've been offered a job in New York!'

'No way! How cool. Are you there already?' Then the penny dropped for Adam. 'Course you are, that's why you sent the dollars!'

'They've set me up with a cool brownstone townhouse, on the Upper East side. You should see it.'

'Stop showing off!' Adam joked. 'Seriously, good for you, Lucy. Rachel would be so proud of you.'

He heard Lucy suck in her breath.

'I miss her,' Lucy said.

'I know.'

'I rang Mum and Dad this morning,' Lucy said.

Adam didn't know what to say to that. Rachel and Lucy had a fractious relationship with them both. The fact that not so much as a card had arrived for their only grandson hadn't been lost on him.

'I don't know why I bothered calling them,' Lucy continued. 'Stupidly, I thought that maybe they'd be thinking about Rachel too, missing her.'

373

'I don't think you'll ever get what you want from them,' Adam said gently. 'Sometimes you've got to just let things go.'

'I think about you and Matthew all the time. I know we are geographically challenged. But even so, I should be doing more. Scrap that. I want to do more.'

'You don't have to do anything. You're always welcome in my house. I want Matthew to know his aunty Lucy.'

'I'm glad you said that. Because I want to step up a few gears in the aunty and sister-in-law stakes.'

Adam heard the sincerity in her voice and he was touched by it. 'Just keep on sending Matthew toys and books and you're gold. And if we ever need a kidney we know who to call,' Adam joked.

'I'd rather give them to him myself. The toys and books that is.'

'You coming to visit?' Adam was delighted by the news. He'd love to see her again.

'That's not what I had in mind. I was thinking more the other way around.'

'I don't follow,' Adam was puzzled.

'Fancy coming here?' Lucy asked.

Adam laughed. 'What?'

'Come to New York. We need an IT guy and if you want the job, it's yours. The firm will sponsor your visa. The house is lovely. Huge, loads of space for you and Matthew, with so much natural sunlight in every room. And it has this gorgeous park close by. I can help out with Matthew. I know it takes a village and all that.'

Lucy paused for a moment, then her voice swelled with excitement and emotion as she finished, 'I'd like to be your village for a bit.'

'Whoa! You've taken me by surprise here,' Adam said. His heart started to beat fast, as adrenalin pumped its way through his veins.

He had always wanted to live in New York. When he'd lost his job, Rachel and he had one drunken evening where they talked about looking for visas.

'My new PA informs me that there is a really good Montessori nursery nearby. We could enrol Matthew there. Or you could get a nanny, if you'd prefer that.'

'My head is reeling.'

'I'm sorry. I know I'm hitting you with a big life-changing decision. Will you promise me you'll think about it? It could be so cool.'

'How long do I have to decide?' Adam asked.

'Take a few days. I know you'll need a little time to make a decision that big. I'll send you an email with some photographs of the house and details of the neighbourhood. Plus a little bit about the job. But you could do it in your sleep. Honestly.'

'I'll ring you back soon,' Adam said.

His hand was shaking as he pressed end on the phone call.

Rachel walked into the room, grinning like the proverbial Cheshire cat. 'Told you I was working on something for you.'

'You took your time,' Adam said.

'Did you ever doubt me?' Rachel asked.

'No, my love, never, not for one moment.'

375

'You're going to say yes, right?' Rachel demanded.

'Are you wise? I can't just up sticks and move to the other side of the world.' The thought of it made his stomach flip.

'Why can't you go?' Rached asked.

'Matthew, my parents, Matthew . . . '

His parents looked up with interest when he walked back into the kitchen. Matthew was crawling between the kitchen and the living room.

'That was Rachel's sister, Lucy.'

They smiled with interest.

'This is the one that lives in Australia, who sent the money?' Mary asked, trying to get it straight in her head.

'That's right, Mum, but as it happens she's moved to New York.'

'Ohhh . . . ' Mary and Bill said together.

He watched Matthew pull himself up to his feet at Bill's knees. Every time he did that, he got a little surer of himself.

'Lucy's firm has offered me a job. She wants us to go to live with her.'

'Oh my God, how exciting!' George exclaimed, then shut up quickly when he saw the shock on both Bill and Mary's face, followed quickly by disappointment.

'And do you want to go?' Bill asked.

Adam didn't answer. He sat down and took a slug of tea. He'd murder a pint right now.

'I've only just found him again,' Mary's voice whispered to the room.

Adam made up his mind, 'I'm not going to go.'

'Why not?' Bill said.

'I don't want to leave you guys. Plus it's better for Matthew to grow up around his grandparents. New York is too far away. I've been dithering about whether to settle in Belfast or in Manchester, unable to make a decision. This is New York for goodness' sake,' Adam said. But as he said the words, 'New York', he found himself grinning.

'Start spreading the news. You want to go!' George exclaimed, clapping his hands together.

Bill looked at Mary, a question in his eyes. She nodded and an unspoken communication flashed between them.

'If it wasn't for me and your mum, would you jump at the chance to go?' Bill asked.

Adam shrugged.

Mary stood up and took Adam's hand. 'When your father and I split up, I let depression eat me up. I fell into it, head first and couldn't find my way out of the dark tunnels for the longest time. I just sat there in the dark, feeling miserable. And in turn, while it wasn't my intention, I ended up making you as miserable as I was.'

Adam thought about how he felt this morning. He understood exactly what she meant by the dark tunnel. He'd been jumping in and out of one since Rachel's death.

'I can still remember the moment that I came out to the light,' Mary said. 'I was watching the London marathon, and all I could see were happy, satisfied, accomplished faces. The runners all kept going until they crossed the finishing line. And it occurred to me that you wouldn't have time to be depressed if you ran a marathon.'

'That's true!' George said. 'So have you run a marathon then? I can't run to the end of the road without keeling over.'

Mary laughed and said, 'Nope. I've always hated getting sweaty. But I knew that I needed to get moving, like those runners, so busy that I didn't have time to think, or worry or fret. So I left Manchester, came home to Coleraine and opened up my B&B instead. And I can promise you that the busier I got, the more light came back into my life.'

Bill reached out and clasped Adam's shoulder. 'We don't want you to let the darkness eat you up. We want you to have such a busy life that only laughter and light is in it. Maybe this is a way for you to accomplish that.'

'I don't want to leave you both,' Adam said.

'Sure we'll be here waiting for you, whenever you do come back. When you're ready, you'll know when it's time to come home again,' Bill said.

'And what about Matthew?' Adam asked. 'Is it selfish of me to bring him to the other side of the world?'

'Matthew will have the most wonderful experience of his young life. He'll get to see a new and exciting world over there,' Mary said. 'Not to mention get to know his only aunty. I would imagine that has to be a good thing. She'll know things about Rachel that only a sister can share.'

Adam himself had questions about Rachel's childhood he'd love to have answered. It stood to reason that for Matthew, that need would be even greater the older he got.

'The Yanks will love you over there!' George said. 'That Irish accent and those twinkling eyes. You'll be mobbed. Just saying.'

'If I went, would you visit us?' Adam asked his parents.

They both nodded immediately. Mary said, 'I could come and stay for a few weeks when you first go, if you like? Help you get settled in, be there for Matthew as you get used to the new job. Say no of course. I don't want to force myself on you.'

'Would you do that for me?' Adam asked.

'Of course,' Mary replied. 'I can close the B&B for a few weeks. One perk of being my own boss.'

'And I'll come during the university holidays,' Bill said.

'Which are practically every second week,' George replied. 'Cushiest number in the world.'

Adam looked at Matthew and asked, 'What do you think, son? Are you ready for another trip, another adventure?'

All eyes turned to Matthew, who looked up from his spot on the living-room floor. He used the arm of the sofa to pull himself up. Then he turned himself towards Adam, saying, 'Dada.'

'That's my boy,' Adam laughed.

And then Matthew took his first steps. Like a drunken sailor on shore leave, he weaved and wobbled his way from the sofa to his daddy's arms.

His first steps.

Towards a new future. For the both of them.

39

The new beginning and the
long goodbye

Manchester International Airport, Manchester

Adam was at the rear of the convoy as they all walked towards the departures gate. He thought to himself how with time, his family of friends had grown and evolved.

Almost a football squad.

He'd said goodbye to his parents earlier that week, but in truth it hadn't been too difficult to do. Mary had already booked her flight to join him in New York the following week. She was closing down the B&B for the month of December and January, as promised, and had booked a flexible ticket so she could stay as long as he needed her.

The loving mother of his childhood was back. He hadn't realised how much he needed and missed her until now. He supposed they would both kick themselves that they allowed a stupid fight last a decade.

Bill was going to fly over in a few weeks too, to spend Christmas with them. And he casually threw in that he might bring George too. When Adam raised his eyebrow at this, he'd smiled and said, 'I thought I might see if true love strikes more than once. Maybe it's time I settled down.'

Adam didn't know if that was possible. But he liked the idea of his father having someone to take care of him. He hoped George was the guy for that. But with his dad, he'd learned that anything — or rather anyone — was possible.

It looked like he would be ringing in the New Year in 2004 with both his parents. That was something he'd never dreamed was possible.

They arrived at the departure gate and the friends made a semi-circle around Adam and Matthew.

David stood to his left, with his arm slung loosely around Robyn's shoulders. They had matching cream sweaters on, tied casually around their necks with a jaunty knot. At a guess, Adam reckoned Robyn had spent time in creating this look for them, earlier that morning.

He was right.

Holding on to Robyn's hand was Josh. He still afforded her hero worship status and it didn't look like that was going to change any time soon. In his head, she'd become a superhero, slaying the dragon teacher. His other hand was holding on to the double buggy that Karen stood behind.

Karen laughed at something Robyn said and David joined in soon afterwards.

How far they had come, Adam thought.

Pete was wearing a baby sling, his pride and joy, Chloe, nestled comfortably against his chest. Chloe, it turned out was the biggest love of Pete's life. Jenny held on to little Adam's arm, who was squirming to get away and run. And boy, that kid was fast. They'd only just retrieved him from his last bolt, which resulted in a mad dash around WHSmith's and the toppling of the latest bestsellers.

Adam, meanwhile, had his own sling on, with Matthew happily resting his head on his chest. He was tired, and struggling to keep his two little eyes open.

Adam loved holding him like this. He much preferred the sling to their buggy. But he knew that this time was already almost at an end. Now Matthew had found his legs and could walk, he rarely sat still.

And last, but never least, standing beside Adam, was Rachel.

She had been quiet this past week as he made his plans to leave and said his goodbyes to his mum and dad. Adam was pleased that she was by his side once more.

A silent witness and cheerleader to this momentous departure.

Now that they had reached the start of the airport security, the atmosphere changed between them. Smiles left faces and an air of solemnity descended upon the group.

Adam hated goodbyes; he'd had far too many of them lately. When he left for Belfast earlier that year, he had quietly slipped off, without a big farewell. But this was different. And there was no way his friends would let him go without them by his side, waving him off.

People bustled around them, tutting at the large group who were messily taking up space right in front of the departure gate's entrance.

Jenny, ever practical, pulled Adam's rucksack from his back. She opened it and rummaged her way through its contents. 'They'll probably make you taste Matthew's baby bottles, you know,' she told him.

Adam nodded. 'Not a bother. I've done it before.'

'I hope he sleeps all through the flight,' Jenny said. 'You make sure and get some rest while he does.'

Adam nodded. It was the strangest thing. Ever since he made the decision to leave, his bad dreams had stopped. He was sleeping through the night with no more dark shadowy figures chasing him down school corridors. He felt energised and rested.

He looked around the group again, and they all looked back, eyes wide and silent. Nobody wanted to make the first move to say goodbye.

'I need to get going. Don't want to miss the flight.' Adam couldn't put this moment off any longer.

In the end, it was Robyn who was the first to break the silence. She moved forward and said, 'My brother lives in New York. He's a good guy, I think you might like him. I've called him and told him to look out for you. He said you should call him too.' She pressed a card in his hand and he placed it in his jeans pocket.

'Thanks, Robyn. I appreciate that.' He leaned in to kiss her cheek and she smiled as she bent down to kiss Matthew's sleeping head.

'I'll look forward to seeing you soon,' Robyn said, and she moved back.

David stepped up, lifting Josh up high, so he could high-five Adam.

'Up high!' Adam said.

'Down low!' Josh replied, then moved his hand away, shouting with glee, 'Too slow!'

They both giggled as if it was the first time they'd done that particular comedy routine.

'Look after those sisters of yours,' Adam said to him. 'Big responsibility being the big brother.'

Josh nodded. Then he spotted a billboard with a photograph of Nemo on it. 'Cool!' he said, running towards it.

'I'll go. You say your goodbyes,' Robyn said to David and Karen.

David moved in to embrace Adam. His voice was gruff with emotion as he said, 'I never had best friends until I met you and Pete. Don't get too comfy over there in the Big Apple. Come back to us.'

'My heart will always be in Manchester, never fear about that. You're a good man, David Marsden. Don't let anyone ever tell you otherwise.'

'I'll need a couple of best men, for my wedding,' David said. 'You better be back for it.'

'Would be my honour. Sure Pete and I already have plans for your stag!' Adam winked at him.

David walked back to Karen and busied himself tucking a blanket around Ellie and Olivia. He was rubbish at goodbyes.

Karen walked over to Adam. 'Looks like it's my turn.'

Adam smiled and kissed both her cheeks. 'You going to be okay?'

'Most days, I think I just might be.' Her eyes didn't leave Matthew's sleeping face. She gently rubbed his cheek with her forefinger and whispered her favourite Dr Seuss quote about travelling to great places.

Adam leaned in and whispered to her, 'You're a cracker of a woman Karen. Don't waste that. Go find yourself a good man. Have some fun. Maybe not with my dad though.' He ended with a wink.

Karen smiled and hugged him tight.

'You can come visit us, you know,' Adam said. 'All of you can.'

'I've already been talking dates with Jenny. We think a girls' shopping trip could be in order for the sales,' Karen promised.

'I'll even carry the bags,' Adam joked.

'He's all I have left of — ' Karen broke off and made a face, trying to compose herself. 'I swore to myself, no tears. Keep it dignified. Best of British and all that.'

Adam smiled and said, 'Sod that. You cry all you like. I've certainly done enough of it lately.'

'He's my godchild and if you need me, anytime, I will always be here for him. I take my role very seriously, you know,' she said, smiling through her tears.

'He's lucky to have you. Goodness knows he'll need someone with some sense to help keep him on the straight and narrow when he's a teenager and probably hating his old man,' Adam replied. 'Be happy, Karen.'

He walked towards Jenny and Pete. They were rooted to the spot, unable to move.

Both were crying.

And for the first time, since he agreed to

Lucy's suggestion, he wondered if he was doing the right thing.

'Just give me a minute, mate,' Pete said. And he walked away to try to compose himself.

'Remember, get in the cab, before you tell them where you're going,' Jenny advised. 'Especially, if you're leaving the borough. And don't eat more than one slice of pizza a day. They're addictive, but not good for your heart.'

Adam did a mock salute.

'If you get lost, don't take out a map. You might as well put a light over your head, saying, 'come mug me'!' Jenny continued.

'Lucy will fill me in on all the dos and don'ts,' Adam said.

'She's only been there a wet weekend. I lived there. I was a New Yorker,' Jenny said. 'Head to Hell's Kitchen. You'll like it there. There's a Greek restaurant that I've emailed the details of to you. Call in, say hi to them for me. Let's just say, I had some fun nights there.'

'Yes to all of that.' Adam smiled at his friend. He knew that she was throwing all this at him, because she didn't want to say goodbye.

'I'm going to be fine,' he assured her.

'Call us when you land,' Jenny said.

Adam saluted again, before hugging her one last time. Then he turned to Pete, who had returned, unsuccessful in his attempt to blink away the tears that had no intention of stopping.

'Mate,' Pete said.

'Mate,' Adam answered.

'Won't be the same without you over here.'

'I know. A hard road ahead of you, Pete my

auld pal, without me by your side to keep you out of trouble!' Adam tried to joke, but his voice cracked at the end.

'I still don't understand why you can't just stay over here,' Pete said. 'With all of us.'

Adam had tried so hard to make them all understand. His parents had just come back into his life, and it would be easy in many ways to just stay in Belfast, or here in Manchester, with the support that each city would give him.

But that wasn't right for him and Matthew. Not now.

He needed to do as his mother said and find his version of a marathon. He needed to run. He needed to get busy.

He repeated his mother's words to Pete, in another attempt to make him understand.

'Don't you see, it would take very little for me to fall into a hole of depression right now. And I can't do that, not with Matthew to think about. I have to keep moving. Going to New York is my version of that athlete running twenty-six miles. I'm just trying to keep the darkness at bay mate,' Adam said.

'I get it,' Pete replied and he swallowed hard on the lump in his throat. 'I suppose, at least we have a good place sorted for David's stag.'

'Vegas baby!' they both said at the same time.

'What's that?' David asked.

'Never you mind. Just make sure your passport is in order!' Pete shouted over to him.

Adam and Pete looked at each other once more — two men, with their babies asleep on their chests. How had that happened? It was only yesterday that they were skipping school to smoke fags behind the old closed-down theatre.

As they looked at each other, a lifetime of memories bounced back and forth between them.

First day of high school. Sports days, where Adam was the captain and he always picked Pete before anyone else. First can of lager and then their first legal pint. First kisses. First loves. First heartbreaks. First friends. All the firsts, always, by each other's side.

Mates.

They moved towards each other to embrace, and bumped baby slings. Chloe started to cry in annoyance and Matthew joined in for good measure.

'Sshhh,' Adam said to Matthew and Pete sang softly in Chloe's ears, until she quietened down once more.

Pete held his hand out, to shake Adam's. 'Probably safer, mate.'

'Aye,' Adam said and he shook Pete's hand firmly in his.

Then he leaned in and kissed Pete's forehead. 'Not mates. We're brothers,' he whispered.

'Brothers,' Pete whispered back.

Adam and Matthew walked towards the security gates, then turned one last time to look at each of their friends, who were standing huddled together waving.

'I love you guys!' Adam said to them.

And then he turned to walk through the sliding doors, towards his next big adventure.

He looked to his right and smiled at Rachel.

'You had me doing things I'd never done before, from the moment you crashed into my life in that red car of yours, in Tesco's car park.'

'That was your fault. You should have been looking where you were going,' Rachel teased. She'd never admitted fault in all their years together.

'And here you are, still making me do things I'd never have thought possible.'

'I'm quite a wonder really,' Rachel answered with a smile.

She stopped walking and he turned back to her.

'Come on, Rach. We better go.'

'I'm not going with you. Not this time, Adam.'

The busy departures hall emptied around him as everything stopped with his wife's words.

Fellow passengers wheeled their suitcases, emptied their pockets into plastic trays and red-faced security guards all faded into nothing. All that was left was Adam, Matthew and Rachel.

He felt fat tears pierce his eyes. 'Why?' he whispered.

'You know why,' Rachel said.

He did.

'Why can't we just keep doing this?'

'That wouldn't be fair on you or Matthew,' Rachel said.

His eyes blurred his vision and he blinked quickly so he didn't miss a single moment of whatever time he had left with her.

'You know that I'm not really standing here, don't you love?' Rachel said.

He didn't want to say yes. He didn't want to admit the truth out loud. Because then there would be no going back.

He'd spent months hiding from this truth. He'd spent months pretending that it was normal to have a relationship with his dead wife. But he always knew that Rachel wasn't really here.

He put his two arms around Matthew, who was snoring softly, in deep slumber.

'I have to let you go now, don't I?'

'And I have to let you go too,' Rachel replied. 'You have to move on. And you can't. Not while I'm here, like this.'

Adam tried to find the words, to argue his case.

'It's not goodbye. Not really,' Rachel said, smiling. Always smiling. 'I'll be here. Whenever you need me. In your head and in your heart.'

'So it's not the end?'

Rachel shook her head. 'This, my love, is just the beginning for you.'

She moved closer and Adam closed his eyes and imagined her touch as she kissed his lips goodbye, before holding their son's face between her hands.

The pain of her death was so profound, but this pain was different. It hurt, but it also felt inevitable, like he was finally doing what he was supposed to do.

Then she was gone. There was nothing he could have done to save her, to get her back. He had spent months in excruciating agony, trying to come to terms with her death.

He knew that for most of that time he was living with one foot in the past and one foot in the present.

He thought of his mother. She had spent years of her life living in the darkness. She had lost her son in the process. He had to learn from that. He had to make sure he didn't follow that path. He had to move forward. Not just for Matthew. For himself too.

He leaned in and kissed his son's forehead. Then he walked towards the security gate.

This wasn't the end . . . it was just the beginning.

Acknowledgements

This book would never have happened if it wasn't for Rowan Lawton, my agent. Her belief that I was the right person to take on this project gave me the confidence to go for it. Her passion, friendship and guidance for my books have been a game changer for me. I shall always be grateful to the talented Mike Bullen, creator of *Cold Feet*, ITV's Shirley Patton and Kate Howard at Hodder & Stoughton for choosing me! As a die-hard fan of the show, I've adored writing this book. Over the past couple of months, I've had the pleasure of getting to know Kate Howard, Veronique Norton and Lucy Howkins in Hodder & Stoughton. And I've seen first-hand how clever they are. My sincere thanks to each of them and the team at Hodder & Stoughton and Hachette who have welcomed me so warmly to their publishing family. Your encouragement and support have been so appreciated.

I'd also like to thank Jimmy Nesbitt, Helen Baxendale, Fay Ripley, Jon Thompson, Hermione Norris and Robert Bathurst who made my job so much easier, because of their incredible portrayals of the characters, who are at the centre of my book. It was an honour to dig a little deeper and show the readers the internal thoughts of the characters. I hope the fans of the show are happy with what I've done. I promise you I worked hard to ensure that I retained the emotional undertones of Mike's wonderful creation, in every chapter I wrote.

I'd like to thank all at ITV and Big Talk Productions, Mike Bullen and the cast and crew for their warm welcome to Roger and me when we visited the set in Manchester earlier this year. Series 7 looks amazing, and seeing the work that goes on behind the scenes to make each episode perfect was a lot of fun.

Special thanks must go to *Cold Feet*'s Line Producer — Margaret Conway. True story — Mags and I went to school together, but we hadn't seen each other since we left Wexford (in two different directions, I might add) at the tender age of eighteen! The universe threw us back into each other's lives recently, through books and of course *Cold Feet*. We're both older, wiser (ahem) and thrilled that we have reconnected. Roger and I feel very lucky to have both Mags and her wife Lisa, in our lives now. A gorgeous couple.

Writing can be a solitary experience, but for me that's never been the case. When I started to write I found my tribe. Too many to mention really, but shoutouts must go to Hazel Gaynor, Fionnaula Kearney, Claudia Carroll, Catherine Howard, Charlotte Ledger, Shane Dunphy, Alex Barclay, Caroline Grace Cassidy, Adele O'Neill, Sheila Forsey, Debbie Johnson, Caroline Busher, Madeleine Keane, Maria Nolan, Louise Hall, Jennifer Burke (thank you for those Robyn legal gems), Margaret Madden, Sharon Thompson and Ruth Long.

I'm also sending thanks to all at Wexford Literary Festival, the Imagine Write Inspire

Group and the Elaine Show, especially Elaine Crowley and Sinead Dalton.

To my family, I send you my love and thanks for the enduring support — Tina & Mike O'Grady, Fiona, Michael, Amy & Louis Gainfort, John, Fiona & Matilda O'Grady, Michelle & Anthony Mernagh, Sheryl O'Grady, Amy & Nigel Payne, Evelyn Harrington, Adrienne Harrington & George Whyte, Evelyn, Seamus & Patrick Moher, Leah Harrington & Ann Murphy, John, Ben, Abby & Sean.

To my friends who held my hand metorphorically and at times physically (Sarah!), thanks for sticking with your crazy writer pal and checking in on me when I disappeared into my writing cave. You all know who you are and I am grateful. There's a proverb that says it takes a village to raise a child. I use this quote in the book actually and it's never been more true for me, than this past year. Like Karen's struggle in the book, I'm a working mother trying to prevent the balls crashing to the floor every day. The juggle struggle is real folks, it really is. With a deadline hurtling towards me at breakneck speed, a number of friends stepped up and welcomed Amelia and Nate into their homes for play dates, often at a moment's notice! Catherine Kavanagh, Fiona Murray, Davnet Murphy, Gillan Jones, Fiona Wickham & Caroline Hodnett, I can't thank you enough for your help. But Queen of my village was Leah, my sister-in-law, who moved into the crazy H house while I wrote this book, and to whom I'll always be grateful.

My great-aunt Margaret (Peggy) died this year.

Her loss broke the hearts of my family. We loved her dearly. It's no coincidence that Adam meets a gorgeous, wise, funny, endearing character called Peggy, while line-dancing. I like to think that somewhere, Aunt Peggy and my Uncle Terry are once again dancing together all night.

Roger, my husband, my best friend, my love and my biggest supporter — every time I faltered and said, I can't do this, you picked me up and insisted I could. My children Amelia, Nate and my stepdaughter Eva, you all make my life a brighter, more beautiful world every day.

And lastly, to you the reader — thank you. I love to write and every time one of you takes time out of your busy day to read one of my books, I am in awe. I truly am. I hope you enjoy your time with the *Cold Feet* gang, as much as I did writing their story.

We do hope that you have enjoyed reading this large print book.

Did you know that all of our titles are available for purchase?

We publish a wide range of high quality large print books including:
Romances, Mysteries, Classics
General Fiction
Non Fiction and Westerns

Special interest titles available in large print are:
The Little Oxford Dictionary
Music Book
Song Book
Hymn Book
Service Book

Also available from us courtesy of Oxford University Press:
Young Readers' Dictionary
(large print edition)
Young Readers' Thesaurus
(large print edition)

For further information or a free brochure, please contact us at:
Ulverscroft Large Print Books Ltd.,
The Green, Bradgate Road, Anstey,
Leicester, LE7 7FU, England.
Tel: (00 44) **0116 236 4325**
Fax: (00 44) **0116 234 0205**

Other titles published by Ulverscroft:

MARRIED QUARTERS

Shane Connaughton

An insignificant Irish border village at the tail-end of the 1950s. The Sergeant is nervous. His men are lined up for inspection in the day room of the Garda station. Chief Superintendent 'The Bully' Barry is on the warpath, and any slip-ups will reflect badly on the Sergeant. But what can he do with the men under his command — all of them forcibly transferred from other more important stations in more important towns? On the cusp of manhood, his son is drawn in by these rough and ready men, stuck in this place and time, when all he wants is a chance to leave and start his life anew. Life at home in the station's married quarters is both comfort and knife-edged, ruled over by his by-the-book father and his gentle, emotional mother.

THIS BEAUTIFUL LIFE

Katie Marsh

Abi Cooper is living her happy ending. She's in remission and is ready to make the most of her second chance. But during her illness, her family has fallen apart. Her husband John has made decisions that are about to come back to haunt him, while her teenage son Seb is battling with a secret of his own. Set to the songs on Abi's survival playlist, this is the story of what happens when she tries to put her family back together — and of why life, and love, are worth fighting for.

I REFUSE

Per Petterson

Norway, 1960s: Tommy's mother has gone. She walked out into the snow one night, leaving him and his sisters with their violent father. Without his best friend Jim, Tommy would be in trouble. But Jim has challenges of his own which will disrupt their precious friendship . . . Decades later, the two meet again by accident on a bridge — Jim is fishing, and Tommy is driving by in his expensive new Mercedes. The fateful day that ensues brings back a torrent of unsummoned memories that defined the adults they would eventually become, and reveals past misunderstandings. The idea of friends who act like family, and family who become foes — and the shifting currents between them — is the crux of this story of friendship, abuse, loss and forgiveness.

TELL TALE

Jeffrey Archer

This new collection of short stories offers an insight into the people Jeffrey Archer has met, the tales he has heard, and the countries he has visited during the past ten years. Find out what happens to the hapless young detective from Naples who travels to an Italian hillside town to find out *Who Killed the Mayor?* and the pretentious schoolboy in *The Road to Damascus* whose discovery of the origins of his father's wealth changes his life in the most profound way. Revel in the stories of the woman who dares to challenge the men at her Ivy League university during the 1930s in *A Gentleman and a Scholar*, and another young woman who thumbs a lift and gets more than she bargained for in *A Wasted Hour* . . . plus ten other original tales.